HUNTING ABIGAIL

JEREMY COSTELLO

To Mervyn
Best wishes.

This is a work of fiction. Names, characters, places, and incidents either are the product of the author's imagination or are used fictitiously. Any resemblance to actual persons, living or dead, events, or locales is entirely coincidental.

First paperback edition June 2020

Cover design by Andrew Heads
Cover photography: Lalesh Alderwish; Alexander Krivitsky; Johannes Plenio
Edited by Terry Flinn

ISBN 978-1-8380901-0-4 (paperback)
ISBN 978-1-8380901-1-1 (ebook)

www.jeremycostelloblog.com

For Kathryn

HUNTING ABIGAIL

When we get out of the glass bottles of our ego
and when we escape like squirrels turning in the
cages of our personality
and get into the forests again,
we shall shiver with cold and fright
but things will happen to us
so that we don't know ourselves

DH Lawrence

2011

A violent shudder passed along the undercarriage jarring her awake. She prised her eyelids up, the dimly lit cabin drifting into focus. Next to her, Milo, her business associate, was sleeping, his head lolling against the headrest.

She leaned forward and checked the rest of business class. Those who were awake didn't seem rattled or panicked.

'Excuse me.' She stopped a passing steward. 'Did we just hit some turbulence?'

'Turbulence?'

'I was just wondering if I'd dreamt it.'

The steward offered up a practiced smile. 'It was a little bit bumpy back there for a while, but there's nothing to worry about. The captain would've put on the seatbelt light if he thought there was.'

She nodded and glanced out the window, streaks of light in the distance splitting the night in two. She closed the shutter.

The plane rocked again, vibrated harshly through strong pockets of wind. This time the captain deemed seatbelts a necessity. Behind her, she noticed a steward replace the onboard receiver and hurry past them. He was being beckoned to the cockpit.

Something was wrong. She could feel it.

'Milo,' she whispered, jabbing the kid's arm. 'Milo, wake up.'

'Uh, wha…what…What is it?'

Emerging from the cockpit, the steward hurried past them again. 'Something's going on. The flight attendants seemed panicked. We've been hitting some pretty harsh –'

As if on cue, the plane was slammed by a violent shock of wind. This time it wasn't brief.

'Ladies and gentlemen, we appear to be hitting some rather heavy turbulence. Please make sure your seat backs are in the upright position, your seatbelts are fastened, and your tables are stowed. We may be in for a rough ride.'

Milo looked up at her and smiled. 'Relax, babe. Everything's fine.'

Perhaps it was just her distrust for all objects lacking self-awareness, but she couldn't close out the peculiar feeling of vertigo. The captain's calm voice had done little to appease her.

Flipping the port cover back up, she stared out into the night. Rain thundered against the side of the plane, hammered there by the battering wind, pale blue tongues of electricity flashing into view and then disappearing like the flick of a switch.

'How much of this can these tin cans take?' she muttered to herself.

'Stop panicking,' said Milo firmly. 'Pilots experience weather like this all the time, it's nothing new to them. These machines are put together pretty well, you know.'

She sat back and rechecked her seatbelt, her watch. The time was gone eleven. They'd been in the air for almost eight hours, which meant they were probably over water.

Driven by invisible hands the elements continued to pummel the aircraft, buffeting her through the sky like she was made of straw.

The flight attendant came stumbling back down the aisle. 'Everybody, please remain calm. Everything's alright. We're just experiencing a little turbulence.'

'No flies on him,' said Milo.

Towards the cockpit door, the attendant tripped and fell through the curtain, crashing against the refreshments trolley as the plane banked sharply to the right. It felt like they were falling out of the sky.

Then, as suddenly as it was born, it died.

The buffeting stopped.

The plane leveled out.

Beyond the curtain, she could see the steward picking himself up from the floor. He smoothed his shirt and brushed off his shoulders. Straightening the curtain, he pulled it across and disappeared from sight.

'Holy shit,' muttered Milo, 'that was intense.'

'Apologies for any discomfort there, ladies and gentlemen. We're flying through some pretty nasty weather so we'll do our best to keep the bumps down to a minimum. In the meantime, if you could keep your seatbelts fastened –'

In that split second, the captain's words became engulfed by the unified screams of the passengers. An impossibly white bolt of lightning tore through the sky and crashed into the wing mere metres from the window. In one swift movement the plane plunged to the left, arching downwards.

As the intensity of the screams pierced the confines, she glanced at Milo, tears spilling from his eyes.

'Focus, Milo,' she yelled.

He didn't reply.

Along the cabin, oxygen masks dropped from the overhead panels. Without hesitation, Milo pulled his down and strapped it to his head.

Another violent shudder; the plane dipped further.

Daring another look out of the window she saw the engine ignite, flames blazing from the rotor.

Falling.

If anybody was still listening, the captain's words echoed hollowly above the terror inside the cabin, its pressure plunging: *'Ladies and gentlemen, please put on the oxygen masks. We've lost the portside engine and the starboard side is presenting difficulties. I'm afraid we have no option but to attempt an emergency landing.'*

His voice still sounded calm.

A front?

A front?

Plummeting.

The shocking vibrations continued to ripple through the carriage as some of the overhead compartments burst open and began vomiting bags and jackets into the aisles, panels splitting from their moorings and crashing into passenger's laps.

As the cabin's odours increased with bodily accidents, an amalgamated truth crept stealthily between the passengers: the next few minutes of their lives were probably going to be their last.

She was yet to put on her mask, didn't need it.

Plunging.

In a terrifying screech, a large section of the wing tore itself free from the plane and disappeared into the night.

This was it.

This was the end.

How much further could they fall before they hit the ground?

Falling.

Falling.

Falling.

The nose of the plane drove into the water, the carriage disintegrating. In the same second, water burst in through the port windows in an explosion of shards.

Propelled forward, the belt tore at her abdomen, dug into the soft flesh as the moorings above her head came loose and crashed brutally against her skull.

It was the last thing she remembered.

Almost.

I

London, England, 1992

Legend has it that in a remote corner of hell there is a solitary room reserved only for the blackest of souls. Very few are considered worthy; fewer still granted entrance...

Detective Sergeant Holly Newport stood quietly at the foot of the bed. She felt like throwing up. The two bodies were arranged side by side on the semen-stained sheets, glowing in their pallid nudity. Each body had been laid upon its back, interlocked fingers entwined between them like fleshy barbed wire.

Newport took in the precise carnage. She was physically small, but carried a big presence. And she'd seen many things.

This was something else.

In her gloved hand she held the small device her superior had found in the bathroom. Together they had listened to its eerily potent message. The individual who made the recording was disturbingly insane, that much was clear, yet from somewhere deep within the subject's mind there was an obvious lucidity. Whoever this person was had planned this with precision, and he'd done so with an overview of toying with anyone who cared.

DS Newport looked back at the bodies. She cared.

At her side was her superior. He didn't speak much, that was his way, and he seldom smiled. Tonight he looked gaunt and tired.

'You want to listen to it again?' DCI Nicolas York asked in his deep west end drawl.

Newport looked to her right and into the eyes of her boss. At forty-two, DCI York remained an attractive man. His thick head of black hair, usually stored beneath a tarnished trilby, helped to prop up his boyishness, despite the salt and peppering of stubble which flirted with his cheeks and the dark bags in which his eyes sat afloat.

Newport took a deep breath. She did want to hear the recording again. She wanted to listen to it until it made sense. Lifting the recorder, she hit the play button, an anticipation of static hissing in prelude...

'Are we born insane, or are life's twisted paths able to corrupt the deepest recesses of our psyches and turn us so? I was once taught of this thing called Free Will, which supposedly was bestowed upon us by the One some choose to worship. The One whose name I'm neither urged to utter nor care about. For is that level of worship not a tailored kind of insanity?

'Some would say it is.

'I would say it is.

'You will label me insane and by your thesis claim that a sane person could not do the things that I have done. Perhaps you're right. I'm of no authority to disagree, nor do I care to. I will not change your minds should I try. Once a

person is labelled insane, every utterance upon his breath will be deemed crazy thereafter, no matter how much he insists on the contra.

'So…'

Newport clicked the device off and looked back at York. His tired eyes told her nothing as usual.

The hotel room had been sealed off by a number of uniforms who were controlling the scene, but all were reluctant to linger. One kid, probably fresh out of training from the IPLPD, had run from the room and thrown up in the corridor. Forensics was going to love him.

At the feet of the victims, Newport pushed her spectacles up onto her nose and took in the macabre playhouse; the bodies, the bloody spectacle. She stayed like this, reeling in the dim light. This was indifference like she'd never seen.

'You'll go blind, staring like that,' York admonished, flipping off his trilby and setting it gently down on the unit by the bathroom door.

Poking his head into the bathroom he already knew well, he flitted into the blue and red flash of lights from the patrol cars in the street. 'Okay, Sergeant,' he said aloud. 'Tell me what you think.'

York did this sometimes, almost like he was testing her. It probably explained why he was so closed down, or why some of the other officers labelled him "genius".

Tucking a loose strand of hair behind her ear, she took a mental inventory of the room for the tenth time: A white tiled bathroom, boxy and unclean; a few pieces of cheap furniture, chipped and scarred; a smashed wall mirror, shattered into infinitely accusing triangles; one grimy window looking out over the equally dour Peckham street; scabby carpet and nicotine yellowed and peeling wallpaper and one queen-sized bed which had recently become the dismal hotel suite's focal point. That was it.

York waited, watching her with steady patience.

'I don't like it,' Newport said finally.

'No?'

'No.'

Pause.

'What's to like?'

'What I mean is,' she added, 'nothing about the scene feels right. There's no passion here, not an ounce.'

York shook his head. 'You're not going down this road again, are you?'

'Do you not agree, though? Where's the anger, the rage? The bodies are –'

'Forget the bodies. Background noise only. Look around, tell me what you see.'

'How am I supposed to –'

'*Forget the bodies*!'

Newport took a deep breath. 'Okay, the room is sparse, dirty. Minimalistic hotel bedroom, used for prostitution. Been a couple of drug problems here in the past, but this doesn't speak drugs to me, or gangland retribution. This has an almost random element to it. The place is probably irrelevant.'

'I disagree,' York cut in, edging his way to the window. 'I think this room tells us something very pertinent. Why have the victims been left to wallow in this pit?'

Newport thought the answer was obvious. 'Opportunity?'

York pulled the trilby back on and glanced out the window. The rattle and reverb of slow-moving black cabs and occasional double-deckers stalked the clear morning somewhere over the building tops, causing minor vibrations to pulse through the floorboards, though nobody mentioned it. From the window he moved to the wardrobe and began rifling the contents. 'Man's Armani suit, woman's Gucci pencil skirt and jacket, it's all here down to the underwear and shoes. All stored away nice and neat.'

'ID?'

'Nope.'

Newport's rogue strand of hair popped free again. 'Okay, so the type of clothes here, assuming they're not imitation, tell us that our John and Jane were well to do.'

York's eyebrows lifted. 'So what are they doing in this shithole?'

She couldn't answer that one. 'Uniforms are knocking on doors but so far no luck. People are in and out of here quickly.'

'What about the manager?'

'Guy named Liam Grayson. He's on his way here now.'

'Uh-huh, what do we know about him?'

'Couple of priors, nothing major, and nothing in his past to indicate he was capable of something like this. Few raids here since he's been running the place, but he's managed to stay off the radar.'

'Oh yeah?'

'Denies all knowledge of anything that goes on in the rooms.'

'Scumbag?'

'Oh yeah, grade A. But this still doesn't smell like him. He's small time.'

York adjusted his trilby; a seemingly common development.

'So what about the smashed mirror? The work of our guy?'

York glanced up at his distorted reflection, fragmented eyes leering back at him. 'No.'

Newport awaited clarification.

'The mirror was broken before the killer stepped foot into this room. Our man would have no reason to break it.'

'Care to clarify?'

'Because he likes looking at himself,' said York. 'Look at the bodies: very precise, very clinical, this is not the work of an angry person. You said yourself it's not a crime of passion. That very notion would go against the killer acting calmly. He's playing God, and I wouldn't've thought God shies away from His own image.'

'You don't believe in God.'

'I believe in this one.'

A forlorn calm fell over the room.

'Okay, your favourite bit,' York continued. 'Tell me about the bodies.'

Newport's stomach turned again as she took in the cadavers. She switched on her blankness, her coping mechanism. Scanning victims this way was an art form. DCI York was an expert and she was getting better.

'The obvious thing is the lack of blood,' she offered.

'I see blood.'

'But it's restricted to the bed. For this type of butchery I'd expect splattered walls, floors, but there's nothing. If you lifted the bed out of here right now, you'd never know a crime had happened at all. It could suggest that the *procedure* took place post mortem – lack of struggle.'

York shrugged. 'Nobody wants a squirming patient.'

'And?'

'Who says there's an "and"?'

'There's always an "and",' Newport said.

The corners of York's mouth lifted slightly. '*And* I don't see butchery, I see surgery.'

Both detectives viewed the still figures. The ashen nudity of each victim, in stark contrast with the crimson linen, begged attention. But those facts paled in comparison to the gaping holes in the chests, the heart of each victim cleanly cut out.

'The hearts?' he asked.

'Not here. Taken as a souvenir, we think.'

'People don't do Big Ben ornaments anymore?'

'Not this person.'

'Okay,' he muttered, 'what else?'

The first thing York noticed when he arrived on scene was the heads. The head of the female lay straight on her pillow, closed eyes to the ceiling. The male's head faced towards the bathroom, eyes wide. Following the victim's line of sight, he'd found the voice recorder in the bathroom.

'It's clear we're being tormented,' she suggested. 'Like a game or something. This guy wants us to look for him.'

York waited.

'Remember Marc Durham?'

'Nope.'

'Come on! That guy who went on the killing spree around Loughton and Dagenham when he found out his girlfriend had been an escort for more than three years.'

'Oh yeah. So?'

'When the girlfriend found out what he'd done, she killed herself, couldn't handle the guilt.'

'Your point please,' York pressed.

'That wasn't nearly as calculated but there are similarities. Durham wanted us to catch him. He admitted when we caught up with him that the guilt was eating away at him. He showed no remorse over the four people he'd killed but he couldn't handle the fact that his girlfriend had committed suicide.'

'There's a big difference. This killer only wants to play with us, I don't think he wants to be caught. Can you imagine this guy feeling guilty about what he's done here? I think you're right, this is a game to him. Guess what that makes us.'

Newport shrugged. 'Inferior players.'

Crouching closer to the bed she inspected the sheets, stained and encrusted with more than one kind of bodily fluid. In amongst the dense clogging of blood, semen splatters were prevalent.

'What do you make of this, guv?'

York fished a pen from his jacket pocket and lifted the male victim's circumcised penis with the tip. 'These splatters don't belong to our John Doe.'

'So whose then? The killer's maybe?'

York shook his head. 'A man who goes to this much trouble isn't going to leave buckets of spunk lying around for us to find. These sheets haven't been changed for a long time. Prostitutes turning tricks in here two or three times a night, you get the picture.'

She winced. 'Charming.'

From the doorway a tentative voice entered the room. It was the young officer who'd puked in the corridor. 'Detectives?'

Both York and Newport stood. 'What is it, son?' asked York.

'Man here to see you. Claims he runs the place.'

'Liam Grayson,' she said to York. 'Would you like to go and make the man's acquaintance, or should I?'

For the hundredth time York adjusted his trilby. 'I think we should both go. It might be less of a blow when we tell him he's going to have to buy a new bed.'

*

The hotel office looked like something from a post-apocalyptic war film. Tiled walls and linoleum flooring, the small workspace had once been used as a kitchen maybe, but now it offered nothing but a cheap pockmarked desk, a single filing cabinet overloaded with junk, and pictures of semi-clad men bent into alphabetical positions. The hotel manager was of another persuasion it seemed.

Sitting at the desk Liam Grayson stared back at the detectives, self-satisfied leer smudged across his face. Newport didn't like the man on sight; like she'd expected anything else. A couple of stone overweight and thinning badly on top, Grayson boasted possibly the best and definitely the worst sunbed tan she'd ever seen.

'Mr Grayson, sorry to have dragged you from your bed so early in the –'

'I wasn't in bed,' Grayson cut in. His voice was surprisingly deep.

York stayed quiet.

'Oh,' Newport added, 'so where were you?'

'I don't see how that's any of your business, Detective,' Grayson replied, examining his ring clad fingers. 'Exactly how many times are you going to pull this shit?'

'Pull what, Liam?' asked York.

The hotel manager shifted his attention. 'Ah, the mechanic speaks.'

York's expression didn't alter. 'My colleague's name is DS Newport. I'd appreciate it if you'd answer her questions.'

'Or?'

'Or,' Newport cut in, 'I put your arse in handcuffs for impeding our investigation and drag you out into the street. Being made to look like a bitch by a woman half your size and weight's going to sting, believe me. Especially around here.'

From the corner of her eye, she caught her partner stashing away a grin. Gone were the days when he had to fight her corner with scum like Grayson.

The manager's smirk disappeared. The last thing he needed was to lose face in an area like this. He'd never recover, and he knew it.

'So,' she repeated, 'want to try again?'

'Look, I know what's going on here. You're trying to accuse me of running a brothel again. Or a drug den, whichever it is this time. I run a legitimate business. If there's tricky stuff going on in the rooms from time to time, I don't know about it. That's what hotels are about, privacy. You think I give a shit if somebody offs themself in some fucked up powder frenzy? The guests don't tell and I don't listen. It's that fucking simple.'

'Touching,' muttered York.

'I'm not the type, Detective.'

Newport waited a second. 'We're not here to accuse you of anything, mate. We're here to inform you that there's been a double murder in one of your rooms.'

Grayson's orange face turned quickly grey. 'What? Nah…this is a windup, right?'

'No windup, sir. Room sixteen has been cordoned off for investigation.'

'What, so they're still here...the bodies?' Grayson spat. 'Where's Danny?'

York glanced at his notepad. 'Your night manager, Daniel Ronson? He's at the hospital. Went into shock when he walked in on the bodies. Probably going to need some counselling.'

Grayson sat back in his seat, eyes glazed. 'Who did this?' he said finally. 'You catch anyone?'

York shook his head. 'We need to know if there's been any fresh custom around here lately? Anyone you don't know, anybody new to the area who's taken a room from you?'

'New faces're coming through here all the time. Could have been any of them. What about the Paki in the shop next door, you talked to him yet? Creepy bastard doesn't miss a trick.'

'He's being interviewed. You keep a ledger?'

'Of course we keep a ledger, but if you were using a room here to snort coke off a pro's tits, would you write your real name down to confirm it?'

York shrugged.

'How about the CCTV?' asked Newport.

'Most of the cameras are in action,' Grayson revealed. 'We run a monthly hard drive before it automatically overwrites.'

The detectives gave each other a glance. Operational cameras in a place like this? Whatever next? 'We're going to need to see that system,' she requested, pretending to write something down.

Liam Grayson wasn't their man. He was way off profile. Still, now they had a potential exhibit A. They thanked him and left the office.

Out in the street, two dark Range Rover 4*4s had arrived and were parked at an angle against the curb by a couple of overflowing wheelie-bins, a sole uniform nearby. The vehicles belonged to Will Graham, the head of field forensics, and his team.

It was no secret around the station that Graham had a thing for Newport, despite her very obvious wedding band. She used to be tolerant of his advances; now she avoided him wherever possible. It had all become a little too weird.

'Want to get some breakfast?' York asked.

Newport checked her watch. It was a little after five-thirty. Daylight was already beginning to beat the darkness into submission, the first rays of the day chasing away the stubborn shadows. If the previous few days of heatwave were anything to go by, it was going to be another scorcher. 'Your turn to buy?'

York adjusted his trilby. 'If you say so,' he muttered.

2

DCI York stood to the rear of the room known as the Pit, as Detective Superintendent Judy Mason, or the Pit Bull as the department furtively referred to her, gave her briefing. York struggled to stay focused.

It wasn't the method of the murders that bothered him, but the way everything had been so carefully executed. Will Graham would not find anything from a forensics angle, York was certain of that, just as the CCTV cameras would show them nothing. Whoever had done this was smart and he had a plan. This wasn't going to go away quickly.

'You'll go crazy, thinking like that.'

Newport arrived at his side and handed him some coffee from the machine in the corridor. 'You know,' she added, 'you've had that stain on your lapel since breakfast.'

York glanced down at his jacket. There was no stain.

'What were you thinking about?'

He stared straight ahead. 'I have a bad feeling about this one, Holly. I think this is going to become personal, for both of us.'

'How do you mean?'

'This guy is clever, smarter than the average. He's going to be watching us. I'll be amazed if he doesn't know our names already.'

'Should I take that coffee back? You sound wired.'

York lowered his tone. 'Twice in as many weeks, did you think of that?'

'Twice what?'

'Do you not read the papers, Sergeant?'

It took a moment for it to click. 'That Fred and Rosemary West thing in Gloucester?'

York shrugged. 'Too convenient?'

'A bit. Are you sure you're alright, boss? You don't look good.'

'I haven't been sleeping.'

'You been to see anyone about that?'

'Yeah.'

The melee of officers listened attentively as Judy Mason talked about the transfer of the two unidentified corpses to Pathology, and of Will Graham's field team bringing in new evidence.

'You're not buying all this, are you?' Newport asked.

York kept his eyes trained on the gathering. 'Buying what?'

'You don't think Graham's going to find anything.'

'I know he isn't. Nothing he wasn't meant to find.'

The briefing over, Superintendant Mason asked for York and Newport to join her in one of the briefing rooms. Something to do with the recording they'd found. It was currently with Jonathan Wheeler, the department's data analyst. Like Will Graham, Wheeler had a room full of toys and he was good at what he did, though what that might have been was anybody's guess.

Slowly the throng of bodies swarming around the Superintendent began to thin. Mason headed directly to the meeting rooms. York caught her eye as she passed and acknowledged her with the slightest of nods. Mason returned it.

'Tell them I'll be there in a minute,' he said to Newport.

'Yep,' she muttered and trailed Mason.

*

'How do you feel?'

York heard the question but didn't reply. Instead he peered into his own charcoal eyes in the bathroom mirror.

There was no easy answer to that question. In truth he felt morally lost. Who was he now? He was a man. He was a police officer. The moral list ended there; the immoral list was longer.

'I asked you a question, Nicky.'

'I heard it,' York acknowledged.

'Are you choosing not to answer?'

'Am I choosing...not to...'

'Yes?'

'I'm choosing to think.'

Twisting the tap, York leaned forwards and splashed his face with cold water. The icy spray jolted him.

In the minute that followed there was silence in the bathroom. York was thankful for that. He wasn't a fan of probing questions. Unless he was the one asking them.

'You can't go on like this, Nicky. You know that, don't you?'

'Like what?'

'You know what I'm talking about. You can't go on punishing yourself.'

Refusing to avert the stiff gaze from his own eyes, York knew what the words meant. 'I feel…'

'Yes?'

'I feel sometimes as though I'm wading through the ashes of my life's remains. And it's fucking slow going.'

A pause. 'Go on…'

'How am I supposed to feel? All I know is anger. Moments of levity actually cause me pain now.'

'Then you must push that demon out.'

York bent over the sink. 'I don't believe in demons, you know that.'

'Choosing not to believe in demons won't protect you from them.'

The density of that remark slugged York in the gut. For a moment he stood frigidly, doused in the subtle bathroom glow. 'What should I do?'

'I can't tell you that, Nicky.'

York gave a subtle nod. Giving his face one more splash of cold water, he turned off the tap and took a step back. The mirror's reflection of the bathroom gave nothing away. Turning, he took in the room with his own eyes and blinked, blinked again.

He was alone.

3

As York entered the cramped and sweltering briefing room, four sets of eyes tracked him.

'Good of you to join us, Nick,' Mason stated in her almost manly tone. There was an edge of sarcasm in the comment, which wasn't lost on anyone.

York didn't mind, Mason's brogue was her way of pressing her authority. An authority few dared question. She was blonde and petite, which gave off a natural air of underestimation. An underestimation some had lived to regret.

'Had to use the bathroom,' he told her, meeting Mason's eyes and holding them.

In the room was Newport, Will Graham and Jonathan Wheeler. Graham stood and shook hands with York as he passed, forever – and happily so – in the detective's shadow. A couple of stone overweight, Graham's shirt, probably bought for him by his mother, stretched over his belly daring the buttons to pop. His trousers, *definitely* bought for him by his mother, dropped about two inches short of his shoes showing off the white of his socks. And no one quite knew what was going on with the moustache he was trying to grow – maybe his mother thought it'd suit him.

'How you doing, Will?' asked York.

'Been up all night, mate, can't be that good.'

York took a seat at the end of the table.

Jonathan Wheeler hadn't spoken yet, but then he barely ever talked. He was the kind of guy who chose his words carefully. As far as York could tell, Wheeler worked out a lot, ate a gargantuan amount of food, and did his job to a high standard. Credentials enough not to speak if you chose.

'Okay,' Mason began from the head of the table, 'here's what we have. Desk takes an anonymous call at three-oh-seven telling us two bodies with their hearts missing are waiting to be found in a crap hole in the middle of Peckham. Not our standard run-of-the-mill crime so we're going to need some quick results. If the press gets hold of this before we take some kind of hold we're going to get eaten alive. Some of those vultures want their own Fred and Rose scoop, and sooner or later I'm going to have to make a statement. I'd like to have something to tell them. Liam Grayson, our charming hotel manager, has already provided us with some CCTV footage, and we've quickly established he's not involved. But that does not mean he doesn't know someone who is. So, who wants to go first? I'm sure you're all itching.'

Mason took a seat and looked around the table. There was a brief moment of fidgeting until Will Graham stood up.

Mason raised her eyebrows. 'Thank you, Will. What have you got?'

With a briefly inappropriate glance at Newport's chest, the forensics man moved to the head of the table. 'Haven't got much yet, I'm afraid,' he mumbled.

'Louder please,' said Mason.

'From a forensics angle we haven't got much to tell yet, ma'am,' Graham said louder. 'We took several semen samples from the bed sheets and several blood samples, both lots of which are being analysed as we speak.'

'How hopeful are we of those being linked to our guy?' Mason asked. 'And don't call me ma'am.'

York interjected. 'Not hopeful at all, guv. This killer is not the sloppy type. Excuse the pun.'

Mason didn't smile. 'Is that your gut, or do you have something concrete?'

'Gut,' he admitted.

'Okay, noted. Fingerprints?'

'We've taken prints from around the room,' Graham continued. 'Items which are most likely to be touched: light switches, taps, et cetera.'

'And?'

'Nothing yet, ma…*guv*, but we're working on it. The room is rife with prints so we should be able to put a list together of suitable candidates within twenty-four hours.'

York stood up and removed his trilby. He placed it gently on the table in front of him. 'Sorry to be a pessimist, Will, but you're not going to find any prints belonging to our killer.' Will Graham went back to his seat, happy to pass the reigns. 'The killer directed us to the voice recorder, he wanted us to find that. Whoever this man is he's playing us, daring us to go after him because he knows we have to. In fact he's banking on it.'

Mason said, 'More hunches?'

York shrugged.

'So the only thing we have to go on at this time is the voice recorder, which he gave us?'

The room's lack of response was affirmation of that. 'What about the CCTV?' Newport asked.

'My guys are viewing it as we speak,' said Graham. 'Nothing so far.'

'Alright,' Mason pressed, 'that's enough. Let's hear the recording, Jonathan.'

Without a word, Jonathan Wheeler snapped on a pair of latex gloves and removed the small voice recorder from the plastic evidence bag. He placed it in the centre of the table and sat back down. Without asking if everyone was ready, he leant forward and hit the play button.

'So, from this point on I would like to make my intentions very clear for the hard of understanding. This is just the beginning. The two… for the sake of argument "people"…in whom I took immense pleasure ending their miserable lives, will not be missed. They are…they were, *as you will discover, at the very core of everything that is rotten. So please, I beg you all, do not shed a tear, and do not mourn Michael and Harriet Fuller. To feel any kind of pity for these people will only diminish what I have achieved tonight. And whether or not you would agree, I have achieved a great deal.*

'The time is 3am. At the conclusion of this recording there is a riddle. I would like the elite few listening to this message to solve it and return it to me within twelve hours. In precisely eleven hours a man will appear opposite your building and he will wait for one hour. He will be wearing a green hooded sweater. You will not speak to him, you will not address him in any way. You will simply hand him an envelope containing your answer and allow him to walk away.

'Now, pay attention, this is the fun bit. If you fail to answer the riddle correctly I will kill a promising young law student. If you succeed, I will kill a convicted paedophile. Either way, somebody dies. Any deviation from the rules, they both die. However, I'm sure we'd all like the same outcome, so I urge you to think long and hard about the solution. A young girl's life depends on it.'

Static…

'An apple begins with me and age too. I am in the midst of a man and foremost in every apprehension. You will find me in everyday and see me in all autumns. It's a pity that you cannot see me in the night, when run must I, hidden from sight.

'Twelve hours…tick tock…'

The quiet in the meeting room thickened, stolen briefly by static. Wheeler reached forward and switched it off.

Eventually York spoke, shattering the tension. 'That's why he left the bodies in that dump.'

'Why?' asked Newport

'He saw Grayson's hotel as a mirror for the victim's souls: rotten and dirty.'

Mason interjected. 'Jonathan, what have you been able to take from the recording?'

'Nothing at all yet, guv,' the techie admitted, shifting his lean frame to the head of the table. Sweat marks were visible at his armpits. 'Whoever made the recording knew what they were doing. They made it within a silent environment so there is literally no background sound at all. Not a single foreign decibel to go on.'

'That's impossible!'

'That's what I thought.'

'So that leaves us with a riddle to solve,' York threw in.

'It's not as simple as that, Nick,' said Mason. 'Solution or not, somebody dies. It doesn't matter who that is, or what he's done, we're the police and we can't hang a man out to dry based on immoral life choices.'

'Tell me you're kidding? We can't hang a young girl out to dry either because we felt like being righteous today.'

'It's not about that, Nick!'

'Then tell me what it is about, guv. Because I'm going to need to hear it.'

'We have a moral obligation as police officers to protect our citizens, no matter what they've done. If this paedophile is back on the street after a conviction, then he's served some punishment and been deemed fit for release. It's not our call to punish him further.'

This time not even a hiss of static betrayed the silence. 'Okay, that's your call,' said York. 'But when this twenty-something girl is found with her heart torn out because we failed to follow simple instructions, I won't be the one talking to her family. The system fails enough people, Judy, let's try and do the right thing here.'

Mason pondered for a moment under the scrutiny of the others, her clear blue eyes unreadable. 'Okay…' she said at last, 'Will, Jonathan, get teams together and solve the riddle. But I want every available resource on this to make sure we never have to make that choice. We have a window of eight to nine hours left to bring this guy in, let's not waste it. Nick, take Holly and find out who Michael and Harriet Fuller are. Get out to their house and see what made them tick. If they are garbage as we're being made to believe, I want to know why.'

York and Newport stood in unison.

'Before you go, Nick,' she added, 'A word in private. Everyone else is dismissed. Let's get cracking.'

Picking up files and evidence bags, everyone but Mason and York left the room. Waiting for the door to click closed, the two officers eyed each other with patience. 'Want to tell me what's going on with you?'

York took a seat and adjusted his hat. 'In what regard?'

'You look like shit, Nick. I need to know if you're fit to work. If I didn't know better I'd say you'd been drinking.'

'Is this because I opposed you in front of the others?'

'Don't even suggest that!' Mason snapped. 'I'm pulling you up because you look like crap, and I don't need to see headline pictures tomorrow morning of our leading detective looking like a bum.'

'I haven't been sleeping. That's it.'

'People on a lack of sleep don't look as rough as you, Nick.'

'Jesus, are you being paid to give me abuse?'

Mason paused. 'Okay, if you say you're alright, I believe you. But if you're lying to me, I'm going to be upset, and my dog doesn't like it when I come home upset. I hope you know what I'm saying.'

'Your dog's hormonal?'

'Nick!'

'I'm not lying to you, Judy! But I did have a request.'

'Go on.'

'I want to be assigned solely to this case. I don't need anyone else.'

Mason didn't react. 'Something going on between you and Newport?'

'No, nothing like that. I just have a bad feeling about this guy. He's going to make it personal and I'd rather Newport wasn't in the crosshairs.'

'It's her job to be in the crosshairs. Are you worried for her husband? Because we can put her house under protection if it comes to that.'

York turned away, the faintest bruise of anguish flicking across his brow.

'Shit, Nick, I didn't mean it like that.'

He brushed it off. 'The logic behind it works, though, doesn't it? Newport's family could be in danger. Mine's gone, Judy, he can't make it personal with me.'

Mason scratched behind her ear to stall. Then she said, 'Request denied.'

York sighed. 'You're making a mistake.'

'Well time will tell, won't it? I want Holly with you on this.'

York stood and headed to the door.

'And Nick,' she added, 'lose the hat, you're not Elliot Ness.'

York shrugged. 'And he wasn't Nicolas York, but he still wore the hat.'

4

Park Lane was filling steadily now, humans flooding the pavements. Bodies were bustling through the streets heading to work, pouring from the Marble Arch underground in multicultural droves, while others not so fortunate lay buried in doorways under rags and self-pity. Gridlocked roads were the next thing on the morning's agenda.

Now that Michael and Harriet Fuller had been identified, their address had been easy enough to find. York stood beneath the towering block and couldn't argue that the couple had taste. It was a converted townhouse building off Hyde Park Corner, and it looked like it should be filled with those cosmetic surgery quacks or Fortune 500 magnates. According to his info, Michael Fuller was a car salesman, his wife a care worker. Neither occupation belonged in this building.

He eyed the flat numbers in the entrance and hit the intercom. As expected, only static replied. Since the couple was dead, the court order to search the property had been granted quickly. Usually these things were cut and dry. The caretaker had been called and was meeting them onsite.

'What do you think?' said Newport.

Shielding his eyes against the sun, York scanned the building's fascia.

'On a beautiful day like today, too,' Newport replied, as if that were somehow relevant.

A nicotine-laced voice intruded. 'You the police?'

Despite the simple black shirt and black trousers, the bunch of keys swinging from his belt loop gave the newcomer away as the caretaker.

York abandoned the intercom. 'Malcolm?'

'Uh-huh.'

The caretaker led the way into the foyer, patently sidestepping York's extended hand.

'You probably hear this all the time,' said York, 'but you look just like –'

'Morgan Freeman, yeah I know,' said Malcolm, dead-panning the comment.

Newport grinned. 'Did you know Michael or Harriet?'

Heading up the steps, Malcolm's keys jangled against his hip. 'As well as anyone. So no, not really. I knew them in passing. Them and their little girl.'

Halting mid-step, Newport said, 'Wait, what little girl?'

'The Fullers!' Malcolm stopped and turned on the steps. 'They have a little girl. You're the police, aren't you supposed to know stuff like that?'

The caretaker huffed as if pleased and continued on up the stairs.

No one had mentioned a little girl.

'What they done anyway?' said Malcolm.

'We're not at liberty to discuss that, sir,' Newport replied.

Bringing up the rear, York smiled. What Newport meant was we didn't have the first bloody idea.

'Here it is,' Malcolm grumbled as they reached the third and topmost floor of the building. The caretaker perused his loop of keys and pushed open the door to the Fullers' apartment, releasing the pungent aroma of class. Intensely modern, the plan opened up into a large living area with huge panel windows showing off a sun-dappled panorama of Hyde Park. The enormous home cinema, the frenzy of artwork, the plush carpets and leather sofas, all spoke lavish.

York whistled in awe. 'How much do these apartments go for?'

Malcolm shrugged. 'one-point-five mil without breaking a sweat. No appeal, you ask me. No personality to them. Only good people live here, though. Everyone trusts everyone. Most of them don't even lock their doors in the day.'

'Have you ever seen anyone coming or going from the building who didn't belong?'

'What do you mean, like one of them Asian types?'

'No, Malcolm. Take a look at this picture.' He plucked the mugshot of Liam Grayson from his jacket pocket. 'You know this guy?'

'Never seen him. Looks like one of them fagg –'

'Thank you, Malcolm, you've been a great help. We can see ourselves out from here.'

Newport walked Malcolm to the door who seemed only too glad to oblige. 'I'll be waiting downstairs,' the caretaker called back. 'And hurry up, I got shit to do.'

From an outsider's perspective the apartment looked like any other, despite the obvious "out of most people's price range" mod-cons. The place was neat and kempt, visibly clean, and smelled of pine. From a detective's viewpoint, the flat was a little *too* immaculate.

Flipping off his hat York stepped into the large, almost clinical kitchen. More pine, this time infused with some kind of cleaning agent. Directly in front of him the refrigerator stared him down. It was a simple household fridge like any other, only this one was bleeding. 'Newport, get in here!'

His partner appeared in the doorway, scepticism splashed across her pixiesque face. 'What is it?'

'Got some gloves?' He pointed out the small patch of cloying blood at the foot of the fridge.

Without trace of hesitation, she fished a pair of latex gloves from her pocket and snapped them on.

'You've got the honours,' he announced.

Newport stepped forward and straddled the dark red pool. Gripping the fridge handle, the door swung coldly outwards. Both detectives stood and eyed the two items sitting gorily on the central shelf atop a large oval meat platter.

Silence ruled for a moment.

'I think we've found what remains of Michael and Harriet,' she uttered.

York nodded thoughtfully. The two human hearts stared at them mockingly.

This is a game to him, and we're inferior players.

York's own words came thundering back. He realised he'd never been so right. He should have felt sick but he didn't. Not even mildly. Breaking the spell, he called the station from a phone mounted on the kitchen wall. Will Graham was going to have a field day here.

'What now?' Newport asked.

York checked his watch. 'I reckon we have about twenty minutes until Graham and his team show up, so let's keep looking. Got to be something here to uproot this fucker.'

Newport turned to York and began following him from the kitchen, their step faltering as a jarring thud reverberated through the laminate flooring. Newport glanced at her superior who was standing motionless, head cocked.

'Malcolm?' she suggested.

York moved to the kitchen window and peered down at the street. Without a word he gestured Newport join him. The caretaker was smoking a cigarette out on the pavement.

'Not Malcolm,' he uttered.

Staying tight, the detectives moved stealthily through the kitchen and into the living room. Perfect rectangular slabs of daylight beamed through the panoramic panes filling the large room with natural light.

Another thud, this time from the direction of the bedrooms.

Edging further in, York found himself in the corridor off the main living area, Newport firmly at his back. He directed her to the first bedroom and stepped into the second: damp and fusty, as if the room didn't see much use. The big space was well lit, two large windows jostled into the wall. King-sized bed, walk-in closet, massive vanity unit and mirror; all in immaculate upkeep.

He halted, waiting for another sound. An instant later, from the depths of some deep, deep lungs, he was obliged. Goosebumps rose on his arms as the echoing crunch and cry of pain echoed out through the flat. A cry belonging undeniably to his partner.

*

Will Graham's unit was buzzing around the apartment block, sealing off necessary areas and annoying the residents. Malcolm the caretaker had been only too willing to avoid all questions, but there was no doubt in anybody's mind that he wasn't involved. He was a stubborn old bigot who had chosen the path to an easy life a long time ago. After recognising the caretaker's evasion as nothing more than sheer disinterest, York had sent him on his way.

'How you holding up?'

Holding an icepack to the back of her head, Newport grimaced. She was sitting in the apartment's living area, keeping her head down.

'Need some painkillers?' York added.

'Had some,' she muttered. 'They haven't made a dent.'

Hearing Newport's scream, he'd bolted from the master bedroom and into the second, smaller room. As he burst through the door into what could only be a child's room, he had been faced with the most surreal vision he could have imagined. Down on one knee, Newport was clutching her head and her consciousness with all she had, while standing against the single bed was a catatonic kid of around nine or ten gripping a baseball bat. The young girl had taken little subduing. After taking away the bat and assuring her that they weren't there to hurt her, the girl had yielded and allowed herself to be placed on a recliner in the corner of the room. Aside from Newport's pride needing a little mouth-to-mouth, she was largely undamaged. Graham and his team joined the party two minutes later.

By the kitchen entrance, he spotted Graham chatting animatedly to one of his unit. He'd changed his shirt since earlier and somehow this one seemed tighter than the last, the buttons fighting for survival. Spotting York and Newport, Graham ushered his guy away and made a beeline for them. Nothing short of a gun to the head could have kept him away.

'Brace yourself,' York muttered.

Newport glanced up and spotted Graham making his way through the knot of officers. She merely reapplied the icepack.

'Now then,' beamed Graham, 'what is it about you two that seems to attract trouble?'

No one replied.

'And Holly, I've seen you reduce grown men to tears, seen you stare down a Rottweiler for God's sake. And now you're being beaten down by a minor?'

Newport peered up, face hidden behind a veil of thunder. 'She was hiding behind a chest of drawers, Will. I didn't know she was there, I'm not Luke fucking Skywalker. And I'm fine by the way, thanks for asking.'

Graham froze, stared back at Newport like her head was on fire. 'Holly…I didn't…I didn't mean…'

'It's fine, Will, forget it,' York cut in. 'Holly's okay. Tell me what you've got.'

Graham's grin promptly returned. 'Not much to tell yet. The hearts probably belong to Michael and Harriet but that's to be confirmed. And there seems to be some kind of markings in one of them. Bites, maybe.'

'Bites?

'I know, this shit just gets weirder, doesn't it?' Graham grinned.

'And the girl?' Newport asked.

'She's been taken back to the station. She's in shock so we haven't got much from her yet, but there's a guy from Social Services coming in to talk to her. We can get a shrink too if necessary.'

'*And the girl*?' Newport stressed.

'Oh, erm, yes, she's the Fullers' daughter. Her name is Abigail, ten years old. We found the family documentation, birth certificates and whatnot. Some photo albums too. It's conclusive.'

Newport went back to the view.

'Will?' York turned to see one of Graham's geeks standing awkwardly outside their circle.

'What is it, Tom?' said Graham.

'I think you and DCI York should come and see this. In the kid's bedroom, we've found...'

The so-called Tom let the sentence trail off, as though finishing it would end everything in chaos. 'It's okay, son,' York stepped in. 'Take your time. What have you got?'

Tom moved nervously from foot to foot. 'I think it's probably best you...see for yourselves.'

Leaving Newport to her icepack, York and Graham followed Tom to Abigail Fuller's bedroom. The atmosphere of the scene suddenly felt several shades darker, like something from a Tim Burton film.

Abigail's bedroom had mostly been decorated in green, with the exception of the *Bill & Ted's* bed sheets and posters, Keanu Reeves's face plastered across most surfaces. Aside from the large *Panasonic* TV and the acoustic guitar propped against one corner, the room was like any other belonging to a ten year old girl. Most girls of that age, though, didn't have a secret compartment behind their wardrobe; one that she probably knew nothing about.

The huge unit had been pulled away from the wall and was being crowded by Graham's nerds. Nobody objected to York's intrusion.

He peered inside the enclosure and was given the answers to a handful of questions, like why the Fullers had popped up on the killer's radar, and how they could afford to live in this building.

He reached in and plucked one of the VHS tapes from the collection, examining the homemade cover. Behind him the room lingered in expectant quiet.

Replacing the tape, he turned morosely, faced the body of officers crowding the room and took a deep breath. 'The killer of Michael and Harriet Fuller told us…he told us that these people were at the core of everything rotten. He wasn't wrong. Some of you may have seen movies like this before, and some of you will again. But the fact that these have been secreted by the parents of a ten year old girl, *in her bedroom,* makes them two of the vilest people I've ever come across. But that does not alter the objectives of anyone in this room. Some of you may feel that Michael and Harriet Fuller got what they deserved, and I wouldn't blame you. But they were murdered by an individual who had no right or authority to deal out vigilante justice. And we still need to catch him. So, now that he has our attention, everybody needs to stay on focus and remember what we're doing here.'

The hush dissipated as the room went back to business and York slipped away unnoticed. This episode had darkened his heart that little bit, and for the briefest of moments he felt gratitude towards the person they were hunting. There were some things out there more despicable than murder, more loathsome. Making snuff movies and hiding them in your ten year old daughter's bedroom was one of them.

5

York itched to be alone.

The lifts out of order, he took the stairs to his apartment. A tornado of desperation bubbled inside him, coiling carelessly around his insides. Sometimes he could suppress the jolts of pain. Sometimes it was pointless to try.

The index finger on his left hand began to twitch. This was a new development. He noticed it for the first time a couple of weeks ago, amazed no one in the Pit had pulled him up on it.

Straight after he and Newport left the Fullers' apartment, they went their separate ways. He'd gone straight from the scene to his flat in Pimlico where he lived alone.

His block was nothing special, his apartment less so, but it was a place to get his head down, and a place he invited no one. It was the only personal space he had left.

Pushing his way in through the front door, he toed a bunch of post from his path and stumbled down the hallway to the kitchen. He hadn't eaten anything since breakfast, but food shopping was rarely on his agenda. The shelves were bare, the fridge likewise.

Thoughts of food dismissed, a torrent of pain struck him below the stomach, like a spike thrusting through his liver. He wouldn't be able to put it off much longer.

Staggering groggily through to the bedroom he tugged off the sweat-damp trilby and took a seat on the end of the unmade bed, a tangle of sheets pushed back against the headboard. His breathing was heavy. He stared at the blank canvass of the wall in front of him, eyes fixed on something beyond. Shoulders stooped forwards, he clung onto the whispery tendrils of denial with all he had.

The hands of the clock ticked on. He had no clue how long he stayed like this, staring in this transfixed, almost hypnotic state.

He waited, trying to recall the face that haunted his dreams each night. He had photographs but they were carefully boxed and taped, stored elsewhere. All the walls in the apartment were bare. Since moving out of the family house and into the flat, he had refused to display memories. Photographs were a fabrication. They spoke of a time when smiling was a part of daily life, laughter was commonplace.

As though on cue his wife's face emerged from the brickwork: painfully beautiful smile, eyes infinitely sad. He knew it was an illusion, the product of a damaged mind; she had been gone a long time, but still Leanne came to him, sometimes Frasier too.

Two years ago his wife had gone on a business trip to Germany, and because York had been up to the eyeballs with an investigation, she had taken their four year old son with her. Saying goodbye to them on that chilly April morning had been the last time he'd seen them alive. That was twenty-something months ago. Leanne's body turned up in Hanover six weeks after the disappearance, gagged, hogtied and dumped in a park like some fly-tipped mattress. Frasier was still missing.

Leanne had been badly beaten and dealt a crushing strike to the back of the neck. Frasier had been taken. Where to remained a mystery, and those German idiots hadn't shone any light onto Frasier's vanishing act in the eight sleepless months of their investigation.

He couldn't imagine what his son might be enduring. Sometimes, he wished him dead. Surely now, dead was better than enduring.

Snapping out of the vision, he tore himself away. He pulled out a small wallet from his jacket, unzipped it and laid it gently on the bed. Tugging off his coat he rolled up his sleeve. He didn't want to do this to himself anymore, but his half-assed attempts at going cold came with wracking pain and despair.

Unsnapping the spoon, he squeezed a small vial of water into it. Next he unwrapped the small brown stone, about the size of a tic-tac and the last he had, and dropped it into the water. The flame danced as he struck the silver Zippo, the orange tongues begging for vocation. He heated the solution, watching carefully as the brown stone dissolved. As the water began bubbling brown, he soaked it up with a cotton bud and drew from it with the syringe.

He paused and checked himself. Then he pushed the needle into an unhealed puncture mark in the crux of his arm and drew a trace amount of blood. The needle was flush. Exhaling deeply, Leanne's face emerged from the smoky confines of his mind. She was smiling.

Pushing down slowly on the plunger, he fell back onto the bed and into the open arms of an uncaring oblivion.

6

Dropping the Ford into reverse, Newport slotted the car expertly into the vacant space. The car park was quiet, which probably meant the wine bar would be too. She was relieved. High volumes would be a distraction, and her next words would have to be chosen carefully.

The back of her head stung like hell. A lump had graced its presence just below her crown and she massaged it. For a second she remained behind the wheel and focused on a broken patch of plaster-wall through the windscreen; a debris of bricks and rubble at the top of the lot which mirrored her thoughts. That moment back in the Fullers' flat, that split second before she realised she was being attacked, she thought that was it, her bucket was kicked. She remembered being the most terrified she could ever recall being. She and York were shrewd coppers, how could they have missed something like that? She shuddered as she recalled the haziness lifting, thankful to be alive.

York had been staring down at her; the distorted image of his tired eyes and battered trilby had been nothing short of beautiful. Her heart was still racing.

Plucking off her glasses and pocketing them, she climbed from the car. There weren't many vehicles around, but next to a long-ago abandoned skip was the green Peugeot she expected. That meant its owner was waiting for her inside.

Straight opposite, a burgundy Vauxhall sat motionless in the afternoon sun. From the glare of the windscreen she couldn't see inside, but someone was in there, watching her. Too broad to be a woman, she thought, but she didn't recognise the car. Dusting the paranoia from her shoulders, she went inside.

At peak time in the day the stuffy heat was growing more intense. She was glad to get indoors, dark and shaded as the lounge usually was. There weren't many punters. Aside from a couple of full booths and a guitarist setting up for the night, the place was deserted. Only one set of eyes tracked her as she entered, and a pleasant shiver danced through her.

Fearing hesitation, she marched confidently to the booth and sat down opposite the petite woman: pretty, blonde bobbed and stony-faced. A moment of sturdy silence hung between them.

'Didn't think you'd show,' the blonde uttered at last.

Newport smiled half genuinely. She realised she was twiddling her thumbs. 'I have to be honest, Kellie, I thought about postponing.'

Kellie dropped her shoulders like she always did when she was waiting.

'A big one opened up today. Another mentalist who likes to play games with people's lives.'

'Sounds familiar.'

'What's that supposed to mean?'

'What's this nutcase all about?' asked Kellie, sidestepping the question.

After the jab left Kellie's lips, she picked up her thin-looking Americano and took a sip. Newport couldn't help but stare, mesmerized by Kellie's plump lips as they met the porcelain cup and sipped at the coffee. It didn't matter that her comment about things sounding familiar was a dig at her, and it didn't matter that she was clearly angry. All that mattered was that she was here with her now, where she could drink from her aura.

'I can't talk to you about an open investigation, Kellie, you know that.'

'You brought it up. Anyway, can't blame a girl for trying to make conversation, can you?'

Taking the question as rhetorical, Newport said, 'It's good to see you, sweetie.' She thought about leaning over the table and taking Kellie's hand, but doubted it would be accepted. A thin smile spread across Kellie's lips and disappeared just as quickly. 'Holly, I asked you here because we need to talk this thing out. I can't go on like this. We're going round in circles and if we don't add some kind of solidarity to the situation soon, I am literally going to implode. This has been going on for almost eighteen months now, did you know that?'

Newport nodded, but in truth she was astounded things had been carrying on that long, and at how good she'd become at covering her tracks. Since the day she met Kellie in that supermarket, Newport's life had been incredible. It had also been a curse. For so long she'd lived a second life outside of her marriage, with a second lover and a second home life. At first there had been guilt. Having the affair behind her husband David's back was something she could never have envisaged, and when she first began seeing Kellie, she had been caught up in a real crisis of conscience. But over time those feelings had rescinded. Kellie was now all she thought about. Her dreams and her future plans all involved her. David had become a blurry second.

Now cooler, Kellie braved a bigger swig of the coffee. 'For a year now, you've been telling me you're leaving David. How long am I supposed to wait for you?'

'I hate that I'm putting you through this, baby, I really am. It's just that David's been away on business a lot lately and I haven't seen him.'

Kellie sighed audibly.

'It's true. I want nothing more than to begin building a life with you, but right now –'

'I met someone,' Kellie cut in.

The words sliced through her, tore at her heartstrings. The silence became so complete, so perfect, it distorted the air. 'Wh…who is she?' The question was childish, but she could think of little else to say.

'Who said it's a she?'

'You've known you were gay since you were fourteen, Kellie. Don't try and tell me I've turned you straight.'

Kellie shook her head dismissively.

Newport felt winded. It seemed like her lover was deliberately trying to hurt her. She reached for Kellie's hand but Kellie retracted it. 'Why are you being like this?'

'Like what?' said Kellie.

'Like a cunt!'

Silence. Then, 'I'll pretend you didn't say that, Holly.'

'Kellie, please…' Newport knew she sounded pathetic, she just didn't care. She had come here expecting a kick in the teeth, but not this.

'I've just had some time to think, Holly. I don't want to give you an ultimatum –'

'Then don't!'

'…but I don't know what else to do.'

'Kellie, please…' she said again.

'Look, something's come up in my life, a new assignment,' Kellie declared. 'I won't be able to see you for a while. Maybe it's the time apart we need. Think about what I've said to you today. I'm begging you, Holly, just think about it.'

'What new assignment?'

Kellie dismissed the question.

'Why are you putting me in this position, Kellie? Can you not see how unfair this is?'

It wasn't unfair, not in the least. Kellie wanted her; nothing in the last eighteen months had changed about that. She had been patient.

Finishing her coffee, Kellie placed the cup gently down. 'The only reason it's come to this is because you refuse to leave David, a man you claim you don't even love. You're not a timeshare flat, baby, I don't want to go halves on you anymore.'

Newport rubbed her eyes.

'What makes it harder,' added Kellie, 'is that I don't even understand why. If you're not in love with him anymore, why can't you leave him?'

It was a fair question. She could've lied, made something up about David's dependability, or waiting for the right time financially, but Kellie would have seen right through it. The truth was, she didn't know why she couldn't leave David.

Kellie stood up and pulled her thin leather jacket from the back of the seat. 'I want to spend my life with you, Holly,' she muttered, leaning over her. 'I do. This other person is great, but she's not you. Please don't make me do this.'

Newport climbed shakily to her feet to protest, but Kellie was gone, the fragrant vapour of her perfume lingering in her wake.

7

Sunshine cast jagged edges onto sharp surfaces. Clear became opaque, opaque clear, and the faces of passers-by took on an almost clown-like manifestation. York revelled in this. It used to worry him, now it seemed more real than when he was sober.

He entered the station by the rear door and stood alone in the darkened corridor. He slapped himself once, twice, a third time. He had to find his game face.

The artificial light from the fluorescent tubes blinded him as he entered the Pit. Blinking until his eyes adjusted, he spotted Newport. She was sitting at her desk, Will Graham leaning over her like a dog in heat. She looked only too glad to see York when he approached. He noticed his partner's eyes linger on him a little too long.

'Got nothing better to do, Will?' he said.

Pushing himself back from the desk, Graham flushed at the cheeks. 'Oh, erm, I was just –'

'You were just wasting time!'

'Actually,' Newport intervened curiously, 'he was updating me on the fingerprint analysis. You okay, guv?'

Newport's words echoed hollowly over his head. He didn't reply. Instead he turned on his heel and walked to his office, feeling the eyes burning into his back as he walked away. Newport was talking after him but the words travelled on a mashed sound wave. He closed the office door behind him and shut the blinds, placing the Pit a million miles away.

He sat down at his chaotic and picture-free desk. A confusion of files, pens and pencils obscured the ring marks to a degree, but couldn't hide the mugs of half-finished coffee, many of which hadn't moved for a fortnight, and the debris of paperwork which hadn't been organised since some time BC.

He didn't need a lot of space and he hadn't been granted much. DCI status was not all it was cracked up to be, allowing him an office no larger than a hefty broom cupboard, a desk, and two cheaply upholstered armchairs facing each other.

He flipped off his hat and rubbed his eyes, the crux of his arm aching from the overused puncture mark. He rubbed that too, the image of Gary 'Tank' Henderson's squashed face worming into his mind. He'd never asked the man why they called him Tank. He just assumed it was on account of the man's size, the term "brick shithouse" being close to literal. Still, he and Tank had an agreement: Tank would continue to supply him with class A's at a discounted rate, and he in turn would leave the dealer alone to conduct his business. It was a sound arrangement.

Pushing some paperwork aside, he eyed the printout in front of him. It was a copy of the riddle from the recording, each sentence, word and letter standing out in a bold font.

He read the whole thing aloud. He hated riddles, had never been much good at them.

An apple begins with me and age too…

What did an apple begin with, a seed, a pip? How did it 'become'?

I am in the midst of a man and foremost in every apprehension…

Who was foremost in every apprehension, a lead detective, a flatfoot?

Eyes fluttering, the phone jolted him alert. 'Nicolas York,' he answered.

Only static hissed across the line. Somebody was there, though, he could tell.

'Hello?'

Nothing, just the muffled breathing of someone standing away from the mouthpiece. Replacing the phone on the hook, he closed his stinging eyes. The phone rang again.

This time he made no move to answer, simply stared at the phone as it rang off the hook. Finally he grabbed the receiver and held it to his ear. Somebody was there again, a ragged breathing and…crying? Given no time to react, he ripped the receiver away from his ear as the piercing scream cut through the static. The hairs on his arms stood on end as the screaming abated, replaced once again by the gentle sobbing.

'*Hello?*'

The line went dead.

'Jesus,' he gasped.

'Nah, just me.' Newport was standing on the far side of his desk. He hadn't heard her come in. 'Who was that?'

York eyed the phone warily. 'Nobody,' he muttered, replacing the receiver. 'You forget how to knock?'

'I did knock! Pardon me for saying, guv, but you look like shit.'

'Yes, I've heard.'

She took a seat on the edge of the desk. He noticed her eyes lingering on his face again.

'Can I help you with something, Holly?'

A pause. 'Any luck with the riddle?' she asked.

He shrugged.

'I'll take that as a no. Just wanted to let you know that Abigail Fuller, the girl who flattened me...she's in briefing room two with the social worker.'

'Okay?'

'Well, I thought you might be interested to hear, she's started speaking.'

*

Abigail Fuller looked so small. He watched her through the one-sided mirror sitting daintily with the social worker, a podgy man of around fifty with thick grey hair and an equally thick beard.

The pair was sitting quietly, neither of them speaking, but the girl, legs dangling over the edge of her chair, looked somehow different. The traces of pallid shock that marred her face earlier were gone. What remained was a healthy-looking, pretty, ten year old girl. Did she know what had happened to her and her parents over the last few days, or was she so zoned out and traumatized by it all, she had blocked it from memory?

She didn't look traumatized, or zoned out.

Pushing his way into the briefing room York was greeted by dubious eyes. He couldn't blame them for their scepticism; it had been a strange morning, and he wasn't exactly a picture of health.

'Hello,' he said with the least fabricated smile he could muster. 'My name's Nicolas.'

Abigail Fuller didn't reply, but the social worker held out his hand. 'Hi Nicolas, I'm Roy. Roy Sunnily.'

He took Sunnily's hand and shook it. The man had a firm grip.

'Abigail,' Sunnily murmured, 'would you like to introduce yourself to Nicolas?'

York decided instantly that he liked Roy Sunnily. Not only did he have the gentlest voice attached to a gentler manner, but his name suited him perfectly.

The girl remained silent, examining York with wary yet strikingly beautiful green eyes. Eventually she muttered, 'Is that your full name?'

York smiled. 'Nope. Nicolas Alfred York is my full name.'

'*Alfred*?'

'Yep, named after my dad's favourite film director, Alfred Hitchcock.'

'Wow,' the girl proclaimed. 'Cruel.'

'Could've been worse. I should just thank my lucky stars I didn't get lumbered with Quentin or Ridley.'

The girl didn't smile. Instead she glanced up to the ceiling, at nothing.

'How are you holding up, Abigail?' he asked. 'Can I get you anything?'

Eyes fixed to the ceiling, she said, 'Keanu Reeves, perhaps?'

York's smile broadened. 'Only if I get Michelle Pfeiffer.'

'Ha, in your dreams!'

'Hey, us oldies are allowed crushes too.'

Abigail offered the faintest of smiles. 'I think I'll just have some water.'

The girl's level of maturity was astounding, York thought, and she seemed incredibly calm, like she was talking with friends in the school playground.

Signalling the uniform outside the room, York asked him to fetch a glass of water.

'So, Abbey,' he continued, 'I'm guessing you have lots of questions about the last couple of days?'

A brief shake of the head.

No.

'You don't? There's nothing you'd like to talk about?'

'I'm sorry I hit that lady,' she uttered. 'I didn't mean to hurt anyone.'

'Holly? Oh, she's okay. She knows you didn't mean it.'

She glanced down at her shoes. 'I…I…'

'Abbey,' Sunnily cut in, 'is there something you'd like to tell us?'

Another shake of the head.

'If there's anything you can remember about the last couple of nights, anything at all,' said York. 'You see, there's a bad man out there and we need to catch him before he hurts anyone.'

'Anyone *else*, you mean?'

York caught Sunnily's eye. The counsellor's apologetic face told him that the subject of the parents had already been broached.

'Abbey, look, I'm not going to try and fool you or treat you like a child. I'm very sorry for what happened to your parents –'

'No you're not! That's just something policemen say to make people feel better. Anyway, *I'm* not sorry they're dead. The world is nicer without them.'

'Abbey,' said York gently, 'do you know anything about a secret hiding place in your bedroom?' He winced at the question, but for his own peace of mind he needed to know if Abbey had ever been exposed to the VHS material. The image of Frasier's face and sandy locks seeped into his thoughts.

'Yes,' she muttered. 'I know about the secret hiding place.'

'Did you ever look inside?'

The girl remained silent and glanced back at her shoes.

'It's okay, Abbey,' he added, 'you're free to speak here, no one's going to get mad.'

'I never looked in there. I wasn't allowed.'

Very briefly Roy Sunnily's eyes flickered in York's direction. The girl was lying.

'Since the last time you saw your mum and dad,' he probed, 'where have you been?'

The girl looked blank.

'Did you leave the apartment, or were you there all along?'

'I hardly left my bedroom. I wasn't allowed out by myself. But my parents weren't there, so I went out for food a couple of times.'

Looking into Abbey's green eyes, he hesitated. 'Was there anyone else in the apartment in the last couple of days? Anybody you didn't know?'

The uniform came back with the water. The girl took it from him and held it with both hands, her gaze fixated on the glass.

'Abbey?'

'One night I was sleeping and a noise woke me. I thought mum and dad were back so I got out of bed and went down the corridor. All the lights were off, which was weird. Then I saw…'

Roy Sunnily rested his elbows on his knees and leaned forward.

'What did you see, Abbey?'

'There was a man. He was wearing black, all black. Like he'd just stepped out of midnight.'

Like he'd just stepped out of midnight..?

'What did he look like, can you describe him?'

'He was…normal. He wasn't tall but he wasn't short. Not fat, not thin. Dark hair. But he was mostly in shadow. He walked into the kitchen carrying some kind of box. I was there in the room but he didn't see me. I stayed behind the sofa. It's dark there. For a while I waited and nothing happened. I could hear noises in the kitchen, and a voice, like he was talking to himself. And then I saw him again. He was still carrying the box, and then…'

'And then what, what happened next?'

Abigail's face changed, like she was recalling something relevant, something potent. 'He just stopped. Stopped right there in the middle of the room and looked straight at me. I could see the glint of his eyes from the street lights. And I just stared back. He was looking at me, *right at me*. And then I had the weirdest thought…'

York raised his eyebrows.

'I wasn't scared of him. Not one bit.'

8

'How was the girl?'

York took a seat on the edge of Newport's desk. 'She's sorry she hit you.'

'She said that?'

'Uh-huh.'

'She say anything else? Like how she came to be alone in that apartment?'

York nodded, his thick locks bouncing over his forehead. 'Three days ago, Michael and Harriet Fuller told their daughter they'd be back later that day. They were going out all afternoon "on business". They never came back.'

'She not think to call the police?'

'She said her parents left her all the time, it was nothing new. They went to Thailand once and left her for three weeks.'

'You're kidding! She's ten.'

'She expected them back at any time. Not that she was devoid of visitors.'

Newport frowned.

'Don't get excited. She described pretty much every five-foot-something this side of the Thames. By all accounts it could've been me.'

'Was it you?'

'Funny.'

Seconds ticked by, an odd silence hanging between them. She wanted to ask York why he looked like shit again, but she knew that'd piss him off. His red-raw eyes were embedded in charcoaled skin around his eye sockets. He looked so desperately in need of sleep. Or food. Or both.

'She tell you anything useful at all, or are we still blowing smoke?'

Her partner slowly shook his head: No.

The thing about spending so much time with somebody was you got to know a hell of a lot about them. You got to know their little tells and giveaways. York was lying, and he'd been lying to her quite a bit lately. God only knew why. He used to tell her everything. Still, it was lucid to her, and probably only to her, that Abigail Fuller had told him something which he felt prudent to keep from her. Now wasn't the time to press him.

'Have you looked at the riddle?' he asked at last.

'No, I've been doing my nails. Come on, guv, what do you think I've been doing?'

'Any joy?'

'There's been a lot of head-scratching going on.'

She examined her partner's face, noticing his glazed eyes. He was looking at the large wall clock over her shoulder.

'Shit,' he uttered, springing from his seat. He pushed through to the window overlooking the building's fascia.

'What is it?' she whispered catching up.

Others joined them at the window, a collage of eyes tracking the figure crossing the tarmac casually.

She understood. There he was, the messenger in the green hooded sweater, walking nonchalantly onto the scene.

His face buried under the hood, everything about this person looked average. Was it the same man whom Abigail Fuller had seen, she wondered? Blue jeans, black shoes or trainers, and that fucking sweater, masking anything of descriptive use.

At the fence towards the end of the building opposite, the man stopped. He leaned back against the panels and dug his hands into his pockets, settling himself in for a wait.

She checked her watch. They had one hour.

*

'Okay everybody, listen up,' yelled York over the buzz of tension. 'Our man across the street is here for our solution to the riddle. If we don't already know the answer then everybody needs to get their eyes down and come up with ideas. If that man walks away with nothing, a young girl is going to pay for our mistakes.

'I know that some of you feel like puppets playing this man's game, I've heard a few of you talking. But the alternative is to sit on our hands and do nothing, hope the killer won't make good on his threat. From what I can gather about this man so far, he's not going to do that. And if we wake up to another body tomorrow, I want to believe in my gut that we did everything we could to prevent it from happening. For now, you, me, we *are* puppets, and we don't have the luxury of controlling our own strings. But if it's what it takes to get closer to this guy, then we'll do as we're told until he makes a mistake. And he *will* make a mistake, mark my words. So, let's get to it. Throw your ideas my way.'

Up on the whiteboard, the riddle had been jotted neatly in block capitals.

An apple begins with me and age too. I am in the midst of a man and foremost in every apprehension. You will find me in everyday and see me in all autumns. It's a pity that you cannot see me in the night, when run must I, hidden from sight. What am I?

Standing before the board, York read the puzzle for the hundredth time. All he saw was the same few sentences of nonsensical bullshit.

Newport joined him. 'We're running out of time.'

York closed his eyes.

'Does any of that make sense to you?' she asked.

'Should it?'

'They do say you're the genius around here.'

'So I hear.'

'So..?'

'So tell me what you think, Holly! Don't just rely on me.'

'I don't know, boss. My bloody eyes are sore, I've read it that many times.'

He took a step back. 'Imagine it's a crime scene, right? What's the first thing you'd do?'

'I'd detach myself from what I'm seeing.'

'So detach yourself and read the first sentence again.'

An apple begins with me and age too…

Newport scanned the board. 'What am I looking for?'

York took another step back. 'I believe the trick with riddles is to apply everything you possibly can to one sentence, and then try to reattach the same logic to the remaining lines. Think about it, how does an apple 'become?'

Newport shrugged.

'I asked myself that question earlier,' said York. 'And I didn't get it then. But now...'

An eerie quiet had fallen over the Pit. Others were listening to York, ears pricked tenaciously.

'What?' she probed.

York took a third step back and scanned the room. 'You, come over here,' he said, pointing out a lad in his mid-twenties who stepped confidently from the assembly. 'What's your name, son?'

'PC Dale Yates, sir.'

'Dale, answer me something, what does your dad do for a living?'

The young constable frowned. 'He's a taxi driver.'

'A cabbie?' York shook his head and ushered Dale back into the gathering. In that same instant, the superintendent forced herself into the fray.

'What's going on?' the commander questioned. 'Some kind of mother's meeting?'

'Guv, perfect timing,' said York. He grasped her by the shoulders and shuffled her to the middle of the floor. 'Your father, what does he do for a living?'

Mason didn't hesitate. 'He's retired.'

'And before that?'

'He was a beat copper. Nick, what's going on –'

'A flatfoot,' he echoed excitedly. 'And you became a copper too!'

'So?'

'So, you might say that the apple didn't fall too far from the…'

A medley of muted voices completed the sentence: '*Tree*.'

Mason looked to Newport, bewildered.

'Look at the whole thing,' he urged. 'An apple begins on a tree. And age? A tree can't produce an apple until it's of a ripe age.'

From the back of the room a voice piped up, 'And the midst of a man? How does that fit in?'

York bit at his bottom lip as he pondered that. 'The midst of a man, Dale,' he said picking out the young constable again, 'is called a..?'

'Torso,' Yates replied.

'Or?'

'A trunk!' Newport cut in.

'You see trees every day, and you see them down to their bare branches every autumn. We pay so much more attention to plants and trees in daylight hours because they're so much more beautiful in the sunshine. It's not that we can't see them at night, but we almost forget that they're there.'

'But foremost in every apprehension?' asked Mason. 'How does that relate?'

Collapsing into the nearest chair, York exhaled heavily. 'I don't know. That's the only bit that's bugging me.'

A sudden hush fell over the Pit.

'Okay,' yelled Mason. 'Let's get an envelope prepped and bugged. We have precisely thirty-five minutes left, that should be plenty. If there are any volunteers to take the package out there, step forw–'

'I'm taking it,' York cut in. 'I want to see what we're dealing with.'

'That might not even be our man down there, Nick. Chances are he's just an errand boy. He probably doesn't even know why he's here. Someone's most likely just bunged him a couple of hundred quid.'

'I'm aware of that, guv, but I also think our guy believes himself so untouchable, he'd risk all just for the hell of it. This is his game, remember, and I'll be fucked if I know the rules.'

*

A warm breeze swept across the blacktop as York traversed the street. He could feel it against his face as he walked slowly forwards.

The messenger didn't move as he was approached; he just waited, hands dug deep into his pockets, his face obscured. There was a menacing, in-control quality about him.

Six feet from his target York came to a halt and checked his watch. They were fourteen minutes ahead of deadline.

'I have something for you,' York said, breaking the ethereal quiet.

From somewhere nearby, a church bell pealed out to remind the good people of London it was time to show their blind devotion. The messenger's hands remained dangerously off-show.

'A package,' he added. 'Is it alright if I come closer?'

Noiselessly the messenger pulled his left hand from his pocket and held it out open-palmed. York edged closer. Arm's length away, he placed the package gently onto the messenger's palm. It disappeared inside the hoodie.

York took a vigilant step back as the messenger pushed himself from the fence and began walking back the way he came.

'You don't have to do this, son,' he appealed as the green sweater passed him. 'Don't be a part of this.'

The messenger didn't stop, didn't even hesitate.

York raised his hand. Further down the street two sets of headlights materialised and two separate car engines popped into existence.

Twenty yards behind, York picked up his pace and fell in behind the messenger. The green hoodie was easy to keep in sight on the quiet pavement, but as the target reached the end of the street, he ducked quickly around the corner.

'Shit,' York muttered, picking up pace. He hit the corner as the messenger climbed into the back of a black cab. Seconds later, one of the unmarked units pulled up next to him, Newport at the wheel.

'Get in!' she called.

He launched himself into the passenger seat. 'He just got into that tax–'

'I saw him. Does he know we're following him?'

'Probably.'

As she pulled from the curb, York heard a distinct whoop-whoop-whoop overhead. The Pit Bull had called in the choppers. Between the eyes in the sky and the bugged envelope, the messenger would have to disappear into thin air to slip away unseen.

Swinging to the left, the cab pulled gently onto Blackfriars, Newport a small procession behind. If the messenger knew he was being pursued he didn't let it be known. And as suddenly as it began, everything changed. At the next set of lights the black cab suddenly punched forward and darted through the red into open traffic, swerving a white van by inches.

'Bollocks!' grumbled Newport. 'Hold on.'

Slamming her foot to the floor, she pulled the same stunt, gunning the unit through the speeding traffic. Other vehicles skidded to a halt in the junction, the smell of torque and burning rubber blitzing the air.

York gripped tightly onto the hand bar above the door. Thudding back and forth in his seat, his hat tipped off into the foot well.

At the next junction the cab didn't even slow for the lights, bolting across at devastating speed. Was the driver in league with the messenger or was he being coerced? York guessed the latter.

This time Newport wasn't so lucky. She gunned it and pounded the pedal as a convoy of vehicles poured into the junction and blocked her exit. Bashing a heavy foot down on the brake pedal, the car fishtailed into the junction, the back end of the vehicle moving out until they were travelling sideways into a swarm of cars and vans at speed.

York screwed his eyes closed. Was this it? Was this how it all ended? Was the last thing he heard on planet earth going to be his partner's intense cursing?

Then came the impact, the screech of metal on metal. He clung to the handrail, squeezed his eyes tighter, tighter, until…

Calm. Utter calm. The only sounds to hear were the occasional car horn or angry driver. York dared open his eyes. Newport was still beside him. She was staring at him, wide-eyed. 'Whoa!' was all she said.

They'd collided with one car only; there was no pileup. He glanced shakily along Blackfriars, the Oxo tower looming dominantly in a trio of iconic letters. He reached for the radio.

Newport climbed from the car and jogged to the vehicle they'd hit.

'This is York,' he said, adrenaline buzzed. 'We lost the suspect. Over.'

A crackle. 'This is Eyes-in-the-Sky. We saw, Nick. You were lucky to escape a bad one there. Over.'

'Do you still have eyes on the messenger? Over.'

'Got some bad news for you. Another junction after he gave you the slip, the cab pulled into a rank. There are dozens of identical cabs parked in there, there was no way to lock down which one was carrying the suspect. Over.'

'For fuck's sake!' York tossed the radio aside, abandoned the car and sprinted in the taxi's wake, Newport at his heel.

As they reached the entrance to the taxi rank, the second unmarked unit showed up, a couple of uniforms inside. 'Stay here and block the entrance,' York advised. 'Don't let any more cabs come in, and sure as hell don't let any leave. Our man still might be here.'

Jogging into the bustle of the taxi hive, York and Newport spread out.

This was a nightmare. Without the messenger, the recipient was smoke.

Slamming his sixth cab door closed, York cursed under his breath.

'Guv,' called Newport from a handful of cabs away. 'You'd better take a look at this.'

As he approached, he prepared for his partner to hammer home that final nail of failure, and she did so brutally. On the back seat of the cab was the envelope, torn open and left behind, bug and all.

9

The twilight sky had turned gun-metal grey and the clouds had begun weeping quietly. The evening remained warm though.

Back in the passenger seat of the unmarked unit, York scooped up his trilby and planted it back on his head. His mind was wandering. Newport had tried to talk to him a couple of times but he hadn't responded. He had to work this out.

He had to *think*.

An innocent girl or a despicable man was going to suffer tonight because of their failings. Because of *his* failings. Was his solution to the puzzle even correct? The pursuit hadn't gone well either, and that had been his doing. He glanced down at his palms expecting to find spilt blood staining his skin.

Newport said something else, but he didn't hear it. He was worried about her. She hadn't admitted anything was wrong but there was something. He just knew. Once she damn near broke a shoplifter's collarbone when she was shopping for vegetables. There was an inquiry. Turned out she and her husband were on the breadline and their house had been repossessed. They'd been living out of relatives' pads for months. She'd bottled it up until a fourteen year old kid lifting a Snickers bar took the brunt force. Now she was hurtling through cross-traffic at seventy miles per hour with a ride-along.

'So you want to tell me what's going on?' he said finally, eyes trained on the dappled windscreen.

Newport smirked. 'That's a bad habit you have, you know that?'

York wiped the foggy windscreen with his sleeve.

'Yes, I want to talk!' she snapped. 'I want to talk about why you keep turning up to work looking like shit. I want to talk about why you don't communicate with me. I want to understand why this partnership feels like a one-man-band most of the time. I mean I've tried, Nick. I try to be a part of what goes on in your head, but you don't let me in. You're so closed down, it's breaking me! Talk to me. Please. Let's get this thing sorted.'

Sitting askew, he peered out the passenger window. He couldn't think of anything to say.

'That's what I thought,' she uttered. 'If you're not going to talk to me, at least have the balls to tell me why, and put me out of my fairytale fucking misery.'

He turned to meet her gaze.

She looked away.

'Have you ever felt like you have a demon inside you?' he said softly. 'Not some little imp lighting campfires, I'm talking Lucifer burning down the fucking world. Someone told me earlier that I need to push that demon out, but I don't know how. Because I know it's not real.'

Newport looked at him like he'd gone mad.

'I know what it sounds like,' he said. 'And believe me, it's not a fairytale.'

Newport waited a beat. Seconds ticked by. 'Is this about Leanne and Frasier?'

'You speak their names, Holly, you'd better know what you're talking about.'

'Is it, Nick? Are we talking about what happened to your family?'

He tore himself away from the streaked window. 'Holly, for fuck's sake!'

'No, we're going to talk this out, Nick! I don't care if you never talk with anyone about this again, you're going to talk to me about it.'

'And why am I going to do that?'

'Because I want to hear it. But mostly because you want to tell me.'

His heart began thumping in his chest. 'Pull over,' he said clearly.

'What?'

'You heard me.'

They weren't far from the station. Newport guided the car to the curb and switched off the engine. Slipping from the car, York pulled up his collar against the rain. He walked to the nearest streetlight and paused beneath it.

Newport perused him into the tumbling sheets. 'What are you doing? You're getting soaked.'

The slosh of running water stole the night's other sounds.

'Nick?'

'Do you remember them, Holly?'

Her face said she did.

'Do you know I haven't looked at a photograph of them since they disappeared? I have boxes full of stuff, all of it locked away. I don't even remember what they look like. My wife was the woman who changed my life, and I can't even remember her face.'

Newport pulled her jacket tighter around her.

Under the unrelenting downpour, he fell to a crouch and buried his face in his hands. His partner made no move to comfort him. There was nothing she could do. The barrier was broken, and only he could pull himself back.

*

By the time they arrived at the station the rain had slowed and the smell of night had settled like a film of dust. York hadn't asked his partner not to speak of his malfunction, she just wouldn't. Not with him, or anybody else.

The pair of them was the focus of attention as they made their way into the foyer. They probably looked juiced, sodden, and white from shock.

At the desk a couple of uniforms waited to sign what looked like a junkie into the register. In front of them was a lone woman who looked like she was straight off the corner of one street or another. She was ranting something about squatters; fairly standard desk behaviour for this time of night.

'What you thinking?' Newport asked.

York almost didn't answer. 'I'm worried. We're not just one step behind anymore, we're in trouble. I get the feeling whoever this guy is, he's going to be angry that we followed his messenger.'

They reached the door to the Pit as the desk phone rang out through the foyer.

Newport shrugged. 'There was nothing in the recording to say that we couldn't.'

'There was nothing in the recording to say that we could, either. And it doesn't mean our guy has to like it.'

She pushed open the office door. 'So what do you think he's going to do?'

'I think he's going to do exactly as he says. He's going to kill somebody.'

Across the foyer, a voice rang out above the din. 'DCI Nicolas York? Is there a DCI York here?'

'I'm York,' he called to the desk clerk.

'Call for you, Detective. You want to take it here?'

The potential prostitute complaining about squatters was giving it some now, adamant she wasn't being taken seriously. She probably wasn't.

He sent Newport on ahead and took the receiver from the desk clerk. 'This is York.'

There was a muffled sound from the other end. A woman, maybe? He didn't know the voice.

'You'll have to speak up,' he urged. 'There's quite a bit of background noise here.' He looked over to the squatter woman. 'Hey, shut up for a minute, will you!'

The complainer looked like she'd been slapped. She gave him the finger.

When the phone voice amplified and repeated the message, his knees jellied. 'Who is this? How did you get my name?'

The voice became clearer with each syllable. '*I know a lot about you, Nick, more than you think.*'

His heart began thumping against his chest again. 'What you said before?'

There was a moment of static. Eventually the voice spoke again. '*I meant it. Your son is in London. He's alive.*'

*

I am not alone.

Enveloped by perfect blackness I tighten the fusty blanket around my shoulders, the insufferable cold creeping in through broken seams and ragged tears.

Stacks of nondescript cardboard boxes surround me. I cannot see them, but I know they're there.

From the darkness come peculiar sounds. I am the only person in the house, yet I'm certain something watches me from another part of the basement.

I am not permitted to be frightened.

It is against the rules.

Outside, snow is on the ground, the fields and woods layered with a thick white bedspread. I saw it earlier, the trees' frozen limbs sparkling like silver and diamonds in the winter sun.

Now, the sun has gone, both from the day and from my mind. Despite the rules I struggle to control my breathing, plumes of my icy breath clouding before me.

I am shivering, but I am not permitted to be cold.

It is against the rules.

Moments ago, there was a cough. But there was no way to be certain I hadn't imagined it. I thought it came from my right, but I couldn't tell. I matched the cough with one of my own. Perhaps the first had been mine.

How long had I been here? A day? Two?

Hours earlier I had devoured the single ration of bread and milk. Now there are stabbing hunger pains in my side. I do not know when the next rations are coming, if they are coming at all.

But I am not permitted to feel hunger.

It is against the rules.

10

King Shaka International Airport, Durban, South Africa, 2011

Today's word: *Carnage.*

Across the table, Milo Stanton prodded enthusiastically at his iPhone. He insisted he wasn't addicted.

Lately he'd become engrossed with a new app. It displayed a different word every day, sometimes exotic, sometimes mundane, but the aim apparently was to try and fit it into everyday conversation. Something to do with extending the vocab. Milo Stanton needed this app, more than he knew.

Despite the coffee shop's tepid effort at a latte, Abigail Fuller, or Abigail Chambers as she was known now, decided she was in a good mood. It was one of the better business trips she'd been on and although Milo's company wasn't exactly ideal, he could usually make her laugh.

Carnage was an apt word; the airport was chaos.

'You should get one of these things,' Milo recommended. 'It's like having a third arm.'

'I've managed fine with just the two my entire life.'

'What are you scared of? Afraid it's going to jump up and bite you on the arse?'

'Technology's going too fast,' she explained. 'It's all going to come crashing down at some point, believe me.'

'Agh, I never thought I'd be given the glorious opportunity to meet such a developed technophobe! What is it that frightens you so much?'

'Fright has nothing to do with it. Trust is a better word.'

Milo flashed his broad and patronising smile. 'I think somebody's watched the Terminator films too many times!'

'People rely too heavily on technology. Nobody knows how to think for themselves anymore, that's all I'm saying. You, me, we're the last generation of children to have actual personalities.'

'Meaning?'

'Take that family there.' Abbey pointed out the perfect nuclear arrangement. 'Teenage son glued to his phone, slightly older teenage daughter focused on a DS. Nobody on that table is talking. Not to one another at least. Technology is killing the art of conversation.'

'Ah, but that's one family. With most people I don't think your logic qualifies.'

'Based on?'

'Absolutely nothing!'

'Not the best of arguments,' she laughed

'Abbey, you don't...'

Milo's sentence trailed off as a large man in an NYC baseball cap stopped next to their booth and stared at them fixatedly. In one hand he held a copy of a sport's car magazine, the other a half-eaten doughnut.

'Help you?' Milo asked.

The man held his stare. He looked confused.

Instead of shying away, Abbey held the man's gaze, green eyes locked onto brown. Something about that seemed to unhinge him. He glanced down at his feet as though embarrassed and walked quickly away, pushing past an elderly man impeding his escape.

'Freak!' Milo shouted after him.

'Shut up, Milton!' she warned. 'We don't want any trouble, especially not from a giant.'

'Don't call me that!' Milton snapped.

Abbey grinned.

'Did you see the way that guy was looking at you?' Milo whispered slyly. 'He looked like you with an iPad.'

'Confused?'

'Angry!'

Whatever that meant.

This was the fourth trip she'd done with Milo. Dennis Smith had been his predecessor but had since retired. The old goat was living out in Canada somewhere now, he and his wife. Dennis had been certain democracy in the UK was on the plunge. The slow downfall nobody was really seeing, or were choosing not to. He talked for a long time about his longing to be back in a community where money was not the governor of society and people were still happy.

She missed him.

If life was a comic book, Milo would've made the perfect archenemy for Dennis. He was quite literally the man's opposite. His love for money was not lost on anybody, nor was his devotion to possessions, and he seemed to be quite proud of the fact that he didn't know a soul on his street.

Still, Milo's two-dimensional attitude aside, she couldn't deny that she liked the kid. At twenty-three he was an up-and-comer in the architectural field. Having been rejected to design the drainage systems for the new Wellington Court financial blocks in north London, he went away and drew up the blueprints off his own back. He submitted them anonymously, and the company ended up going with his designs instead of their own. Though no more efficient, he'd managed to reduce the amount of required project materials by sixteen percent. When word got out that it was Milo who'd come up with the design, those up above began looking at him as the next household name.

'I can't do any more of this coffee,' Abbey grumbled. 'I'm going to have a walk around, see if I can find something to read on the flight.'

'Hey, don't forget we need to've gone over these proposals by the time we land in North Shore. I want the commission on this one, Abs.'

'Keep your hair on, Whiz!' We're set to hit it for six.'

'I'm just saying, one more green light in New Zealand and we'll be flying home with a hat-trick. And you know what that means - new BMW for me.'

She pushed herself out of the booth and climbed to her feet. 'There're more things to life than cars and money, Milo.'

'Only poor people say that!'

Joining the multicultural ebb of people moving through the airport, she recalled a bookstore she'd seen at the top end of the terminal. Wrestling through the human traffic, she stepped into the congested store, noticing the shop assistant's eyes lingering on her. Did she have something written on her face today, she wondered?

Idly she began to browse a few paperbacks, trying wholeheartedly to ignore the assistant's glare. Skipping the newspaper stand where almost every nationality's paper was headlining the Will and Kate hitch, she found herself at a sales-bin absently leafing through a battered second, third, eighteenth-hand copy of a violently graphic book entitled, *The Blood Diamond Insurgency*. As she put it back where she found it, she felt eyes on her again.

Slowly she glanced up from the sales-bin and met eyes with the giant from the café, his NYC baseball cap sitting primly atop his head. Like before he was staring fervently, his expression carrying an anxious twist.

'Your mother never teach you it's not polite to stare?' Abbey said calmly.

Like in the café the giant turned away awkwardly, pretended to be perusing the magazines – *Pregnant Mothers, Monthly?*

It was strange, despite the man's size she didn't feel threatened by him. The way he turned away abashed, he resembled a twelve year old who'd been caught scanning the underwear section in one of his mum's catalogues.

'Were you following me?' she asked moving closer.

Instead of answering, the giant picked up *Housewife & Home* and began flicking through the pages, eyes glancing up every few pages.

Another step. 'What's your name?'

Replacing the magazine, the man turned his huge body towards her. He continued to look down, his eyes locked onto the nasty green tiles beneath their feet. 'I learned the alphabet,' he muttered. His accent carried the faint trace of Australia.

Hand to her mouth, Abbey took a step back, embarrassed. 'You...you did?' she mouthed. 'Well that's no easy thing, is it?'

The giant shook his head. 'No, but I can do it first time,' he said proudly. 'Want me to show you?'

'You don't need to do that. What's your na –'

'A...B...C...D...G...F...'

She placed a hand on the big man's arm. '*What's your name?*'

He thought about that for a moment. 'Eric De Boor,' he said confidently. 'You can call me Eric.'

'And who are you travelling with, Eric De Boor?'

'You're very pretty.'

'Eric, I think you might be lost. Who're you trav –'

'I saw what the man had under his jacket!' Eric cut in.

She looked around hoping to spot someone looking for their son, brother, *father*, but the airport was too busy.

Eric shuffled from foot to foot. 'He was trying to hide it but I saw.'

'Who are you travelling with, Eric?' she persisted.

'I'm with my mother, Elaine De Boor. But I don't know where she is. She went to find *something-hot-to-drink*.'

Abbey couldn't help but smile as Eric repeated his mother's words. 'So she's at the café?'

'I don't know. She went to find *something-hot-to-drink*.'

She sighed, frustrated.

'Are you mad at me?' he said glumly. 'Sometimes people get mad at me.'

'Of course not,' she assured him. 'I'm just trying to help you get back to your mother.'

'My mother's name is Elaine De Boor. She went to buy *something-hot-to-drink*.'

Rubbing her eyes, she said, 'I'll tell you what, Eric, go ahead and tell me the alphabet.'

*

It wasn't easy but Abbey finally managed to extract a gate number from Eric, and thankfully it was the same as hers. Like she and Milo, he and his mother were travelling to Auckland through the night.

At the gate she found Elaine De Boor nursing a cardboard takeaway cup, head buried in a Bible. Since Eric was forty-ish, she guessed Elaine to be somewhere in her late sixties, early seventies, but she carried no air of frailty. Abbey guessed a lifetime of raising a challenged son had carved her out of wood, and as she approached with Eric, Elaine De Boor climbed to her feet with the ease of a teenager.

'Where was he this time?' Elaine asked. And then to Eric, 'I swear to god, they'll be prizing you off the runway one of these days!'

'Found him in the bookstore at the top end of the terminal,' Abbey said. 'Is he alright wandering off on his own like that?'

'Look at the size of him, darl! You'd have to be an idiot to antagonise him.'

Growing immediately impatient Eric was off again, heading back towards the café.

'He remembers short term things fairly well. So long as he knows the gate number and what time to be back, I let him go explore. Means I can read in peace.'

Abbey smiled. 'Well, I'm glad I took the time to bring him back then.'

'God bless you, darl,' Elaine replied and went back to the Bible.

Mixing back into the throng of travellers, Abbey made her way back to the café wondering if Milo had waited, but the booth was empty.

As she turned to leave, that's when she met *him*.

Bumping into the person behind her, she watched as the coffee flew from his hand in slow motion and crashed down onto the table to their left, lid popping off the cardboard cup and erupting over the nuclear family and their lack of conversation.

How.

Embarrassing.

Through a blizzard of apologies and the angry ramblings of the father, she finally took a proper look at her collision partner.

'Hi,' he smirked and held up a hand in greeting.

For a second she stood transfixed. The man was about her age, with sandy blonde hair, clear blue eyes and a cheeky grin. To call him handsome would have been an insult to his face.

'I…I…' she stammered.

'Coffee was lousy anyway,' said Blue Eyes, his smoky American accent delivering the words to her on a bed of silk. 'I was about to hurl it at that old guy over there, but I guess the family deserved it more.'

He waited for a reply. When none came, he said, 'I'm James,' and held out his hand.

'Erm, Abbey,' she stuttered and shook the man's hand. There was more to say, she was certain.

'Well, Abbey, it was lovely to meet you,' he said at last.

For heart-stoppingly long seconds he held her stare, and then without another word, he moved past her and disappeared into the crowd.

Carnage.

*

Wasn't it true that once a downed aeroplane began burning, you had ninety seconds max to get out, or you burned with it?

Abbey was sure she'd read that somewhere.

'You're looking a little pale there, Abs,' said Milo Stanton as he dropped into the next seat and fiddled with the table in front. 'This that whole technology thing again? Let me tell you, planes do not drop out of the sky anymore. It's like one in a bah-zillion flights or something goes down.'

Abbey wedged the picture of her husband into the corner of the locked table, wishing she'd brought some miniatures on board. 'Jesus, don't start with the statistics before we're even off the ground!'

'Just trying to make you feel better. For me, all I have to do is picture that lovely, gleaming, shiny, sparkly new BMW and guess what…'

She raised her eyebrows.

'It puts a grin right on my face!'

'Well instead of daydreaming about flash cars why don't you get your laptop out and go through the proposals? You can kiss the BMW goodbye if we don't nail this one.'

'I can't 'til we're in the air, that burly homosexual steward will kick off at me.'

'How do you know he's gay?'

'Like I know my cousin is gay,' he revealed. 'I just know.'

'And there was me challenging your sexual integrity.'

'Nothing wrong with me, girl!' Milo said defensively. 'I'm all man.'

She smirked. 'Relax, Milo, I was being facetious.'

'Face-*what*-ious!' he grumbled. 'You know I don't like it when you do that.'

'Do what?'

'Use big words. Why do you think I'm trying to extend my vocab?'

'I know you can't backchat when you don't know what the hell I'm talking about.'

'Touché,' he ceded. 'Nevertheless, I do have the uncanny ability to talk my way around long words.'

'Is that so?'

'Yeah, that *is* so, Miss Fetus.'

'Facetious.'

'Whatever.'

As Milo began to get settled in, she spotted blue-eyed James stowing his bag several rows in front. He caught her looking and waved. Never had she clammed up so badly in front of a man before, not even Edward, her husband. But then she didn't think she'd ever met a man quite so good looking. Edward was handsome in a rugged, Gerard Butler kind of way.

She went for rugged. Rugged did it for her.

James, though, he was beautiful. It turned out beautiful did it for her too. Was she horny, she wondered? It had turned into a kind of ritual between her and Edward to wash away the weeks of frustration within minutes of her being home. Sadly, home was six thousand miles away.

Slowly the plane began to move along the tarmac as the final few passengers took their seats. For several minutes they taxied, waiting for their turn to take off. Milo had his eyes closed now, headphones plugged into his ears. He looked downright calm.

The plane lurched to a stop. She gripped the armrests tightly. Milo was looking at her now, and she couldn't tell if he was amused by her fear or concerned. The stewardess who gave the safety demo did a final check on seatbelts. Abbey's was fastened; she'd checked it religiously since snapping it closed.

Reaching the end of the aisle, the stewardess took a seat and buckled herself in.

Milo leaned over. 'You ready?'

The Rolls Royce twin engines kicked in and the plane rocketed forwards, tearing down the runway. Teeth grinding, Abbey locked her eyes onto the picture of Edward and his reassuring smile. His confidence that always made her feel safe.

Shaking and vibrating, the plane left the tarmac and soared up into the sky as though it was light as a feather, rather than the thousands of tons of steel and moving parts it actually was. The rumbling grew more dramatic for intolerably long seconds before finally,

Finally…

the plane leveled out. Minutes later, the seatbelt sign vanished.

'You can loosen up on those armrests now, Abs,' suggested Milo. 'Wasn't so bad, was it?'

She exhaled loudly. 'Speak for yourself.'

Unsnapping the belt, Milo went back to his iPhone. 'Good thing I brought this.'

'Your third arm?'

'This flight is going to put it to the test. Can *Apple* entertain me for sixteen hours?'

She closed her eyes. 'What about the in-flight movies?'

'What about them?'

'See if there's something good showing,' she suggested.

He began prodding the screen in front. 'It's usually a bunch of chick-flicks on these things. I've seen *Moulin Rouge* six times since we left Heathrow.'

'Well, you could always do what I'm going to do.'

'Yeah, what's that?'

'Sleep.'

'Since when have I been able to sleep on public transport, woman?'

'Well then, the proposals it is!'

'Nah,' he replied. 'We've already got it sealed tight. Nothing can go wrong.'

'I can think of one thing.'

She knew Milo was looking at her. 'Is this where you tell me to shut up so you can sleep?'

Abbey closed her eyes.

'Point taken.'

'Good,' she smirked. 'Shut your trap and watch *Moulin Rouge.*'

'Fine, if it's like that, I'll just put my earphones back in and watch…' he fiddled with the panel again. '…*Casper, the Friendly Ghost.*'

Abbey's smirk evolved into a giggle. That was funny.

'No no,' he said, 'don't feel guilty. Me and Casper are going to be just fine.'

'I don't feel guilty.'

'I don't want you to.'

'I don't.'

Finally, Milo quieted down and went back to his headphones.

She suddenly realised how tired she was. So far they'd spent three days in Riviera Maya in Mexico, three in Brasilia, and almost a week in Durban. After Auckland they were home dry. No more proposals, no more hotel rooms with broken air-conditioning. No more flying.

She sat back and attempted to close out the white noise around her, the soothing rumbling of the engines quietly wooing her. Seconds later, she drifted off.

II

He couldn't move, his entire system paralysed. And unless that changed in the next sixty seconds, he was going to drown. Synapses somewhere were not transmitting signals as they should, and messages leaving the brain were not reaching their destination. Everything below the neckline was a numb wasteland, leaving him at the mercy of the disinterested waves.

Beneath him was sand. He knew that much because grains had crept into his ears, his mouth. Moreover, he could see just fine. Waves crashed over him, covering him totally, and then rolled back allowing him a few seconds of oxygen. Inch by inch he was being dragged further away from the beach with the tide.

Move, you dumb bastard, he willed himself. You want to die out here?

He recalled the plane hitting the water, the devastating impact. For literally seconds he must have been out, because when he came around, chaos was still churning around him, the plane tossing violently.

But the quiet. The quiet didn't match the devastation, as if he'd been the sole passenger aboard the plane. Somebody nearby was crying. He could hear it, like he could suddenly hear the torrential riptides tearing at the carriage.

Snapping off the belt he'd hauled himself up and stepped into two feet of tepid water. Bodies were strewn, smashed, torn apart from the impact. In the aisle floated the corpse of an eight or nine year old boy, half his head missing, oxygen mask still strapped around his frail neck, trying to escape in the rushing water.

At the top end of the aisle he found the crier, the blonde stewardess who'd served him a Heineken no more than an hour before. She was trapped beneath a stanchion, the water rising around her.

She'd pleaded, begged him to help her. He'd told her everything was going to be alright. He'd told her he was going to get her out. The next thing he remembered, he was swimming alone for the huge dark mound two or three hundred yards away.

It was an island or a peninsula, he knew this for sure. Parts of the aircraft had crashed to the beach, flames dancing in the gales. Hitting the shore gasping, he had tumbled to the sand. But that had been the start of it. The second he fell, his body had shut down. It was not exhaustion. Something else was wrong.

That was then. This was now.

Move, god damn it!

He held his breath as the next wave tumbled over him. This time he was under for longer. And longer still.

He willed his fingers to move, to claw at the wet sand.

He was pulled under again and dragged away from the beach, his head filled with images of the blonde stewardess, petrified, placing all her faith in him.

And whether it had anything to do with divine intervention or just a stroke of blind luck, he felt his collar snag on something, preventing the currents from whipping him away. Then he was being hooked under the arms and dragged backwards onto the sand.

The rain struck his face. Saltwater erupted from his lungs as he was pitched forwards, his skeletal form a tin can of pins and needles. His entire body was wracked with fire.

And then he heard her. She was asking if he was alright. She was asking if he knew of any more survivors. The Blonde stewardess?

'I can't move,' he spluttered.

'You made it to the beach, didn't you?' the voice yelled above the wind. 'Did someone drag you here?'

'I…I swam.'

'Then you can move!'

'I could,' he replied. 'I mean…I woke up in the wreckage, managed to get out and swim to shore.'

'Then it's in your head, James,' said the voice. 'Get your arse up.'

James?

'How do you know my name?'

'This isn't the time for a meet-and-greet, soldier,' the voice said. 'You need to get it into your head, there's nothing wrong with you. There may be other survivors, I need your help.'

'You saved my life,' he stammered. 'Tell me your name.'

Behind them the wind tore at the palm trees lining the beach. Rain pummelled them, lightning cracked all around, and the only thing offering illumination were the multiple fires aglow along the beach, refusing to blow out.

'*Tell me your name*,' he insisted.

Blocking his view of the bruised sky a face appeared over him, dark hair tangling in the wind.

'Abigail,' she said. 'Abigail Chambers. Now are you going to get up, or am I throwing you back to the fish!'

*

The sensation in James Bailey's legs slowly returned. The pins and needles had transformed into feeling and he was able to stand shakily.

What had caused the paralysis he didn't know, but he was standing now. With one arm over Abigail's shoulder she helped him along the beach. They battled the gale together, trudging slowly along the sand. Of all the people to have found him, he couldn't believe it was *this* girl. Dark locks, tangled and wet. Perfect green eyes. He tried not to stare.

A couple of hundred yards offshore, dark leviathans disappeared beneath the surface of the water, huge sections of the aircraft swallowed whole.

'Where the bloody hell is everybody?' Abigail yelled above the wind.

He'd been wondering the same thing. There didn't seem to be any bodies, alive or dead, anywhere.

'Gone down with the plane, probably,' he shouted back.

'I don't think so. There were a handful of bodies in my section when I left the plane, but most of the seats had been ripped out, gone, passengers along with them. I expected the beach to be littered.'

Navigating their way gingerly through the fires and debris, they paused to catch their breath.

'I think I can manage now,' he gasped.

Abbey unhooked her arm, her eyes casting upon the bigger fire dancing around the huge chunk of aircraft that had beached and wedged itself against the trees, propped up as if the rest of the plane was buried beneath the sand.

'Do you see that?' she called.

A figure was moving around near the tailfin, a silhouette against the backdrop of the fire. It was a man. Straggly blonde shoulder-length hair plastered to his head, thick stubble. He looked like a surfer, board-shorts and flip-flops. He appeared frantic, flipping luggage, one suitcase after another tossed aside, hurled into a pile already discarded.

'What're you looking for, friend?' James called out.

When he realised he wasn't alone, the man's head snapped up in a spray of rain. 'I *know* it's here somewhere!'

James approached wearily and placed a gentle hand on the man's arm. 'Are you hurt?' he asked. 'Do you have any injuries?'

'I need to find my suitcase,' the man insisted, pallid and wild-eyed.

'What's your name?'

No response, just a passive glance.

'Hey, can you hear me? What're you doing out here?'

'Get away from me, mate!' the surfer yelled back, his accent heavy east coast Australian.

James took a step back. 'I think you're in shock, friend. I just want to help you –'

'I'm not your *friend*, dude, and I'll let you know when I need your help! *Shock*. . .Jesus Christ!'

Over his shoulder, James caught a glimpse of Abbey walking back to the shoreline. He was close to abandoning the Australian and joining her. 'Listen,' he yelled. 'I don't know what your problem is and I don't know what you're looking for, but when you're ready to talk we'll be around, alright.'

'The only problem I have is I can't find my bag!'

'Like I said. . .'

'You'll be around,' muttered the Australian dismissingly. 'Good to know.'

'Will you at least tell me your name?'

'Sol,' he answered without hesitation. 'Sol Delaney.'

'Have you seen any other survivors, Sol, or is it just you?'

Sol shook his head. 'I was flying alone. You're the first people I've seen since we went down, but you know, I haven't really been looking.'

'Why the hell not, Sol?'

'Forget the bodies, dude,' he muttered. 'They're smoke.'

'What do you mean smoke?'

'Look around, mate, the passengers are history. If you want to look, look. Me, I have to find my suitcase.'

'Yeah, you said. And if you were out there dying?'

Sol glanced away impatiently. 'Well I'm not, dude!'

'What kind of attitu –'

'*We done?*'

Sol went back to the bags, unhinged.

James backed away. The conversation with Sol had strangely filled him with sadness. Never in his life had he encountered such an apathetic approach to death, such a blankness. As he watched Sol ruthlessly rooting through the luggage, blonde locks lashing in the wind, he felt sorry for the man, a deep sense of pity sitting on a shelf high above Sol's selfishness.

Turning morosely away, he jogged after Abbey.

12

The next bay lay peppered with debris like the aftermath of a battlefield. From the top of the rocky bay partition, James and Abbey looked across the devastation, the handful of bodies, the slabs of steel and seat rows jutting from the sand amidst leaping campfires.

'My God,' James heard his companion whisper. He made his way down the rocks and stepped in amongst the ruin. He sensed Abbey at his heel, her footsteps pressing into his own. They moved between the wreckage like wandering scavengers, one by one flipping the twelve or fifteen bodies onto their backs, probing them for signs of life.

'Over here!' Abbey bellowed. 'I've got a live one.'

At her side, James examined the young girl Abbey had discovered; eleven or twelve and at a glance unhurt. Aside from the ill-fitting dress, she wore a small locket around her neck dangling from a thin silver chain.

He leant down and lowered his ear to the girl's breast, finding the steady thump of a heartbeat. With a little coaxing and relentless rain, the girl came gingerly around. She pushed herself into a sitting position and coughed some water from her throat. Her eyes wandered confusedly.

Brushing the hair away from her face, Abbey asked her if she was in any pain.

A shake of the head.

'She's okay,' Abbey said to James, 'I'll stay with her.'

James began moving once again through the few remaining bodies, finding each one stone cold, beaten, life having abused them, death having claimed them.

He made his way back towards Abbey and the girl. In the firelight he could see Abbey's lips moving, attempting to cajole words from their new companion.

Pausing next to a burning seat, he sat in the sand and let the rain wash over him. Was this shit actually happening, he wondered? It was the twenty-first century for Christ's sake, wasn't being stranded on a desert island a couple of hundred years out of date?

The rain finally managed to extinguish the flaming seat in a plume of blue smoke. He faced the heavens, his eyes heavy. So far they were a band of four, if he included Sol Delaney, and four was not enough to begin picking up the pieces here. As he trained his eyes back on the two females, one question leapt to the forefront of his mind: did anybody, on the island or off, have any idea where they were?

Before he had time to contemplate, his head jolted out to sea and to the disappearing mass of aircraft, the scream of a woman ringing out across the bay.

Somebody was alive out there.

*

He scrambled to his feet and ran to the shore, damp shirt trying to free itself from his back.

'James!' Abbey bellowed. 'Don't be a bloody idiot!'

Abandoning the confused girl, she sprinted to James's side and snatched his arm, tugging him away from the water.

'The hell are you doing?' He jerked his arm away and shoved her back. 'Don't pretend you can't hear that!'

'Don't do it, James,' she urged. 'She's gone. You'll never make it back!'

'I made it to shore.'

'Barely. And it's different this time. That section is almost totally under, it's a bloody tomb!'

He stripped off his shirt. 'I can't leave her. I can't just stand by and do nothing. Don't tell me you can turn your back on it.'

For a handful of seconds he stood silently and held Abbey's gaze. Then he said: 'I'll come back,' and crashed into the waves, rag-dolled and dragged under. He kicked against the currents and thrust himself up, plunged through the surface and began crawling out to the vanishing wreckage. Despite the raging wind the water remained tepid. He reached the looming shape in one piece and gripped a torn section of metal shredded away from the carriage.

He kicked at the water and tried to pull himself up, but he couldn't move. His leg was snagged. He kicked harder and realisation crashed home. The currents surging in towards the shore were clashing with those diverted by the carriage, creating something else entirely: a riptide.

His legs rolled like pistons but he wasn't strong enough, not by a long shot. He was whipped under, dragged into the uncaring stream. This close to shore the water was shallow, no more than six feet deep, but it was enough. He couldn't breathe. The current gripped him, took him, dragged him along, his hands finding only insubstantial sand.

No longer was he battling the ebb, no longer would his body allow it. The last of his air supply was being ravaged from his lungs, the reserves of his strength stripped away. For the second time in minutes he was a dead man, and this time a dead man with no one to pull him from the clutches.

With nothing left to cling on to, he relaxed, rode the current carrying him away from the shore, the wreckage. He didn't know how fast he was travelling as his body struck the solid shape at his back. He didn't feel the collision. But from somewhere buried deep, he reached out and gripped something solid.

The current held his feet fast, but couldn't take hold. He flipped his body and lunged upwards gripping something else solid, and something else again.

As he broke the surface, his lungs flooding with sweet oxygen, he realised he'd struck a huge chunk of a wing and grasped a smashed flap.

He rubbed his eyes, clearing them of salt. He could see the beach, he could see Abbey scanning the waves for him, he could see the section he'd been torn away from; not as far away as he thought.

A scream.

The stewardess?

Without hesitation, he dived from the wing and began crawling back the way he'd come.

*

A girl.

A tattoo on her neck.

A piercing...

Several piercings!

She was screaming, thrashing in the water, a jammed overhead panel wedging her tightly down. The rising water was lapping around her shoulders, pouring in from every crevice. She was not the stewardess he'd been expecting. She was someone else. She was someone new.

A gap.

He was next to the tattooed girl, as deep in the water as she. He could feel it pulsating around him. The girl was crying, cursing. She called him a cunt. A useless cunt. She was terrified.

He asked her to feign to one side as he levered himself under the panel attempting to move it. It shifted slightly but did not loosen.

The girl called him a faggot.

He ignored her, considered abandoning her.

A gap.

He saw the tattooed girl with her face pressed to the ceiling. She was trying to gather the remaining oxygen before the water consumed her. He was doing the same. The panel had shifted considerably, but the girl was still not free.

She disappeared under in a splutter of bubbles and curses. He reckoned he had about thirty seconds until he went under with her.

With one final brace against the port shutter, he lunged against the panel, the sturdy rack refusing to budge. The water rose over his face and filled his nostrils. He began to sink.

A gap.

The rain struck his face as he lay afloat on the water. He was free of the wreckage and was being dragged. He could hear grunting as the waves thrashed around him. It was a man's voice.---

Where was he being taken?

How was he alive?

What had become of the tattooed girl?

A wave crashed over them, filled his mouth with saltwater and a curious taste of metal. He decided his mouth is bleeding.

A gap…

13

James rolled onto his side to a scramble of voices, male and female: *Is he alright?* He's breathing. *What happened?* Found them this way. *What about you, Teri?*

Teri?

He lifted his stinging eyelids. The rain had gone, taken by the night which had also vanished, replaced by bright morning calm. From somewhere nearby, birds were singing as they dried their feathers. And the smell, the raw aroma of a tropical beach surrounded him, tainted with death.

'He's awake!' someone yelled.

At the tiny patter of sandy footsteps, the girl leaning over him shaped into focus. Both ears heavily laden with studs, one through her eyebrow and one through her left nostril, she wore a tribal tattoo which snaked up over the collar of her black t-shirt and spread up the side of her neck. There were more on her arms and hands.

'What happened?' James muttered.

'Welcome to hell,' the girl deadpanned.

'*Move*, Teri!' Abbey arrived at his side, shouldering the tattooed girl away. 'Oh, thank god you're okay, you bloody moron!'

He sat up and rubbed the confusion from his eyes. Aside from Abbey and the tattooed girl, two others lingered. The first was the teenage girl in the shabby dress. Her blank expression hadn't altered. The second figure was a newbie, a middle-aged balding man with a dark tan and rotund belly. Standing behind Abbey, hands in the pockets of his tattered grey suit, he watched the scene closely, unsmiling and serious. He was smoking something thin.

'How long was I out?'

Abbey took his face in her hands. 'Couple of hours. What did I tell you? No one can fight currents like that, you're lucky Sebastian came along when he did.'

James glanced up at the smoking man. 'You pulled me out of there?'

'I was in the area, chief,' Sebastian replied, the hint of a smile creeping onto his face.

Shakily, James climbed to his feet and ran his fingers through his hair. It was knotted, sandy. Stepping to Sebastian, he held out his hand. The smoking man shook it.

'Thanks,' he muttered.

'Yeah,' said Sebastian, heavy traces of South African in his accent.

'He rescued Teri too,' Abbey threw in. 'Dragged you both right out of the wreckage in one go.'

Finishing his cigarette, Sebastian flicked it into the nearest dying fire. 'I was a coastguard in a former life,' he revealed. 'It's no big deal. Besides, I literally was passing. I was swimming to shore from further out when I came across you guys. What was I supposed to do, let you drown?'

'How about you, Teri?' asked James.

'How about me?'

'You okay? You hurt?'

'I'm alive, aren't I?' she murmured. 'No thanks to you.'

Abbey reeled. 'You ungrateful bitch! James risked his life for you last night, so the words you're looking for are *thank you.*'

'Chill down, Oprah,' Teri said. 'Before you go getting all righteous on me, perhaps you'd like to ask yourself the question, did she *want* to be saved? Did this girl who, judging by her appearance is severely damaged, wish to be rescued by the knight in slightly off-white armour and carried away into the sunset?'

'You ungrateful bitch!'

'You did that one.'

'You sure as hell sounded like you wanted to be rescued,' James threw in. 'We could hear you screaming from here.'

'Instinct, cowboy,' Teri countered.

Done with the argument, Teri backed away and headed for the tree line, the back of her t-shirt shredded revealing more ugly black patterns on her skin. 'When the search party turns up, I'll be over here smoking a cigarette.'

'Let her go,' James advised. 'She's not going anywhere.'

'Who does she think she is?' Abbey fumed. 'Wish I'd known her attitude stank last night, I would've gone out there myself and held her under.'

'Does it matter?' said Sebastian.

'Teri's not the problem,' James agreed. 'But she's right about something, we should sit tight until help arrives.'

'How do you know it will?'

'Because it's twenty-eleven, and when planes disappear, people notice.' James smiled reassuringly. 'Okay, here's what we do. We check every human body, try and find pulses. We need to gather all survivors for when the cavalry arrives, and we count heads. The last thing we need is folk wandering into the jungle if a boat turns up.'

'Why do we all need to stick together, chief?' Sebastian asked.

'We don't *need* to do anything,' he said. 'But there is safety in numbers.'

'Tell that to six million Jews. Besides, we've checked the handful around us, there aren't any more.'

'They were on the plane, Sebastian, so they're here somewhere. Two hundred-plus people don't just evaporate.'

'This two hundred-plus people do.'

At the tree line, Teri had planted her behind on the sand and was toking on a cigarette. Like the Australian, they would have to abandon her and catch up with her later.

Already James could tell the day was going to be a firetrap, the rising sun beginning to get serious.

'What do you suppose that is?' Sebastian piped up finally.

In the adjacent bay a huge towering chimney of smoke funnelled into the sky.

'Looks to me like a fire's just gone out,' Abbey suggested.

James agreed. 'Looks to me like a good place to start.'

14

With the fires blown out and most of the charred debris cooling, it was easy to cross the beach. Single-file, Abbey led the group. Behind her was the girl who seemed to have taken a shine to her. She wondered why the young girl hadn't requested they search for her family members. Instead she'd merely followed the pack as though in a trance.

Nearing the end of the inlet, a thin gulley of water streamed from the jungle and flowed into the sea. It wasn't wide enough to give them any problems. Directly beyond the separating outcrop, the stack of smoke dispersed into the bluing sky.

'Want me to go first?' James called from the back of the line.

'No, I got it.' Hauling herself up onto the first boulder, Abbey glanced down at the trio watching her from the sand. 'Piece of cake,' she grinned.

Her confidence grew as she bounded from one rock to another, Sebastian behind her, then the girl, and finally James. Her eyes lingered too long on James as he climbed, and she glanced away coyly.

One by one the others reached the top of the divide, their eyes settling on the source of the smoke. Buried in the white sand halfway along the next beach was the first hundred feet of the plane, part of one wing still attached. Its jet engine, still attempting to rotate, coughed out the pale grey smoke. The nose cone had ploughed into the sand and created a furrow right up to, and beyond, the tree line: an object and a location sharing no common ground. The remainder of the beach was largely untouched.

'Wow,' James muttered at last. 'Does anybody else feel kind of…'

'Yeah,' Sebastian agreed.

'But also kind of…'

'Yeah.'

'You know what it's going to be like in there, right?'

Abbey began making her way down the rocks and across the sand. At the wreckage she paused at the hatch door. It was hanging from its enormous hinges, a thin residue of rainwater dripping steadily from it. Beyond the door was blackness.

'You sure you want to go in there?' James had arrived at her side, his clear blue eyes scanning her face.

'Give me a boost, will you.'

Sebastian and the girl arrived at last, both of them eying the oily darkness.

'I think I can speak for both me and the girl when I say we don't want to go in there,' Sebastian declared.

'You don't have to,' said Abbey. 'Stay out here, James and I will take a look.'

'We will?'

'Yeah, we will. Come on, give me a boost.'

As Sebastian took the girl back along the beach, Abbey tensed as James moved closer to her, brushed a few strands of hair from her face. 'You don't have to be the hero,' he muttered.

'There might be people inside who need our help,' she replied quietly.

'There's also going to be a lot that don't.'

'It's not about being a hero,' she uttered. 'It's about doing what's right. You had your moment at the beach.'

He looked at her with gentle eyes, something behind them she couldn't quite read. It took everything she had to break the connection and turn away.

Today's word: *Guilty.*

*

Most of the shutters were down inside the cabin, and the open end where the plane had split in two was crushed inwards, only a trace amount of light breaking through. Water lapped gently against the open deck.

Moving slowly along the first aisle, Abbey probed the darkness.

'Hold on,' said James at her back. 'You hear that?'

Abbey paused and cocked her head. 'I don't hear anything.'

Stepping further into the blackness, she could smell blood. Or thought she could.

'There it is again,' he insisted.

'There's what again?'

'Voices. I swear I keep hearing people talking.'

'These people are dead, James. Are you going nuts already?'

Abbey leaned across the nearest seat-row and grabbed a shutter, light pouring in through the panel. She yelped and jumped back as a man's agonized face appeared in front of her own, neck at an impossible angle.

'What is it?'

In better light the rest of the carriage appeared to them. She heard James exhale behind her, a long drawn out sigh.

There must have been thirty or more bodies strewn throughout the scattered light, most of them still buckled firmly into their seats. It was a collage of destruction, a meat carnival. Here: a teenage girl, earphones still plugged into her ears, her eye socket caved in, grey matter visible. There: an elderly man with a ceiling panel wedged through his shoulder, separating his arm from his body. Here: a young boy no older than five or six, draped into the aisle, the whole left side of his small body dappled in blood from some unidentified wound. There: a young couple holding each other tightly, the impact unable to tear them apart as they took their final breaths, both bodies lurching intestines from where their belts had torn into their stomachs.

'Holy shit,' James murmured.

'Yeah.'

'Poor bastards.'

This time there was no mistaking the voices coming from business-class, loud enough to be heard, quiet enough to be incoherent. Moving hurriedly back through the carriage, Abbey pushed her way through to the front, an obstacle course of curtains, trolleys, bodies. The voices grew louder as she neared; several different voices, male and female.

She bustled into business-class to be met by three males and one woman standing agape. She knew two of them.

'Elaine?' she whispered. '*Eric*?'

'Abigail!' beamed Eric. 'We was in a crash!'

Abbey felt her body go numb as James arrived behind her.

'Well now,' Elaine De Boor smiled, looking James up and down, 'if it's God's will that I'm to be stranded on a desert island, He's seen fit to provide the eye candy. Not to mention your good timing! We have a bit of a situation here.'

There didn't seem to be any bodies in business-class. Aside from Eric and his mother, there were only two others. Standing to the rear of the compartment was a man in his late forties, early fifties, mildly disfigured with a birthmark covering a big chunk of his face. It stretched from his left eye socket right down to below his collar.

The other was lying flat on his back beneath a dislodged row of seats. He was a geeky looking black kid, early twenties and sporting a thick afro. He looked oily skinned and frustrated.

'This is Anthony,' Elaine introduced, pointing out the branded man. 'And this charming young buried fella is Oliver. Oliver who prefers to be called Oli.'

'My parents still call me Oliver,' he grumbled. 'It's only a short step from Oliver to Rupert or Tarquin or something. There's no way to cool up those names no matter what you do.'

'He's nothing if not sunny,' Elaine explained.

'Are you here to help Oliver?' Eric asked.

'*Oli!* the kid insisted.

'What exactly is the problem?' Abbey asked.

Finally Anthony spoke, his bass-tone voice rich with Deep South America, Georgia or Alabama maybe. 'We can't move this row of seats. Where the carriage has caved in, it's wedged the row in tight.'

James stepped in. 'What about you, Oli, are you hurt?'

'Yeah, my afro's messed up, man!'

'I'll take that as a no,' he said. 'Okay, here's what we do. Big guy, what's your name again?'

'Eric.'

'Eric, you come around here, we're going to need your strength. Anthony, if you brace yourself beneath the seat row and I'll try using some good old leverage to prize her up.'

Abbey watched as James rallied everybody into position as he snapped a steel pole from the overhang and plunged it into the darkness beneath the seat row.

'Okay,' he said. 'Everybody set?'

A rumble of grunts.

'On three, everybody push. One, two, *three*!'

The seat row began to shift, jarred backwards with the pressure. Eric's pure brute strength was paying off, and Oli slid free and stepped away, Elaine wrapping him up in motherly arms. 'Oh thank God, thank God, thank God. For a minute there I had images of us bringing you food and water every day and taking it in turns to keep you company in here.'

'Alright, alright,' grumbled Oli trying to smooth his afro, 'you can put me down now. I think I got it.'

'Not just a pretty face, your husband!' Elaine grinned, nodding to James.

'Oh…no,' Abbey corrected. 'He's not my husband.'

'Oh I'm sorry, darl. Me and my big mouth.'

Abbey chanced a peek at James. He was smirking.

'Well,' Oli threw in, 'I hate to break up the party, but since you're all here on my behalf, I hope you won't mind if I depart. I do believe the sun's coming out. I need to work on this tan.'

Abbey waited for Anthony to second the notion. Instead he stayed back, the gloom absorbing him.

James led the way out, trailed obediently by Oli, Elaine and Eric who lumbered clumsily after them.

Looking back to Anthony, Abbey said, 'You coming?'

Silence.

'Anthony?'

'In a minute,' he murmured.

'Okay,' she frowned. 'We'll be outside.'

15

'You're doing *what*?' Abbey gasped.

'We need to see what we're up against,' James replied casually. 'It's no big deal.'

'It's no big deal?'

'No.'

She took a step back. 'What is it with you? Have you got a death wish, or something?'

Throwing a couple of water bottles into a rucksack, James turned and looked up at the towering and rocky tor overlooking the north of the island.

'It's bloody suicide, James! And in this heat? I don't know if you've noticed, but the sun has burnt away every last bit of cloud, and there will be no shade up there.'

Tightening the cord on the bag, he said, 'Don't worry about it.' He rose from his haunches and faced her, placed his hands at the tops of her arms. 'I'm coming back.'

'You'd better! I can't take care of this lot alone.'

Some of the others were scattered along the beach staring out to sea, preparing themselves for some miraculous rescue. Others were prying their way into suitcases, seeing what they could salvage. Anthony had finally turned up, his birthmark starker in the afternoon sun. Teri too had made an appearance. She seemed to have raided a man's case and substituted her torn clothes for a pair of khaki shorts and a large checked shirt, which looked too heavy for the weather. Everybody except Sol Delaney, the elusive Aussie, was accounted for.

'Listen,' James said quietly. 'Everybody's frightened. There are no leaders here, so we have to get organised. Get them working while we're gone. Build shelters, keep them occupied. You have a couple of accomplices in Eric and Elaine. Use them. They'll do anything for you, it's obvious.'

'Shelters? How long do you suppose we'll be here?'

'I don't know,' he replied truthfully.

'Hang on a sec, you said *we*. While *we're* gone. Which crazy bastard have you g –'

'You all set, James?' interrupted Oli. He too had changed. Now he boasted a pair of faded Bermuda shorts and a t-shirt which insisted Frankie was back.

'Wow!' James replied. 'Who's the eighties throwback?'

Abbey stashed away a grin.

'What?' Oli examined himself. 'Nobody. I found my own case over by the tailfin.'

'These are *your* clothes?'

'What's the problem?'

'There's no problem,' James grinned.

'You guys crack me up!' Oli deadpanned. Pushing between them he stormed into the jungle.

'Oops,' Abbey smirked. 'I think you'd better go and apologise.'

'I think I'd better.'

Glancing down at her feet, she murmured, 'Please come back, James. I meant it when I said we need you. I can't take care of this lot by myself.'

'I'll be back by tonight. I promise.'

*

It only took a half-mile for James to realise that Abbey had been talking sense. It was too damn hot for this crap. Earlier he'd changed into a sky-blue baggy shirt and knee-length khaki shorts, and in a suitcase not belonging to him, he'd found a good pair of walking boots which fit.

'Can you remind me,' Oli gasped from thirty yards back. 'At what point did I agree this was a good idea?'

Taking a seat on a fallen tree, James waited for Oli to catch up. 'It's that afro, it's weighing you down.'

Dropping his rucksack, he took a seat next to James, panting. 'Don't be dissing the afro, man. It's what sets a brother apart.' Oli took a couple of big swigs of water and handed the bottle to James. 'So how much more of this feral garden do we have to conquer before we reach the base of the hill?'

'We're nearly there. But if the jungle is killing you, you'd better turn back now. The hill is going to be worse.'

'How'd you figure? There's got to be fewer bugs up there. I'm like a fricking banquet to the little assholes.'

James took another swig of water and bagged the bottle. 'Sweet blood, that's what my mom always used to say. When I was a kid, I was never bitten. She always said I had sour blood. Sucking on it was like biting into a lemon. You, my friend, are a strawberry.'

Oli swatted the back of his neck. 'Awesome.'

'Where are you from anyway?'

Oli hesitated and examined his shoelaces.

'It's not a trick question.'

'Tinsel Town,' Oli said coyly. 'Hollywood. But don't judge a book by its cover, man. There's more to me than meets the eye.'

'I wasn't judging. What's wrong with California?'

'Nothing wrong with the place, per se,' Oli clarified. 'It's the people I have an issue with.'

'Plastic?'

'Some of them make Barbie and Ken look positively real, in appearance and personality.'

'So what sets you apart?'

Swat. Slap.

'Simple, I'm organic,' said Oli with a wink. 'I'm studying law at UCLA. It seems there're only about one in ten people in Hollywood not trying to become an actor or a singer or something, so that makes me the one in ten. Anyway, I wish I could say my time at university was passing amiably. I'm not exactly jock material which, in the current narrative of society, makes me a nerd. And there doesn't seem to be much of an in-between.'

James frowned. 'What's in New Zealand?'

Again, Oli hesitated. 'I was on an excursion with some other students. They weren't on the plane. I lost them in Port Elizabeth. Or they lost me if you want to cross-examine. Went to use the bathroom in a restaurant and when I came back they'd taken off. I don't know if they ditched me or just didn't miss me. Either way, it made me feel pretty crappy.'

James shook his head. 'There were no tutors taking headcounts?'

'It wasn't an official trip. The Student Union put it together. We're considered adults so the lecturers left it up to parental consent.'

'So you just wanted to continue alone.'

'Yeah, screw them!' Oli said venomously. 'The trip was bought and paid for so I figured I'd finish it.'

James had to admit, he'd got Oli all wrong. To carry on alone with a tour like that took guts. In the same situation there would've been many a kid - and no doubt some of the jocks - quickly on the phone to their parents crying to them to get them home.

'So what's your story?' Oli asked.

James raised his eyebrows.

'You originate from somewhere, right?'

'I'm from West Virginia originally, but I've spent some time in London recently. Went there for a job.'

'Doing what?'

James paused, then said, 'IT.'

'Oh yeah,' Oli grinned. 'What field? I'm pretty useful with a computer.'

'Never would've guessed.'

'Come on, what field?'

'I can't get into it, Oli. Some of it's classified.'

'Oh, come on, man, don't be like that.'

James leant forward and rested his elbows on his knees. 'Just drop it,' he muttered with a note of finality.

Holding up his hands, the student ceded. 'How did you come to be on that airplane?'

'I was on my way to see my brother in Wellington. Haven't seen him in years.'

'So why not fly into Wellington?' Oli probed.

'North Shore was the only flight I could get yesterday.'

'Was he expecting you?'

'He and his family, yeah.'

The gap between them brimmed with quiet. Finally, Oli muttered, 'They're not going to find us, are they?'

James raised his eyebrows.

'The Indian Ocean is enormous, how could they know where we are?'

James climbed to his feet and stretched his back. 'You know, for a law student, you ain't that bright, friend.'

'Gee, thanks.'

'Three things. First of all, because of satellite, over ninety-five percent of the world's islands are now discovered. Hell, this one probably even has a name. Secondly, we were on a flight plan that's recorded at both ends of the journey. And finally, hidden amongst that mess on the beaches is the Black Box, which gives off a locating signal. So, bearing that triple whammy in mind, combined with a bitch of a walk up a steep hill, I'd say you should sleep soundly tonight!'

'You state your case solidly,' the student admitted. 'Have you ever considered a career in law? Still, I put it to you that nothing could be working after that crash. If the Black Box was giving off a signal, it sure as hell isn't now.'

'They say those things are indestructible,' argued James.

Oli appeared to relax. The reality was, James had only spoken a partial truth. Yes there'd be parties looking for them, no doubt about it. Whether or not they find them was a different story. None of them knew if the plane had been on course when it went down. If they'd been dragged off the flight plan, Black Box or not, the search teams would be pissing into the wind. If they didn't find any wreckage along the route, what then?

He said, 'We still have a hill to beat. You all set?'

Oli climbed to his feet. 'As I'll ever be.'

*

Reaching up over the edge of the plateau, James probed the rocky surface for some kind of grip-hold. Thrusting himself up over the lip he rolled onto his back, winded. He opened his eyes to a cloudless sky. The sun was floating directly overhead, beating down on them cruelly. Minutes passed before Oli clambered up over the lip and lay beside him, wheezing.

'Is it easier on the way back down?' he panted. 'Some Chinese tortures aren't as nasty as that.'

James grunted.

'You didn't think I'd make it, did you?' Oli gasped.

'Never doubted you!'

'Oh ye of little faith. Tell me again why we did that?'

James climbed to his feet and held out a hand to Oli. 'Stand up.'

At the southern edge of the table, the pair feasted on the view. 'Whoa,' muttered Oli.

'Agreed.'

Laid out before them was the island in its entirety, every inch of beautiful scenery waiting to be explored. Putting to bed any doubt that they were on an island and not headland, the only colour visible offshore was the different hues of blue meeting over the horizon. About four or five miles around, something like fourteen or fifteen bays skirted the trees.

Below they could clearly see the front end of the plane, mangled back end spanning out into the water. In the next bay over, the tailfin stood out like a shark's fin. And out in the clear water huge dark shapes lay visible beneath the surface, sections of the plane lying dormant on the seabed.

Further along the same beach they could see the others moving about like ants.

The density of the forest became far more apparent from the plateau. They'd traversed a good mile and a half through the thicket to the foot of the hill.

'What do you suppose that is?' Oli posed.

James moved to the student's side. 'What are you looking at?'

'Right there. You see that open clearing about a half-mile away?'

Scanning the expanse below, he spotted it. A couple of hundred feet around, the clearing was surrounded by trees at odds with the other greenery: a lighter shade.

'I don't know. Seems strange that a different kind of tree should grow inland like that.'

'Hmm,' Oli mumbled. 'As interesting as the shades of leaves might be to some people, I wasn't talking about the trees. If you cast your eyes into the centre of the clearing, something stands out as a kind of focal point, if you know what I mean.'

Oli was right. There was something there for sure, some kind of structure.

'What the hell is that?'

Back at the northern edge, Oli gasped, 'Never mind that…what the fuck is *that*?'

Tearing his eyes away from the mysterious clearing, James stepped over to Oli, his breath catching in his throat.

'James?' the student pressed.

Stretching out into the water like a pan-handle, a natural pier had been formed out of an arm of solid rock. It did the job of separating one bay from the next. Pressing against it in the mild tide was a dark mass, parts of it broken away and resting on the sand.

James placed a hand on the kid's shoulder. 'Enigma solved, Oli.'

'I didn't realise we had an enigma.'

'We sure did. You just found the rest of the bodies.'

Oli took an uneasy step back from the ledge. 'No, that's not possible! Look at the wreckage, how did they get way over there? The geography doesn't work, man!'

'I don't know. Strong currents must've swept them beneath the surface to the eastern bay. If they hit an eddy they would've been whipped around and thrown back on themselves. That outcrop must've caught them.'

'Awesome,' Oli mouthed quietly. 'So what now?'

James shrugged. 'Guess we go check it out.'

The student sighed. 'That's what I thought you were going to say.'

16

The trek down the northern slope proved to be a walk in the park compared to the plateau climb. From the base of the hill, the walk through the trees back to shore measured only about a mile.

They pushed their way onto the beach about two hundred yards from the outcropping, the rocky handle splitting the Indian Ocean in two, its beauty grotesquely marred by the large black mass pressing against it.

'There it is,' James said quietly.

Oli's gaze settled on the abomination, ebbing and flowing gently with the tide. Visibly he paled, hesitated.

'Oli, it's okay,' James sympathized. 'I've got this.'

'No, I'll…I'll be fine.'

James took another look. 'There're sights down there that will probably stay with you forever. Honestly, is it worth it?'

'What, and let the jocks be right about me?'

Hesitantly they walked towards the bodies. As they neared, Oli's pace slowed further.

Several of the bodies had made it onto the sand, split from the pack as though trying to escape.

When the two of them reached the first cadaver, it was clear the small broken figure was that of a child no older than six. She was lying on her back, the scorching afternoon sun baking her.

Oli turned his back and vomited.

James crouched by the slightly bloated figure of the girl. He guessed she'd been out of the water for most of the day, one of the first to break from the group.

He understood Oli's nausea. This girl wasn't meant to die here, so young, and in such an horrific way. How could it be that she'd wound up on a beach in the middle of nowhere, small desecrated body on exhibition? It didn't make sense.

Oli had relinquished his bravado. He'd retreated towards the trees and planted himself down on the sand, face buried in his hands.

The stench of death inhibiting, James was finding it difficult to move closer to the mass. He glanced back at the student. 'What did you say?'

Oli looked puzzled. 'Nothing! I didn't speak.'

He turned back to the sea. 'Come on, James,' he muttered to himself, 'get a grip.' He placed one foot forward and watched it sink into the sand. A second step; one more dry footfall.

The notion of the third rolled away on the waves. 'Oli, seriously, shut the hell up!'

Oli raised his hands, palms up. 'I told you, man, I'm not making a sound.'

'I just heard a cough,' James insisted.

'You're going insane, man!'

'Oli, I'm sure of it.'

'The sun's getting to you.'

Running from body to body, James began flipping those facedown, checking pulses. Six had made it onto the sand. Only one was breathing. Lying on his side, the large black male coughed again.

'Jesus, Oli, this guy's alive!'

Oli sprinted over. 'Holy shit, you sure?'

The man had colour, and it had nothing to do with his origins. Easily in his fifties, he had closely cropped hair and a big round belly.

'Oli…look at that,' James whispered.

Oli examined the man's clothes. 'Is this who I think it is?'

'Who do you think it is?'

'If I didn't know better, I'd say we've found the captain.'

*

'He doesn't look too hot, man!' Oli announced.

Despite the pilot's functioning internals, his externals had taken a hit. Grazes and scratches aside, James couldn't tear his eyes away from the open wound above the man's knee, stretching halfway up his thigh. The gash was wide open, angry red flaps of skin peeling away from the oozing mess. If it wasn't infected already, it soon would be.

'We need to get him back to the camp,' said James. 'Maybe one of the others will know what to do with him.'

'I don't know if you noticed but this dude ain't no prom queen. No way the two of us can carry him that far.'

Running a hand through his hair, James agreed. 'Abbey's setting up camp about a half mile in that direction. Run back there and fetch help.'

'What about him?'

'I'll stay with him. This is important, Oli. If any one of the survivors has any kind of medical background, have them prepare as best they can.'

The student began to back away.

'And Oli,' James added. 'Be quick. I don't know how big our window is.'

The student began jogging along the beach, a spray of white sand at his heel.

Shrugging off his shirt, James tore it into strips and began bandaging the gaping wound. Wadding the rest together, he lifted the pilot's head and placed it underneath. There wasn't much else he could do.

Spread out before him like a giant blue blanket, the ocean sparkled beneath the afternoon sun. The presence of death was not lost on him, bathed in the unnatural calm to which the island had succumbed. All these people, all but the meager handful of survivors, dead.

Gone.

Growing up with Christian parents, he'd been led to believe that God, if He existed, was kind, that no matter what your sin or bad deed, He would understand, He would forgive you and pat you on the head. If that was true, what the fuck was this about?

He lay down next to the still form of the pilot and scanned the sky. There were no birds anywhere. Wasn't that odd?

Were there other forces at work that determined the way this sort of thing worked, he pondered, or was it all down to chance? Could it be that the survivors shared some sort of illogical connection, each person a cog in the machine that would eventually spell their way off the island?

Time was their only friend now. Time. And almost three hundred corpses cooking in the afternoon sun.

Next to the pilot, James lay still and quiet, wondering where all the birds were.

*

Almost half an hour after his departure, Oli had returned with Sebastian and Anthony carrying a flat section of metal salvaged from the wreckage. Still in the tattered grey suit, Sebastian's South African accent became a blur of excitable and colourful language.

Anthony was the opposite. Clearly a man of few words, he said nothing as he swept his eyes across the dismal collage. He moved closer to it as though in a trance. It was only when Oli called out to him did the others realise he was crying. What was going on under that birthmark? James wondered.

'Has he come around yet?' Oli asked.

'Not yet.'

'What're we going to do about these bodies, chief?' Sebastian asked. 'We can't leave them here, that's for sure.'

James climbed to his feet. 'The bodies aren't going anywhere. We need to get this man some medical attention.'

'Yes, yes,' Sebastian agreed. 'But after that, we need to –'

'Shut up, Sebastian!' Anthony's deep voice intruded.

'What's stoked your boiler, chief?'

Anthony didn't acknowledge the question.

'Look,' James interrupted, 'you girls can argue amongst yourselves at your leisure. This man's in a bad way.'

Anthony turned his back on them and began once again examining the bodies.

'Brought this as a stretcher,' Oli said pointing out the sheet of flat steel. He looked to James hoping for a nod of approval.

Without Anthony's help, they hoisted the pilot carefully onto the makeshift stretcher. The big guy was about as heavy as he looked.

'Hey, Anthony, little help here!'

Anthony whipped around, fresh tears snaking down his cheeks.

'You okay, man?' Oli asked skeptically.

Anthony wiped his face and began up the beach towards them.

'*Obra del Diabo*,' Sebastian murmured.

The others looked up.

'The devil has been here,' uttered Sebastian. 'I can feel his presence.'

'The devil?' Anthony said at last. 'The devil has been here?'

Only the waves responded.

'There is no God,' Anthony declared. 'There is no devil. There is only you, me, and every other blood-sucking parasite calling themselves human.'

'Wow, never heard you say so much,' Oli threw in.

'You think this man is your saviour?' Anthony pointed to James. 'Nobody can save us from this.'

'Whoa, whoa,' James interrupted. 'Who said I was the saviour of anything?'

Anthony turned to face James. 'Exactly.'

James stood quietly, perplexed.

Nobody moved.

'This is not about you, Anthony,' James whispered. 'And it's definitely not about me. It's about getting these people to safety. It's about getting this man some medical attention. I don't want to be here any more than you.'

Anthony bent down and grabbed the corner of the metal sheet. He waited silently, almost as if James had never spoken.

Eying the birth-marked man cautiously, the other three paused.

James hesitated. Something about that situation had been far from normal, something about Anthony likewise.

Gripping the adjacent corner, James caught the man's eye, hoping to see some hidden emotion, something to explain his motivation, but there was nothing.

17

Since Oli had returned and absconded with Sebastian and Anthony, Abbey had felt better. James was okay, and so too was Oli.

There was definitely something about James that she felt drawn to. Whether he knew it or not, he carried with him an aura of confidence. Who was she kidding, of course he knew. Whatever the case, she felt safer when he was around.

At present only she and the girl were at the camp. Still wearing the frumpish beige dress, Abbey watched as she propped sturdy branches in the sand, fitting together the framework for the tents like Abbey had shown her.

She still hadn't spoken, and Abbey had begun to wonder if it really was shock. Perhaps she was a mute. Whatever the reason, it hadn't stopped her working. The kid was a grafter.

Way over in the west, the sun was beginning to fail, the blue of the ocean slowly melting into a golden shimmer.

Earlier she'd sent Elaine off with her son to salvage the wreckage. In a haze of cigarette smoke, Teri had volunteered to go with them. It wasn't pretty in there, but somebody had to do it. Everybody was doing their part. All except Sol Delaney, the evasive Australian; nobody had seen him since he was flipping suitcases. Nobody missed him either.

Elaine and the others had been gone for about three hours. In the meantime, Abbey and the girl had built six temporary quarters along the sand. They'd lashed some branches together in bizarre frameworks, and thrown blankets over them for protection from the sun. So long as it didn't storm again any time soon, the tents would hold up just fine.

Collapsing onto the sand, she coaxed the girl to sit with her and watch the setting sun. With no apprehension, she sank down onto the sand and rested her head on Abbey's shoulder as they watched the dazzling spectrum of colour washing over the horizon.

Chancing a peek at the girl, Abbey spotted the damp in her eyes. She hugged her closer, both of them shivering in the evening heat.

18

'You really want to go back in there?' Teri asked.

'No, not really,' Elaine replied. 'But Abbey's sent us for supplies. No better place to look.'

Teri stepped back. 'Fuck that!'

Elaine glanced at Eric who was idly examining the underside of the battered carriage. 'Please don't use that language in front of my son.'

'What, *fuck*?'

'Or in front of me.'

Teri flicked a cigarette butt on to the sand. 'I don't see what the problem is. Eric hasn't even noticed. You're the only one bitching?'

'Listen, you little brat,' Elaine uttered vehemently. 'I don't care what you do in your own time, and I don't care who you do it with. But while you're in the company of me or my son, you will refrain from using foul language.'

Teri smirked. 'Or what?'

'Or for the love of God, I will put you on your lily-white arse, and believe me, you won't get back up.'

'Whoa,' Teri uttered. 'Momma bear got some *stones*.'

Elaine held her stare.

Shying away, Teri sparked up another cigarette.

'Mom, are we going back inside?' Eric called out. He was eying the darkness from beneath the emergency exit.

Earlier that morning, they'd exited through this very door. Nobody wanted to go back inside, not a soul. But somebody had to. They needed water and blankets. Cushions. Food provisions. Anything that would aid the preservation of those left alive. And if this was her duty, her contribution, she wouldn't argue.

'I'm not going in there,' Teri declared. 'I'll stand watch.'

'Stand watching for what?'

Taking a drag, Teri said, 'I don't know, cannibals. Or something.'

'Cannibals?'

'Look, I don't know. Whatever involves me not going in there, man.'

'We're all going in, Teri, no exceptions. Eric, you okay with that?'

The big man whipped his head around. 'Okay with what?'

'Of course he's okay with it,' Teri grumbled. 'He retarded. *I'm* not okay with it, *entiendes*? *Me*, I'm not.'

'I don't care what you're okay with, Teri! It's very simple. The sun will be gone in the next hour and I'm fairly sure you don't want to go in there in the dark. I'm not standing here bickering about this anymore. Get your tattooed backside onto that plane and help us search for supplies.'

'Christ...' Teri mumbled. 'Gimme cannibals any day!'

Elaine smirked. 'The amount of ink in your skin, you'd be like chewing on a pen.'

One after the other, Eric boosted the women into the darkness then hauled himself up. In the gloom, Eric and Teri waited for Elaine to give them instructions. When she was through, the three of them peered hesitantly into the dim cabin.

'Can I get my magazine, mom?' Eric asked.

'Another time, pumpkin. Right now we just need the essentials.'

'But I hadn't finished reading it,' he muttered glumly and moved away into the darkness. 'It has to be here somewhere.'

The magazine was long gone, thought Elaine. She had just avoided broaching the topic with her son.

The first layer of dust had now begun settling over the bodies, the smell of decay denser than before. Nothing else had changed and so they passed quickly through. Between the cockpit and business-class, Elaine remembered seeing supply cupboards. It was as good a place as any to start.

Eric still didn't seem too perturbed by the devastation. He moved nonchalantly along the aisle as though the death and carnage all around was merely a performance. Until now, the only death he'd know was their pet cat, Whiskey, but that didn't stop her wondering just how he'd cope when she suddenly wasn't there one day.

No longer visible in the gloom, she assumed Teri had gone in the opposite direction. Or back outside.

Thankfully the area behind the cockpit was body-free, the small recess lined with steel lockers. Inside they found small tins of Pepsi, bottled water, bags of peanuts, sandwiches.

The cockpit door slightly ajar, a narrow bar of light sliced into the gloom. Gingerly she reached out and pushed the door inwards, the evening sun filling the recess with quiet light.

A crackle startled her, and she registered it for what it was: a hiss of radio static.

'My God,' she gasped, pushing her way into the tiny control room.

Before her, two uniformed males were sprawled, pushed up onto the instruments with the brute force of the impact. With the pips had come the responsibility of several hundred people, on top of the burden of having your skull pulverised in the event of an emergency landing. Once the plane was down, all pips became null and void, and both pilots had shared the same fate.

The third seat off to the right was vacant – the navigation officer seemed to be absent.

'Mom,' Eric asked. 'What's that noise?'

'Just stay there, pumpkin. Mom needs to check something.'

Probing the cockpit, she scanned the equipment for the radio receiver. She prayed for it to speak again. Then it did, the quietly distorted voice filling the cockpit – directly beneath the co-pilot.

'Bugger,' Elaine muttered to no one. She rubbed her eyes.

Was it cruel to involve her son in the hideous task of moving the co-pilot's body? Did it make her a bad mother, or was she just doing what was necessary? The fact remained, she couldn't lift the man alone, and Eric could.

Upon request, he casually hauled the co-pilot from the panel and gently placed him back in his seat, the whistling crackle amplifying. Leaning over the panel, she fiddled with the controls and blurted desperately into the receiver. 'Hello…is anybody there?' Nothing responded. She tried again but only white noise sang back at her.

Teri appeared in the doorway. 'I found a first aid box and a tool kit. Threw them out on to the sand. Stewardess was clinging onto the medical kit like her life depended on it. Whatever the bitch's life depended on, it wasn't that.'

Elaine explained to her about the radio. 'I just don't know how to use the damn thing.'

'Can I get my magazine now, mom,' Eric persisted.

'Pumpkin,' Elaine said firmly, 'another time, okay!'

'But I hadn't finished reading it.'

'I know that, kiddo, but we don't have time right now.'

'But mom, I was reading about the new –'

'Forget the fucking magazine, retard!' Teri snapped.

Eric reeled like he'd been slapped. His eyes widened into large confused discs.

Elaine stood rigid. 'What did you say?'

Teri didn't hesitate. 'I told this big goofball to forget the goddamn magazine!' And then to Eric, 'Don't you get it, dumb ass, we were in a plane crash, your magazine is gone. It's smoke, dust, fucking *ash*!'

Elaine took a step forwards. 'How dare you –'

'Save it, Grandma, you don't frighten me! I've seen autopsies with more life in them than you!'

'It's okay, pumpkin,' Elaine assured her son. 'We'll find your magazine.'

Teri scoffed. 'Whatever.'

'Just get out of here!' Elaine yelled. 'You've done enough damage, you snotty little brat. You think you know hardships? You couldn't walk a *day* in my son's shoes!'

'They wouldn't fit me,' Teri smirked and turned on her heel, leaving a wake of devastation in Eric's head.

The big man was frantic, disorientated. He was focused on his hands, his twiddling thumbs. Nervously stepping from foot to foot, he didn't know how to stand.

Rallying to her son, Elaine began to soothe him with practiced words and platitudes. It would take at least an hour to bring him back, she knew this from experience. It broke her heart to see him this way. Eventually he would push the attack from the forefront of his mind and into a box in a shadowy corner like he'd learned, but the process of getting him there was a hardship nobody needed right now, least of all Eric.

The crackle of static continued to interrupt the silence.

Elaine's eyes rolled gently closed. They hadn't come here for this.

19

The final whispers of light had retreated over the horizon by the time James and the others staggered back into the camp. The moon seemed too close, illuminating the white sand in long glowing strips. Waiting patiently, Abbey prayed they'd be returning with good news.

And they were, for sprawled out on the sheet of steel was the still form of a man, his chest rising and falling gently beneath his shirt. She couldn't help noticing James, toned and golden, wearing only shorts and boots, the remnants of his shirt wrapped around the unconscious man's leg. She shifted her gaze away when he caught her looking.

'My god, you weren't joking,' she gasped.

'Did you ever doubt me?' Oli wheezed.

'This way,' Abbey directed. 'We'll put him in one of the tents.'

Without a word, Anthony abandoned his post and walked down to the shore. Watching Anthony leave, Oli looked to James in confusion.

'Just let him go,' James muttered.

'What! How is that fair?'

'Oli,' he said firmly, 'let him go.'

'Fucking slacker,' Sebastian grumbled, earning raised eyebrows from James. 'I'm just saying out loud what everybody's thinking, chief. Don't see why we should break our balls when your man gets to shirk off. He's bloody weird anyway.'

'I second that,' Oli agreed.

'You saw how he was with the bodies,' Sebastian said. 'You telling me that was normal?'

James shrugged. 'One problem at a time, huh?'

They raised the pilot once again, Abbey taking the absent corner. It took only a couple of minutes to get him settled into one of the tents and feed him some water. Sebastian too decided he was shattered. He told the others he was going for a walk along the beach to clear his head, and when he came back he insisted he was going to sleep like one of the deceased.

'Where's Elaine and the others,' James asked.

As if on cue Teri came sauntering along the sand alone, the lit tip of her cigarette dangling from between her lips. She was carrying something.

'Speak of the devil.'

'Yeah, literally,' Oli murmured.

As Teri neared, she dropped her goods onto the sand. 'Happy? First aid box and a tool kit.'

'Where are the others?'

'God knows. The retard had some kind of breakdown, so I left them to it.'

Oli bent down and scooped up the first aid box. 'If I didn't know better, I'd think you were talking about Eric.'

'Smarter than he looks, this one.'

'So how about calling him Eric?' James suggested.

'Whatever,' Teri scoffed and walked away, planting herself down in her usual spot by the trees. She lit another cigarette.

All eyes turned to the pilot's tent as a soft moan emanated.

'What's wrong with him?' Abbey asked. James glanced away casually, but for the briefest moment she caught a fleeting shadow pass over his face.

'Oli?' Abbey pressed.

The student didn't seem to know how to stand. He thrust his hands into his pockets, withdrew them again. Shifting from foot to foot, he couldn't meet Abbey's eyes. Instead he muttered, 'I'm going to leave you two lovebirds to it.'

'Look at me, James,' she insisted. 'What's going on?'

'The pilot's in a bad way,' James said at last. 'I mean, most of his wounds are superficial, they'll heal fine.'

'But?'

'He has a huge gash on his thigh, opened right up. I've wrapped it, stemmed the flow of blood, but I can't even imagine what'll happen if we don't get the man some drugs. If gangrene sets in…well, you do the math.'

Scooping up the abandoned first aid box, she said, 'What about this?'

'What about it? It'll have clean bandages and wraps, but there won't be any drugs. First aid boxes like this don't carry them.'

Abbey skimmed through it quickly. There was nothing inside in tablet form, not even painkillers.

'Tomorrow, we'll begin a search through the luggage for penicillin, and I'll dive the wreckage, see what I can find out there. Somebody on that plane will have some antibiotics.'

'You dealt with anything like this before?'

James shook his head.

Abbey exhaled wearily. Neither had she.

*

Having returned from his walk, Sebastian had quickly smoked a cigarette and disappeared into one of the tents, the soft hum of his snoring spilling out onto the sand.

Anthony had not returned.

Placing stones in a small circle, Teri had built a crude campfire in front of the tents. Now she was loading it with twigs and shredded paper. The night had grown cool, forcing Abbey to throw on an extra layer – a thin pink cardigan she'd found amongst someone's clothes. James too had pulled on a black v-neck sweater and pushed up the sleeves. Elaine and Eric had still failed to show.

'I'm starting to get worried,' said Abbey. 'They should be back by now.'

Standing by her side at the shoreline, James didn't respond. Instead he stared out to the darkened horizon, his eyes glazed over.

As Abbey began to stress her point, Elaine walked wearily towards them, arms linked with her son. Eric looked mildly distressed, his enormous figure taking small infantile steps, his arms rigid by his sides.

'We were about to send out a search party,' Abbey said as they approached. 'Did you get lost?'

'Eric did,' Elaine replied. 'In a sense.'

'Everything okay?'

'It is now,' muttered Elaine. 'Would you mind watching him for a second?'

Not waiting for a reply, Elaine marched up the sand, beeline made out for Teri. The tattooed girl was still loading up her campfire.

From the shoreline Abbey watched the scene unfold like something from a movie. Following the word "Bitch", spat vehemently from Elaine's lips, was the most vicious punch to the nose Abbey had ever seen delivered by a woman. Teri went down like a lead balloon, clutching her burst nose, blood spraying down her heavy shirt.

'The next time you speak to my son that way, God help me I will literally pop your head open! How's that for stones!'

With that she walked back towards the shore to collect her son. In her wake, Teri writhed on the sand clutching her bloody nose.

'Jesus, Elaine, what the hell was that?' Abbey gasped.

'She had it coming.' Elaine didn't smile. 'I can defend myself, Eric can't. When someone abuses that fact, I defend him. Which of the tents are free?'

'On the end.'

Elaine took Eric by the arm and led him away, disappearing into the end tent.

James still hadn't moved, his fixed gaze unbroken. She placed a hand gently on his arm. 'James, you alright?'

The physical contact seemed to wake him up. 'Hmm,' he murmured. 'Fine. You?'

She tilted her head. 'Come on, let's take a walk.'

Sticking close to the shoreline, they moved away from the camp. In one direction they would pass the aircraft, in the other the mass of bodies pressing against the arm of rock. Death would be their companion, whichever way they went. They chose the aircraft.

'How're you holding up?' James murmured warily.

'I'm okay. I'm not worried about me.'

'Eric?'

'Everybody. My husband's going to be going out of his mind.'

'I didn't realise you were married,' said James.

Abbey smiled. 'Why would you?'

'You're not wearing a ring.'

She fanned out her fingers. 'I was on my way to a sales pitch in Auckland. Always take my ring off in case I need to flirt a little to seal the deal. When all else fails…'

He smiled at last. 'So your husband, he knew which flight you were on?'

'I usually text him the flight numbers so he can check that I landed safely. He's going to know by now that the plane went down.'

James didn't reply.

'I miss him, James. I've been threatening for so long to give up my job and stay home. God knows we can afford it. But I kept putting it off and putting it off. Just *one* more year…I've been saying that for a *long* time.'

Wrapping an arm gently around her shoulder, he said, 'We're going to get off this island, Abbey. You'll see your husband again, I promise.'

'You can't promise something like that, James. The truth is, my husband thinks I'm dead.'

'You don't know that. Any guy who can get a girl like you is no fool. All he knows is the plane went down. We haven't been found so they won't write us off just like that. If the media haven't, then I can guarantee your husband hasn't either.'

She smiled through thinly pursed lips. 'How's a guy like you single?'

'Who says I'm single?'

'Oh, you're single! Here's me jabbering on about Edward and you haven't uttered a single word about a loved one.'

Shirking the topic, he asked, 'Who were you on the plane with? I'm assuming you don't travel alone.'

'My colleague, Milo. Shit, he was such a good kid.'

'What happened?'

'I don't know,' she said honestly. 'The plane struck the water, I was knocked out. When I came to, Milo was just sitting there. There was no blood, nothing. But when I lifted his head his neck was so twisted, all gnarled, as if something had been yanking on it, trying to rip it off. I threw up in his lap, right before I got out of there. I was the only one left alive in my section.'

'And then you found me?'

'Saved your drowning arse, you mean?'

He offered a subdued smile. 'I'm sorry, Abbey.'

'For what?'

'For Milo, for Edward, for being stranded in the middle of nowhere with me.'

They walked on in silence, the cool breeze dusting them as they strolled. They passed the aircraft and carried on walking, the silence between them strangely comfortable. When it seemed like the right time to speak again, James said, 'So what's the story with the girl?'

'I really don't know,' Abbey replied resignedly. 'She hasn't spoken a word but it doesn't seem to be shock. One minute she clings to me as though the floor is giving away around her, the next she's throwing up tents like they're made out of Lego.'

'Do you know who she lost?'

'I don't know anything, she has no ID. The only thing she does have is the flimsy locket around her neck, but she won't let me see it.'

'Could be a family heirloom. We should probably pin her down and take it.'

Abbey smirked. 'Yeah, that'll help with her trauma.'

A little further along the bay, James paused in the sand and lay down flat on his back.

'What're you doing?'

'Lie down,' he said.

'I'm not lying in the sand, it's freezing.'

'It's not cold,' he assured her.

'It is cold.'

'Trust me,' he said patting the sand.

Reluctantly she lowered herself down and lay back.

'See, I told you, it's bloody freezing.'

'Ignore it,' he muttered. 'Look at the sky. Did you ever see anything as beautiful as that?'

Draped over them like an enormous black duvet, the sky twinkled back at them, a million stars in perfect lucidity. They appeared closer than she'd ever seen them.

'My mom always used to say that no matter where you were in the world, you're seeing the same night sky as a billion other people. Somehow it always made me feel closer to home.'

Abbey didn't reply. She just absorbed the moment.

'It's going to be okay, Abbey,' he murmured. 'You're going to see Edward again. They'll find us.'

*

My neck is bleeding. I can feel the sticky patch against my skin.

The month is January and today is my birthday. Frost has bitten the ground and transformed it to stone. When I fall, it hurts like concrete. By means of incentive, I am allowed only underwear.

I am not permitted to fall.

If I do, I am punished.

From head to toe I am covered in scrapes and bruises, and my arm is bent at a funny angle. I fell from the frame and landed on it. There was no crack, but now it's swollen, and it throbs.

I am not permitted to react to pain.

It is against the rules.

Each time I fall, I am dragged back to the base of the frame, the objective: complete the itinerary before sundown. There will be no food should I fail.

I must do it until I get it right.

I must do it until I get it right.

I must do it until I get it...

The words are ingrained, yet they do not assist me. Knowing the assignment is different from completing it.

Stepping onto the frame, I imagine my arm to be uninjured and haul my body-weight up. I realise now the source of the blood. With each rung, I bite into my bottom lip. It stops me from screaming. I tongue the paper-thin skin. I have almost bitten right through.

On the far side of the frame there is a cargo net, after that a rope swing, a frozen crawl tunnel and a water pit, recently filled.

The water is not yet frozen, but it soon will be.

Unable to climb further, I topple from the frame and crumble onto the uncaring frost. In an eruption of blood, I am lifted from the ground by the kick to my ribs. It takes a moment to realise the blood is mine, the remains of my lip spraying it in a haze across my small chest. But I do not scream. I do not cry.

I am not permitted to react to pain.

It is against the rules.

I am nine years old today.

20

London, 1992

A heavy blanket of mist had descended upon Wimbledon as Derek Holliday walked. There was no need to rush. He sauntered in hazy contentment, solidified by the carefully rolled blunt secreted between his index and middle finger. The streets were empty, the thick mist giving him a dank chill.

He rarely left the house anymore, and when he did he would wait until all those judgemental cunts were tucked up in bed. He didn't mix well with others. Not that he gave a shit. The fewer people knew about him the better, but of late some people had begun probing into his affairs. The guy down at the corner shop told him only that morning that people had begun asking questions about him, the mysterious new bloke living in their street. He was an unknown, an outsider. If word got out who he was, *what* he was, he imagined he'd be fucking lynched. He didn't need that. Not again.

Overhead, a low guttural thunder rumbled. He looked up. Seriously, tonight he could do without rain.

He crossed the street to the park entrance. Pausing between the two tall gate pillars, he relit the blunt. Fucking things were always going out on him. As the flame licked, he was inhaling deeply when he spotted the dark patch in the fog across the tarmac.

Everything suddenly felt too calm. There were some real weirdoes around here. Whoever was watching him never moved, just stood there.

Holliday took another drag and turned his back. Weed was making him paranoid. No one would be stupid enough to be out in this weather, least of all any self-respecting smackhead, and there weren't many of those.

Flicking the roach into the nearest drain and hitching up his ill-fitting jeans, he tried to disregard the silhouette and headed into the dark tangle of trees.

He hated this park. It was a breeding ground for cottagers, muggers, dealers. He didn't belong here; he was not a predator, not anymore. Since his release from Frankland he had adopted a different lifestyle. The Board had deemed him fit for society but there was no way to turn off the urges. It wasn't a bloody tap. All those fucking suits thought they knew the score. Truth was they didn't have the first fucking idea. His current solution was working well. He had developed a strict "look but don't touch" policy, which was all good, but it didn't tick all the boxes. He still needed to purchase new material a couple of times a month, and for that he needed his trader.

He considered sparking another blunt. The extra buzz would help pass the minutes. Last time the bloody arsehole had kept him waiting for over an hour.

Unexpectedly his discomfort returned. As the first few drops of rain began falling, as he headed deeper into the bowels of the mist, as he searched in vain for the clearing, he realised he was lost.

He steadied himself and tried to pick a direction, but stopped dead, heart bouncing double-step. Standing ten yards away was a motionless figure, thin grey tentacles of mist swirling like vapour around him.

Panic spread slowly through Derek like syrup. Backing stealthily away from the apparition, he could feel his fists clenching, his arsehole too. In one fluid motion he turned his back on the figure. And ran.

*

The smell out the back of the club was horrendous, but Janine Bluestock needed a minute to herself. She pushed away from the wall, distancing herself from the wheelie bins. They reeked of stale beer and pee.

Pulling down her little dress against the evening damp, she fished in her purse for a cigarette and sparked one up, savouring the first drag. It helped calm her.

She was so angry with Andrew. He just didn't get it. They'd only been seeing each other for a year and already he was suggesting things like moving in together and engagement. Was he crazy? She was only twenty-three, he a year older, and they both had their whole lives ahead of them. They hadn't even completed their Masters' yet. It was way too early to consider committing to anything that drastic.

Wasn't it?

Tonight they were out with Jay and Charley. It was supposed to be a double date of sorts, but Andrew had pulled her aside after only a couple of drinks and told her he loved her. They'd said it to each other before, no biggie. This time, though, she hadn't said it back. Janine was old school. Her mother had always taught her that to say those three words when you didn't mean them was sacrilege, unforgivable. The problem was, she didn't know if she could say them to Andrew with conviction anymore. In the last couple of months that spark seemed to have extinguished. She'd asked herself if it had just been infatuation, mere animal lust. Anything was possible.

In the early days, she'd been mildly obsessed with Andrew, his puppy dog eyes, his big shoulders. But although the sex was still good, she wouldn't call it "making love", not in a classic sense. To her it had always been "fucking".

Listening to the dull whumping beat coming from inside, she took one final drag on the cigarette and flicked it to the ground. She didn't feel like going back in but the thought of a couple of tequila slammers sounded good – anything to wash away the nostalgia.

A slow rumble of thunder rolled across the London sky. She shivered, hugged herself. Rain was coming.

The beat growing louder, the door swung open. Andrew stood in the doorframe eying the surroundings in disgust. 'There you are, babe. I've been looking for you everywhere.'

Suddenly she needed another cigarette. 'I wanted some air.'

'You've gone for the fresh variety, I noticed.'

'Better than in there. What are you doing out here, Andrew?'

Pushing the fire door closed, he stepped into the small courtyard. 'Just wondered where you were. I lost you after you hit the dance floor.'

She didn't respond. Instead she plunged back into her purse in search of another cigarette.

Andrew moved closer and placed his hands on her hips. 'Babe, what's going on? You haven't seemed yourself all night.'

She cursed as her search for nicotine became futile. In the name of cutting down she'd only brought a couple out. When they were gone they were gone. And they were gone.

'Janine?' he pressed, his voice almost pleading. 'You're freaking me out here.'

'Nothing's wrong. I just need a cigarette and I'm out. Quitting's overrated.'

Andrew took a step back.

She didn't know what to tell him. Instead she tried to compose herself, looked him up and down. He was wearing the grey sweater she'd bought him a couple of months ago. Right at that moment she hated the very sight of it. She hated the very sight of Andrew.

He caught her by the arm. 'Jan, are we going to talk–'

'I don't think I love you anymore,' she blurted looking into his big brown eyes. She began to add more. Thought better of it. Charley had said earlier that night that alcohol had a way of loosening the tongue. And grass is green and the sky is blue.

Andrew looked amused. Then he realised she wasn't joking.

'You…you…what?'

'I'm sorry, but I just can't do this anymore, Andrew. All I want to do is concentrate on my studies, my career, and all you seem to want is me. You're living in your own little world. I'm not ready to move in with you, I'm not ready to be the happy little housewife you seem to have me down for, and I'm sure as hell not ready to be in love.'

Andrew's face contorted into a twist of shock. He took another step back.

'You don't mean that. You can't!'

'I'm sorry, Andrew. I just need to be away from you for a while.'

'A while? What does that even mean, babe? Is this a break? Or are you ending it?'

'I just need to be away from you for a while,' she said again. 'Take my keys, go back to my place, I'll stay at Charley's tonight.'

'I don't understand this, Jan –'

'I'll be back around midday. I need you and all your stuff gone by the time I get home. Please, Andrew, just do this for me.'

She moved for the door leaving Andrew standing. He looked like a lost little boy, surrounded by garbage and stale odours. As she reached the door she heard him call over the music. 'I won't let it be over, Jan. I love you. I'm not going to give up on us that easily.'

She pulled open the fire door and dissolved into the music.

*

Derek Holliday tried not to look over his shoulder as he ran blindly into the mist. He was tripping out, he thought, had to be. But the thick fog was no illusion, nor were the slapping footsteps in his wake.

Eyes wide, he ran in a wild panic. Someone had found out about him, there was no other explanation. Someone had joined the dots and discovered he liked little girls. Like-liked little girls! But they didn't know everything, how could they? He was a changed man now.

Holding the jeans up around his belly, he dashed sightlessly through the huge park. Trees came at him from the mist, but there was no way to tell if he'd passed them before.

If he could just keep moving…

The quick footsteps in pursuit were gaining on him, he was certain.

The damp grass underfoot his enemy, he slid to his knees and slumped onto his front, the breath knocked from him in a sludgy whump. He rolled onto his back and gulped at the air, lungs emptied. He needed to climb back to his feet, keep moving, but there was no use. He was done.

From the mist his pursuer emerged. Derek closed his eyes tight and tensed, arms outstretched pathetically.

'Derek,' he heard the voice say. 'That you?'

He chanced one eye open. Standing above him in his trademark beanie was the trader.

'Donovan?' he gasped. 'Oh, thank the fucking Lord.'

'The fuck you doing in the mud, Holliday?'

Derek climbed to his feet and brushed himself down.

'You fuckin paedos are all alike,' spat Donovan. 'Sickos, the lot of you. Got me chasing you through the park like some bastard relay! What the hell was that about?'

'You got the stuff?' Derek managed to splutter.

Donovan held out two blank VHS boxes. Holliday snatched them and turned to leave, relief washing over him.

'Hey, sicko!' Donovan called. 'You still owe me for last month's stuff. Don't make me come to your house.'

The park responded with silence. Derek Holliday was gone.

*

Muscling her way to the bar Janine Bluestock caught the attention of one of the bartenders, the best looking one in an open collar black shirt and dark tan, small pendant dangling from his chain. She wanted to flirt with him, take on an instant rebound, but he was dashing around, too busy to stop and talk with her. Instead she ordered three large tequila slammers and hammered one back.

'One of those for me?' a voice at her back yelled above the music.

She turned to find Charley's grinning face beaming back at her. She and Charley had been friends since forever, and she loved her like a sister. With her long legs, peroxide locks and fake double D's paid for by one sugar daddy or another, the boys loved her too. Janine always felt invisible by comparison.

'Go for it,' she said, handing Charley one of the slammers.

They clinked glasses and tossed them back in a wince. 'So listen,' said Charley. 'Where's Andy? Jay's bounced. Pussy's got a lecture in the morning.'

Janine shrugged, unknowing.

'Well that's good, cos I spy a couple of hotties ripe for the picking. Check it out, end of the bar.'

Janine leaned forward. Two guys waiting to be served looked over, faces buried beneath cheesy grins and squinty eyes.

'Get some more drinks, okay?' said Charley. 'I'll go put in some groundwork.'

Charley disappeared into the masses only to reappear between the two guys, all fluttering eyelids and fake giggles.

Janine didn't order drinks, didn't hang around. Instead she pushed herself away from the bar and made for the exit. Charley wouldn't be mad. She probably wouldn't even notice she'd gone until later in the dorm room when she discovered her in bed.

Outside, Janine found herself enveloped by the loitering fog which had descended over Clapham High Street, the muted whumping fading behind her. She began to shiver, her tiny dress doing little to ward off the chill. It started to rain.

Stepping off the main drag she took the deserted Nelson's row. The sooner she was out of the rain the better, and cutting across to Park Road would shave ten sodden minutes off the walk.

In her high heels, she clicked hurriedly along the empty street. For the love of God she needed a cigarette. If there was ever a night to break the regime it was tonight.

As she reached the end of the street a car drew slowly to the curb and stopped ten yards in front of her. No one got out. She paused, suddenly dubious. There was no light on the roof, no licence over the plate. It was not a taxi.

Edging forwards, she moved closer to the fence, eyes trained on the mysterious car. Five yards away, four…

It might just be somebody after directions, but something about it felt wrong. She couldn't explain why.

Three yards, two…

The passenger door burst open and a figure charged her. Instinct taking over, she turned to bolt but she barely made it off the spot. Strong hands caught her from behind and pulled her roughly backwards. She flailed her arms, kicking, punching. She tried to scream but a large hand gripped her mouth, cut off her vocals. A second arm tightened around her throat, lifting her from the ground.

Consciousness began slipping; she could feel the darkness creeping in. Where the hell was everybody? Please, this couldn't be happening.

The last thing she felt was the hot tears running down her face. Then she faded away, the misty street swallowed up.

21

Standing beneath a flickering tube York dropped the receiver. As the strange woman's voice reverberated he tried to piece together the five syllables:

Your son is alive…

He'd asked her to repeat it.

There had been no mistake.

Back to the wall he slid to his haunches and removed his hat, running moist fingers through his thick hair. 'What're you looking at!' he snapped at the curious desk clerk. The young officer turned coyly away and went back to the raving woman going on about squatters next door. A giant of a man with what looked like a vandalized pot plant under his arm had joined the queue.

York picked himself gingerly up and left the reception desk circus. Heading straight through the Pit, he avoided eye contact with everyone and shut himself in his office with the familiar stuffy odour. He stood with his back to the door and took several deep breaths. What the fuck was going on? For a man whose emotions changed like the weather, the most frequent being rain, he couldn't quite dispel the tingling in his gut. Was this what sunshine felt like? Could it be true, could Frasier be alive?

In front of him were the two facing armchairs, battered and scuffed. He'd bought them for his living room, but they'd never made it further than his office.

Falling into the left-hand chair, he stared solemnly at the empty one, the bustle outside the door stepping into his silence. It took him a moment to shut it out.

'Here we are again,' he said aloud.

Slowly he moved into the opposite chair. 'Yeah,' he muted. 'Been a while. You missed me?'

He moved back to the first chair, didn't answer.

He knew if anybody ever caught him using the chairs this way, effectively talking to himself, there'd be questions. Some coppers already thought he was nuts.

Come on, Nick, let the nice men take you away...

'I don't get it,' he said at last. 'It just doesn't click.'

'What's to get?' he questioned himself, moving into the opposite chair.

He hopped instantly back. 'Why send a messenger to pick up the package when he could've just as easily come himself? It doesn't add up.'

'He likes playing games, we know that. Coming himself would have made him feel powerful, even more in control than he does already. And he knew we couldn't chance nicking him. If he wasn't our guy, both targets would have been murdered. That would have been considered tampering, wouldn't it?'

He moved quickly back to the opposing chair. 'Whichever it is, he didn't want to be followed. He made a break for it.'

'Yes,' he acknowledged. 'But where was he going? This guy is organised, calculated. He's somebody's next door neighbour, somebody's friend, probably charismatic. Most likely has a job, colleagues that have no idea who he is.'

'Married?'

'Don't know, possibly.'

'So how do you keep that kind of thing hidden from relatives?'

'You don't, it's impossible.'

'So he's not doing all this from home. To keep it hidden from his family, he'd have to have a separate life away from home, one that his significant others know nothing about.'

Pause.

Switching back and forth in the chairs was making him dizzy. 'Agreed. I'd say he has a lair away from home, some address he can give his messenger. An empty house. That way he can come and go and no one will question him. Probably turns up dressed like a maintenance man, or something.'

'That doesn't make sense!' he mused. 'We're determining that he has a lair away from home, somewhere away from watchful eyes. But somebody's got to notice. If the messenger is a whole other person, then *two* bodies are coming and going? Come on, that's got to raise question marks.'

He rose slowly from his seat. Something was nagging him. 'You're right, somebody would definitely see him. He's a stranger in a strange street, an unknown. Surely someone coming and going from an empty house would raise some suspicion, no matter how much you dressed it up.'

Moving back to the first seat, he clammed up, bugged to death.

Then it came.

Springing from his seat, he bolted from his office and back through the Pit, wary eyes tracking his frantic path. Without question, Newport sprang from her chair and pursued.

Back in the foyer the giant with botany issues had reached the head of the queue. Aside from the clerk, the reception was deserted.

'The squatter woman,' yelled York frantically, 'where did she go?'

Following the clerk's outstretched finger, York sprinted for the door and out into the car park, Newport hot on his heels.

'Guv, what's going on?' he heard his partner say.

He spotted the woman at the end of the damp lot, heading out towards the road. She was on foot.

'Hey!' he called out.

The woman stopped and turned, frowning.

'Hold up.'

She suddenly looked wary.

'What's your name, Miss?' York asked.

'What's yours?' she countered.

'Oh, of course,' he muttered breathlessly. He pulled out his wallet and flashed his credentials. 'DCI Nicolas York.'

'Ah, the rude one.'

'Excuse me?'

'You the one who told me to zip it?'

He nodded. 'Yeah, sorry about that. Your name?'

'Angelina,' said the woman sceptically. 'What's it to you?'

Newport loitered in the background waiting for development.

'You want to come back inside, Angelina? I'll put the kettle on.'

'What for?'

'I want to talk to you. Can't let a charming personality like yours come into my life and not take advantage.'

'Oh that's a shame, you sarcastic prick,' smiled Angelina. 'For a minute there I thought you gave a shit.'

'Angelina, I heard you talking about squatters. I want to hear it.'

'DCI? Don't you like, deal with like, killings and stuff?'

'Sometimes.'

'Like I said to that lad in there, I don't know nothing really. All I wanted to do was give the address and have someone come and have a butcher's. Not much to ask, is it?'

'It's not,' York agreed.

'I don't want them to get settled. Few strange noises at night but that's all they done.'

'How long have they been there, Angelina, a week, two weeks?'

'Something like that. Last time it happened I had to move. Coppers wouldn't do nothing. That's why I came down here.'

The sky began to grumble again. More rain?

'Inside,' he urged, moving closer, 'you said someone else turned up tonight. How'd you know?'

Angelina stared at him like he was stupid. 'How'd you reckon? I saw him.'

York went to say something else but stopped.

Newport waited.

Angelina said, 'You want me to tell you what I saw? Easy. He was going into the house when I was going out. I saw him over the fence.'

He glanced over his shoulder. Newport was checking her watch.

'*Angelina...*' he pressed.

'What do you want me to say? Tall, white, dark hair. And he had these cold eyes, looked right through me. Gave me a bloody chill. Handsome, though. I remember him because he looked like he'd been running, all sweaty and that. But he couldn't have been because he was wearing jeans. No one runs in jeans, do they? Mind you he was wearing a sweater. This bulky green thing with a hood.'

22

Clocks had ticked past midnight. Rain had stopped. Mist remained dominant. An unnatural quiet hovered over the residential street, a macabre, almost sinister noiselessness.

No one spoke.

From the staging area, a tactical unit parked a hundred feet from the house, York and Doug Player silently viewed a plan of the street. Player had been in charge of CO19 Special Firearms Command for as long as York could remember. He liked him. Hair severely graded down, shoulders like engine pistons, the forty-something bulldog resembled a machine; no-nonsense, no bravado, just precise and efficient. Each member of his unit was likewise. York knew some of them well. They lived for this.

In the background, Newport and Mason donned stab-proof vests and were waiting patiently for Player to give the nod. His unit was patterned strategically along the street, obscured in the convenient mist.

The only reason Mason was here was to take the credit if the raid was successful. If they captured the suspect it wouldn't take long for the street to turn into a media catalogue, and Mason was a public relations guru. York had no qualms with that; credit could gladly be hers.

Masked behind a row of conifers, the target house was still. No one had gone in or out since they'd been watching. If anybody was inside, they were keeping quiet.

Doug Player gave the signal.

York stood enthralled as the shadowy forms emerged from their positions in perfect unity and advanced on the terraced house. From the back, Doug Player co-ordinated via a headset, talking his guys through it. The indiscernible unit reached the house, waited, instructed to listen for internal sounds. Whispers came back over the radio: it was quiet inside the house. Through the uncurtained windows only empty and bare rooms were visible. Same thing at the rear.

The team leader, a snappy character with cropped red hair, asked Player if they were certain this was the right house. Player assured him it was.

'Okay, take it down, Williams,' he instructed.

From where York was standing, he heard the crunch as the Enforcer, a huge battering ram, slammed into the front door of the house, tortured hinges screeching in agony. Over the static came the muffled sounds of the unit filtering into the premises, clearing rooms. After what seemed like an eternity, Williams emerged from the front of the house and jogged towards them, eddies of mist swirling in his wake.

'No one's in there,' he reported to Player.

'Shit!' spat York as Mason and Newport joined them. 'You certain?'

'Went over it twice, sir,' Williams assured him. 'But I'd recommend you get CSU down here. There is something you're going to need to see.'

*

Inside the house smelt fusty, unused, but certain factors begged the contra. Footprints in the dust, an open kitchen window, drip patterns in the sink, all indicated recent activity.

With no electricity provider to the property, Will Graham and his team had set up bright battery-powered lamps to work under. Jonathan Wheeler had arrived too, chewing on a huge baguette, and asking if another recording had been found.

Team Leader Williams waited patiently as York milled on the landing. Finally he nodded and followed Williams into the master bedroom.

Barely over the threshold York stopped dead, a thick bubble of saliva catching in his throat. He edged across the thin carpet, taking in the message scrawled on to the back wall. He could have sent Williams away, have Player ready another staging area, but he did nothing.

Edging further into the dim room, he became overwhelmed with a need for a hit. Beneath his jacket he had begun to sweat. His back felt wet, his chest tight. His vision began to blur as he read the jeering sentences again, scripted neatly in red.

'Blood?' he asked Graham quietly.

'Original, isn't it.' said Graham.

Next into the room was Newport. She read the message. 'What is that, Nick?'

It was uncommon for Newport to use his first name, especially on scene, but he let it go. He backed into the opposite wall and sank to his haunches, eyes fixed on the blood.

'Anyone hear me?' Newport snapped. 'What the bloody hell is that?'

Nobody responded, not even Graham.

'What does that crap even mean?' she almost yelled. 'Williams? Graham?'

She turned on the forensics man like a tiger on prey.

'Holly, I...I don't know what you want me to say.'

'I want you to explain that to me!' she snarled, nodding at the blood. '*That* is not your everyday occurrence, Will, even in our profession. And you!' she turned on York's bland expression. 'How can you be so calm about this? I mean, what's wrong with you, you bloody robot!'

'Holly...'

'No, don't try and brush me off, Nick. This is getting stupid and we're not even twenty-four hours deep! For Christ's sake, show me some emotion, show me you give a shit!'

York pushed himself back up, wincing as Graham took Newport's arm in an attempt to calm her. She grabbed the forensics man by his thin wrist and spun him away, pushing his arm up against his back and driving him into the wall. 'Don't fucking touch me, Graham!' she bellowed into his ear. 'Don't you *ever* fucking touch me, understand?'

York wrapped his arm around his partner and yanked her away. 'Outside,' he snapped at her. 'Now!'

Newport's face suddenly changed. 'But I – '

'Did I stutter, Sergeant? Get out!'

Knowing she was beaten, Newport glanced at the wall once more and then back at York. Then she left the room.

Will Graham massaged his wrist. 'My God, Nick, what was that all about?'

'You alright?'

Graham nodded meekly. He looked ready to sob, like a bullied kid.

'When you have something, you let me know straight away!'

The forensics man nodded again.

'Williams, get a message to Doug. Tell him to move the unit.'

'Already on it, sir.'

'Straight away, Graham, okay!' York said again and followed Williams down the stairs.

The student or the paedophile, Nicolas, which will it be?

Three houses down, my friend, one, two, three!

23

With little need for discretion now, marked police units had arrived on the scene, flashing beacons painting the street in a brushstroke of primary colours. Mason was blasting out instructions to uniforms, one of which was cordoning off the area from the advancing crowd. At the tactical van he could see Doug Player talking animatedly with Williams.

Along the street, precisely three doors down, was another *For Sale* sign standing lonely in the mist, guarding the soulless house. Three doors in the opposite direction, a couple was standing in their yard rubber-necking.

He spotted Newport, still in the stab vest, perched on the bonnet of a marked unit. As he neared she looked up, hard eyes showing no remorse. He took a seat next to her, stared ahead. He sniffed and adjusted his trilby.

'You going to lecture me now?' she said at last.

'Nope.'

'Then what? I'm guessing I'm off the case?'

'No,' he said again.

She looked sideways at him. 'You're not making this very easy, guv.'

'Neither are you, Holly. You want me to be on your side, you want me to open up to you? Then you need to reciprocate. You want to tell me what that was in there?'

She examined the blacktop. 'I don't know.'

'I think you do.'

'Then why are you asking me?'

He ignored the question. 'Who's Kellie?'

Newport's head snapped up. She didn't question how he knew the name. 'Kellie is none of your business!'

'*You're my business.* You just lost it in there, almost broke Graham's wrist, and I think the reason you're so fucked up is because of something going on backstage. So, want to try again?'

Doug Player's team was advancing on the second terrace, their method and efficiency equalling the first. An excited gasp travelled across the wave of gatherers, hoping for another Fred and Rose West scandal right on their own doorstep.

As the door of the empty house caved inwards with a resounding crunch, Newport said, 'I just need you to trust me on this one. Please. I need time to take care of something.'

York paused thoughtfully. 'One more incident like that, Holly, and you're off this thing, do you understand? These guys rely on us to keep it tight. When we fall apart, they fall apart. So get your shit together! Is that clear?'

'Crystal,' she acknowledged. 'It won't happen again.'

York nodded. 'I want you to apologise to Will, and then I want you to grab a couple of uniforms and interview the crowd.'

'Interview the crowd, are you kidding?'

'Sometimes these guys return to the scene to watch us stepping on each other's toes. Gives them a hard-on, you know that. Find out where all these people live, what they're doing here, everything.'

She looked morosely into the gathering of spectators. 'You're not letting me into the house this time, are you?'

He turned and looked her in the eye. 'Nope.'

She simply nodded, eyes sad.

Then turmoil broke out by the front of the house. Both York and Newport jumped from the car and sprinted to the terrace, Player and Mason too. One of Player's team had burst out the front door, assault rifle hanging limply around his neck, and was retching on the path, a tendril of vomit stretching from the corner of his mouth.

York ground to halt at the gate. This kid's violent response had nothing to do with a living suspect.

This was all about the dead.

*

They found the body in the master bedroom. A young girl in her early twenties lying naked on a wooden trestle table, arms by her side, gaping hole in her chest. The rest of the house was empty as predicted. Williams and his team had taken seconds to clear it.

'Pretty girl,' Judy Mason declared. 'Do we know who she is?'

Nobody did.

'And I suppose this means the paedophile gets off scot-free,' she added. 'Not the way you planned it, is it, Nick?'

Will Graham and Jonathan Wheeler moved solemnly into the room, pushing through the small gathering of officers milling on the landing. York turned away from the body.

'How do you suppose he knows your name?' Mason pressed.

York didn't answer. He felt steam-rolled.

'Nick,' Mason pressed, her cold eyes penetrating. 'I'm talking to you!'

He turned to the Pit Bull, focused in on her chips of ice. 'I told you this was going to happen. Didn't I tell you it was going to get personal?'

Mason held his stare. 'I didn't disagree with you.'

'He knows my name, Judy. And he's not afraid to let me know. He's saying "Come and get me, I dare you," because he knows he's untouchable.' From the background, Graham and Wheeler stood eavesdropping, their faces masks of bewilderment. 'How can he be gone from this location before we get here? How is it he knows my name? How is it that he's one step ahead on every single level? He's smarter than us. He knows that and he's exploiting it.'

'Almost sounds like you admire the bastard!'

'Admire, no,' he replied quietly. 'Respect…of course.'

Mason's hard boyish features softened. To blink would be to miss it. 'Okay,' she said aloud. 'Listen up. Will, I want you to comb every surface of both houses. Look for a hair, a fingerprint, anything. Jonathan, use Will's team to search for another recording. If this bastard's the cocky shit I imagine him to be, he'll want to brag again.'

'And me?' York asked.

'You take Holly and go see Charles Kilroy. He should have finished with the Fullers' bodies by now, see if there's anything to learn.'

He nodded and turned to leave. 'Wheeler, you'll find the recording in the light fixture.'

Fighting through the drama of badges, York found himself in the terrace's tiny back yard. It was deserted. Closing the door behind him, he took a seat on the single garden chair. It looked like it had been placed there solely for him.

Scratching at the crux of his arm he closed his eyes, tried to shoo away the burn. He began to shake, almost convulse as several sharp stabbing pains punctured his midriff. He doubled over, cramming a hand into his mouth to stop him from crying out.

'Still playing this game, Nicky?'

York looked up, rubbed his eyes.

'You're going to keep on punishing yourself until it kills you, you know that? And you're still no closer to pushing that demon out. Are you?'

Stamping down the agony, York tried to clear his blurry vision. From somewhere within, he managed to find some vocals. 'I don't know how.'

'Your son may be alive, Nicky. You and I are the only ones who know that. Do you think the demon can be driven out by the truth?'

'Everybody has demons,' he muttered. 'Theirs are just less compelling.'

'Theirs are countered by an angel. The demon in you is more dangerous than the one you seek in reality because there is no black and white. There isn't even room for shades of grey.'

'What are you saying?'

'There is only black.'

York continued to pick at the scabbing needle marks. 'When my family left me, I died inside. My faith has gone.'

'Oh, listen to yourself, Nicky. Woe. Is. Me. My heart bleeds. *Children* believe in Santa Claus, the Tooth Fairy. Some of them even believe in God. Are you telling me you have no fight left? I don't believe it. I *won't* believe it.'

'I just need some time,' he insisted. 'I just need to get my head straight.'

'I know you do, Nicky. I know.'

He turned his head at the sound of the door clicking open behind him. Newport stepped through. 'Boss? What you doing out here? Mason wants us out of here. Kilroy's waiting for us at the Dungeon.'

He climbed from the seat.

Newport glanced around the yard. 'Who were you talking to?'

York dismissed the question and filtered back into the house.

24

In the catacombs beneath the Pit, Newport grimaced at the stench. Intolerably sanitised, the green-tiled tunnels reeked of pine disinfectant and death, like the entranceway to some recently cleansed abattoir. She hated it down there, but like every other aspect of her life she displayed a bravado that wasn't necessarily real. York would tolerate no weakness, not now.

She'd been itching to ask how he knew about Kellie. She thought she'd kept her affair completely severed from her working life, and her home life. His perception infuriated her.

Next to her, York took long confident strides through the tunnel, hands dug deep into his jacket pockets. She had to struggle to keep up. He once told her that he liked it in the Dungeon, as it was nicknamed, that he could happily work down there. She'd asked him why and his reply had been simple: the dead don't talk back.

Pushing through the double doors she followed her partner into the Dungeon: metal slabs lined the floor, only two in use for Michael and Harriet Fuller, thin plastic sheets covering their departed modesty. The ancient brickwork of the room curved above them in graceful reinforced arches, modernisation and dim florescent tubing having done little to tone down the room's morbid depth.

Charles Kilroy was writing a toe-tag at his desk when he realised he wasn't alone. He looked up, a huge beam splashed across his face.

'Nicolas, my boy,' he sang, 'how are you? And Holly, my-oh-my, look at that face. I swear you get younger every time I see you.'

Kilroy climbed to his feet, white lab coat covering one of his trademark ill-fitting suits, and limped towards them. Nobody quite knew why the aging pathologist walked with a limp, or how old he actually was. Nobody ever asked. Newport had him pegged for somewhere between fifty-five and a hundred and five, and yet his tidal wave of silver hair helped him maintain an almost handsome edge. He hadn't bothered to wage war with the indifference of time, graceful was his way. But one thing that was certain about the man was his utter charm. Never married, most officers in the building believed him an inveterate womaniser. It was an easy rumour to accept.

'You don't look well, Nicolas, my boy,' said Kilroy sporting a paternal frown. 'Have you been sleeping?'

Newport glanced down.

'I'm fine, Charles, really.'

'And how about you, Holly?' the pathologist asked, redirecting his attention. 'My word, if only I was younger. You really are quite lovely, aren't you?'

Newport couldn't help smiling. 'I'm very well, Charles, thank you. Which is more than can be said for these two.'

The three of them moved over to the steel slabs.

'You're right about that, my love,' Kilroy agreed. 'These two were dealt the Devil's hand, no question.'

'They were playing the Devil's game, it's what happens.'

'Yes indeed.'

York had fallen silent. Newport took the lead. 'So what can you tell us about them?'

'Actually I can tell you very little you won't already have guessed.' He pulled the sheet back exposing Harriet Fuller's naked torso, a fatal black abyss where her heart should've been. 'I ran the tissue comparison on the two hearts, and they do indeed belong to our two vics, no doubt about it. What worried me were the teeth imprints.'

'What about them?' York muttered.

Kilroy looked back to York. 'Are you sure you're okay, Nicolas? You look positively awful.'

Newport turned to her partner. The doctor was right, he'd turned bed linen pale, his face moist and clammy.

'I said I'm fine!' he snapped. 'Why does everybody keep asking me that?'

'I'm just concerned, my boy.'

'Can we just crack on? Thank you,' York said firmly. 'How were they subdued? Can't be easy to incapacitate two targets at once.'

'Agreed,' Kilroy acknowledged. 'But there was nothing in the bloodstream of either of them, no toxins whatsoever. My guess is they were chloroformed. Heavy anaesthetic. If you apply enough to the facial orifices, you'll down an elephant.'

'What about sexual abuse?' asked Newport.

'Nope, nothing. I checked the walls of the female's vagina, and the anus of both vics, and there's no evidence of tearing or forced entry anywhere.'

'So we're back to basics. What were you saying about the teeth imprints?'

'Well…' Kilroy hesitated.

'Charles, what is it?' Newport pressed.

'It's quite disturbing, but the teeth marks are human. I ran it twice, there's no question. I sent it off to the lab for the boys to make a mode-imprint. Hopefully we'll get a dental match.'

Unexpectedly York stumbled backwards, falling against Michael Fuller's cadaver.

'Guv?' mouthed Newport. Running to her partner's aid, she pushed her weight under him. He was too heavy and he was going over one way or another. He looked gonzoed, totally out of it.

'Jesus Christ, Charles, help me!'

Charles came limping hurriedly around Harriet Fuller's block, but it was too late. Newport danced out of harm's way, and York went down like a sack of potatoes.

25

'Where the hell is York?' Mason growled.

Standing with her arms folded to the rear of the briefing room, Newport shrugged. 'Don't know what happened, guv. He just collapsed.'

Mason rubbed her eyes. 'For the love of..! Where is he now?'

'Left him in the Dungeon with Kilroy. Said he'd take care of him.'

'Kilroy specialises in corpses, Holly. Are you sure your partner was still breathing?'

'He's still breathing,' she confirmed.

'Good, you can brief him later, presuming he's still alive. Moving on. Will Graham and CSU are still on scene, we're waiting for their report to come in. The girl's body has been cleared by the coroner and is on its way to the Dungeon. We'll know more once Charles has had a look at her. Holly, without me reading the official autopsy report, what can you tell us about Michael and Harriet Fuller?'

Stepping up to the table Newport reeled off everything Charles Kilroy had said, right down to the human teeth marks in Harriet Fuller's heart.

Jonathan Wheeler physically shuddered. On the opposite side of the table was the station newbie, Tony Braddock, a criminal psychologist transferred in from MI5. Mid-forties and more serious looking than a dose of Hep B, the man never flinched. 'Kilroy said with confidence that the MO is not sexual?'

'There's no evidence to suggest it, Newport confirmed.'

Mason nodded. 'Then until we know more, we have to assume the new vic will be consistent. Jonathan, what about you?'

The large man rose to his feet and slid the plastic evidence bag into the centre of the table, a small voice recorder sealed tightly inside. 'York was right, the recorder was in the light fixture.'

'And?' pushed Mason.

'Again there wasn't much to clear up, the recording is impeccable.'

Wheeler sat slowly back down, avoiding eye contact with everyone. The room intolerably hot, Newport noticed fresh sweat marks at the man's armpits again.

'Well, Jonathan,' urged Mason,' are you going to mince around all day or are you going to play the bloody thing?'

Displaying no reaction, Wheeler leaned forward and hit the play button, introducing the familiar static preceding the calm, calm voice…

'Hello again. I'm going to assume I'm addressing the same officers, or I might just get the impression you're not taking me seriously.

'Firstly, I'd like you to know that I did not enjoy taking the life of Janine Bluestock. It made me feel somewhat cheated. She was a charming young girl. Very promising law career ahead of her too, until you failed her. Nevertheless, I do feel a valuable lesson has been learned. Maybe now you'll realise just how grave your situation is.

'Because of your perpetual errors, a paedophile is still walking the streets. I've been watching him. He's trying so hard to be something he's not, but it's only a matter of time until he abducts another little girl. His resolve is wearing somewhat thin. How does that sit in your stomachs?

'The next riddle will be more difficult and the same rules will apply. If you solve the riddle within twelve hours, I will kill a wrongly acquitted gang member responsible for the death of a garage worker. And if you fail, I will kill a police

officer. This time if the messenger is pursued, I will kill them both. The rules are simple. How *simple will be down to you.*

'Have you decided yet if I'm insane? Ooh, exciting. I almost wish I was in the room. I mean, come on, am I the only one having fun? Oh and FYI, you don't need to worry about Abigail Fuller. I didn't hurt her when I dropped her parents' belongings round to their flat, I'm not going to hurt her now. What kind of monster do you think I am?

Static…

'No legs have I to dance, no lungs have I to breathe, no life have I to live or die, and yet I do all three.

'If anybody was wondering, the answer to the first riddle was the letter "a".

'Kicking yourself, Nicolas?

'Tick tock…'

Silence fell like a thick duvet over the room.

Pushing the hair from her face, Newport exhaled heavily. It was the second time her partner had been singled out. She could feel the anger rising inside. Why York? Why now?

Mason pushed herself up from her chair, steely eyes scanning the room. 'I don't like this guy,' she declared sharply. 'Janine Bluestock, name mean anything to anyone?'

It didn't.

'No one?' she pursued. 'So she's a random. Holly, find out who this girl is, where she lives, everything, you know how it works. Then get Nick out of bed and get round to her house. If she lives alone or with a partner, make the personal trip to the parent's home and inform them.'

Newport nodded, wide-eyed. She wanted to smash something.

'Anybody else?' Mason added. 'Let's start being a little more vocal, people.'

'He sounds different,' Wheeler offered quietly.

'What?'

'Yeah,' Braddock agreed. 'And you know what it is?' The question was directed to no one in particular. 'He sounds jovial. In the first recording he sounds more philosophical. Now he genuinely sounds like he's having fun. And I don't think the amusement comes from taking lives, it comes from mocking us. This man like is likely to be suffering from some form of childhood deprivation.'

'Leading him to dress up in his mother's clothes kind of thing?'

Braddock didn't laugh.

'So the murders are just to get our attention, is that what you're saying? His actual purpose here is just to fuck with us?'

'Oh no,' said Braddock, 'there's definitely a more potent issue at work here than that. I think this guy craves attention, probably didn't get it from his parents growing up, or got too much. One thing's for sure, he's incredibly smart.'

'Nick said the same thing, smart, smart, smart,' blurted Newport. 'I'm tired of hearing this crap over and over. We *know* he's smart, we *know* he's ten steps ahead, and we *know* he seems to have a hard-on for my partner. How about something solid, Braddock, something we can go on. Like what's the significance of the hearts? Why does he take them, why does he return them, why does he fucking eat them in between?'

Braddock shrugged, unphased. 'Perhaps some failed surgeon out to get even, thinks the world owes him a favour or a career? Or an underground ring selling organs on the black market? Who knows until I begin building a profile?'

'So start building!' she snapped. 'What else do you have to do?'

'Holly, right?' asked Braddock rhetorically. 'I understand your anger, I really do. Your partner's name has come up a couple of times now and no one knows why, including me. But pointing fingers isn't going to achieve anything. I'm here to help, that's all. I'm not the all-seeing eye, Holly, I'm just a psychologist.'

Newport glanced away. Braddock never raised his voice, never lost his cool. Smug prick.

'Okay, that's enough,' said Mason. 'Braddock, start your profile. And while you're at it, look into any gang members who escaped jail time after killing a garage worker recently. There can't be many. Maybe we can get a heads-up on his next target.'

Braddock shifted his ample shoulders to the right. Was that his affirmation?

'I have to go and issue a statement' said Mason. 'The press have got wind at last, the fucking vultures. Apparently they're already naming the killings "The Valentine Murders."'

'Inventive,' said Newport.

'Isn't it!'

26

Frasier.

Leanne.

From the inky blackness they emerged, disappeared.

Emerged.

The images of their beautiful, anguished faces swam in and out of focus. In and out.

He wanted to reach for them. But they were hazy, distant and insubstantial. He cried their names but his voice was thin, weak. They didn't know he was there. Nobody knew. And he understood. It was not his wife and son who were vapour. It was him.

In the darkness he waited, his patience undeterred. He couldn't bear to look upon Leanne's features, twisted and torn, Frasier's likewise.

He had failed them.

Where was he when his wife was being beaten and hogtied? Where was he when his son was being sold to some rich Arab for amusement?

He reached out again, could feel his outstretched arm plunging into the dense blackness, searching, groping, the feeling of solitude inching in again like slowly seeping cancer. Leanne was gone. Frasier was gone. And he was entirely alone.

*

Groggily his eyes peeled open and the blurry angles of the Dungeon edged into focus. Charles Kilroy was standing over him, peering down like a concerned father.

'Welcome back, my boy,' he said. 'How are you feeling?'

Rubbing his eyes York pushed himself into a sitting position. He was on a transfer gurney tucked stealthily into the corner of the room. 'Like I've been hit by a bus,' he grunted, pinching the bridge of his nose.

'Head clearing up?'

York coughed. 'No, not really. Where's Holly?'

'She's gone to the briefing. Something about another recording. She helped me load you up here first. Stronger than she looks, that one.'

'Shit,' York cursed and tried to push himself off the gurney.

'Whoa, whoa.' Kilroy laid a gentle hand on his shoulder and pushed him back down. 'Just a sec, Nicolas.'

'I have work to do, Charles, I feel fine.'

For an infinitely long moment, he was penetrated so intensely by Kilroy's gaze he didn't know where to look. 'How long?'

York frowned. 'Come again?'

'I'm not kidding, Nicolas. How long have you been using?'

York paused, a phantom itch breaking out in the crux of his arm. 'Using what?'

Kilroy sighed. 'You think I don't know the signs, son? I was in this game before you were a twinkle in your mother's eye. The second you walked in here today I saw the jolts of pain, the shakes, the sweats. Want to tell me what's going on?'

York looked down at his dangling feet. 'Did you tell Holly?'

Kilroy shook his head slowly.

'Thank you.'

'Why are you using, Nicolas?'

York rolled up his sleeve and found a freshly wrapped bandage over the bruised puncture marks. Kilroy had administered a patch job while he was out. 'Why do we do anything?'

Kilroy raised his eyebrows. 'What's that supposed to mean?'

'What makes you think something's wrong? I'm an addict, Charles, plain and simple.'

Kilroy watched him carefully. 'Nope, you're too smart for that. Try again.'

York didn't know where to start. Lots of people knew about his family, but only Tank Henderson knew about his addiction. Until now. He scanned the room. Kilroy was not going to let him off the hook, that much was evident. 'Do you remember Jack the Stripper?'

'Jack the Stripper, should I?'

'Not necessarily,' York murmured. 'Jack "The Stripper" Devlin. We were running surveillance on him a couple of years back. Owned two high-end strip clubs, one in Chelsea, one in Kensington. We got an anonymous tip that he was using the clubs as a front for dealing smack. It was an organised operation. Devlin never went near anything, his hands were clean, had a bunch of kids running for him.

'Anyway, this local kid, Robbie Plank, supposedly one of Devlin's runners, turns up dead one afternoon. Some poor bastard walking his dog came across him, two bullets in his heart.'

'Robbie Plank,' Kilroy cut in, 'I do remember him. I took the fragments out of his chest.'

York nodded. 'Once it was conclusively a murder, the drugs bust was no longer just a drugs bust. That's when I was brought on board. I was to go in, become friends with Devlin over time, gain his trust. Hopefully if we became tight, he'd tell me all his dirty little secrets.'

'And did he?'

'Oh yeah, we got him, but it took seventeen months of staying undercover. He had a one-point-eight million quid a year business going off on the side of his clubs. Robbie Plank had been taking the stuff himself, with no means to pay off what was owed. That's what earned him the two bullets.'

'So how do you end up with needle marks?'

'As part of keeping up my cover and building Devlin's trust, I had to hit it. I went in as a buyer, so there was no way around it. Like any buyer I had to test the authenticity of the product. I would have been transparent otherwise. I thought I had it under control, I *did* have it under control, but a week after the collar my family disappeared. That's when the control slipped. I've been hitting it ever since.'

'Jesus, Nicolas.'

'Don't judge me, Charles, you don't know what it was like, what it's still like. I'm living in a fucking nightmare.'

'You think I don't know?' Kilroy pushed. 'I had two daughters, now I have one. Julie was thirty-two when cancer took her. Hannah is battling it now, twenty-nine. We all have our ways of dealing with tragedy, Nicolas, no human goes unscathed.'

York shifted uncomfortably. 'I didn't know, Charles, I'm sorry.'

Kilroy glanced down to his shoes. 'Yeah...'

'So how do you cope?' York detected an almost needy edge to his question. 'What's your way of dealing with it?'

'I haven't coped, my boy, I'm just a master at disguising it. But I do still find moments of alleviation. We just have to dig deep. It is within you, Nicolas, I promise. It's within us all. Some of us just need more guidance than others. Opiates may offer you a temporary reprieve, but that's exactly what it is: temporary. Real guidance comes from the people who know, the people who've been there, the people who have found that peace.'

York jumped from the gurney. 'And I thought you were going to say women.'

'Them too,' smirked Charles. Then his smirk transformed into an infectious laugh and suddenly York couldn't help joining in. It was what he needed. When the laughter died down, he plucked his hat from the side and rested it on his head. 'So what do I do, Charles?'

'While you were out I administered a dose of Methadone. That should help with the cravings for a while. Come and see me tomorrow and I'll give you some in tablet form. And look, I'm here if you need me. I can always use a conversation. I don't get much down here.'

'Charles, about the Methadone…'

'Off the record, Nicolas, you have my word.'

'I appreciate it,' he murmured.

Then he was gone.

*

Roy Sunnily had disappeared from the room. Abigail Fuller was alone. Roy said he'd gone to fetch some water. Perhaps he had.

Abbey shifted uneasily on the seat and fingered the pages of a tattered celeb magazine. She'd heard them talking in the background about packing her off to some facility until they could relocate her, but she didn't fully understand what that meant. It sounded okay, though. Maybe there'd be others there who she could be friends with.

Images of the dark man flashed into her head like snapshots. The steely glint of his eyes in the light from the streetlamps, the way he attracted shadows, she'd been mesmerised. The way he'd moved, the way he'd *shifted* across the room, there was something magnetic about him. She wanted to see him again, though she wasn't quite sure why.

Pushing the thoughts down, she glanced up when she heard the door click open. That sad-looking policeman with the funny hat was back. What was his name again? Nicolas, that was it! She wondered what was wrong with him. He didn't look well, like he had a bad cold and hadn't slept.

'Couldn't find him,' the Nicolas muttered as she sat down opposite.

Abbey frowned.

'But he's around here somewhere, I'm sure,' he added.

'Couldn't find who?'

'Keanu Reeves. I thought you wanted me to find him for you?'

Abbey smiled. 'Shut up.'

Nicolas smiled back.

'You think I'm stupid, don't you?' she said suddenly. 'Just another stupid kid.' Nicolas held her eyes, his silly hat perched on his head. 'I'm not, you know. I know how to take care of myself.'

Still, Nicolas remained quiet.

'The first time they left me alone, I was seven,' she revealed. 'They filled the freezer with pizzas and took off. Said they'd be back in a couple of weeks. I walked to school and back every day while they were gone. I cooked my own food. Still don't know where they went, but they came back with tans. And the second they walked in the door I was their precious little darling. After they did it a handful of times I knew I wasn't precious to them, I was no more valuable to them than some fancy jewellery or expensive watch.' She paused thoughtfully. 'One day it just kind of hit me. I realised I was on my own. I knew this wasn't normal, only because other kids at school talked about their lives and their mums and dads and their homes, and I knew I was the freak, not them.'

As the room descended into quiet once again, she watched Nicolas's tired face carefully.

'It's okay. You don't need to say anything. I know what people think of me.'

Nicolas leaned forward and took her hands in his. She noticed the sadness in his eyes again. 'I don't think you're stupid, Abbey. That's the truth. I think you're quite remarkable.'

'I'm a freak.'

'No, you're not,' said Nicolas vehemently. Your parents were the freaks for not wanting to watch you grow up. Things will only get better for you now, I promise.'

She listened to the detective's words. Just listened. She didn't know if he meant what he was saying, but she couldn't help liking him and his big sad eyes.

'Nicolas,' she uttered, 'are you my friend?'

The sad detective nodded. 'Of course I am.'

Abigail glanced back at her shoes. 'But you'll leave me too. Everybody does.'

27

The mist had lifted and the bruised clouds had blown over by the time York and Newport reached Janine Bluestock's flat in Clapham. The sun was on the rise, colours flowing across the sky in long purple brushstrokes. With no wind, the day was looking to be another hot one.

The law student's flat sat in a courtyard just off the Common, centred in a modern block. Judging by most of Clapham the little estate was a diamond in the rough, a genuine find. Standing in the dusky morning smog between a Mercedes and a Lexus, York looked the building up and down - too high end for a student. Daddy's dollar perhaps?

'So what did he say?' Newport asked, fracturing the morning still.

'What did who say?'

'You know who I'm talking about.'

'Do I?'

'Fine, you don't want to tell me, I can live with that. Next time you collapse, your arse stays on the floor.'

He looked sideways at his partner. 'I know you're wondering how I know about Kellie,' he threw in. It was the one thing he could think to say to get her off the topic.

'You *don't* know about Kellie.'

They found the narrow staircase and began the ascent.

'Maybe I should,' he said.

'And maybe I should know why you collapsed!'

Eyebrows raised, York turned to look at his partner. 'Kilroy thinks I might be diabetic.'

'Bollocks, Nick. You're doing it again, telling me what you think I want to hear. It's not going to cut it anymore.'

'I'm allowed some secrets, Holly.'

'Not from me you're not!'

'Listen, you asked me to trust you, I have pushed you no further. Why can't you extend me the same courtesy?'

Janine Bluestock's door was a subtle shade of blue. It felt kind of appropriate.

Bringing up the rear, Newport had fallen quiet. 'You're right,' she muttered. 'I'm not being fair. The Kellie situation has got the better of me.'

York pounded on the blue door. 'Look, Holly, I don't know who Kellie is, and I don't need to know. It's your business. But if you want to talk about it, you know where I am. I'd like to think the same comes back to me.'

Newport looked almost ashamed. 'It does. Of course it does. But seriously, how do you know about her?'

York winked at her.

About to knock again, the door suddenly swung inwards. A young guy standing in pyjama bottoms greeted them with sleep in his eyes.

'Yeah?'

The detectives flashed their ID and York introduced them. 'We're here in connection to an incident, sir. Can we come in for a minute?'

Stepping aside, the guy opened the door all the way. He rubbed his eyes as they passed.

'Out last night, sir?' asked Newport.

'Yeah, yeah I was. And it's Andrew.'

'Thanks,' she said. 'We're sorry to bother you so early, we didn't expect anyone to be here. This is Janine Bluestock's flat, yes?'

Blinking himself more awake, Andrew glanced up sharply. 'What's happened? Oh my god, is Jan okay?'

'There has been an incident, Andrew. I'm sorry to have to tell you, Janine was found dead this morning.'

'Oh god no,' shuddered Andrew. He began sobbing in big wet gasps, grabbing for nothing. He stood, sat back down. Stood.

'I know this is not easy, Andrew, but were you Janine's boyfriend, flatmate, relative?'

Fighting for breath, the kid sat back down. 'Oh my god, we were going to move in together, get engaged…'

'Andrew?'

He looked confused. 'She was my girlfriend. Well, last night...'

Moving from the window, York joined the conversation. 'Last night?'

'Yeah, we were at *Black Crystal*, you know, that club on the high street. We had a row…of sorts. Jan said she didn't want to be with me anymore, said I was getting too full-on, you know. Wanted to concentrate on her career or something. It was only temporary, she didn't mean it. Anyway, she disappeared back into the crowd. That was the last I saw of her. Oh, Jesus, what happened to her?'

He stood again.

'Sit down, Andrew,' Newport urged. 'If you rowed, why are you here? Do you live here with her?'

'Oh no, I'm in halls. Jan's parents own this flat, they let her live here rent-free. She gave me her keys last night, wanted me to clear my stuff out. But I was drunk. I came in and crashed.'

The detectives shared one of their glances. York disappeared into the kitchenette. Newport began to stand. 'Andrew,' she said slowly, deliberately, 'have you been anywhere near the fridge since you came here?'

'The fridge? No, I told you, I went straight to bed.' Andrew began to stand too. 'What is this?'

From the kitchenette York suddenly yelled, 'Holly, get him out of here, right now, go!'

Without hesitation, she grabbed the student by the arm and yanked him across the room. 'Time to go, Andrew!'

'Hey wait, you have no right –'

'Listen, Andrew, if you want to see something that will scar you for life, be my guest, stick around.'

*

'Taken a full bite this time, huh?' said Will Graham excitedly. 'Whoa, he's really beginning to enjoy himself, isn't he?'

Graham was kneeling at the fridge examining the human heart sitting on a dinner plate, centre shelf. It was bathed in a small pool of coagulated blood. Behind him, York chewed a plastic straw he'd picked up off the counter. Other uniforms were rifling through the small apartment, that familiar buzz and static filtering from one room to the next.

'Where's Holly this fine morning, Nick?'

York shifted his stance. 'Holly's married, Will. Remember that gold thing on her finger?'

'Oh...yeah, I didn't mean...erm...'

'Besides which, she almost broke your wrist earlier. What's wrong with you, you got a death wish?'

'Maybe I'm into the whole fem-dom thing, you know,' Graham smirked. 'Whips and chains and all that.'

York plucked the half-chewed straw from between his teeth and threw it at Graham. 'Concentrate, yeah?'

'Yeah...I mean I am concentrating...I'm just, you know...what's going on with you anyway, Nick, you look awful. Wheeler told me you collapsed earlier, is that true?'

'True enough.'

'Wow, someone's got some sand in his vagina this morning! Need some sleep? Hey, I've got a joke about that. This old woman, right, she walks into this Chemist –'

'Will! Con-cen-trate.'

'Fine.' Graham went back to work as Newport pushed her way into the flat.

'How's the boyfriend?' York asked.

'Pretty shaken up,' she replied, the anger back in her eyes. 'He doesn't have anything to do with it. If he does he should be on stage.'

He noticed Newport's gaze shift attention to Graham. She shuddered slightly.

'What is it?'

'Nothing,' she muttered. 'Graham just gives me the creeps.'

York smirked. 'I think your little stunt back at the house has made things worse. It turned him on.'

'You're kidding!'

'Anyway, forget that. Notice anything about the front door?'

'Yeah, no forced lock again.'

'So?'

'So Janine Bluestock didn't have her keys, she gave them to her boyfriend. He was going to clear his stuff out and leave the keys outside. Janine always hid them in the light fixture over the door.

'But Andrew never left.'

'Exactly, so how'd the killer get them? How did he manage to get Janine Bluestock's heart in the fridge without waking the boyfriend?'

'We don't know that it's Janine's heart.'

'Yes we do.'

'So our boy's good at picking locks, so what?' said Newport.

York shook his head. 'I think it's simpler than that. Anyone can pick a lock with enough know-how. But this guy gets off on watching. He knew where to find those keys.'

'The keys were never outside. He has to be picking locks, guv, there's no other explanation. He let himself into the Fullers' apartment and he let himself in here. He came and went when he thought no one was home, but both times he wasn't alone.'

'Both times?'

Newport nodded. 'He knew Abigail Fuller was watching him, guv, he says so in the recording.'

York paused for a long moment, one solid thought slapping him across the face. 'Jesus, Holly, how did we miss this?'

She looked back at him perplexedly. 'Miss what?'

Pulling his partner to one side, he whispered, 'Abbey told me her parents didn't allow her to leave the apartment when they were away. But she did. She went to the shop for groceries. Our man didn't force entry, Holly, he was already inside, both times.'

'No, that doesn't make sense…'

'Think about it! Abbey goes out to the shops, doesn't lock the door. Remember the caretaker telling us that no one locked their doors during the day. Our man slips in while Abbey is at the shops. He hides. And he watches her. When she goes to bed, he plants the hearts and leaves. It wasn't about Abbey, it never was. He knew she was there, because *he* was there, hours before!'

Newport leaned against the wall. 'Jesus.'

'And he's been here before tonight too. The keys weren't there last night because Andrew had them inside. But he's been watching. He knew where to find those keys before now. He waited. Waited until Janine went out. Yesterday, the day before, who knows? Came along here, took the keys and made copies, and then returned them before Janine came home. He was in here last night when Andrew got back. He watched him come in, get into bed, watched him fall asleep. Then he put what remained of Janine in the fridge and left.'

Newport filled her lungs and exhaled loudly.

'Listen,' he said, 'I want you to go over to *Black Crystal,* check out the CCTV. Then I want you to go home and get your head straight, okay?'

'I'm fine, guv.'

'No, you're not. Go home, get some sleep, speak to Kellie, whatever you need to do. I'll see you back at the station in a few hours.'

'Guv, really –'

'It's not a request, Holly. If you want to keep on working with me on this, you'll do as I ask.'

He spied Graham looking over his shoulder, trying to eavesdrop.

'Fine,' she muttered. 'But I'm not the only one who needs sleep, you know.'

He nodded. 'Right now, you are. My battery backup just kicked in.'

28

Three streets away, Newport rolled the car up next to a phone box and shut off the engine. Beyond the windscreen the morning had become pallid, a none-event. One or two people were out and about now, heading towards Clapham South tube, milling around the coffee shops and avoiding eye contact with one another.

She reclined the seat and tried to relax, and suddenly the tears were spilling from her eyes, snail-tracking down her face. The crying grew harder and harder until her stomach was wracked with spasms. She pounded the steering wheel, ground her teeth, jarred herself back and forth, letting it all go. Kellie, the bodies, Abigail, Kellie, York, the bodies.

Kellie.

Kellie.

Kellie.

What was happening to her? All these other people going about their day, she envied the smug bastards. Why should they have it so easy? Her life had never been such a shambles. She'd always maintained the structure, the spine. So long as the backbone was in place, everything else just kind of worked out. Now her entire existence was a train wreck.

Slowly the tears dried. She settled back into the seat and took large heady breaths. She had to regain control.

She climbed from the car and went inside the phone box, pocketing her glasses. It only took two rings for Kellie to answer, and immediately she could tell something was wrong. Can't talk over the phone, she said. Don't know who's listening. She sounded jittery, anxious.

Newport asked if she was okay. She said she was fine. But they should meet. Thirty minutes at St Paul's Cathedral, the little café with the Andy Warhol replicas.

*

This time Newport arrived first and ordered two espressos before choosing a table near the back. She looked a mess but what could she do? Any time with Kellie was good time.

Minutes later, Kellie walked in and took a seat opposite. She too looked a little sleep deprived. Her pale green blouse was wrinkled and her pixiesque face bore no makeup.

'I had to see you,' Kellie said, slightly frantically. She picked up the espresso and knocked it back.

'What's going on, Kellie? You worried me on the phone.'

Kellie kept glancing over her shoulder, around the café. 'I don't know if they're on to me, Holly.'

'Who? What're you talking about?'

'Keep your voice down, please.' There was desperation in her tone, her eyes, an almost naked trepidation.

'You want to tell me what's going on?'

Kellie took one more look around, waved to the Barista for another espresso. 'Remember yesterday, I told you I was working on something. Something big. Well I think it's caught up to me. I'm in trouble.'

'What have you done, Kellie?'

'Don't be so judgemental okay, I'm asking for some help.'

Newport shrugged. 'The last time I saw you, you were moving on. You'd met someone else. Now you're in trouble you need me again?'

'Fine,' Kellie snapped. She got to her feet, looked wired. 'You don't want to help me, I get it. I'll just go. You can get back to your nutcase.'

'Sit down, Kellie,' Newport urged resignedly.

Kellie did. Instantly.

'Start from the beginning. Don't leave anything out.'

Running a finger around the lip of her espresso glass, Kellie said, 'I was following a lead for a story, nothing more. I didn't think it would actually go anywhere.'

'What story? Has that fucking paper threatened you with your job again?'

The Barista arrived with two more espressos. Newport hadn't finished the first.

'No, no, nothing like that. A week or so ago, I went to meet this bloke in Brighton. A contact. I've used him before, had one or two stories out of him. He's generally been pretty reliable. Anyway, he tells me about this European child trafficking ring operating out of London. Mostly closed-market, need-to-know stuff. Apparently it's a group of Eastern European labourers. Disguised as such at least, that's their cover; plumbers, sparkies, the like.'

Newport put down her coffee. 'Kellie, there are scoops and there are scoops. And then there's stupidity.'

'But just imagine, Holly. Imagine if I break this story and snag the exclusive. Every tabloid this side of the Thames would want me. No more shitty articles for Mr Fat Prick editor.'

'So what's happened since?'

'I chased it, didn't I!' Kellie's head snapped back and forth. 'I was put in touch with another contact, bloke named Reggie Hayes. He gave me an address in Camden where these guys were supposedly operating out of. So I staked it out. I watched it for days. People were coming and going, mostly men. Any women going in looked like whores, you know, fishnets up to their tits. But the men definitely looked Eastern European, Poles or Romanians or something. Their dress sense was fucking hideous.'

Newport narrowed her eyes. 'So why haven't you been to the police before now, Kellie? This is fire you're playing with.'

'You're the police.'

'You know what I mean.'

'I haven't got to the best bit yet,' she insisted. 'I followed one of these men to a bar one night, decided to chat him up, see what I could find out. He wouldn't give much up but that night I went with him back to this house. And get this, I heard all sorts of conversation about someone called "The Face." No one would tell me who The Face was, just that I'd do well not to mention it again. And they were saying it in English, like maybe it was an English bloke running things. But I kept pushing. Eventually they freaked and threw me out of the house.'

'Kellie, are you fucking *insane*? What were you thinking?'

'I wasn't thinking! And now I reckon I'm being followed. Strange people hanging around outside my house, blokes behind me in the street. I'm not imagining it, I'm certain.'

'So why haven't you been to the police?'

'Are you nuts? This exclusive is still alive, Holly, I can still get this. If I blow it open now, The Face will just disappear, materialise somewhere else. But this Polish bloke, he likes me. I can try to meet him again, see what else I can find out.'

Newport shook her head. 'Kellie, listen to me, okay. I know you want this scoop like nothing else right now, but a scoop is nothing if you're dead! These guys don't mess around. This is big business for them and they'll kill anyone who interferes. Our laws mean nothing to them. If you're right and they're watching you, then they're doing it to see if you pose a threat. You need to let it go. File a report with the police and leave it alone.'

Kellie looked across the table at her like she was crazy. 'You can't ask me to do that, Holly. I'm so close to this, you have no idea what it means.'

'It means me dragging you out of the Thames at 3am with a concrete block chained to your leg. You're already scared. Do you have any idea what these people will do to you?'

Kellie blinked, a subtle eye movement that shot across the cafe. She genuinely did look nuts. 'I thought you were going to help me. I thought you might want to see this through with me. Now I can see I'm wasting my time.'

She stood up to leave.

'Kellie, don't do this, please. Go to the police. Or at least give me the address and I'll file it myself.'

'I can't do that, Holly. I have to see this through.' And she turned to leave, pushing her way to the door.

Quickly, Newport climbed to her feet. 'Kellie!' she called, random stares shooting in her direction. 'Don't do this, I'm begging you.'

In amongst the other diners, Kellie had vanished.

*

Visitations to inform loved ones never got any easier. After he and PC Dale Yates had called in on Janine Bluestock's family – mother, father, brother – to notify them of their daughter's fate, York had felt so incredibly low he was fastened to the driver's seat of the car, firmly in park. Their faces had shown so much anguish, but most of all, they had shown compassion. Love for each other and for the girl whose legacy had simply become a shortened branch on the family tree.

He hadn't told them the gruesome details of their daughter's death; they hadn't asked and they didn't need to know. They had learned only the surface details, the icing. Their daughter was dead. That was enough.

He stared ahead into the day and for the first time since his family was lost to him, he was frightened. They had no leads. They would continue to have no leads. They were losing.

He was losing. How many other families would he have to visit? How many other fathers and mothers would he have to look in the face and tell them their child wasn't coming home?

He slowly took off the handbrake, started the car and pulled away.

Switching the engine off in the station car park, the crux of his arm began itching beneath the bandages. How fast could he get to Tank's place, he wondered? The methadone was doing its job. The sweating had stopped. So had the stabs in his gut. From his reflection in the rear view mirror, he appeared just about human.

The reception was busier than it was last night. As he passed, he asked the desk clerk if he had any calls. The answer was no, nothing.

The Pit was livelier now. Jonathan Wheeler was back, sitting at Newport's desk, eyes down. The current hot topic was the latest riddle. York looked at the wall clock. The morning was nearly gone. So was their time.

Over by the chalkboard The Pit Bull stood staring at the new riddle. Stepping up next to her he said, 'Any ideas?'

Mason's stare remained fixed on the board. 'I think if I looked at this for the rest of the day I'd be none the wiser.'

York waited, sensing Mason had more to say.

'The papers are calling us lax, inept, and I don't think I can argue it. We're nowhere, jumping through hoops for this bastard. He has us right where he wants us.'

'Yep,' said York scanning the riddle.

No legs have I to dance, no lungs have I to breathe, no life have I to live or die, and yet I do all three.

'He's back,' someone called out. York and Mason turned to the see PC Dale Yates standing at the bay window looking out.

York and several others joined him. The man in the green hoodie had returned, standing exactly where he had the first time, hands in pockets, back casually to the fence.

'You want me to take our answer out this time, ma'am?' Yates said to Mason.

'Don't call me ma'am, Dale,' said Mason.

A thin smile crept onto York's face. 'There's nothing to take out there yet. If we don't find the answer to this riddle soon, someone we probably know isn't going to see the night out.'

Yates looked back to the figure in the street. 'How do we even know there is an answer? All that shit on the board, it means nothing to me!'

'There's an answer. Giving us something unsolvable is not his style.'

He spotted Roy Sunnily walking into the Pit hand-in-hand with Abigail Fuller. It looked like they were leaving.

'Going somewhere?' York asked cutting them off. Abbey looked back at him with gentle green eyes.

Roy Sunnily smiled. 'We were just released. Apparently you don't need us anymore so I'm going to take Abbey here down to Social Services, get her on the register. And afterwards we're going to go hit KFC, right, Abbey?'

'What's this?' asked Abbey walking demurely over to the chalkboard.

'It's a riddle,' said York. 'We play games in here too, you know. We're not a bunch of boring sods.'

Abbey's smile broadened. 'Ha, well you're not very bright then, this is an easy one!'

The majority of the room heard the girl drop the bombshell.

'What...what did I say?' she muttered.

'You know the answer to this?'

'Of course, I love riddles! Jeez, grown-ups are soooo thick sometimes!'

Silence.

'Okay look,' she said, exasperated, 'what dances, other than human beings? Fire, of course! Fire needs oxygen to breathe, and a fire comes to life and then it dies, simple!'

Turning to the Pit crew, Abigail offered a small curtsey.

'You heard the girl, *go-go-go*! Prep the envelope again. No bugs this time. There will be no pursuit!' Then York knelt to Abigail Fuller's height. 'Abbey, I think you're the most amazing ten year old I have ever had the pleasure of meeting.'

'I know,' she smiled. 'I'm pretty cool.'

'Keanu Reeves doesn't know what he's missing.'

Roy Sunnily stood patiently behind the girl, tugging at his beard.

'I'm going to have to go now, aren't I?' she murmured.

'I don't know what's going to happen, Abbey,' he replied honestly. 'Roy's going to take care of you for a while. But I'll keep up with your paperwork. If I know where you are, I can drop in on you from time to time.'

'You promise?'

'If it earns me a hug.'

Without encouragement, Abigail Fuller wrapped her tiny arms around him and squeezed.

'Not too hard. I'm an old man.'

'Oh, I know,' she grinned.

Sunnily stepped forwards. 'We should be going, Nicolas. Lots of paperwork to fill out, you know how it is.'

It had been eighteen months since he'd held a child in his arms, or felt that genuine feeling of warmth and vulnerability only children emitted. There was a big age gap between Frasier and Abigail, but the effect was the same. For just a moment, a split second even, his loneliness had abated.

'I'll see you soon, Abbey,' he said quietly.

She stepped forwards and kissed him on the cheek. 'Bye, Nicolas,' she murmured, and Roy Sunnily led her out of the Pit.

29

This time as York crossed the street more people were filtering through the morning, mice lost in a maze, passing the hooded figure with little or no interest. Clutching the envelope tightly he stood before the messenger and waited silently.

In the bright daylight, the messenger pulled the hood further down until only his lightly stubbled jaw line was showing. Mirroring his first visit, he reached out, palm upwards, and waited for the package to be placed into his hand. York obliged, and the envelope disappeared into the hoodie. Then the messenger began to walk away, mixing subtly into the crowd.

Clenching his fists York let out a yell of pure frustration. Heads turned his way; others gave him a wide berth.

For fuck's sake! His adversary was the one cordoning off areas with yellow tape, restricting places he needed to see. He yelled again, the frustration pouring out of him. More people strode wide of him, some crossed the street.

He dug his hands into his pockets and leaned against the fence where the messenger had stood, watching as a handful of minutes ticked by. When his perspective didn't broaden, he crossed the street and headed back inside.

'He say anything?' asked Braddock who had since appeared. 'Inspector, *did he say anything*?'

York glared at the MI5 man and pushed past him.

'I'm here to help, Inspector,' said Braddock stepping on his coattails. 'If he said anything, I need to know.'

York stopped and turned on his heel. 'He didn't say a word. And neither did I. I jumped through another hoop and the one solid lead we had just walked away again. I couldn't talk to him, I couldn't follow him, and I sure as fuck couldn't reason with him.'

'What do you mean?'

'The man's a robot. It's like he's programmed, or something.'

Braddock blinked. 'Maybe if I'd gone out there, things would've been a little different.'

York stopped suddenly. 'Come again?'

'I'm a criminal psychologist, graduated at Cambridge. Maybe I know how to talk to these people better than...others.'

York ground his teeth. 'Do you even know what's happening, Braddock? Since you're here I'm assuming you've heard the recordings. *I wasn't allowed to talk to him*! That is unless you wanted two bodies instead of one, then you could've recited fucking Shakespeare. Congratulations on your qualifications and your undoubtedly framed certificates, but honestly, I could not give a shit *where* you attained them, and I can't think for the life of me why you'd drop that into conversation.'

'Well, I –'

'I'm assuming you were trying to impress me. Well the only thing that does impress me is my ability to catch bad men, and others' abilities to aid me in catching bad men. If you're here to help, help. Otherwise pack up your school books and your stories about Oxford and go home.'

'Cambridge.'

'Jesus Christ.'

Braddock looked confused. 'Lot's of pent up aggression in you, isn't there?'

York stopped and turned again. 'Who are you, anyway?'

'Hey!' Mason yelled from the door of her office. 'You two ladies, in here, now!'

Trailing Braddock into Mason's office, York closed the door behind him and leaned against it.

'Nick, what just happened?'

'I was frustrated,' he explained. He removed his hat, the band inside slightly damp.

'Screaming and shouting at passers-by? Like we need the complaints. Tony?'

'I ran checks on garage workers recently killed. Came up with only two names. One in Peckham, one in Brixton. Both times the assailants scrubbed up well, had alibis. John Harker-Williams had been with his girlfriend, she testified to it, and Winston Jackson was apparently in Glasgow the night of the attack. Their fingerprints were all over the crime scenes, but neither was convicted. They both admitted to using the respective garages all the time. Anyway, I think we have a couple of winners for the next target.'

'Which one?' she urged.

'It's a photo-finish.'

'Send a couple of cars out to both addresses, see that these guys are okay. We're assuming we got the riddle correct so we've got to assume he'll go after the offenders.'

'I don't think so,' York interrupted.

'Excuse me,' said Braddock.

York didn't move, didn't reply.

'Explain, Nick? You've been wrong once in the last twenty-four hours.'

'I've been wrong a lot more than that. Why would he go after someone he knows it'd be easy for us to check. We have profiles on every loser in the city. *Of course* we can check acquitted individuals.'

'So?'

'This guy, whoever he is, he's way too smart for this. He's throwing us a bone, and like every time before, we're going to chase it, just like we're supposed to.'

Braddock smiled pleasantly. 'So what're you saying? He's going to go after a copper just to sucker-punch us? That's outrageous. Ma'am, you're not buying into this crap are you? Our guy has never broken his pattern, not from the get-go. Why would he change now?'

'Don't call me ma'am,' warned Mason. 'Nick?'

'Man makes a good case, Judy, I just think it's a bit too convenient. We continue to not give this guy the respect he deserves, and he continues to make us look stupid. I'm not saying you shouldn't send those cars, I'm just trying to get one step…'

He paused abruptly.

'Nick, what is it?'

He closed his eyes slowly. As his eyelids peeled back up, he glanced from Mason to Braddock.

Back to Mason.

Oh shit...

Holly.

30

Queuing up behind a silver sports car, Newport switched her driving glasses for shades, the dying sun blinding. She fiddled with controls, couldn't concentrate. Kellie had left her stunned. She had shown her a side Holly never knew existed, dangerous and idiotic.

Exciting.

As the thoughts coursed through her head, a pleasant shiver passed between her thighs. She visibly quivered.

At first, as Kellie's words passed through her, she felt that familiar pulsation of jealousy; Kellie out with another man, burning the midnight oil. She'd almost asked her to stop, cease talking. She didn't want to know, even if she *was* talking about some Neanderthal halfwit. But as the story sped along unwaveringly, and she began to push aside the envy and incredulity, it felt good to just roll with it. After Kellie had left the café and the dust had settled, she realised she was mildly turned on.

Amidst the jarring blare of car horns and curses, she began to wonder if there really had been another woman or if Kellie had fabricated the entire thing. Judging by this unexpected new side, anything was possible. In the heat of the moment she'd made no effort to read her. From countless interrogations, she'd grown good at spotting character traits and imperfections. She could tell when someone was telling the truth. And she could tell when somebody was concealing it. She just had no idea which category Kellie fell in to.

Finally, the car in front began to move. First gear. Second.

The buzz from the espressos began to wear off and behind the sunglasses her eyelids started to droop. It suddenly dawned on her just how tired she was. When was the last time she slept?

David wasn't going to be home, that was one positive. She wouldn't have to engage in small talk - You manage to close that Bates account, David? No, you manage to catch that psychopath, Holly? - and she wouldn't have to make an excuse to not make love. Again.

The cars were moving now, the traffic breaking up. Second gear. And third.

Fighting to keep her eyes open, she focused on an image of her bed. It was beautiful, and if she was lucky she might get a full two hours.

*

As she neared her house there was more night than day around, but it didn't take a genius to see she was being followed. She recognised the car. It was the same burgundy Vauxhall she'd seen yesterday at the bar, its driver still obscured neatly behind glass and velocity.

She flicked on the indicator and turned into her street. The Vauxhall went speeding past. At the back of her head the lump began to tingle again as she recalled the jeering message left for York at the scene, the taunting voice on the recordings. Mark my words, York had said, this is going to get personal. And now she was being tailed. A shudder ran along her spine. Did he always have to be so bloody right!

Pulling on to her driveway, she shut off the engine and paused. David's car was there.

Frowning, she climbed into the warm evening and took off the sunglasses.

David was supposed to be in Middlesbrough, though she couldn't deny she was glad he was there. The strange Vauxhall had unnerved her.

She let herself in and lingered in the deserted hallway. Sitting primly on the laminate floor was a suitcase, one of David's full-sized bags and too big for a quick trip up north.

She found him in the living room. He was sitting in the centre of the sofa and in silence, leaning forwards, a glass of golden fluid nestled between both hands. As she entered he glanced up with his ocean grey eyes and placed the glass on the coffee table. She loved those eyes. They were the first thing she noticed about him when they met in that coffee shop seven years ago.

'Didn't expect you to be here.' She edged further into the room.

'I decided to stay home,' David muttered. There was no welcome in his voice, no spark.

'What's going on, David?'

'Sit down,' he said, eyes more piercing than sexy.

'Are you going to tell me –'

'*Sit down,* Holly,' he said firmly.

Doing as asked, she began to grow concerned. She perched herself in the armchair, stared straight ahead.

'You can't even look at me, can you?' said David.

She didn't know what to say. So she didn't say anything.

'I knew something was wrong. That trip to Jersey, the entire time, you were never there.'

'What do you mean? Of course I was there.'

'But you weren't *there,* Holly! I tried to talk to you, but you were off somewhere else. You had this…blankness in your eyes. At first I just thought it was some case you were wrapped up in, but it didn't take long to work out you were seeing someone else. Those little telltale signs.'

'David, I –'

'When we got home I hired someone. I had to know.'

Newport took a deep breath, tried to compose herself. 'Does this person drive a maroon Vauxhall by any chance?'

He looked up.

'Jesus, David, I'm in the middle of an investigation to track down a killer and I keep seeing this car everywhere. I thought I had a deranged psychopath following me around, what the fuck were you thinking!'

'What the fuck were *you* thinking, Holly?' He hurled the remote controller across the room. 'Huh? When were you going to tell me you'd gone off cocks? I mean I know we haven't been having much sex lately but good god, if I'd known you were a rug-muncher I wouldn't've bothered trying!'

'Oh, don't be so crude, you righteous prick!' She climbed to her feet. 'Do you think it's been easy for me? I've tried to tell you, I just didn't know how. And now you throw it in my face like I'm the root of all evil. I was lost, David, okay. You were never here and I was lost. I met Kellie and she was a friend when I needed one.'

'Kellie,' he mouthed. 'So it has a name.'

'Look, David, I never wanted to hurt you. Bloody hell, I don't even know *what* I want anymore. But Kellie was there for me when I was lonely. I'm not making excuses, I still shouldn't have done what I did. But you don't know how bad it was. You were so wrapped up in your work I became a piece of furniture to you. I was about as far from happy a person can be.'

Reaching into his jacket, David withdrew a small envelope and dropped it on the coffee table. 'Then you should've talked to me, Holly. You should have come to me. But not this. I didn't deserve this.'

Swigging back the remainder of the whiskey, he climbed to his feet.

'Where're you going?' she uttered.

'Staying with my dad for a while until I figure this out.'

She inched closer. 'You…you don't have to go.'

'Yes, I do.'

Closer still. 'Please, David, I want you to stay.'

'Why, Holly? We don't have anything more to say to each other. You've fucked up something good. How do we bounce back from this?'

She took his hand. 'I don't think you want to go.'

He tried to pull away. She held tight, a sliver of their past pulsing like lightning through the contact. She kissed him hungrily and David responded. She yelped as he grabbed her hair and yanked as he kissed back, his aggression flooding out in waves.

'You want to cheat on me, you bitch!' he growled into her ear. 'Huh? You want to fucking cheat on me?'

'Yes, I cheated and I fucking liked it.'

Grabbing her throat, he mashed his whiskey tasting mouth to hers and slammed her up against the wall, a scattering of picture frames crashing to the floor. She tore breathlessly at his shirt, the buttons popping open to reveal his stubbled chest. She raked her nails across his skin and he grunted, jarred.

Spinning her to face the wall, he grabbed her hair again, his free hand yanking down her pants, knickers. As he freed himself from his jeans he grunted, 'This is how I treat dirty little cheats, you fucking whore!'

She pushed her arse hungrily back against him, desperation gripping her, and he thrust himself roughly into her from behind. He grappled ruthlessly at her breasts through her shirt as he ground in and out, tugged at her hair, gripped her throat tightly. Tighter. Bang, bang, bang, the two of them panting in unison, unceremonious grinding, sweat dripping from their noses. Aching and hurting, she allowed herself to be abused, battered, thrust ruthlessly into, bodies colliding together, backs moist, until in minutes they exploded as one, great gushes erupting from each of them, leaving them quivering, breathless, hearts pounding.

They remained as they were against the wall, David's chin resting on her shoulder, sharp gasps exhaling. It took only a moment to free himself; another to pull up his jeans.

She turned to look at him but he wouldn't meet her eyes. Instead he tucked in his shirt, stood still and eyed the carpet, blinking uncertainly.

'David...' she murmured. 'I'm sorry.'

He glanced at her once, eyes filled with sadness, and walked into the hallway.

She pulled up her underwear and wiped the moisture from her eyes.

The front door slammed shut.

*

In a screech of tyres York tore into Newport's street and spun the car into the driveway. His partner's vehicle lay dormant in front of the dark house. David's was gone.

Despite the car the house looked vacant, zero signs of life.

He climbed from the car and jogged to the front door, hoping to God that she was in bed.

Others had emerged from their homes, pairs and groups of excitement deprived neighbours.

Back at the station Braddock was sitting at Mason's desk, phone glued to his ear hoping Newport would pick up. By the time York left, the psychologist had struck out.

Tentatively, York gripped the handle and pushed the door inwards.

The phone in the hall was ringing...

*

…ringing, ringing, but the sound was incoherent. Newport had poured herself some of David's whiskey and taken his place on the sofa. Around her the silence felt comforting, frightening.

How had she managed to fuck things up so monumentally? David was gone, York was pissed off at her, and Kellie hated her. And what about the sex? How pathetic was she to assume she could get David to stay with the offer of lovemaking.

Lovemaking?

Hardcore fucking.

He'd abused her and she'd deserved it. One thing was for certain too, David hadn't been the only one who'd enjoyed it. Tacked onto the end of the electrifying conversation with Kellie she'd been horny, and David had been in the right place at the right time.

Picking up the glass, she swigged back the whiskey in one wince. The phone began to ring again, the only sound for a million miles. This time she acknowledged it. Perhaps it was David to accept her apology, or Kellie to say she was backing down from her assignment.

Neither was likely.

She crossed the carpet groggily and wandered into the hallway, eying the place where David's case had stood. Pushing her hand tentatively through the nostalgia, she reached for the phone, but in a flash was dragged back as the strong hands grappled her from behind, lifting her off her feet. She swung a sharp elbow upwards connecting with bone, hopefully an eye socket. As she fought, only two things tore through her mind, cutting a path inside her own unequivocal terror:

He was already inside.

He'd been there all along.

*

The cacophony of the shrill ring set York on edge as he entered the shadow laden hallway. The entrance remained vacant and soulless.

He wanted to call his partner's name but held back. Instead he bent down and unplugged the phone, the chimes dying away echoingly. His eyes began to adjust and he moved stealthily into the equally dark living room, enough light from the street dappling the space with vision. In the centre of the floor, a sole glass stood empty on the small coffee table.

Slowly he took off his hat and laid it on the table next to the tumbler. And then he saw her.

'Oh shit, Holly!' he called. 'Oh, *shit-shit-shit.*'

He found the wall-switch, flooding the room with light. There, on the floor next to the kitchen door in a small pool of red, red fluid was his partner, unmoving, one arm up over her head, legs twisted unnaturally, peppered with photographs of herself and a cute blonde woman.

He rushed to her, fell to his knees and saw where the damage was focused. In her side, high enough to have punctured one of her lungs was a serrated blade thrust in at an angle.

'Oh, Jesus, Holly,' he moaned.

Down in the blood, he drew closer. He brushed her hair aside and pressed his fingers to her throat, his palm to her chest. He felt no pulse, no rhythmic whumping of her heart. His partner was not sleeping. She was dead.

31

Since the discovery of Newport's body the scene had become a circus. Press parasites were lingering around outside, as were do-gooders from the neighbourhood, insistent of knowing every scrap and morsel of gossip. On top of that David was back. Having reached his perfect alibi of a father, he'd decided to come back and talk things out with his wife. Apparently they'd had a bust-up. Instead he walked into a crime scene and spent the next ten minutes clutching his wife's body against his chest, splatters of blood on his cheek, his forehead. It took two officers to haul him off.

Despite his father backing the story, David had been taken to the station for questioning. The photographs of his wife with another lover scattered over her body were a little too damning, even for a man with an alibi. But York had known David for a long time. He wasn't their man. He wasn't anybody's man now.

Slouching in the armchair, York rubbed his tired eyes and watched the officers working. Will Graham was attending to Newport's corpse, his eyes red and puffy. Yates buzzed around like a worker bee throwing out instructions to his colleagues. He had no real authority, but they were responding regardless. York gave him a nod. The kid was growing on him.

'Hey,' said Mason quietly. She took a seat on the edge of the table, takeout coffee cup in hand. 'How you holding up?'

He shrugged.

'I know this is difficult, Nick, we're all going to miss her. Holly was a good copper –'

'She was my friend, Judy.'

Mason nodded slowly and examined her shoelaces. 'Listen, I just want you to know that I'm here if you want to talk. There's a psychological evaluation you'll be required to attend, but if you wanted to talk to someone who isn't a robot…well, you know where to find me.'

'I tried to talk to you,' he uttered. 'I told you this would happen. I wanted her off this case, I wanted her off this assignment altogether.'

'No decision I make is easy, Nick, you know that. You were my best team –'

'Yeah, *were*!'

'You were my best team,' Mason said again, 'but I stand by my decision.'

'You stand by your decision?' he echoed. A few sets of eyes turned their way. 'Look around, Judy, what's left to stand by? Holly was the one good thing I had left in my life. Now what, huh? Where do we go from here? Because from where I'm sitting, we're dropping like flies.'

'You still have your work, Nick. These guys depend on you, you've become a rock to some of them.'

'Let me show you what I've *become,* Judy,' he snapped, taking off his jacket and rolling up his sleeve. 'You see this? This bandage covers marks in my arm that have been there since my family disappeared. They don't heal, because I keep opening them up with the needle I use to inject heroin. I'm a junkie, that's what I've become. You want to preach, Judy, do it to someone who gives a shit, because as far as I'm concerned he's won, he beat us. You think it matters if we catch him now? There's no way back from this.'

Mason sat in stunned silence, her icy eyes more penetrating than ever. 'Nick, I'm so sorry. I had no idea. You think I don't get it, but I do. I've seen other officers turn to one addiction or another after losing someone, but you know we need to talk about this! I can't have an addict on my team, heads would roll.'

'I'll make it easy for you, Judy. First thing tomorrow morning you'll have my resignation on your desk. I'm done with this shit.'

With nothing more than a subtle shake of the head, Mason rose to her feet. 'Tomorrow, okay, we'll talk some more.' And she walked over to Graham.

His threat was empty, he knew that. So did Mason probably. Newport was about to become a symbol, by all accounts a legend, and he owed it to her to not rest until somebody's head was on a stick, even if it meant his own.

In the last couple of minutes Jonathan Wheeler had arrived and was rolling around the scene, kit box in one hand, half-eaten banana in the other. When he clocked York he made a beeline for him. The audio man didn't look at Newport's body. In fact he seemed to downright avoid it.

'Guv,' Wheeler began, 'any sign of another voice recorder?'

York tugged down his sleeve. 'No. There's probably not going to be one, son.'

Wheeler frowned. 'Why not?'

'He came after Holly, where was the consistency in that? We got the riddle right and still we're punished.'

Wheeler glanced over at Newport's unmoving corpse and quickly looked away. 'Why would he do that?'

York sighed, ignored the question. 'You know something, Jonathan, I don't think I've ever heard you talk this much.'

'Silence is golden,' the big man said.

'Amen! It's good to know you have a heart in that chest.'

'Speaking of hearts, what happened to Holly's?'

'Still inside her ribcage. He didn't take it,' said York.

'That doesn't strike you as odd?'

'Everything was rushed this time, things didn't go according to plan. I think Holly fought back.'

Wheeler finished the banana and pocketed the skin. 'Wouldn't expect any other.'

York shrugged.

'He must've made a quick getaway. He wouldn't leave something like this unfinished unless he was forced to. I mean, would he?'

York climbed to his feet. Wheeler had a point. Their guy was meticulous, exact, had been from the start. This was not his MO. If he hadn't finished the job, something must have scared him away. Had York walked in on him while he was centre-stage? Once he'd killed the ringing phone, he recalled no other sounds in the house, only sinister tranquillity.

Only two possibilities remained. Either their guy had been long gone when he arrived.

Or he was still there.

32

'Jonathan, don't make any sudden movements. I want you to look around and tell me if there's anybody here you don't recognise.'

'No,' he murmured. 'I know everyone in the room.'

York plucked his hat from the table and perched it on his head. 'Here's what I want you to do. Head upstairs and look around. Take your kit so it looks official. If you spot anybody you don't recognise, find me.'

'What will you be doing?'

'Same thing. And Jonathan, not a word, okay? Keep this between us. If these people knew there was a cat amongst the pigeons, they'd freak. Not to mention our guy, who knows what he'd do to get out of here.'

York began moving casually away, but he paused beside Will Graham. The forensics man was covering Newport with a plastic sheet. The en-route Charles Kilroy would need to clear the body before he could examine it further.

Pushing through the ensemble of uniforms gathered in the kitchen, he scanned each of their faces. They looked back at him sceptically. He recognised them all. 'Come on, you fucker,' he muttered to no one. 'I know you're here. You wouldn't miss this for the world.'

He left the kitchen through the side door and stepped into a dining room. Devoid of furniture, devoid of anything, it looked like Holly and David had been in the middle of decorating. The walls were bare plaster, the floor carpetless. The room lay bathed in shadow, and only one man resided. Back to York, he was examining something in his hands.

York stepped further into the room. 'What're you doing in here, son?'

The figure didn't respond. He remained motionless, focused on whatever was in his hands.

Another step. 'I'm talking to you, constable…'

York inched further forwards. Touching distance.

'I'm going to ask you one more time,' he warned. 'Who are you, why are you off-post?'

Reaching out, he grabbed the figure's arm and spun him around. The young officer freaked, pager in hand. 'Oh my god, I'm so sorry, guv. I know I shouldn't be in here.'

He took in the kid's mid-twenty-ish face. 'Why didn't you answer me, what're you playing at?'

'It's my girlfriend,' he stammered.

'What's your name?'

'Barlow, sir. Colin Barlow.'

He reached down and took the device from the officer's hand. 'Want to tell me what's going on, Barlow?'

'It's my girlfriend, sir, she's sick. I know I shouldn't be in here but I just needed to see if she'd contacted me. I was only gone for a minute.'

York sighed and handed Barlow the pager back. 'In future when somebody's talking to you, Colin, answer them! I had images of me explaining to your parents why I put you in hospital.'

'I will, sir,' Barlow nodded. 'Sorry, sir.'

'Go on, get lost.'

As Barlow scampered from the room, York moved to the patio doors overlooking the back garden. He peered out into the heavy leaf of shadow overlapping the fence, the hedges. The evening was calm.

He took a deep breath, the aromas of bare wood and plaster filling his nostrils. A cat sauntered idly across the black blades of grass. The large oak in the far corner ebbed in the gentle breeze. Nothing else moved.

He squinted and looked back to the oak, the base of its trunk swallowed in the oily dark. Something *was* moving out there. Unhitching the lock he stepped outside, narrowed eyes locked on the tree. He wondered if it had been an illusion, nothing more than a trick of the mind brought on by an impossibly long day, and narcotics in the mix.

A few more steps.

Only ten or so yards from the tree now, he paused to glance over his shoulder. He could see officers inside the house; likely he was invisible to them.

He turned back to the oak and right there, in full view was the silhouette of a man standing with his back to the fence, eyes glinting in the moonlight. York held his ground, held the stare, his heart in his mouth. Perhaps twenty seconds passed. It seemed like a week. The silhouette's eyes altered, turned up at the corners.

He's smiling, York thought. The bastard is smiling.

As quickly as he appeared, the figure turned and scrambled over the fence with lightning agility. No hesitation, York plummeted forwards and thrust himself up, vaulting the fence and landing in a narrow alleyway, cats scarpering at the sound of his slapping feet.

Left.

Right.

There. Towards the end of the passage his target disappeared into a garden. He gave chase, dashing along the alley to find the gate locked. He kicked it hard, the flimsy lock shattering away from the jamb.

In time to see the figure disappearing into the house and locking the patio door, he sprinted through the garden picking up a cracked gnome as he ran. The glass door erupted inwards as the ornament struck it and he followed the debris, the crunch of glass under his feet.

Passing quickly through a living room, TV blaring out a rerun of some Australian soap, homeowner cowering against the back wall, he found the front door swinging on its hinges. He ran for it, realising the mistake, the red herring.

The target hadn't left that way. He hadn't left at all. He turned in time to catch the silhouette emerging from the shadows on the staircase, arms raised. York threw his hands up in time to deflect the swing of something solid and fell backwards through the open front door. He collided with the concrete path as the figure stepped over him and sprinted for the main road.

Back on his feet York lunged on, arm burning from the attack. Across the main street, heavy streams of traffic surged back and forth, killing machines made of steel and glass. In a screech of tyres and a blare of horns he ran out into the road, slid across the bonnet of an emergency stop and fell onto the opposite pavement, hip aching from the collision. Up ahead the suspect vanished into a small café, pushing aside patrons, product stands.

York followed, muscling his way into the coffee shop. Only two tables were in use, the parties of both staring at the scene in wild fascination. The barista merely pointed to a door at the back, feet glued to the spot.

Through the back of the café he found himself in a small courtyard, stacks of cardboard piled on one side, empty crates on the other. From the far side of the fence, he heard a grunt – his target had gone over.

Scaling the fence as quickly as his aching body would allow, he crashed down on the other side. Another alleyway, only this time he got lucky - his fleeing target had chosen the wrong direction. York didn't move, but he didn't have to. One end of the dark alley terminated with an unscaleable brick wall. The dark shape paused in the shadows, glancing back at him, peering to the top of the obstacle.

York caught his breath and edged forwards, the figure turning to face him. He still hadn't seen the man's face, but at that very moment it didn't matter. The only thing that mattered now was the next few moments. Who was the stronger willed? Who was the stronger physically?

Who had who cornered?

There was only silence and a shock of airlessness in the alley, like they were standing at an elevated altitude. What followed was another stare down. This time there would be no running.

'You killed my friend,' York said at last. His voice carried confidence. At least he thought so.

The silhouette didn't reply, simply stood motionless, watching, his face pulling in the shadows.

'You went back on your word, you fuck!'

Still nothing, just the concentration of careful observation.

'I can stand here all night,' York assured him. 'I've got nowhere I ne–'

'You talk too much,' the figure finally murmured in a low guttural grunt. There was no fear in the tone, not even a trace.

York took another step forwards. 'You don't talk enough.'

'Maybe.'

'Who are you?'

'Does it matter, Nicolas? Do you think it will change anything to know who I am, what I've done? What I'm going to do?'

'Oh, I know what you've done.'

'Is that right?'

'Yes, it is.'

'Your partner was a fighter,' the voice grunted. 'Real spirit. It was almost a pity to put her out of the game.'

'Is that what this is to you, a game?'

'No. As a matter of fact it's not. I believe disposing of your partner has taken us past the stage of riddles and messengers. That was just my bit of fun.'

'People have died, son, that's not my idea of fun.'

'I've given you a purpose again, Nicolas,' said the figure cryptically. 'Are you going to begrudge me that?'

York frowned.

'Since your family disappeared you have had no real focus in your life. You cling on to each day in the hope that your son may still be alive, and you shoot that crap into your veins because it gives you a reprieve on your excuse for an existence. You think you're any different to me? We both have our escapisms, mine is just a little more…inventive. Bottom line, Nicolas, you need me.'

York took a step back this time, suddenly apprehensive. 'How do you know these things?'

'Because I watch. I observe. And I especially see people in turmoil. I saw you, Nicolas. You stood out.'

'I don't need you,' York muttered uncertainly.

'Who are you trying to convince? Only two of us here.'

'Fuck you! You're through. It's over. I can't let you leave here, you know that.'

'You can't stop me, Detective,' the voice murmured firmly. The defined glint of a sharp edge appeared in the darkness. 'No one can. I chose you because you were damaged, a broken man. I figured you'd provide the best sport and you haven't disappointed. But this little rendezvous is over. Now you're going to step aside and let me pass.'

'And why am I going to do that?'

'Because, Detective, I will not hesitate to gut you where you stand.'

York paused a moment, stood fast. 'Let me ask you something. Do you think I have anything left to lose? Morning after morning I wake up and curse the daylight, devastated that I haven't died in my sleep from an overdose. I'm not afraid to die, son. So if you think I'm going to step aside so a punk like you can walk away, think again. I can see your knife. Well, I'm unarmed. What do you suppose my chances are?'

'Oh Nicolas. Nicolas, Nicolas, Nicolas...'

York took a step forwards. 'Bring it on, you degenerate fuck!'

In the blink of an eye the silhouette was on him, the glint of his blade slicing through the air inches above his face. Grabbing a handful of hair, York yanked viciously back, his assailant tumbling off him, rolling away into the shadows.

Instantly back up he leapt onto the figure's back, swinging hooks at any part of the body, any connection a good connection. Some of the jabs landed, others found air.

Pitched off to the side with unnerving strength, York tumbled through the air and landed with a solid thump on the concrete, springing back up in time to feel himself being picked up and slammed into the wall of the alley, a reverberating whump as his head cracked the brick. Glitter and closing darkness danced before his eyes, but his consciousness gripped. With his arms pinned he swung his head forwards feeling the hard connection. His release and the agonising grunt came hand-in-hand as he pushed himself away from the wall, his assailant reeling.

York charged forwards flailing into the dark, arms wind-milling, but not a single blow landed. From the shadows, a large arm snaked around his neck from behind, lifting him off the ground, crushing his throat. He couldn't move, couldn't breathe.

He closed his eyes and waited for the inevitable. His assailant obliged. He gagged as the serrated edge of the blade was pushed into his lower back. At first there was no pain, only the cold feeling of despair, failure.

As the chokehold loosened, he dropped to his knees feeling the blade twist slightly as he fell. As if in slow motion he crumbled onto his side, unable to move. He refused to pass out. Then the pain came, and he began to fade away to a soft voice in his ear. 'No need to thank me, Nicolas. I just pray death is all you hoped for.'

York tried to reply but no sounds left his mouth.

'I'll see you on the other side.'

From his perspective on the ground, he watched as the killer walked casually away free from pursuit, his footsteps rescinding into the darkness, the serrated blade dripping with blood.

His blood.

Moments later the alley vanished, and he slipped into the silky black place he'd visited many times before.

*

Leanne.

Frasier.

His family was with him, their beautiful faces forming. From the shadows they emerged, evaporated. Emerged.

Something was different this time. He was standing at an odd perspective, almost oblique. Like he was closer to them in some way, nearer.

Still they couldn't hear him. His lungs bellowed out the words he needed them to hear but only silence emanated, as though they weren't meant to hear him, or weren't permitted.

He closed his eyes and watched the faces of his loved ones dissolve away again. When he reopened them, the blurry definitions of the dark alleyway reappeared, disappeared.

Leanne again, standing at the kitchen sink wiping plates, bubbles clinging to her soft hands. Frasier runs into the kitchen, holds up a drawing he's finished, his face full of pride. Look, Daddy, he grins, it's our house. Leanne turns to see, her smile broadening. She flicks bubbles at Frasier and he squirms away giggling like any other child. Any other child.

The scene dissolved again, and the alleyway reappeared. His back felt warm and damp. He decided there was no cause for optimism. Blood was escaping his body at an alarming rate.

'Keep your eyes open,' a soft voice whispered into his ear. 'Help is on the way.'

A woman's face appeared into his line of sight, blonde. All other details were lost in the haze.

'Remember this, Nicolas,' said the voice. 'Remember me.'

He tried to ask her name but his vocal cords refused to operate. Something was being slipped into his jacket pocket.

'Keep your eyes open,' the voice said again. 'Whatever you do, don't go to sleep.'

The only thing to follow was the click of heels as the mysterious woman hurried away. Despite her advice, five seconds later he slipped into unconsciousness.

Leanne.

Frasier.

He liked it here.

*

Why have I come here? Nothing has changed.

I stand at the head of the driveway eying the soulless structure. It seems smaller now, but no less threatening. The inhabitants have long since departed by various means, the remnants of their legacy standing firm amidst overgrown bracken and ivy.

My father is gone.

My mother is dead.

I am a different person now, and without prejudice or discrimination I function in the real world with unique qualities. Ordinary people will know my name, but it is not notoriety I seek. Ordinary people will be sickened and disturbed by me. Ordinary people will fear me as I have feared the waking day.

In each hand I hold a canister, the contents sloshing as I advance upon the house. I place them on the steps and peer through the stained window into the hall. Nothing remains, not a chip of furniture. The floorboards are bare, as they always were.

I empty the first canister over the porch and steps, the flecking paint crumbling away as if thankful. The second canister I splash over the side of the house, the rich scent of gasoline dominating the air.

I haven't brought enough, though the house is an amalgamation of flammable materials. I stand back and strike a match, tossing it into the cloying pool of golden liquid at the foot of the steps. The house erupts in a burst of orange, the blast of heat forcing me backwards. Beyond the far corner of the structure, I spy the briefest glimpse of the frame at the foot of the yard. For no longer than one frigid second, I contemplate returning with extra fuel and razing the diabolical monstrosity to the ground.

The notion passes, and I quickly become consumed by the blazing spectacle before me. Already the chimney has collapsed. Inside, a fallen crossbeam hangs ablaze across the stairs. Once more I ask myself why I came here. One by one, memories will burn, childhood scorn will perish, and I will be left standing.

My father is gone.

My mother is dead.

Ordinary people will know my name.

33

Somewhere in the Indian Ocean, 2011

Abbey forgot where she was. In the stuffy heat of the tent she rolled onto her back. Here last night, the girl was now missing. Slipping into a shirt, she poked her head through the blankets and scanned the sand. Halfway along the bay was Sol, the obnoxious Australian, lying face down and unconscious on the sand. Nobody else was around.

Last night's fire kicked out only smoke, its flames long since dead.

Crawling onto the sand, she stood and stretched, the perfect blue overhead making it hard to believe there'd ever been a storm. The vestige of wind was barely enough to stir the fronds.

'I'm guessing you must be Abbey,' said an unfamiliar voice at her back.

Startled, she turned to see the injured man in the pilot's uniform, blankets drawn up around his tent. The man's skin was ashen and oily, though he managed to bare his faintly stained teeth with a boisterous smile.

'What, no cheerful greeting?' he added in his thick West Indian accent.

'I'm…I'm sorry,' she muttered. 'I thought I was alone.'

'No need to be sorry, gal. In the gravity of our situation' – *sichueeeshan* – 'I am required to be as forthcoming as possible. Forgive me for making you jump. My name's Gibson. Gibson Sommerfield. I was the navigation' – *navigeeeshan* – 'pilot onboard.'

In an instant she liked Gibson Sommerfield. He gave off a warming aura. There was little doubt he was a father. Abbey took a seat in the sand and asked him how he was feeling.

'Like I've been in a catastrophic accident,' he replied. 'I can't imagine that to be true, though, gal, otherwise I'd have heard about it on the news.'

Abbey smiled coyly and nodded at the bandage. 'You mind if I check this out?'

'James took a look earlier. Apparently I'm in need of some kick-ass penicillin. Not to worry, I'm sure there's some knocking around here somewhere.'

'Sure,' Abbey replied dubiously.

'James has been up since dawn,' the pilot revealed. 'Searching the wreckage for drugs. Then he took off with that kid with the afro. And the young girl. They went into the jungle to find some odd clearing, or something.'

'Some odd clearing?'

'I don't know. You'd have to ask him. Saw it from the hill apparently.'

He went on to explain about the others he'd met that morning: Elaine and Eric had gone inland to find fruit and Sol had returned in the middle of the night. After failing to find a spot in one of the tents, the Aussie had flaked on the sand and hadn't moved since. As for James, she found it amusing that Oli had become his second shadow.

'Elaine tells me she heard static in the plane's cockpit?' said Gibson, interrupting her thoughts.

'Yeah, for what good it was.'

'It's probably just broken. If I can get my hands on the correct components, I might be able to do something with it.'

'You can get it working?'

'Not exactly. I'm trained in radio communications. With the right working parts there's every chance I can construct a pulsing shortwave frequency transmitter.'

'And for those of us from earth?'

Gibson flashed his teeth. 'Sort of an inside-out radio. But one that sends out a continuous signal. If any traffic passes nearby, we'll pop up on their screens.'

'What about this Black Box thingy that James was talking about? Doesn't that thing give off a signal?'

'Only for thirty days. I'd like to think I can build something a little more permanent. Nothing like being prepared. I did so many long hauls, one of my flights had to go down eventually.'

Abbey sat back, unable to tell if Gibson was joking. 'About that. What happened up there, Gibson? I thought we were in more danger crossing the street.'

Gibson shook his head. 'People do get run down, gal.'

'Million-to-one shot, my arse!'

'We're alive, is that not enough? When the elements turn on you, all the fail-safes, all the precautions in the world can't help you.'

'You're blaming this on Mother Nature?'

Gibson shuffled painfully onto his side. 'We were levelled at thirty-six thousand feet. When the weather picked up, we climbed a little further to try and avoid the convective clouds. We figured if we could rise above the boundary layer we could smooth things out. At the increased altitude we were fighting draughts from below and above, nothing like any of us had seen before.'

'But it wasn't the turbulence that brought us down, was it?' Abbey questioned. 'My seat was near the wing. I saw the lightning hit.'

'Lightning hitting an aircraft is not unusual, gal. But in most scenarios it's harmless. Unless it hits one of the engines or the fuel tank it'll normally just pass right through the plane's shell. There'll be a lot of static, everybody's hair will stand on end, but then the charge will exit the plane through the tailfin or another extremity. In our case we were already having trouble with the starboard engine. It was no big deal, the portside would've easily picked up the slack. But that brings us back to your million-to-one theory.'

Abbey exhaled. 'Should've put the lottery on.'

'No point, gal. You're not around to collect.'

Pushing herself back up, she said, 'All this is academic, though, isn't it? Because in your next sentence you're going to tell me that you know exactly where we are, and search parties will know precisely where to look.'

The pilot's ashen face remained stony.

'Gibson...'

'We were having some technical problems with the navigation equipment,' he revealed hollowly. 'North Shore was directing us in...but we lost contact with them forty minutes before we went down. There was no way to tell if we were still on course.'

The words left the pilot's mouth with an undertone of apology, as though he was embarrassed. He struggled to meet her eyes.

'Terrific,' she murmured. 'We're on an island in the middle of the Indian Ocean and we might as well be on Mars.'

'In a nutshell, yes.' Gibson confirmed. 'We could be anywhere within a three hundred mile radius.'

34

The further into the jungle they trekked, the denser the bush became. James had little energy for conversation so he was pleased his companions consisted of the silent girl, and Oli, who was unusually quiet.

Protected largely from the sun, there was still no relief from the sweltering heat. With no breeze reaching them, their backs were sodden, the trek turning out to be worse than the hill. It took almost another hour of searching before they stumbled upon the clearing. Grimy, sweaty, and in need of water, they sat for a moment and passed around a tepid bottle of *Evian*.

The clearing was exactly that, a clearing. A couple of hundred feet around, it quickly became apparent why the leaves appeared lighter from above.

'What is this place?' Oli muttered. 'I've never seen trees like this before.'

'Because they're not trees,' James clarified. 'They're plants. This is a banana grove.'

Unexpectedly, the girl split from the pack and wandered further into the clearing, that peculiar trance-like expression hugging her face. She looked almost happy. It was the first time James had seen her smile.

'So what's the script with you and Abbey, anyway?' Oli asked.

'The script?'

'Yeah, you know…you like her, right?'

Glancing over his shoulder, James locked eyes with the student. 'You do know she's married, Oli? There is no script.'

'Ah, bet you wish there was, though, huh? I've seen the way you look at her.'

'Oh yeah, how's that?'

'With that like glazed look, like you're totally blown away by her. I've seen it, man, you got it bad.'

James smirked. Refusing to play the student's game, he followed the girl into the clearing. At the far end he could see the odd structure they'd spied from the tor.

'She is hot, man, I'll give you that.'

'Oli, be quiet.'

Catching up with the girl, James held her back, the fixated expression lingering with her. She was barely breathing.

'And those green eyes. I mean, wow!'

'Oli, if you don't shut up, I'm going to tie you to a tree and leave you for the birds.'

From where he was standing he couldn't make out what the structure was, but amazingly it looked manmade.

'Think this place has got the girl spooked,' Oli observed.

James knelt before her. 'Sweetheart, are you okay?'

He expected no response and wasn't disappointed. It wasn't until he laid a hand gently on her arm that her head whipped around as though startled from a bad dream.

James backed away a tad. 'What is it, sweetie? What's got you so frightened?'

'It's this grove, man,' said Oli. 'I'm telling you. We should get her back to the camp.'

The girl didn't seem to want to move. Her blankness was beginning to disturb him.

'Oli, keep an eye on her for a couple of minutes, will you?'

James climbed to his feet and headed cautiously towards the structure, tentatively stepping along the patch of infertile ground. His suspicions were confirmed as he neared – the structure was manmade, some kind of hut propped up on stilts. The whole of one side had collapsed but it was still accessible, if uninhabitable. If somebody had once lived here, they were long gone now.

'Hey, James,' Oli called. 'Want me to grab some bananas?'

James didn't reply. Instead he began up the three small steps and went inside. Part of the roof was still intact, but the majority had caved in. He shifted some of the fallen roofing, an escaping bird startling him. Beneath it was the remnants of habitation: a silver-plated whiskey flask, some curious-looking rags which had probably been clothes once, and right at the bottom was a black and white photograph preserved in cellophane.

He held it up to the light. The image was of a beach somewhere. It looked like England. The men in the picture were wearing shirts and braces, the legs of their pants rolled up for paddling. Some of them wore handkerchiefs on their heads, knotted at the corners. Most of the women idled in deck chairs wearing full bathing suits and identical hairstyles, tightly curled from hours in rollers.

The focal point for the cameraman was an open-shirted gentleman and a woman standing next to their chairs, saying cheese. Around the man's neck, a golden medallion rested against his hairy chest. At odds with the women in her proximity, the female was a stunner.

He flipped the picture to find an inscription that had refused to fade. In eloquent looping scripture, it read:

Me and My Beautiful Betty.

Blackpool Beach, 1922.

Standing quietly in ambivalence, James placed the picture carefully into the pocket of his shorts. He didn't know how he should be feeling. Like them, somebody had been stranded here almost ninety years ago, long enough to build a shelter substantial enough that it should endure. Several questions nibbled at him. Only one seemed pertinent. If somebody had been around to build the hut, where was the body?

Back outside, Oli was plucking bananas from the untapped source and stuffing them unceremoniously into his rucksack. The girl hadn't budged.

'What'd you find, man?' Oli asked through a mouthful of banana.

'Nothing,' James lied.

'What do you mean nothing? Somebody built that thing.'

'It's empty now.'

'Then whoever built it was rescued, right?' Oil said hopefully.

James knelt in front of the girl. 'Okay, sweetheart, are you ready to head back to the beach? We can come back another day, okay?'

Never in his life had James witnessed such unwavering fascination, if that's what it was.

'We ready to go?' said Oli, bag bulging with bananas.

'I don't think so.'

Bending forwards, Oli looked into the girl's eyes, her pupils suddenly dilating, catapulting her back to the present. Startling them the girl locked eyes with Oli and screamed the scream of the damned.

James winced, Oli reeled, birds erupted from the treetops. The unfamiliar cry of an animal returned the girl's call with a chilling shriek of its own. Whatever it was didn't stop until the girl did.

'Jesus Christ!' Oli cried covering his ears. 'I know I'm no looker but *come on!*'

Gently taking the girl's head in his hands, James looked into her eyes. They blinked and peered back at him, confused. She appeared to be back. More importantly, she was breathing again.

'I've got goosebumps,' Oli declared. 'They must've heard that at the beach.'

James wrapped his arms around the girl's slender shoulders as tears trickled down her expressionless face. In his grasp he could feel her frail body shivering.

'I think we may be ready to leave, Oli,' he uttered. 'Get your stuff together.'

This time as he urged the girl from her spot, she didn't protest.

35

'I don't think I like this,' Abbey grumbled.

James looked sideways at her. 'It was your idea.'

'Don't remind me. Does it feel to anyone else like we're in violation of one of God's laws, or something?'

Anthony snorted.

'Something to add, Anthony?'

'God's laws…' the scarred man mumbled. 'You people have a warped sense of morality.'

From further along the line, Sebastian took a brave step forwards. 'You think there's something morally righteous with what we're about to do here?'

'Yes,' said Anthony flatly.

'Then you've got some serious issues, chief.'

Anthony made no effort to respond.

'I notice the Aussie isn't helping again,' Sebastian observed. 'What's his deal?'

'He graced us with his presence for a few hours this morning,' said Abbey. 'Thankfully he was sleeping. When he woke up, he vanished back into the jungle.'

'Anyone know where he's spending his time?'

Nobody did.

'So come on,' James piped up, 'who's going first?'

Sebastian grinned. 'Well, you know what they say…ladies first.'

Abbey hesitated. She supposed she was as good a person as any to make a start. Even James seemed tentative.

Spread out before the four of them was the mass of bodies swimming against the rocky outcropping, the rancid stink of the bloated corpses polluting the air. It didn't take an undertaker to work out what needed to be done. The bodies couldn't be buried – no lye; the putrid odour would penetrate the surface of the sand. They couldn't be dragged out to sea – the tide would just whip them back to shore. Only one conceivable method remained – the bodies would have to be stacked into some kind of grizzly bonfire and reduced to ash.

Abbey waded out into the murky water, the first of the bodies billowing towards her. What she was feeling was odd, an almost indifferent emotion. Standing amongst so many unmarked graves peculiarly felt no different to standing amongst the marked ones of a graveyard.

Gripping the corpse of a medium-sized woman beneath the arms, she dragged her from the water, the woman's heels leaving twin tracks in the sand. Following suit, James headed out and picked a corpse of his own, pursued Abbey to the centre of the beach and laid it down.

Soon the four of them were back and forth, gag reflex down to a minimum. They transferred four bodies in one journey, some missing limbs, others twisted in horrific and gnarled ways. Between trips they introduced wood and other flammables to the pile.

Anthony was working hard, Sebastian too. Since starting work the birth-marked man hadn't uttered a syllable. In turn, Sebastian hadn't shut up, his suit jacket now off, the sleeves of his tattered shirt rolled up.

Teri passed them by as she walked, eyes blackened from Elaine's assault. She didn't offer to help, didn't speak to anyone, merely eyed each of them with contempt as she passed.

She was ignored.

The sun went down in quiet splendour as they worked, reminding them how long they'd been at it. As the last body went on, the daylight vanished altogether.

Dropping onto the sand, Sebastian wiped beads of sweat from his forehead and observed their work. 'Is it wrong that I'm happy with the results?' he wheezed.

Picking up a few straggling items from the sand, Anthony tossed them onto the pile.

Around seven or eight feet high and twenty feet long, the gruesome bonfire held their solemn attention. Abbey wanted to say something of meaning, but appropriate words failed her. Instead she said, 'How're we going to light it?'

'With one of these, presumably.' Sebastian was holding up a lighter.

'I'm not talking about the flame. The bodies are damp. We're going to need some kind of accelerant.'

Sebastian pocketed the lighter. 'I don't know if anybody's noticed, but there don't appear to be any gas stations around here.'

'Leave the accelerant to me,' said James. 'I have that covered.'

From the end of the line, Sebastian sniggered. 'I love this guy. Everything's so dramatic.'

Abbey grinned and turned to look at James.

'Don't encourage him,' James smirked.

Gradually her smile transformed into laughter, she couldn't help it. Sebastian's comment had tickled her. Soon after, Sebastian and even James joined in with the gratuitous chuckling, caught up in the somehow hysterical moment. Only Anthony remained quiet. His eyes lingered unwaveringly on the gory effigy.

'Something funny about death?'

Elaine had approached stealthily along the beach, the sand aiding her silence.

'We weren't laughing at that, Elaine,' James explained. 'The laughter was at my expense.'

Hardly appropriate, though, is it? Standing before the shells of so many departed souls. Do you think God would approve?'

Anthony's quiet sneer was lucid to all.

'I say something funny, Anthony? Are you mocking God's name? Because I can assure you, you'll pay for it when you're kneeling at His feet.'

Anthony turned his back. 'Better watch out for that then.' The sarcasm wasn't lost on anybody.

'How dare you stand before me and ridicule my beliefs! Jesus Christ died for your sins.'

Anthony offered a humourless smile, mouth full of crooked teeth. 'What sin exactly, The Tree of Knowledge? I have some depressing news for you, Elaine, that story is a metaphor. Only a moron would believe it as fact.'

'Blasphemer!' she cried. 'This is how you choose to exercise your free will, by ridiculing God's name?'

'No, I exercise my free will to not believe in Him.'

Elaine was visibly paling. 'He didn't give you free will for that purpose, Anthony. He gave it to you so you make good decisions in life, and strive to be a good man.'

'Says who?'

'Says our Lord, Jesus Christ!'

'Your Lord, not mine.'

Taking a step back, Elaine reeled in disbelief. 'Are you not thankful for surviving the crash? Do you not believe it a miracle you're still alive?'

Anthony's face visibly darkened, the moonlight bathing one side of his face in shadow. 'A miracle? And what about these people?' Slowly he turned to face the stack of human devastation. 'Are you going to tell the families that their loved ones are dead because a miracle took place?'

'God will welcome these souls into Heaven, Anthony.'

'How convenient.'

Tears in her eyes, Elaine uttered, 'I shall pray for you tonight. I shall pray that God has looked upon these remarks with sympathy.'

Anthony turned away. 'Prayer means nothing.'

'How can you say that? Prayer is the most powerful tool we have.'

'Talking to thin air is not power, it's called gullibility.'

'Let me tell you something, Anthony,' Elaine said firmly. 'Last year I was in Daga Medo, Ethiopia, doing some volunteer work. Their colonies were dying out. Crops dehydrated to the point of decay, land infertile. It hadn't rained in months. The starvation there was breathtaking.

'One evening, three colonies came together and prayed for water, and you know what happened, it rained. *The very next day.* So the next time you think about ridiculing prayer, why don't you spare the people of Daga Medo a thought? Try telling them prayer isn't powerful.'

Anthony was stony-faced. 'You think I'm a virgin to prayer? For *years* I knelt by my bed and prayed. I prayed that my father wouldn't come through the door, whiskey on his breath, and take my sister away with him. For years he brutalized her, his only daughter. He destroyed her in every way imaginable. I prayed to God for it to stop. I prayed for *anything*. And when He didn't answer, I realised the truth. I was speaking to nothing but empty space. Your God can go fuck Himself.'

Elaine paled further. 'Anthony,' she murmured. 'I'm so sorry. I didn't mean to…I didn't…'

Waving a hand in dismissal, Anthony walked towards the shore. Abbey went after him.

'I am truly sorry, Anthony,' she called out. 'I…I honestly didn't mean to…'

Intervening, James said, 'Okay, Elaine, leave it alone.'

'But I didn't mean –'

'I know. But what's said is said. Let him cool off.'

Backing away, Elaine fell to the sand and buried her face in her hands. For the first time, she appeared her age, frail.

Further along the shore they could make out Abbey talking with Anthony. The conversation wasn't long. In under a minute she came walking back towards them, the light evening breeze teasing her hair. 'He's okay,' she said rejoining the group. 'Just wants to be left alone.'

'I didn't mean to upset him?' Elaine assured them.

Abbey took a seat next to her and wrapped an arm around her shoulder. 'So, what next?'

Looking to the top of the human structure, James took a deep breath. 'I guess we light it.'

*

After commandeering Sebastian and disappearing for nearly forty minutes, James returned with several large water bottles stuffed into his rucksack, the South African likewise.

After revealing that amongst the wreckage he'd spied the fuel tank, he and Sebastian had filled the empty bottles with the remaining *avgas* – aviation gasoline as Gibson had reliably told him it was called – and returned, prepared to douse the beach's centrepiece.

Everybody took a bottle and began liberally soaking the bodies, the wood. Advising everybody to step away, James said, 'When we light this thing, it's going to burn a hole in the sky. It'll be going all night. If any transport passes, they won't be able to miss it.'

Elaine said coyly, 'Does anyone mind if I say a prayer? It seems appropriate.'

In Anthony's absence, no one objected.

Interlocking her fingers, Elaine began reciting a homemade prayer. Watching transfixed, Abbey clung to the woman's words. They were eloquent, sugar-coating their bleak predicament; words of departed souls, God's infinite love, Heaven and water. Anthony was not mentioned. Only silence followed the Amen, the subtle breeze rustling the fronds in the darkness behind them.

Pulling the lighter from his pocket, Sebastian rolled the flint, each of them drawn to the tiny orange flame flickering with the tide. 'Any volunteers?'

Nobody spoke up.

'Didn't think so,' Sebastian murmured.

'If you don't want it,' said James, 'I'll do it.'

'And let you take all the credit? I've got this, chief.'

Sinking to his haunches, Sebastian held the flame out in front of him, flickers of uncertainty passing across his face. Nobody breathed.

As the flame touched the grizzly spectacle, it sprang up into the night sky, the first of the corpses engulfed in blue tongues. Abbey took a step back as the heat licked outwards, the others following suit. Soon the entire human structure was ablaze, the tips of the flames casting off flicks of ember into the torched night sky. All present stood hypnotically in gruesome awe as skin frazzled, flesh melted.

The smell wasn't so bad, thought Abbey. Beef or pork maybe? The coppery tinge of blood. She couldn't look away, drawn in like a child. The scene was brutal, carnage, but it was beautiful; a magnificence was being shared between the living and the dead. For those condemned to the flames, it was judgement day, redemption day for those who were not. Offering a departing gift of beauty, the deceased displayed their glory in spectacular unity, the living receiving it with open arms.

Noiselessly, they watched the flames for over an hour. Then, one-by-one they began to depart. James disappeared first, then Sebastian, Elaine, the others. Eventually, only Abbey remained.

With no one else around, she watched the flames lick higher, another soul depart. There were no words for what had taken place here, there was no splendour. Death lived here now. Only death.

Today's word: *Fuck.*

36

Cutting into the dim confines of James's tent, a single shaft of light speared through the blankets, waking him from a dreamless sleep. Outside he could hear excited voices accompanying birdsong, melodious notes carried upon the morning.

Pushing his way onto the sand, he found a handful of the survivors standing around Elaine and Eric, animated and impatient. They were keyed up about something. Even the girl was smiling.

As the group began to split, he noticed Sebastian sitting by the tree line smoking a cigarette. The South African wasn't involved in the gathering. Instead he watched solemnly from afar, his unreadable eyes trained on the girl.

Keeping his eyes on the South African, James headed over to Elaine. 'What's with all the excitement?'

She too had her eyes on the girl. 'I'm not supposed to say.'

'Keeping secrets now?'

'No,' Elaine smiled. 'Not particularly. God gave us a gift yesterday, and today we're going to share it.'

'Sounds intriguing.'

'Trust me.'

James yawned. 'I don't like surprises, Elaine.'

Finally Elaine took her eyes off the girl. Sebastian did not.

'Just indulge an old lady for a little longer, dear.'

From the corner of his eye, James spotted Gibson lying at an uncomfortable angle. The pilot was waving him over. Picking at half a coconut, Gibson grinned as James approached. His moist face looked paler than last night, James thought, eying his congealing bandages. Hiding his disquiet, James sat down in the sand. 'How you feeling?'

'Like I have a horrific wound!'

'Where'd you get the coconut?'

'Elaine not tell you? They found a stack of trees somewhere inland. There'll be all sorts of fruit here if you know where to look.' James frowned. 'Too much TV,' Gibson clarified.

'See anything on how to catch fish?'

'The next challenge, huh?' Gibson laid back and exhaled deeply. 'You're doing good, lad. I have confidence in you.'

James pushed himself onto his knees. 'What do you mean?'

'Come on, look around. Only eleven of us survived that crash and I'm not going to be around much longer to talk about it. No one here has what it takes to keep morale up the way you do. Morale is vital, otherwise deprivation will lead them to frustration, which leads to anger, and finally conflict. I don't need to tell you, the last thing you need here is these people turning on each other.'

'Sounds like you have it all worked out.'

'I haven't had much else to do.'

'Well you have me all wrong, Gibson. I don't know how to lead these people.'

'That's not what I think. It's not what Abbey thinks either.'

He frowned. 'Abbey?'

'She believes in you,' Gibson revealed.

'She told you that?'

'Didn't have to. It's written all over her face.' Gibson flashed his pearly whites. 'Everybody's woken to zero signs of rescue this morning, even though the fire burned all night. They should be disillusioned, but they're not. Just keep that hope alive, that's all I'm saying.'

James laid back and tried to digest what he was being told. It was a fact that none of the survivors were leaders, Gibson had that right. He just didn't know what the pilot wanted him to do about it.

Along the beach Sebastian hadn't moved, the cigarette pinched between his fingers, his gaze still idling on the girl.

'Pretty weird, huh?' said Gibson. James turned back to the pilot. 'Sebastian can't take his eyes off the girl. Want to see something weirder? Look at Eric. He can't take his eyes off Sebastian. It's like some incredibly wrong love triangle.'

'You're sick,' James grinned.

'What do you suppose is going on?' said Gibson.

James shook his head. He had no idea.

Shuffling uncomfortably, Gibson let out a moan.

'You okay?'

'Leg's stinging like mad,' the pilot grumbled. 'Check it out for me, will you.'

Kneeling back down, James began unwrapping the bandages. Gibson winced as the congealed wraps lifted free.

'Close your eyes,' James suggested.

'What, you think I'm a pussy?'

Peeling away the last of the bandages, James recoiled. Evidence of infection was more severe than yesterday. It reeked.

'Holy shit,' Gibson muttered.

Clear signs of gangrene had set in, the flaps of serrated skin growing angrier. With no oxygen getting to the wound, the dead skin would be crawling with bacteria. No wonder it stank. Today the skin was pale, tomorrow it would turn red. When it reached purple, they were in real trouble. By that time Gibson would be in remorseless pain and all the drugs on earth wouldn't make a dent.

'Don't sugarcoat it,' Gibson murmured.

James reeled off everything he knew, down to the angry skin and gangrene. When he was through, the pilot fell into silent contemplation. They both knew the single remaining option if they failed to find drugs, but neither said it.

'We're going to find penicillin, Gibson,' he promised. 'It has to be out there somewhere.'

But the pilot wasn't listening. Instead, he rolled over and faced out to sea.

*

James headed down to the shore to join Eric standing in the spill, cotton slacks rolled up, baseball cap turned backwards. When he realised he was no longer alone, the big man became more attentive, like a red-handed kid in a sweet shop. Wading out to the breakers, James greeted Eric with a "good morning", but received no reply, only morbid fascination and big cow eyes.

Trying again, he said, 'James to planet Eric…anybody there?'

Eric changed positions and screened him once again. 'I woke up early today, James,' he said spontaneously.

Irrelevant, but James couldn't help smiling. 'Did you see the sunrise?'

'I like it here,' he revealed. 'It's always sunny. I like the sun.'

James offered a single nod, hoping Eric would continue.

'Are you American?'

'Yes I am,' James confirmed. 'How did you know?'

'I've been to America. I went to Disneyland.'

'Oh yeah? In California?'

Eric narrowed his eyes. 'Disneyland in America.'

'How did you like it?'

'Why are you talking to me, James? You've never talked to me before.'

Feeling slightly deflated, James pressed on. 'Sorry, Eric, I didn't mean to neglect –'

'I know I'm not smart,' Eric intervened. 'My dad used to tell me. But I'm kind. My mum always tells me it's important to be kind.'

'Your mom's a smart woman.'

'I think you're smart.'

'I'm probably not as smart as you think,' said James.

Darting past his feet, a brightly coloured fish caught the big man's attention.

'How'd you like everybody else?' James asked casually.

'I want to be a racing driver,' said Eric randomly. 'I was reading a magazine on the plane about cars. Did you know that some cars are more expensive than houses?'

'No kidding.'

'It's my favourite magazine…' Eric assured him.

Another fish.

'Eric?' James said hesitantly. 'Do you like the other people here?'

Smile fading, the big man faltered. He didn't like that question, nor did he reply.

'Eric,' James persisted. 'Did you hear me?'

'I like it here, it's always sunny.'

James bit his lip. 'Why won't you answer my question, Eric? Do you not like the others?'

'I like Abbey.'

'Me too,' he agreed nonchalantly. 'What about Anthony, you like him?'

'The man with the scar on his face?'

'The birthmark, yes.'

'I don't think so,' Eric said dubiously. 'My mum told me to stay away from him.'

Understandable.

'My favourite is Sebastian,' James revealed. 'I like him a lot.'

Eyes to the water, the fish.

'Eric?' he urged. 'You like Sebastian?'

'I don't know him.'

'I thought you did,' he said casually. 'I saw you looking at him earlier so I just figured you were friends.'

'I like the sun…'

'Why were you staring at him?'

'It's always sunny…'

'Eric…I'm asking you a question.'

'I think I'm going to go back to sand now,' he said, unable to meet James's eyes.

Frustrated, James backed off and watched the big man turn and flee.

Meeting him at the shoreline, Elaine welcomed her son. Despite the distance, James couldn't make out what she was saying, her voice muffled by the gently tumbling waves.

Sebastian hadn't moved from the tree line, James's eyes settling on him from afar. He was no longer looking at the girl. Meeting James's gaze, the South African was staring stonily back. Like he knew they'd been talking about him.

37

Like a procession, they marched into the jungle following the narrow estuary flowing from somewhere within. Sticking close to his mother Eric took second place, then James and Oli, and bringing up the rear was Abbey, shadowed by the girl.

As tired as the rest, Abbey gulped in deep breaths of the stifling air and began to grow light-headed. 'How much further, Elaine?' she called from the rear.

'Not much, dear.'

'You said that about a hundred miles ago,' she gasped. 'Since then I've had at least two strokes.'

Blowing out a breath of frustration, James intervened. 'We should probably stop for a minute, Elaine, catch our breath.'

Chuckling, Elaine said, 'Are you saying you've all been outdone by a sixty-seven year old with a dodgy hip?'

'I didn't say anything,' Oli protested. 'I think we should soldier on!'

'You would say that, you pansy,' said James. 'You wanted to stop every five minutes when we climbed to the plateau.'

'Every six as I recall,' Oli corrected.

'It's irrelevant anyway,' Elaine interrupted. 'We're here.'

Familiar with the surroundings, Eric pushed through some thick undergrowth and disappeared.

'Anybody else hear that?' Abbey asked.

Elaine smiled as the group fell silent, the faint gushing sound riding the air around them.

'I hear it,' Oli confirmed. 'What is that?'

'Euphoria,' grinned Elaine.

'Euphoria?' Oli quizzed. 'What does that mean?'

'This way.'

Taking the same route as Eric, it soon became apparent what was creating the sound. 'Elaine, is this what I think it is?'

'What do you think it is?'

'If no one's around to hear it...'

Elaine pushed aside some heavy branches. 'Now's not the time to get philosophical, darl. It's merely a time to marvel at one of God's better designs and have some fun.'

They pushed through some dense vegetation, and finally there is was: Elaine's utopia. Almost thirty feet high, a shelf of rock towered above the crystal-blue lagoon, the perfect white spray of three small waterfalls tumbling delicately onto the surface of the water. More boulders bordered the lagoon's edge in a gentle rise to the stone shelf. They hung there like a wonderfully crafted natural ladder, spanning out into the water and forming small stepping-stone islands. To the left, a sheer rock face rose out of the ground dappled with greenery, extending across the topmost shelf of rock and flowing down the opposite side where a small cave was hollowed out of the rock.

'Watch your step,' Abbey admonished as they joined her at the water's edge.

Already in the water was Eric, clothes peppered on the nearest rock.

'Whoa.' Oli.

'Oh my god.' James.

'Told you,' said Elaine.

'People...' James tugged the damp shirt from his back. 'We are officially in paradise.'

He ran and plunged headfirst into the lagoon, surfacing seconds later, sandy hair slick to his scalp. 'Holy shit, it's freezing!'

'Freshwater, darl!' Elaine revealed. 'We left the salty stuff at the beach.'

'*Fresh*water? Does that mean…'

'There's a small rivulet running parallel to the waterfall. Anyone carrying bottles, feel free to fill them.'

Stripping down to her white bikini, Abbey toed the lagoon. 'You mentioned water in your prayer last night, Elaine.'

'Had to thank the Big Man for it,' she acknowledged rolling up the legs of her pants.

Standing on one of the boulders, Oli looked hesitant. 'Just how cold is it in there, man? My body's sensitive to extreme climate change.'

'Just get your pale ass in the water!'

Like a kitten with cotton wool paws, Abbey crept up on Oli with predatory silence, flashing a "shush" to anyone who clocked her. Still reluctant, the student was shoved unceremoniously from his rock. '*You biiiiitch*!' he screamed, windmilling, grabbing at insubstantial air, and crashing into the water headfirst.

Coming back up for air, he gasped breathlessly.

'Stop your whining, you big fairy,' she giggled and jumped in next to him, pinching her nose closed.

'Oh yeah?' Oli grinned pushing her head under. 'How'd you like them apples!'

For over an hour the six of them frolicked in the lagoon, in the sun. None of them had laughed so hard for days. The braver ones took turns jumping from the shelf into the cool water, even Oli and the girl with enough encouragement. There was not a defensive word, not a cussed remark as they enjoyed the happy moment.

As they grew fatigued, one by one they began to exit the lagoon, scrabbling around for their clothes. Only Abbey and James remained in the water.

Standing beneath the biggest of the waterfalls, she watched as the water cascaded across James's shoulders, flattening his hair. He'd begun tanning nicely, his eyes seemingly bluer than before. In silence he stared back at her, brushed the dark strands of hair from her face.

'You think it's possible that a group of survivors can keep it together long enough to get home?' He asked her.

Abbey broke eye contact. 'They're good people, James. They deserve to get home.'

'That's not what I asked.'

'Do I believe in our ability to survive?' she murmured. 'Yes I do.'

He smiled. 'Good.'

Their eyes met again. She wanted to look away but something was stopping her, an enticement in the invisible space between them.

'Please don't look at me like that,' she whispered.

'Like what?'

'Like that,' she said softly.

Holding her gaze for a few seconds longer, he said, 'Sorry.'

'James, I –'

'Won't happen again, I promise.'

He disappeared through the tumbling water, leaving her reeling, goosebumps on her arms. She thought for a moment he was going to kiss her. Perhaps he would've done if she hadn't stopped it, and then how would she feel, guilty? Distraught? Neither of those words felt satisfactory. Almost not wanting to think it, she believed the word she was looking for was "Relieved".

Poor Edward.

Poor Edward.

38

Sitting alone on the outcropping now free of bodies, Abbey surveyed the charred stack of human ash in the centre of the beach. Having returned from the lagoon with a warmer heart, it was now beating remorselessly cold. Was this the soul's way of balancing elated and disconsolate, she wondered? From gliding gracefully through clouds to scraping the barrels of depression? She began to cry. Then she began to sob.

She'd considered walking over to the charred remains. In the end she stayed away. There had been too much death; she didn't want to see anymore. Besides, her blackened emotions had little to do with the waste of human life here, and much more to do with Edward – the husband who thought she was dead. The husband who would be emotionally torn to shreds, for he worshipped the very ground on which she walked. The husband who was possibly, at that very moment, considering himself a widower.

How long would it be before he moved on, met somebody else? How long would it be before he began dating again? Would he remarry, begin a new family, a new life? Would he have the children she had never given him? A feeling of nausea expanded in her gut, and for a brief moment she thought she might throw up.

And then there was James.

James wasn't five thousand miles away. He was alive and more importantly, he knew that she was too. Her thoughts edged precariously towards turmoil, beaten solemnly against the black wall in her head. Her fragile mind had never seen such disorder, had never been put to this kind of test.

Aided by the waves breaking peacefully against the shore, she began to calm down. Unwilling to show signs of weakness, she had stepped away from the group prior to her impending breakdown. The timing had been perfect.

Recently any actions of consequence were being passed through her, as if the others had appointed her in command alongside James. This she could handle. This she *needed*, the power of occupation helping to rebuild her crumbling walls. For the others it was nothing more than an astute generation of hope, placing her in the position of metaphorical shoulder, but for her, vocation was the distraction she pined for.

Climbing to her feet, she took one more look at the beach's appetite for chaos, refusing this time to succumb. Emotions raw, she started back to camp.

✡

Armed with a shopping list from Gibson, Abbey was boosted back into the plane by Eric. The big man was unusually quiet. She wondered if something was bothering him.

She knew what to expect as she sidled into the murky cabin. The open tomb appeared no more ominous than it should, each body unmoved. She almost laughed. What did she think, the corpses were playing musical crash-positions in her absence? Disturbed dust mites swimming in the air, she drew a hand to her mouth, reluctant to breathe.

Behind her, Eric and Anthony had clambered silently aboard. What a pair she'd brought with her, she thought – the mentally challenged and the mentally scarred. Anthony had his uses if nobody mentioned religion, and Eric was there solely as brute strength, should they need it.

In the gloom she eyed Gibson's shopping list, the entire compilation a mystery. Most of it was electrical; circuit boards making use of ceramic capacitors, trimmer capacitors, variable capacitors, batteries, fuse holders, fuses, resistors. She would also need to find a speaker, lengths of enamel wiring, switches, and to cap it all, a wire coat hanger and a cardboard toilet roll tube. They already had a soldering iron from the toolkit, but no means to plug it in.

She hoped the pilot knew what he was doing.

Pushing her way into the cockpit she ignored the uniformed bodies, and instead asked Eric to move them into the cabin. The big man obliged, astonishing her. She knew Eric was strong, he *looked* strong, but he lifted the two bodies from their seats like they were filled with candy floss. Standing quietly she listened for the static that had alerted Elaine.

None came.

'What exactly are we looking for?' Anthony muttered deeply.

Abbey handed him the shopping list. 'Gibson said everything electrical on the list is in the cockpit somewhere,' she explained. 'He gave me pointers on where to look. He doesn't want the individual components, just the circuit boards. He'll take it from there.'

Narrow eyed and unsmiling, Anthony stared until she began to grow unnerved.

'You going to help me look?'

Holding the gaze for a few seconds longer, he said, 'Where?'

She and Anthony searched together while Eric sat in business-class next to the corpse of a woman. He looked so sanguine, anyone would've thought he was enjoying an in-flight movie.

It took them almost two hours to find everything they needed. When they finally exited the cockpit, they were sheathed in grime and sweat.

*

Daylight had turned to dusk while they'd been inside the plane, and by the time they made it back to camp the sun was losing the battle. Teri's campfire was ablaze, a handful of survivors surrounded it in a circle, their faces a palette of shifting oranges and blacks. Only Gibson spied their stealthy return.

With a steady eye Abbey settled next to the pilot, his almost translucent skin more evident. The subtle shivering wasn't lost on her either, a well dug-in fever having taken hold. 'How you holding up?'

'Why does everybody keep asking me that question?' said Gibson resignedly. 'Take a look, sister.'

'Sorry,' she muttered.

Anthony and Eric joined the others around the fire, James glancing over his shoulder. He nodded to her.

'I think we got what you need,' she revealed.

'Great! Just need to build it now before I kick the bucket.'

'Don't talk like that, Gibson, you're going to be fine.'

'If you say so, gal.'

Growing concerned with the pilot's tone, she uttered, 'Gibson...'

'Don't worry about me,' he said, shifting uncomfortably. 'If I work through the night, it'll take the edge off. I don't think I'm going to be sleeping any time soon.'

'You've done this kind of thing before?'

'Crash on a desert island?'

'Irony's not abandoned you, I see! The radio?'

'Hundreds,' he assured her. 'Bit of a nerd as a kid, wasn't one for parties. I would stay home and build stuff. It was just a hobby, you know. Better than getting wasted every night on keg beer and cheap vodka.'

'You just described my college days,' she smiled. 'On the flipside, if you had misspent your youth like so many miscreants before you, we'd be further up shit creek than we are already.'

'It's probably going to be my crudest contraption to date, gal, you're aware of that?'

'So long as it works, it can look like John Merrick for all I care.'

She watched the pilot trying to get his wracked body comfortable, unable to look away.

'Who's waiting for you at home, Gibson?' she asked. 'Anyone to welcome you with open arms?'

'I should hope so, gal,' he grumbled, settling down. 'My wife and I are separated but we're still close.'

'Kids?'

'Three,' he announced proudly. 'Gabriel, Janet and Thandie. Still kids to me anyway. Gabriel's twenty-nine and has a stake in a retail firm with a salary that would make you blush. And my gals just had their twenty-first birthday.'

'Twins?'

'You wouldn't guess it. Thandie is the lead singer in an all-girl rock group and Janet's studying philosophy at NYU.'

Abbey smiled. 'Contrasting angels.'

'You should hear the arguments they have,' he recommended. 'Thandie insists she's the only one in the family not a "slave to the system." I'm beginning to think she's right.'

It was hurting the pilot to talk of his family, emotionally and physically. Dropping the subject, she lay back onto the moonlit sand and peered at the stars.

No matter where you are in the world, you're seeing the same night sky as a billion other people...

Her eyes traced the constellations from star to star, and from star to star. Did she feel closer to home? She couldn't tell.

'Nostalgia,' she almost whispered. 'Today's word: Nostalgia.'

'If you say so, gal,' Gibson uttered.

The group around the fire began breaking up, James and Eric heading their way. Eric was gripping the white carrier bag like his life depended on it. 'We got your things, Gibson Pilot,' he said excitedly. 'I found the coat hanger and the toilet roll.'

'I never doubted you, Eric,' said Gibson flashing the best smile he could muster.

They watched as the pilot delved into the bag, rummaging through the contents like a child. With Eric's fascination unwavering, James led Abbey along the sand towards the campfire.

'What is it?'

'Sol is still missing,' he said quietly. 'He's been gone all day.'

'So what?'

'You don't find it odd?'

'He's a grown-up. He can do what he likes.'

James glanced over his shoulder at the empty beach. He seemed on-edge.

'Why the sudden interest in Sol?'

'It's not interest, it's concern. No one should be in that jungle alone, it's an assault course out there.'

As they spoke, Teri came ambling along the bay, surprisingly without a lit cigarette.

'Mind if I join you?' she asked, her eyes still decidedly dark.

She received only questioning eyes.

'If it's too much trouble, fucking *forget* it,' she grumbled and turned away.

'Teri…' James said. 'It's your fire.'

'Thanks,' she mumbled, and began warming her hands.

Behind them, Eric was following Gibson's instructions, fishing items from the carrier bag and handing them over in the meagre light.

'Where've you been?' James said to Teri.

'Why?'

'Because I'm concerned about people being out there alone.'

Expecting some sharp remark, Teri simply said, 'Couple of bays along, that's all. Wanted to be alone.'

'Did you find a beach free of wreckage?' he asked.

'Why?' she said again.

'Because I'm going over there. Want to go back?'

'You're going over *where*?' Abbey stepped in. 'It's getting late.'

'Little project,' he grinned. 'Who's with me?'

39

Having managed to elicit the interest of only Oli and Teri, James led the way past the human bonfire and beyond to the adjacent bay. The idea was to find an untouched beach and lay an enormous SOS on the sand, a symbol that couldn't possibly be missed from the sky. A fire would always burn out, a watchdog would always sleep, but even if a storm hit, a well-entrenched message would remain.

'So what you're saying is,' Oli grumbled, 'we're here for more strenuous shit?'

'For fuck's sake!' Teri's input.

James grinned, the moonlight catching his white teeth.

Despite their bickering, the two co-workers cracked on, shuffling back and forth from the tree line and transferring materials onto the sand. James laid them out in cipher. Made up of boulders, rocks, heavy branches, wreckage from the previous bay, the thing was enormous. There was no way a low flying aircraft could miss it.

James checked his watch. The minute-hand ticked past midnight as they hauled the final piece into place. Standing back, they admired their efforts.

'We done?' said Teri impatiently.

'Oh, we're done,' Oli wheezed. 'I'm not lifting another finger tonight.'

The two of them fell to the sand at gravity's request.

'Man, I am whacked,' the student added. 'I think Eric and Sebastian would be far more capable if you had the crazy notion of, oh I don't know, doing more of this.'

'I'll bear that in mind,' James replied, grinning. He waited while Oli and Teri caught their breath, neither of them seemingly willing to move, before suggesting they headed back to camp.

'One more minute,' Oli begged.

'Fuck that, man, I'm all set!' Teri climbed to her feet and lit a cigarette. 'I'm not fucking staying out here all night.'

'Ever the charmer, Te -' James double-took the tree line.

'What is it?' Oli asked.

He shook his head. 'I don't know. Did you guys see that?'

Eying the trees, Oli frowned. 'What're we looking for?'

'Freak,' Teri threw in.

James didn't respond. The beach seemed to slow down as if in stasis.

'James, you're freaking me out here,' said Oli nervously. 'What the hell's going on?'

'Call me crazy,' James murmured,' but I just saw something in the trees.'

'Saw what exactly?'

'I think somebody's had a loooong day,' Teri suggested impatiently.

'I didn't imagine it!' James said calmly. 'I looked to the trees and saw movement. I thought I was mistaken. When I looked back, it was there, large as life.'

'What was there?'

'A light,' he muttered. 'The faint glow of a light.'

'Bullshit,' Teri groaned.

'You've had too much sun, man.'

'Jesus, Oli, I know what I saw. somebody was standing right there in those trees, watching us!'

'So it was someone from the camp,' Teri suggested through a plume of blue smoke.

'Yeah,' Oli agreed. 'Who was still awake when we left?'

'Or what about that fucking loser who's never around,' Teri added. 'What's his name?'

'Of course,' said Oli. 'You saw that Australian guy with the long hair, erm…'

'Sol,' James finished. 'Yeah, maybe. But why hide from us, huh? The man's odd, not creepy.'

Oli sat up. 'James, what do you even know about Sol? Maybe he's the kind of guy who likes the whole voyeurism thing. Perhaps he just likes checking out sweaty men carting shit about. He's probably watching us right now, whacking one off.'

Teri sniggered.

Shutting out Oli's foolish words, James kept his eyes trained on the trees.

'Listen, James,' if you saw something in the trees, you would've seen it again by now, right? There's nobody out there, man, I'll stake my reputation on it.'

'You don't have a reputation.'

'Well I'll acquire one from this situation.'

'I know what I saw,' James said stubbornly.

'Whatever you say, captain.' The student climbed to his feet. 'It's time for Oli to flake.'

'A-fucking-men,' Teri added.

'You two go,' James uttered. 'I'll be right behind you.'

'Safety in numbers, man, remember?'

When James didn't reply, Oli began walking across the expanse of white sand, tattooed girl silently in tow.

Firmly rooted, James eyed the trees for several more minutes, praying something moved or shone again, but the more he stared, the more his optimism faded. Nothing seemed out of place in the eerily still night, nothing moved, yet he couldn't shake the chilling notion that he was being watched. Oli and Teri were already reaching the end of the bay, walking silently side-by-side. He followed in their tracks, every few steps glancing over his shoulder.

The beach remained vacant.

40

The most obvious change to the camp in their absence was the extra personnel. Beside the fire, twenty yards from Gibson and Eric, was Sol Delaney thoughtfully chewing a banana. He shoved in the last mouthful unceremoniously as James approached, and tossed the yellow skin into the flames. Wearing only a pair of knee-length denim shorts and a Stars and Stripes bandana, he braved the chilly night with only the amber glow of the campfire for warmth.

Hands out to the heat, James took a seat across the flames. 'Hey.'

A grunt.

'How long have you been back?'

A shrug.

'Am I invisible, Sol?' James pressed. 'I asked you a question.'

Sol exhaled impatiently. 'I don't know the answer, man. Can't a brother get some peace at one in the morning?'

'Yeah, no problem. I'll leave you alone when you answer my question.'

'Fuck knows, dude. An hour ago, or something.'

'One hour? You sure?'

'That's what I said,' the Australian grumbled sleepily.

'And if I ask Gibson the same question, what do you suppose he'll say?'

'I don't think Gibson's been anywhere, dude, he's like all fucked up.'

'About *you,* Sol.'

'He can tell you what he wants,' said Sol calmly. 'I've been *here,* man.'

James didn't think the Australian was lying, he didn't look capable – which meant he hadn't been loitering in the trees three bays along either. Changing tack, he said, 'Where do you keep disappearing to, Sol?'

'Ah dude, more questions? You said you'd bail.'

'I know what I said.'

'So fuck off then!'

'It's about time you told me where you go all day. These people are scared, and if they find out somewhere down the line that you're hiding useful information from them, I imagine you're going to get lynched.'

Sol looked uneasy. 'I like my alone time, dude, what do you want me to say?'

'That's it, alone time?'

'That's it.'

Unwittingly interrupting the conversation, Eric came running over to reheat the soldering iron. Breaking eye contact with Sol, James said, 'How's the transmitter coming along, Eric?'

'Erm…' the big man seemed aware of the tension into which he'd walked. 'I'm helping Gibson Pilot. He said I'm a good ass…ass…'

'Assistant?'

'I like Gibson Pilot. He's been teaching me all sorts of neat things – *Ouch…*' Eric leaned too far into the fire. Sol turned away sniggering.

Following Eric over to the pilot James noticed Teri down by the shore, alone, lit cigarette glowing. Oli had vanished.

The pilot's damp brow didn't seem plausible in the evening chill, the inky smudges beneath his eyes sinking away into his dark skin. James said, 'How's it going?'

'It's going,' said the pilot.

'Finished by morning, you think?'

'You mean will I get it built before I check out?'

'I didn't say that.'

'It's coming along fine,' the pilot assured him. 'Couple more hours, all being well.'

Keeping his voice steady, James said, 'You're clearly some kind of genius, huh?'

'Not really, I could build one of these things in my sleep. But something tells me by your tone that the transmitter isn't your primary concern.'

James shrugged.

'What is it?' Gibson asked.

James took a seat on the soft sand, slightly agitated with the trees at his back. He waited for Eric to reheat the soldering iron before speaking. 'When's the last time you checked under the blanket?'

'I haven't,' the pilot admitted. 'Couldn't bring myself to.'

Leaning over the pilot's leg, James lifted the sheet, careful to keep the wound hidden from its owner. He recoiled at the stench. The flaps of loose grey skin confirmed the spread of infection, the sweating gash oozing a viscousy liquid, neither blood nor mucus. The lips had darkened to the predicted angry maroon, the infected area in the late stages of bacterial build-up.

'First light, Gibson,' he said quietly. 'First light, I'm snorkeling the wreckage.'

'It's okay, lad, you don't need to bullshit me. I'm ready.'

'Christ,' James cursed softly.

As the two of them took a trace of solace in a moment of solicitous silence, they noticed a silhouetted figure climbing from one of the tents. Female and slim: Abbey yawning.

'What on earth are you lot still doing up?' Her voice was small in an early hours kind of way.

'Back at you, sister,' countered Gibson.

'Can't sleep,' she replied. 'Thought I might go for a walk.'

James forced himself to shy away from Abbey's bed look; shaggy hair, sleepy eyes. 'Walk?' he asked. 'Walk where?'

'I won't go far, boss,' she smiled. 'Just want to work off some energy.'

'I don't like you walking out there alone.'

'He's right, gal,' the pilot cut in. 'Think of all them cannibals – canneebaaals – we've seen!'

'Gibson, not helping,' James admonished.

Placing a hand on James's arm, Abbey said, 'Come on, James, what do you think is going to happen? I'll be fine.'

He wanted to tell her about the light he'd seen, but panic was nobody's friend. 'I would just prefer it if we all stuck together.'

'I'll go to the end of the bay,' she smiled sleepily. 'No further, I promise.'

'Just stay attentive, okay? And the first sign of anything amiss, you scream, got it?'

'What's got into you tonight?'

'And stick close to the water,' he added hastily. 'Stay away from the trees.'

Frowning, she walked down towards the shore. He watched her until she slipped into the night and out of sight.

'What's going on, lad?' the pilot asked. 'Gal's going for a walk on the beach, not downtown Baghdad.'

James scratched his stubble thoughtfully. 'Can you keep a secret?'

'To the grave, which by all accounts isn't going to be too long.'

Sitting back down, he said quietly, 'Three bays over, I saw a light in the trees. It was only there for a second but I know I saw it. Somebody was out there, watching us.'

'Anybody else see it?'

'Just me.'

'What about Sol, he's never around?'

'He was tonight,' James muttered. 'Said he'd been here for over an hour.'

'He had,' the pilot confirmed.

'Then it wasn't him. I'm telling you, Gibson, somebody was there.'

'I can promise you, lad, I've been here all day, but everybody's been coming and going, it could've been any of them.'

'Shit,' he grumbled. 'It's weird, Gibson. I know what I saw.'

'Maybe this island is messing with your head.'

'Yeah, I had all that from Oli. Do I sound insane to you?'

'No, you do not, which leaves one possibility.' James met the pilot's bloodshot eyes. 'You saw a light.'

Gibson went back to fiddling with the transmitter as Eric came wandering coyly back, the soldering iron held out in front of him at arm's length. 'Gibson Pilot, is it okay for me to come back now?'

'Come on, lad,' the pilot smiled. 'Let's get this thing wrapped up.'

'Are we going to be able to use it tomorrow?' James asked.

'The higher the ground the better,' said Gibson. 'If you and Oli fancied a trek again, the top of the hill will be the best place for it.'

James grinned. 'He'll be thrilled.'

Scanning the opaque sand he could see Abbey nowhere. But it was a long bay, and she did say she wouldn't go near the trees. He checked his watch: almost 2am.

She'd be fine.

41

Porcelain skin.

Thick curls of dark hair.

He liked breaking things, things of beauty, and upon impulse he would act with unnerving efficiency, the prospect presenting itself on a sweet-smelling bed of petals. Her pale skin and slim body suggested eminence in variety, the opportunity unmarrèd by pestilence or noise.

From the trees he watched...

The perfect calm.

The graceful pace of her step against the quietly lapping water.

...as she carefully examined her surroundings, residual emotion flowing from her in waves.

With every footfall, she drew nearer to the tree line, his insistence for silence unmarred.

She would not ruin it for him.

He would not allow that.

Closer to the trees she drew, a heavy and black smudge of burden pressed against her good sense.

A chance peek over her shoulder.

Another silent footstep.

Closer.

Directly in front of him, she stopped.

Anybody could wish for damnation. Anybody could refute it. In this moment, she was of the wishing kind, though she didn't yet know it. Close enough to touch, she admired the view.

He admired it with her.

Sharing was about to become part of her life, the very meaning to her existence. Sharing would be her final gift.

At breaking dawn, the resilient group of "survivors" would wake, the persistent wedge of anxiety driven through the very heart of their hope. It was about to begin. Begin with the translucent skin before him, and the urgent desire to destroy something beautiful.

Porcelain skin.

Thick curls of dark hair.

It was about to begin.

42

At first light, James hit the sunken wreckage with the snorkeling gear. As he'd hoped the morning was calm, the only sounds drifting across the sand coming from the groaning pilot, the blankets drawn up over the flanks of his tent.

With no breeze, the water was as still as it was warm. He waded out wearing only a pair of board shorts, plump fish shooting between his legs. Most of the larger portions of the wreckage had thankfully settled close to shore, the nearest no more than ten feet deep. Parts had broken the water's surface, too large to be engulfed.

Strapping the mask to his face he disappeared beneath the surface in time to spy a plethora of fleeing fish. Only some were spectacular, but all were graceful in the arcing shafts of the immature sun.

Clawing deeper he hauled himself into a long flat section of what looked like the hull, the snagged form of a cadaver startling him as he glided into the luggage compartment. It was a man, one side of his face torn away. Sea creatures too small to know better probed the corpse with curiosity, while some of the larger ones fled into nearby crevices. No luggage remained.

For over an hour he swam between the three main sections of the fallen craft, each one offering little in the way of baggage or medical supplies, but he hadn't struck out completely. Strapped around his shoulder he towed along two pieces of hand luggage and gripped tightly in each hand were two suitcases, courtesy of – according to their respective nametags – a Mr Adams and a Mr Zachariah.

He surfaced to pandemonium.

Something was happening within the camp, a screaming, a bellowing. He could hear his name being called, Abbey's too, a throng of bedlam journeying out across the bay.

Bounding through the shallow water, he crashed panting onto the sand, luggage forgotten, pushing past the incoherent Oli, the inaudible Elaine, and in nothing more than a haze he was by Gibson's side. The man writhed in agony as Anthony and Sebastian attempted to pin him to the sand. Glaring on in confusion were Eric and the silent girl, their faces a similarity of age, despite the years between them.

'Get them out of here!' James screamed.

Senses clicking, Elaine led them away, her hands placed gently over the girl's ears.

'Gibson,' he said firmly. 'It's James.' The pilot's rolling eyes drifted in his direction, any sense of recognition hidden beneath several thick layers of pain. 'I'm going to look at the wound, okay. Try to calm down.'

He lifted the blanket, the wound visibly much the same as he'd last seen it.

'Jesus,' Sebastian gasped.

'Come on, Gibson, stay with me.' Then to the others: 'Does anyone here have any medical knowledge? Anyone... *anything* at all?'

A collage of frightened faces peered back at him.

'Look at him!' Anthony bellowed. 'Do something.'

James hesitated, scanned the beach. Where the hell was Abbey? He needed her! As the world slowed down he closed his eyes, blocked out the screams and the curses. The moment he'd been dreading had arrived. He wasn't prepared for something of this magnitude, neither by expertise nor equipment.

Anthony's pleas had become indistinct, as too had the pilot's screams. He looked to the birth-marked man, watched his slow-moving lips silently bellowing for action, and Gibson, whose own cries should've been bringing down the trees. Sebastian was the only one to remain composed, his eyes limpid pools of calm.

Snapping out of his ethereal state, all five senses returned to him at once like a slap in the face. With somebody else's arm, he reached into the toolbox and withdrew the serrated saw. Somebody else's fingers gripped the handle, and it was somebody else's idea to remove the blanket and position the instrument's teeth above the pilot's wound. He glanced up at the student. 'Oli, hold his legs down. Whatever you do, don't let go.'

'I…I can't, man!' The student's horrified face was sheathed in sweat. 'Not me, no way!'

'Hey!' Anthony snapped. 'Do it.'

'Oli,' James said calmly. 'You need to do this now or the man is going to die, do you understand? Sit on his legs and face away.'

'You can't do this, James. We…we can find drugs, we can -'

'It's too late for drugs! There's only one way to stop the infection, and we need to do it *right now* before he has a heart attack!'

Oli stood fast.

'Look, man!' James roared. 'Take a look. The infection's eating him alive, and we have no way of stopping it. This is what it's all about, right here! This is where you prove to the jocks you're every bit the man they say you're not!'

The sobbing student straddled the pilot's legs and held them steady.

Exhaling heavily, James placed the saw on the sand and tore a strip from the blanket, wrapping it above Gibson's wound as a tourniquet. Retrieving the saw, he replaced the teeth an inch above the wound, an inch below the tourniquet. Sweat was trickling into his eyes.

He looked to Sebastian, then to Anthony, and finally back to Sebastian, their subtle nods of approval jarring him. Then, hesitating no longer…

He thrust forwards, the jagged edge of the saw sinking deep into the pilot's thigh with the first incision. Gibson's screams amplified as the cut opened up, blood erupting from the new wound. Dragging the saw back, he thrust again, this time cutting into the tough sinuous flesh of the thick quad muscle. A third thrust finally found bone, grinding into the femur and rupturing the muscle further. Blood spurted from the next drive, shooting across James's shoulder and splattering his face. The pilot had fallen eerily quiet, eyes rolled back into his head.

More laborious thrusts and the huge bone split in two, Anthony taking the brunt of the spray to the face. Another moment of grinding commenced, before finally the brutal display came to an end. He instructed Oli to release the pilot's legs and threw the dripping saw aside. No longer any need to hold Gibson down, Anthony and Sebastian stood back as James tugged the appendage loose, free-flowing blood squirting from the wound. The pilot was fast losing consciousness.

'Anthony!' he screamed, 'Keep him awake. Don't let him pass out.'

Leaning over the dying man Anthony lightly slapped Gibson's cheek, the man's eyes popping open groggily. Gripping each end of the tourniquet James pulled it taut once more, the blood continuing to flow onto the sand.

'How's he doing, Anthony?'

Anthony peeled up the man's eyelids. 'He's sliding! I can't keep him awake.'

'Keep trying. Oli, get something to put under his thigh. Let's keep the leg up, maybe gravity can help.'

'Wait a minute,' Anthony intervened. 'His pulse has gone.'

'Shit!'

Springing back to Gibson's side, he held his ear to the pilot's chest.

Nothing.

There was nothing.

Interlocking his fingers facedown, he began the artificial beats of CPR, convinced the real ones could be reignited.

'It's not looking good, chief,' said Sebastian.

'One, one-thousand, two, one-thousand, three, one-thousand, yeah thanks, Sebastian.'

Ear to chest.

Still nothing.

'One, one-thousand, two, one-thousand, three, one-thousand, *come on, man!*'

'James...' Oli muttered.

'One, one-thousand, two, one-thousand, three, one-thousand...'

'It's over, James,' Oli said again.

'No! No...One, one-thousand, two, one-thousand, three, one-thousand...'

This time Sebastian placed a steadying hand on James's shoulder. 'Come on, chief...he's gone. Let him be.'

Springing to his feet James turned his back on the scene and ran bloodied fingers through his hair. '*Fuck!*'

He paced back and forth, the enormity of his decision dropping like a lead weight in his stomach. In the spur of the moment he'd made a choice. Drugs may well have turned up in a suitcase tomorrow, a rescue team could've well hit the beach the day after, but right then, right at that moment, there'd been him, several terrified and clueless individuals, and a serrated saw. In the heat of it, he believed he'd taken the correct path. But now...

Turning to the trees, he vomited.

'James?' said Elaine.

Standing behind him was Eric's mother. He hadn't seen her return. Without another word she put her arms around him, hugged him fiercely.

'It's okay, James,' she murmured. 'You're not responsible for everybody here.'

'It's not okay,' he replied quietly. 'It's not okay.'

She continued to hold him tight.

'He trusted me, Elaine.' Releasing her, he took a step back and inspected Gibson's mutilated body, the others splattered in the man's blood. Oli was still crying quietly.

'Are you going to be okay?' Elaine asked.

James eyed his blood-smeared palms. 'What do you think?' he said quietly.

*

In the aftermath of the amateur amputation, Gibson Sommerfield's body had been re-covered with the blanket, the leg roughly pushed back into position.

Anthony had disappeared, probably to get cleaned up. Everybody else stood around looking remorseful and dejected. They had just slipped from eleven to ten, and the notion wasn't lost on anybody.

'You okay, chief?' said Sebastian, sitting down next to James.

'Never better,' James muttered.

'Pretty amazing thing you did back there.'

James snorted. 'Killing a man? Not one of my best achievements.'

'Depends how you look at it,' said the South African. 'I thought it was pretty heroic.'

James didn't react.

'You want to break it to Abbey?' asked Sebastian. 'Or you want me to do it?'

'Abbey? I haven't seen her all morning.' In fact, if he thought hard enough about it, he hadn't seen her since last night when she decided to go for a walk. When Sebastian had no answer he looked to Oli, Elaine. In unison they shrugged, and all he could picture was the light in the trees, the faintest glimmer of their mysterious voyeur.

'Don't look at me,' said Oli. 'I haven't seen her.'

'I haven't either,' said Elaine. 'And I was one of the first up.'

'Shit.' Sebastian's input. 'What you thinking, chief?'

'Look, she can't have gone far,' said Oli. 'We're on a desert island for Christ's sake.'

'It's a big island, darl,' Elaine challenged.

James held up his hand, hushing everyone. 'The island is about five miles around. That's about the size of a small town.'

'Seems to me everybody's blowing this out of proportion,' said Anthony re-emerging from the trees, shirtless, free of blood. 'Do I need to remind everybody just how unpredictable the female of the species is? The woman has probably gone off to the lagoon for a swim.'

'You know this for a fact?' James asked.

'No, sir, I do not. But I *do* know I'm the only one speaking any sense around here. Ya'll have your heads mashed up, convinced Little Miss Wet Dream is in all kinds of trouble, when actually, she's off picking fruit somewhere inland, whistling with the birds.'

James noticed that when Anthony spoke, nobody intervened, like he commanded an unnatural authority nobody knew how to cope with.

'Seems to be a lot of guesswork there,' James questioned.

'Just telling you how it is.'

'How what is?'

Anthony smirked slyly. 'Mark my words, sir, Abbey is going to be just fine.'

'Somebody mention my name?'

Idling from the jungle Abbey appeared, her white bikini at wonderful odds with her tanning skin. Five sets of eyes homed in on their co-survivor, oblivious to their concern, oblivious to the mutilation in her vicinity.

No gloating, no smirking, Anthony turned and walked back into the jungle to do whatever it was he did in there.

'Abbey,' Elaine said, 'thank goodness you're okay. We've been worried sick.'

'I've been exploring,' she revealed. 'I was up early so I just took off. Found that hut you were talking about, James. It's amazing to think…what's that?'

Eyes focused on the outline of Gibson's corpse, Abbey shuddered.

'We tried to save him,' said Elaine softy. 'He was in so much pain, we had to do something.'

Edging forwards Abbey knelt by the pilot and lifted the blanket, a single tear snaking down her cheek. 'Oh my god…'

'We did all we could,' Elaine echoed. 'We had no drugs, no proper means to treat his injuries. It was inevitable. Even Gibson knew it.'

A second tear followed the first. 'He didn't deserve this. My god, what did you people do?'

James stepped forward, his head pounding. 'What would you have suggested, huh? A nice hot bath? Let me make this clear, Abbey, the man was in so much pain he didn't know where he was. He was delirious and he was scared. Who the hell are you to judge what we did?'

'James, I –'

'We had to make a split-second decision. We had no equipment, no anaesthetics, and you stroll in here now and tell us we should've done things differently?'

'James, please –'

'Next one's on you.' Turning his back on the group, he headed to the shore. Nobody tried to stop him. It had been a long day and he'd been awake less than two hours.

Wading out into the spume, James stared out over the horizon. There had to be something out there that could bring this chaotic morning into clarity. Perhaps another climb to the tor's peak could shatter the anarchy. He could take Gibson's transmitter, the man's legacy, try and activate it and build the thing a shelter. Unable to recall seeing it, he wondered where the contraption might be. He began turning over the events of the last twelve hours and continuously, he arrived back at the same answer.

Eric.

43

No more than half an hour after the death of Gibson Sommerfield, two more bombshells rolled through the camp in quick succession. After suspecting Eric of taking the pilot's transmitter – perhaps for safekeeping, perhaps for some other purpose – James had to approach the situation with kid gloves. Eric could be temperamental and so calm would be his middle name, composure his last.

Back on the sand he could make out Sebastian and the girl at the end of the bay, sitting together on the sand. God only knew how that conversation was going. Abbey was sitting alone by Gibson's body, her quiet voice masked by the distance.

Passing Elaine, James asked of her son's whereabouts and she pointed to their tent, the blankets drawn down to obscure the sun. Inside was stifling. Eric was sitting alone at the rear of the tent. Tears lingered in the man's eyes, the remains of the transmitter in his lap.

'Eric,' James muttered, 'what on earth have you done?'

The big man's eyes remained focused on the smashed transmitter. 'Don't shout at me,' he said miserably. 'My dad used to shout at me.'

'I'm not shouting, Eric,' he said quietly, edging further into the tent. 'I'm asking you a question. Why is the radio in pieces?'

'Why does she like that man?'

James shook his head. 'You mean Sebastian?'

'I like her. I want her to be my friend, not his. He's a bad man.'

James sat back, suddenly interested. 'What do you mean he's a bad man?'

Eric failed to explain further.

'Eric, do you think Sebastian is a bad man because he's befriended the girl, or for some other reason?'

'I want her to be *my* friend,' Eric repeated, eyes still glued to the useless radio.

'This is important, Eric,' James urged. 'Has something strange happened with Sebastian you need to tell me about?'

'I don't like him, that's all. Nothing wrong with that. I don't have to like him if I don't want to.'

'No you don't,' James agreed. 'But I need to know why last night the transmitter was almost finished, and now it's in pieces.'

'Gibson pilot's *dead!* said Eric.

'That's not what I asked you.'

'He was my friend and he's *dead*.'

Taking a pausing breath, James said, 'What's going on, Eric?'

'Soon everybody will be dead. No one will find us and we'll all die here.'

'Okay, that's enough. You wouldn't want your mom to hear you talking like that.'

The big man paused consciously and went back to the sabotaged transmitter. He almost looked ashamed having betrayed his mother's faith. Prodding the radio's components, he seemed confused. They needed that transmitter working and there wasn't anybody left alive with the genius to repair it.

'Eric, I'm going to ask you this one time, okay, and I want an honest answer. Did you break Gibson's radio?'

Pausing to contemplate, Eric's face revealed nothing. 'I didn't break it,' he muttered.

'Eric...'

'I said I didn't break it.' No hesitation this time.

'But it's in your lap,' he pressed.

'So? I didn't break it.'

'Then who did?'

Eric wiped his eyes. 'I want to go back outside.'

'First tell me who did this,' James said firmly.

'I don't know.'

'In that case the onus is on you, pal. I don't know why you'd do something like this, but your mother's going to be very disappointed.'

James pushed aside the blanket to leave, bright shafts of sunlight flashing through the tent.

'Wait,' the big man mumbled.

James glanced back.

'I didn't do it. Cross my heart.'

Sitting back down, James said, 'You understand the importance of promises, Eric? If you make one, it's vital you keep it.'

'I do promise.'

'Then who broke the transmitter?'

'I swear I don't know,' he said. 'Last night when Gibson Pilot had nearly finished making the radio, I was falling asleep. He didn't need me no more, so I went to my tent. I was real tired, James.'

'So how did it end up here?'

'When I heard Gibson Pilot screaming before, I ran to him before anybody else. I didn't have good dreams last night. I dreamt I was –'

'Eric...'

'...When I got there, the radio was lying next to him like this. I brought it in here to fix it, but I can't make it work again.'

'Shit,' James murmured.

'I promise, James, it wasn't me. Do you think Gibson Pilot smashed it himself? Because if he did, he smashed it good.'

Nothing seemed coherent. There was no chance Gibson would've stayed up all night building the transmitter and then decide to smash the damn thing. That made no sense at all. Spite wasn't in the pilot's toolbox. He believed Eric too. The man just didn't seem capable of something like this. So who?

He was interrupted by Oli poking his head inside the tent. 'James, you'd better get out here.'

'What is it?'

'Just come take a look.'

'Kind of have something going on in here, Oli, can't it wait?'

'Not really,' said the student. 'We think it's Teri. You'd better come see.'

44

Jogging alongside Oli, flour-soft grains pushing between his toes, James's wish for order seemed a million miles away. How naïve he'd been to assume they could simply set up camp and wait for the cavalry. That too seemed far away now, like the blistering shimmer on the horizon. Oli pointed out the others further up the beach. Sebastian and the girl were standing with Elaine around an unidentifiable spot.

'What is this?' James asked as he neared.

Nobody replied.

Stepping into the circle, he took a closer look.

'Nobody's seen Teri since last night,' said Oli.

'So?' said James casually. 'Wouldn't be the first time she's wandered off.'

Elaine placed a worried hand over her mouth. 'I think this may be my fault. Goodness, I shouldn't've hit her.'

'This has nothing to do with you, Elaine.'

'We assumed she'd gone wandering too,' Oli explained. 'Then we found this.'

Dropping to his haunches, James examined the disturbed sand, a thin trail of dark spots leading from fat to thin. 'What is that?'

'We think it's blood,' Oli confirmed.

'Somebody cut themselves?'

'No,' he said, pointing out the path-like ditch heading to the tree line. It looked as if something had been dragged into the jungle.

'Okay,' he said firmly. 'Here's what we do. If we're assuming the blood belongs to Teri, we also need to assume she's nearby and injured. So we fan out and search. Sebastian, you go to the left, Oli to the right. About a hundred yards over, dip into the trees and head back this way. Elaine, find Abbey, get her over here.'

Elaine hurried away.

'What about you?' asked Oli.

'I'll head straight in from here. I'll see you in there.'

Oli nodded to the girl. 'And her?'

'I don't mind taking her,' Sebastian offered.

James eyed the South African. 'She comes with me.'

He expected the man to protest. Instead he simply walked away in the direction he'd been instructed.

For a moment, Oli burned a hole into the South African's back. When he caught James watching him, he turned and headed sheepishly in the opposite direction.

James offered his hand to the girl who took it without uncertainty. Closer to the trees the ground was less disturbed, as if whatever had been dragged had then been picked up.

Hesitant to step further, the girl began dragging her heels.

'What is it, sweetie?' Images of the banana grove flooded his head. 'You don't need to worry, I'm right here.'

With little more coaxing the girl edged forwards, stepping into the shade of the fronds. 'Atta-girl,' he said, holding her hand tight.

No more than ten yards in, the tracks began to fade. In thirty, there were no signs at all that anybody had ever been there. At one-hundred yards the girl abruptly stopped for the second time, cautiously eying the surrounding foliage with big saucepan eyes. Her features softened dramatically when Oli's voice floated to them from nearby. 'James? Where you at?'

'Over here.'

Through the tangle of greenery Oli stepped into sight. 'Find anything?'

'Nothing, you?'

'Nope,' said the student. 'She's got to be here somewhere. This is the same bay as the camp. If somebody's out there preying on us, he's got some balls snatching one of us this close.'

Sebastian appeared, stepping tactlessly between James and the girl. 'Who's talking about snatching people? You guys losing the plot, or what? We're on a *deserted* island.'

'Then who took Teri?'

'*Nobody* took Teri,' said Sebastian. 'Do I have to remind you, we were all panicking about Abbey no more than an hour ago?'

'Something's not right on this island, I can feel it,' James countered. 'Last night I saw a light in the trees a couple of bays over, and today Teri's missing and Gibson's transmitter has been sabotaged.'

Sebastian's face altered. 'Sabotaged?'

'Busted beyond repair.'

'So Gibson didn't finish it,' said Oli.

James shook his head. 'He finished it. I saw the almost completed thing last night, and it looked a lot healthier than it does now.'

'Eric?' Oli suggested.

'No, I talked with him already. I don't think he did it.'

'So what're you saying?' Sebastian probed. 'You think the two incidents are related?'

Looking from Oli to Sebastian, James murmured, 'I don't know.'

Behind the group the girl waited patiently, ears pricking at the sound of Abbey's voice. Moving back into the gathering, she reached out for James's hand.

*

Abbey examined her fingernails, the blood encrusted beneath them. Earlier, when only she and Elaine had remained, she had insisted they move the pilot's body to beyond the tree line and out of sight. Nobody wanted that kind of human mutilation in their midst, least of all a confused twelve year old girl. He'd been heavy, but between them they'd managed it – in two goes.

From the trees, James emerged hand-in-hand with the girl. Unexpectedly she stayed by James's side instead of rushing to her. Close behind was Sebastian and Oli, both looking pissed off.

'Find anything?' she asked.

'Nothing.'

'What do you mean nothing?'

'I mean nothing, *nada*, zip!'

'Apart from this?' Abbey muttered, toeing the spots on the sand. 'So we should expand the search, shouldn't we? A girl doesn't just vanish, and it's crazy to assume she's okay just because we can't find her in the immediate area.'

'The size of the job hasn't altered. This island is a big place.'

'So what! If Teri is out there, scared and alone, she's going to be praying somebody comes for her. We owe her that much.'

'You think we owe her something?' said Sebastian. 'How about recalling what the freak is like before we get all sentimental.'

'How about exercising a little compassion!'

James intervened. 'Look, if somebody's taken her, they're going to hide her. She could be anywhere by now.'

'So that's it then,' said Abbey, 'you're just going to abandon the poor girl? What if it were you out there, James, or you Oli?'

'I'm not suggesting we should forget about Teri. I'm just saying it's no good blundering into the jungle and expecting to find her. We need a search plan.'

'By which time she could be dead.'

James sighed in frustration. 'I'm just trying to be realistic, Abbey.'

'Realistic?'

'Yes, realistic! Jesus, I am sick of the "I'm Abigail and I know best" routine. Maybe, just maybe, you could have a tiny bit of faith in me!'

'Is that what you expect, all these people to have faith in you, James? You snap your fingers and they jump to it, is that it? Well, come on then, give us something to believe in. Tell us what we should be doing!'

'We should be talking about Teri and formulating a search plan, not bickering like children. We need to talk about *how* to look for her, who goes with who, and make sure we don't cover the same ground. As for the faith, I'm not a robot, I make mistakes just like anybody else, but at least I'm *trying, Goddamnit*!'

Elaine winced.

Abbey paused. Then, 'No, it'll be too late by then. We move now.'

James began laughing at nothing and fell on to the sand. The girl sat down with him. 'My God, this is insane. She's probably gone for a walk.'

Abbey shook her head. 'And the blood?'

'She cut her foot on a rock,' he suggested. 'It happens.'

'Either way, I'm going to grab some provisions and circle the island. If she's anywhere near the coastline, you'll still be talking about it by the time I find her.'

'No, we stick together,' James said.

Abbey noticed the girl slip her hand into James's. 'Why? Nothing's amiss, remember?'

'You know what, Abbey, go for it,' he ceded. 'You're twisting my words to suit yourself.'

'I'm a woman, I'm good at that. And yes, I'm going whether you like it or not.'

She eyed James's face, expecting a sharp reply. Instead, he simply said, 'I think we should stick together, I'm just going to say that. If you're adamant about this, make sure you take plenty of water and try to be back before dark, that's all I ask.'

'Fine.'

He turned to the girl and placed a hand on her cheek. 'Come on, sweetie, let's get you something to eat.' Climbing to his feet he walked towards the tents, shoulders slumped in defeat. The girl hurried after him.

*

Last night's campfire smoldered, kicking thin grey smoke into the air. Next to it was the illusive Sol reading a book, American flag bandana pressing down his scraggly blonde locks.

It was unusual for him to be in the camp this time in the day, James noted. Perhaps he was getting lonely.

The girl disappeared into Eric's tent, her presence undoubtedly welcome. Eric's fixation with the girl's friendship was beginning to outweigh Sebastian's, which James was almost thankful for.

Sitting across the fire, James eyed the Australian silently through the smoke. He was angry with Abbey, but had no clear right to be. There was nothing official about his leadership here, she didn't have to listen to him. But he wasn't making up guidelines for the good of his health, and he wasn't ignoring suggestions from the others either. He was trying to do the right thing, and whether or not that meant a little faith had to be thrown his way, he didn't think it was too much to ask.

'You alright?' he asked Sol.

The standard grunt, eyes rooted to the book.

'Busy?'

'What's it look like, dude?'

'I don't know, Sol,' he sighed. 'I guess people have forgotten how to converse around here…'

Sol shrugged.

'So I need your help with something,' James added. Sol stared as if he'd just asked him to swim for help. 'You game?'

'Depends.'

'On?'

'On the game.'

Headache returning, James pinched the bridge of his nose. 'We need to bury Gibson. I'd rather not do it alone.'

Expecting the Australian to refuse, he climbed doggedly to his feet. 'Okay, let's go. Then I suppose I might get some peace. Paradise my arse! Get me back to Bell's Beach.'

Gibson waited just beyond the tree line, detached limb akimbo. He looked dismal, even pathetic. It took only a few minutes to locate a suitable ditch to inter the man, and only a few more to lower him gently in and cover him with bracken and shale. When they were done there was no trace of the pilot, no evidence there was even a body four feet beneath them.

Kneeling next to the burial site, Sol wheezed, 'We done?'

'You think maybe one of us should say a prayer or something?' James suggested.

'Knock yourself out, dude, if you believe in all that.'

'It just seems respectful, you know. Only I don't really know any. Do you?'

Sol smirked. 'Oh yeah, dozens. I know the Bible backwards.'

'Point taken. A minute's silence?'

A noiselessness surrounded them. Sol appeared quite tranquil sitting next to Gibson's resting place. Maybe he just liked the quiet. For more than the agreed minute the two survivors maintained their silence, their unshared reasons no doubt varying. When respects were paid and platitudes were whispered, James slipped peacefully away leaving Sol to his peculiar resolution.

Back in the camp Anthony was prodding the fire, a dented steel tray of fish lying by his side. Abbey was talking animatedly to him, about what, James could only guess; the conversation looked remarkably one-sided. So many things seemed to be going awry. Teri's disappearance, the smashed transmitter, the rift developing between himself and Abbey; it felt like the whole thing was coming down around them. Strange happenings were occurring within the camp, bizarre lights in the trees. It was beginning to feel like a torrent of burden was weighing down upon him, pressing doggedly against his better judgement. He glanced solemnly across the camp.

Gradually, despair was taking over.

45

The terrain had become unfamiliar, though it hadn't varied much from the ground already covered. Each new bay presented itself in different length or width. Some were harder to reach than others, some hardly bays at all, but in essence they were just more sand, more trees and water.

Walking alongside Abbey was Anthony. He hadn't uttered a word since agreeing to come along, not even so much as a "watch your step." She got the impression chivalry was something Anthony avoided rather than being incapable of. He had grown up with an abused sister, an abusive father, and a birthmark buying up permanent real estate upon his face; all things most others lived without, never had to cope with. Yet the man was still standing. She figured that had to be worth something.

Climbing down onto what she assumed to be the northernmost shore, Abbey waited as her companion jumped down after her. As his feet hit the sand he continued walking, not a word in her direction. So far there had been no sign of Teri, not a shred of evidence to suggest the tattooed girl had even been this far. Abbey began to curse her own hot head. What if James had been right? What if Teri had never strayed far from the camp and they'd found her already. Tail between her legs came to mind.

'you don't talk much do you?' said Abbey at last. 'Nothing wrong with that, not much of a talker myself.' Anthony just blinked. 'But I'll just...think aloud if you don't mind. Helps me get my bearings.'

He glanced at her impatiently, his eyes saying clearly, "If you must."

'You're not the only one with a messed up childhood, you know,' she told him. 'I grew up in foster care, made new brothers and sisters at a late age, though

I was fortunate enough to be placed with a good family. But it wasn't until I met Edward that my life began properly. We were college sweethearts. Right from the outset I knew he was going to be the one I'd marry. Before him I'd been trying to tick the boxes of what I thought I needed in a man, but with Edward there were no boxes to tick. He was just...Edward.'

No reaction from Anthony. Was he listening? Was he tuning her out?

'I would've married him after our first date, you know. I've never told anybody that. But he always joked he wouldn't marry me until he could afford to divorce me, the bastard. I suppose in a lot of ways, we were made for each other. I'm not exactly a picnic to live with, either. But when Edward's dad died a couple of years ago I promised I'd always be there for him. It was like an unofficial renewal of our wedding vows. He already knew it, but I could see what it meant to him to hear the words aloud.'

'Dying is easy,' Anthony said quietly. 'Living is the hard part.'

Abbey stopped dead in the sand.

Anthony paused and turned. 'What happened to your real parents?'

'What do you mean dying is easy?'

'What happened to your real parents?' he said again.

Unable to explain why, she wanted to respond to Anthony's insistence. Was it excitement, she wondered, sharing things with a stranger? 'They were murdered,' she mumbled.

'Speak up,' he said sharply.

'I said they were *murdered!*'

No reaction. 'How?'

'I was ten years old when it happened,' she began solemnly. 'Don't remember much. My parents used to leave me alone all the time, go on holidays and business trips. One day they never came back. They later turned up in a slum in south east London with their hearts missing…'

'Don't stop.'

'I was home when the killer visited our flat. He had this thing about returning the hearts he'd taken. I was hiding in the living room. He didn't know I was there, not at first, but on his way out the door he stopped. Just stopped and looked straight at me. I wasn't scared. A stranger was standing in my home no more than ten feet from me, pitch black, but he didn't frighten me.'

They began walking again.

'For years I tried to rationalise it. I was ten years old, I should've been terrified. Finally I realised, the man before me was responsible for taking away my parents, and I was…*grateful.* I think maybe I knew all along, I just didn't want to admit it. I mean, what kind of monster would that have made me, worse than my parents? But that feeling of warmth that spread through me was the feeling of freedom. I know that now. I'd been freed by this dark man, this stranger, and I couldn't ever remember feeling happier, more liberated.'

'Then what happened?' said Anthony.

'I got on with my life,' she said simply.

Approaching the end of the bay they fell back into their ponderous silence. Anthony made no attempt to reciprocate with tales of his own, nor did he probe Abbey's stories further. Instead he led the way to the top of the next rocky partition, pausing at the peak. At the base of the rocks, splitting them from the sand was a large crevasse, twelve feet across and seemingly bottomless. 'You've got to be kidding,' Abbey gasped. 'What's caused that?'

'Evolution,' Anthony replied quietly.

Stepping down as far as she could, she peered over the edge, a sight propelling her backwards. 'Jesus, Anthony, there's a man down there!'

She moved closer to the edge and poked her head over the side. Twenty feet down, sitting on a shelf or rock protruding from the face of the east wall, was the human skeleton of a man, scraps of fabric remaining to cover his modesty.

'Who do you suppose he is?' she probed.

'One way to find out. I'll lower you down to take a look.'

Abbey stepped back from the edge. 'You're bloody kidding! I'm not going down there.'

Anthony picked at his teeth with a twig and flicked it over the edge. 'You faced your parents' killer without fear. This is a walk in the park by comparison.'

'You don't get to pull that one, Anthony. I didn't tell you those things for you to use against me.'

'Are you telling me you don't want to do this?'

'Don't try and twist thi –'

'Are you telling me you don't want to do this?' he said again.

She hesitated. Something about the danger of it all did appeal, she couldn't deny that, but the simplicity of circling the chasm's edge and forgetting about it appealed immensely too.

'What's it going to be?' he said. 'Since that day when you were ten years old, there's been something inside you, hasn't there? A burning *need* to understand that feeling you can't turn off. I see it in your eyes. Something's been amiss all your life and you're dying to learn what it is. That chasm may not have the answers, but the closer you are to death, the closer you are to understanding.'

Never in her life had anybody spoken to her like Anthony. He understood her, knew how she'd suffered inextricably behind the facade of her perfect existence.

She stepped back from the edge and looked into Anthony's perplexing eyes. 'We're going to need some rope then.'

*

Coiled beneath her rump, the tree vines dug into her skin as Anthony lowered her down. In the absence of rope, the sturdy vines were more than adequate to support her weight. Up top, Anthony had tied the vines off against the trunk of a palm tree, the slack coiled at his feet.

Inch-by-inch she descended into the tapering crevasse. The lower she went the damper it became, the smell of saltwater filling her nostrils. Her feet touched down on the shelf without incident.

Leaning against the wall of the chasm, the man had died on his back. Arm raised, he was propped against a protruding boulder, tibia bent out at an odd angle. Edging closer, she guessed he would've been tall, maybe six feet, with narrow shoulders and a sloping chest. Around his neck hung a medallion, stubbornly clinging to him, surviving countless tropical storms.

Anthony was peering down.

'He's wearing a medallion,' she revealed. 'Same man as in James's photo, I'm certain. I reckon we have our hut builder. Looks like his leg's broken. If he fell down here, no way he could've climbed back out. He would've died of dehydration long before his leg healed.'

'Anything else?' Anthony called down.

She took a step back. Above the dead man's head was an inscription carved into the rock, etched deeply to last. She leaned closer and squinted: *Jerry Benton – 1925.*

'Anthony, this guy's been here for eighty...eighty-six years!'

She looked up. No birthmark loomed over her. Anthony had slipped out of view.

'Hey!' she called. 'I'm done down here, pull me up.'

Nothing.

'Anthony! This is not funny, get me out of here.'

Then came the jabbing moment of despair as she watched the vine sail past her, untied and pitched into the chasm. Hurriedly she stepped out of the makeshift harness before the weight propelled her forwards.

'*Anthony!*' she cried.

She hugged the wall, eyed Jerry Benton's skeleton, and suddenly had grim thoughts of her own body found here in ninety years by some other poor fool who braved the descent.

Jerry Benton's lifeless skull seemed to be smiling.

'*Anthony!*'

*

The light was failing and Abbey had not returned. James's mind began wandering into patches of shadow. They should've been back by now.

Fire roaring, Sebastian was preparing the fish he'd caught earlier in the spill, offering his catch to others. It was a welcome change from fruit.

Everybody bar Sol and Teri were accounted for, and so his concern was not unjust; Abbey and Anthony had been gone too long.

'Chief,' Sebastian called. 'You want some of this?'

James waved in acknowledgment as he panned the coast, the moon already high in the sky. When the light failed entirely, the situation would become a whole other entity. He would no longer be able to sit on his hands.

And then he heard his name being called, faint and indistinct. It was Abbey's voice, he was certain.

James!

The second call was clearer, some of the others turning their heads.

He narrowed his eyes to the west.

'Where are you?' he uttered to himself.

James!

There she was, stumbling over the rocky panhandle, Anthony draped over her.

'Oli!' yelled James. 'Eric!'

He sprinted towards them, covering the bay in seconds. Standing before the bedraggled duo, he paused in awe. Abbey looked disorientated, confused, her eyes harbouring bloodshot panic.

'What happened?'

'Take him!' she cried.

'Abbey, what happened?'

'*Just take him*!'

As James shouldered the burden of Anthony, Abbey crashed to the sand. Anthony looked barely conscious, his hair matted with dried blood.

As Oli and Eric arrived on the scene, James said, 'Eric, take Anthony. Carry him back to the camp and lay him down in Gibson's tent.'

Without question, the big man hoisted Anthony over his shoulder.

'Oli,' James said, 'help me with Abbey.'

She waved them away. 'I'm not injured, just exhausted. Had him over my shoulder for more than two miles.'

'What happened out there?' Oli cried. 'Were you attacked?'

She closed her eyes, fell onto her back. 'We're in trouble,' she gasped. 'We need to get off this island.'

*

For over an hour Abbey sat with James and Elaine, the others out of earshot, and filled them in as best she could. When she brought up the discovery of Jerry

Benton's skeleton, James fished the photograph from his shorts and ran his thumb over the image.

'Unbelievable,' he murmured. 'He's still here.'

'Been here since 1925. He carved it into the rock face.'

James shook his head in astonishment. 'What happened after that?'

'Anthony vanished,' she replied, her head shaking. 'I screamed for him to pull me up but he didn't answer. Next thing I knew, the vine was being thrown into the chasm. Whoever threw it over intended to keep me down there.'

'Did you see anybody?' said Elaine.

'Nobody. It was weird.'

'So how did you get out if *this* guy never managed it?' said James tapping the picture.

'Jerry Benton was injured, broken leg,' she revealed. 'The climb wasn't so tough. If Jerry had been able-bodied he wouldn't have died on that shelf. When I reached the top I found Anthony face down in a pool of his own blood. He can't remember what happened, just remembers hitting the deck, a scuffle of feet around him, and then lights out.'

Elaine appeared anxious. 'What does this mean?'

James eyed the picture.

'Come on, guys,' Abbey said resignedly. 'Get your heads out of the sand. It's obvious what's going on here, isn't it? This island isn't as deserted as we thought.'

'Whoa, that's a bit of a jump, Abbey!' James challenged. 'What about Sol, what about Teri, they're both roaming around out there.'

'They didn't do this. We know enough about Sol and Teri to rule them out.'

'What do you *know*? You met them three days ago.'

'I know enough. Sol's a deadhead and Teri's twenty-one years old and angry. Neither of them is insane.'

'What about fresh footprints? Another camp, anything like that?'

'No, nothing.'

In the subtle orange hue, Elaine fixed Abbey with a concentrated stare. Then she shifted her gaze to James. She seemed fidgety, nervous.

'Elaine, you okay?'

Elaine shook her head and glanced warily over her shoulder.

'We're alone, Elaine. What is it?'

'There's something I have to tell you,' she revealed quietly. 'I think I know what happened to Teri.'

A pause.

'Elaine,' said Abbey, 'I would really appreciate you telling me this information came to light *after* I left.'

Elaine continued to scan the sand, doggedly refusing to meet Abbey's eyes.

'*Great*,' Abbey uttered. 'Fantastic.'

'Look, all I had to go on was Eric's word. I honestly didn't think it was relevant. I've raised him for forty-six years and you just kind of get used to his strange stories. Most of the time they're nothing more than adaptations of something he's seen on TV.'

'What is actually wrong with Eric, Elaine?' James asked.

Glancing up warily, Elaine said, 'When I met Eric's father, Graham, he was a good man. Strong-willed, handsome, motivated. He was involved in rugby in a big way, a local hero in our community. It had been his dream since childhood to one day play for the All Blacks, and when he turned twenty, things started happening for him. He was playing for a lower league club when he was scouted by the Wellington Hurricanes, but during his second week of training, his left knee was bent ninety degrees the wrong way. After that he was never able to play in competition again.'

Further along the sand, Eric was laughing at something Oli had said.

'Predictably Graham took to the bottle. He became abusive and brutish, but somewhere along the way I fell pregnant with Eric. I should've seen it coming, but by then I was so blinded and living in fear that I ran out of bargaining chips.

'Eric was born a perfectly healthy child, and he remained that way until he was twelve. He loved to read, spent most of his time in the library. God knows, he was a smart kid. Graham didn't like that, not one bit.'

Sebastian called out a final request for fish.

'What happened after that?' said James.

'Graham could see his son growing big and would one day rival, if not surpass him, in size. So he got it into his head that Eric should be playing rugby. There was a vicarious undercurrent to what was happening, I saw it a mile off, and it didn't take long to escalate into a full-blown obsession. But Eric wasn't sporty in the least. All he wanted to do was read. One day his father came home drunk and angry. I was out at the store, was literally gone for thirty minutes, and when I got home I found Eric battered and beaten and lying in his own blood at the foot of the stairs.'

'My God,' Abbey murmured.

'Graham had finally cracked. Eric would never become the man Graham wanted him to be, the man *he* never was, and he couldn't handle it. As unpredictable as Graham had become, never in my wildest dreams did I think he could raise a hand to his son. Eric never thought about much else again after that day.'

A respectful silence hung in the air.

'Eric was hospitalized,' Elaine went on. 'Repeated blunt-force trauma to the head. He was unconscious for four days. When he woke up…well, you see the result. Eric is a seven or eight year old boy trapped in the body of a forty-six year old man.'

'What became of Graham?'

'Sentenced to three years for ABH and assault. We never saw him again. The second he was behind bars we moved to Auckland discreetly. Eric still asks now where his dad is. He has no memory of the attack, and I pray to God every day for that small mercy.'

In the awkward silence, Abbey uttered, 'I'm so sorry, Elaine.'

'It could have been worse, darl,' she said smiling weakly. 'Eric is alive and I still have my boy. We are truly blessed. Of all the times God has looked out for us, I don't find it surprising we survived the crash. It was simply another miracle granted to us, God correcting wrongs done.'

'I don't mean to sound insensitive,' James cut in, 'but we've deviated. You were telling us about Teri.'

Elaine lowered her voice further. 'Eric told me something. And now I know it's not just one of his stories, he's telling the truth.'

'How do you know?'

'I just do,' she insisted. 'Mother's intuition. Eric believes he saw somebody at the airport wearing handcuffs.'

Abbey stiffened. 'He was trying to tell me something too, back in the terminal. He said he'd seen beneath the man's jacket. I didn't pay attention.'

Elaine looked up. 'Now he's saying he saw the same man on the plane. He was with a second man, an escort of some kind.'

'It's possible, James mused. 'A convict being transferred on a commercial jet to save taxpayer's money.'

Face tightening, Elaine leaned forwards. 'An hour ago, Eric told me the cuffed man is here.'

James massaged his temples. 'And there's the flaw. If the man was in cuffs, he still would be. How would he get them off?'

'I'm one-hundred percent about this, James,' she defended. 'Whoever was wearing those handcuffs is one of the remaining ten.'

'Have you not asked your son who he saw?' Abbey asked.

Elaine nodded. 'He won't tell me. But I'm working on it.'

46

The scream pierced the night and jolted Abbey awake. The girl lay beside her, snoring softly. Had she imagined it, she wondered? Had she dreamt it? Tentatively she lay back down and closed her eyes.

The second scream was louder, a shrill and desolate note. Poking her head from the tent, she scanned the beach. Not a soul in sight. Furtively she moved from tent to tent, certain the scream had come from further afield. Already missing were Teri and Sol, and now the tent shared by Sebastian and Oli stood vacant too, the blankets drawn. She found James where she expected him to be, fast asleep on his front.

Yelping, Abbey spun sharply as her shoulder was grabbed from behind. Inundated in the moon's backdrop, Anthony stood before her, palms defensively forward. 'It's me!'

'What do you think you're doing?' she whispered. 'You scared the shit out of me.'

'You woke me when you invaded my privacy.'

'Invaded your privacy?' she whispered angrily. 'I carted your unconscious arse halfway round the island earlier, how about a bit of gratitude?'

Anthony turned away and scanned the trees. Any notion of his injury seemed to be forgotten.

'Did you hear the screams?' she asked.

A single nod.

'What do you suppose we should do?'

Anthony began gliding silently towards the trees, his face unmarred by fascination or fear. Abbey nipped at his heels. 'Maybe we should wake James.' When she received no answer, she said, 'Do we have a torch?'

'Leave it,' Anthony instructed.

In amongst the trees she could see only black. No sinister eyes shone back, but she struggled to shake the sensation of being watched. Going in there without a torch seemed like insanity.

The first dabs of perspiration appeared on her brow as she stepped into the trees. She wiped them away. As her eyes adjusted, the terrain became more accessible. Outlines of trees presented themselves, and in patches the moonlight broke through their leafy ceiling showing them a path. They trod carefully in no particular direction.

Shrieking through the trees, the fresh scream turned her blood to ice. Anthony glared at her, unsmiling, birthmark sitting ominously in shadow. 'This way,' he whispered.

Following Anthony's nose, the pair descended upon a small clearing blanched in moonlight. Grabbing her wrist he stopped her from going further, huddling down next to her by a series of misplaced boulders.

'What is it?' she uttered.

He silenced her with a hand gesture and pointed across the clearing. Two unidentifiable people were out there, silhouettes against the moon's backdrop. Though only a mere twenty yards across the clearing, it was obvious what was happening. One figure was kneeling before the other, breathing heavily, soft gurgling sounds caught in the throat. The second figure was pacing the ground deliberately, tauntingly.

Abbey jumped as Anthony spoke, almost forgetting she wasn't alone. 'We should go,' he whispered calmly.

'I think that's Elaine,' Abbey murmured. 'We can't leave her.'

'We should *go*,' he insisted.

'*No!*' she said firmly. 'We need to see this.'

Falling silent, Anthony seemed to appease her and rested against the boulder. The pacing silhouette continued to bide his time until God only knew what, the kneeling figure shuddering groggily.

'Seen enough?' Anthony whispered.

Abbey hauled herself up and edged around the boulder for a better angle. As she pushed from the rock a clatter of stones fell away, rolled along the side of the boulder and came to rest in the undergrowth. Anthony closed his eyes in resignation as the pacing silhouette's glinting eyes snapping in their direction.

She held her breath. The figure took a few paces their way, head cocked. Then he turned and walked steadily back to the kneeler.

Abbey couldn't have anticipated what came next; nothing on earth could've prepared her. Without hesitation the pacer drew a blade from somewhere, looked directly at the cluster of boulders, and jammed it into the kneeler's throat, twisting. The churning gurgle carried across the clearing as the blade was withdrawn. The body crumpled to the floor.

Abbey held a hand to her mouth, stifling the scream. She turned to find Anthony. He was gone.

Back in the clearing the knife-wielding silhouette was walking towards her, dripping blade an extension of his arm. Unconcerned for Anthony, she turned and fled. Trees came at her, disappeared behind. Intact branches swung for her head, the fallen kind grabbing at her feet. Over her shoulder was forbidden territory. Only once did she tumble into the undergrowth, her left knee taking the brunt of the impact. Unhindered further, she crashed onto the beach by the plane's nose, minutes from the camp. Staying by the water's edge she sprinted across the sand, the dying embers of the campfire flickering a million miles away.

Fifty yards from the camp.

Forty.

Startling her, Anthony pushed through the tree line unharmed. 'Wait, Abbey,' he grunted, catching her around the midriff. 'It's okay, it's me... *it's Anthony.*'

For a moment she forgot where she was. Tugging at his shirt, she freed herself from his grasp and spun in the sand disorientated. Finally, she screamed.

*

'Abbey, I love my sleep, so for Christ's sake tell me what's happening!'

Stepping in for the distraught Abbey, Anthony said clearly, 'We don't know what we saw.'

'What!' Abbey wheezed. 'James, you need to listen to me, okay. Something is happening here. I don't know what, but we're in serious danger!'

'It was dark,' Anthony interrupted. 'We could've seen anything.'

Abbey's face dropped. 'What're you saying? You were right there, you saw what I saw.'

With the slightest movement of his head, Anthony picked out Eric who had joined the affray. James spotted the gesture. 'I'm just saying, it was dark, our minds were probably playing tricks.'

'I think what Anthony's trying to say,' James cut in, 'is there's probably a more appropriate time to discuss this.'

'No…*no*!' gasped Abbey, close to delirium. 'We talk about this now. Everybody needs to hear this. You too Eric.'

Unconvinced by his own judgement, James ceded. 'Fine,' he muttered. 'Go ahead, tell us what happened.'

Everybody was awake now, absorbing the remaining heat from the dying fire. The girl stared into the flames in nonchalance, Oli ghostly pale. The student looked sick.

'I was woken by a scream,' Abbey mouthed, 'scared the shit out of me. When I checked the tents, a handful of people were missing.'

'My mum's not in our tent,' said Eric, confused.

'Anthony was awake too,' she went on. 'So we decided to take a look.'

'I thought Anthony was injured,' James observed.

'Still am,' the scarred man said.

Turning back to Abbey, James said, 'Why didn't you wake me?'

'We don't need you for everything,' Anthony interrupted. 'In fact we don't need you at all.'

James narrowed his eyes in confusion. 'Someone better tell me what's going on. Enough games.'

'We…' she paused, anxious expressions waiting eagerly.

'Abbey?'

'We saw somebody being murdered.'

An ethereal quiet descended upon the camp.

'You…you what?'

Abbey reached for her grazed knee, brushed away the stubborn dirt.

'You both saw this?'

'He saw it too,' she answered for Anthony.

'Who?' James asked incredulously. 'Who did you see being murdered?'

'It was too dark,' she uttered. 'But he knew we were there, James. He knew he was being watched. It was almost like he wanted us to see!'

James planted himself down on the sand. He believed Abbey, no question. Was this the convict Elaine had told them about? Had she been punished for divulging? He glanced from frightened face to frightened face. More questions. No answers.

Spying movement along the sand, unified heads turned to see Sol wandering shirtless into the camp. He stopped flat when he found the others still awake. James bore down on him as he walked amongst them. 'Where've you been, Sol?' he began coldly. 'And no more of this "I like being alone" bullshit, that's not good enough.'

Away from the moonlight, he swore the Australian smirked. 'That would be none of your fucking business, dude.'

'Well let's just say that the escalation of events has made it my business.'

Sol ran a hand through his matted locks, fingers snagging in the knots. 'You're barking up the wrong piss-pole, people. Whatever's going on here, you self-destructive freaks figure it out for yourselves. Leave me out of it.'

'Mum?' Eric called out suddenly, pathetically.

'When I first saw you that morning, Sol, you were pilfering luggage. What were you looking for?'

'I told you, man,' he said defensively. 'Just needed my stuff.'

'That's not going to cut it,' Abbey growled. 'You were searching for something specific.'

'Go fuck yourself.'

Without warning Anthony went for the Australian, wrestling him to the ground. Sol writhed beneath him, squirmed, cried out as a jab landed. Anthony was heavier, tougher, and he battered Sol mercilessly, emotionlessly. Nobody interjected.

'You can make him stop, Sol,' said James. 'You can make this go away.'

A sickening crack echoed along the bay as Sol took a flattened fist to the jaw.

Abbey stepped in. 'Isn't this a little extreme?'

The camp watched hypnotically as Anthony climbed to his feet and swung a vicious kick to the Australian's ribs, another crack signifying a second breaking bone.

'*James*!' Abbey cried. 'Stop this. Whoever's out there, this is what he wants.'

Sol rolled into a fetal shape, the sand absorbing his wracking sobs. 'Okay!' he screamed. 'Stop, please. I'll tell you, *I'll tell you*!'

Stepping back, Anthony gasped heavily and turned his back on the group. James watched him walk past Eric and disappear into the shadows along the bay.

Holding his ribs, Sol climbed tentatively to his knees. 'You guys are so *fucking* warped, do you even know who you are anymore?'

James grabbed his hair and yanked. '*Where do you go, Sol?*'

'I get high, *okay*!'

James wasn't sure he'd heard right. 'High?'

'*Yes*,' Sol cried. 'That's it. *Fuck*, dude!'

Releasing the man's hair, he peered down wearily at the Australian.

'Where do you get drugs out here?' Abbey interrupted. 'Unless…'

Sol looked nervously from face to face.

'You're a smuggler,' James confirmed.

Massaging his tender jaw, Sol said, 'Not quite. I mean I was smuggling, this time. But it was only a one-off.'

'That's why you were looking for your case.'

'What were you smuggling,' Abbey asked.

Sol sniffled. 'Just Class C's.'

'Class C's?'

'The chronic… *weed*, dude! Whacky baccy, skunk, resin, pot, draw, *marijuana*. Look, I'm a dealer back home, okay. A couple of months ago, a friend of mine comes to me with a proposition. He knows some guy in Durban with this real killer stuff, but it's only a one time offer. All I've to do is get from South Africa to Australia. I got the stuff dirt cheap, no way I could've passed it up!'

'Great,' she murmured. 'A scumbag drug dealer.'

'Not at all, what do you take me for? I sell to my mates and surfers on Bell's Beach, and never anything harder than weed.'

'Oh, you're a regular saint.'

'You arseholes can scoff all you like, but that's all I've been doing, smoking my own product. It takes the edge off. You don't believe me, that's your business. Like I give a fuck.'

'What does this prove?' Abbey said firmly. 'He could be getting high and killing people, it's possible to do both.'

'*Killing people*!' Sol gasped. 'Just what the fuck are you people into here?'

James crouched. 'Somebody was murdered tonight, Sol. Teri is still missing and you keep vanishing. Do you see our dilemma?'

Sol glanced around looking for support where there was none. 'Why are you hassling me?' he moaned. 'Where's that big South African, I don't see him anywhere. Go and bother that guy.'

As if on cue Sebastian came striding along the beach, buried beneath the tattered grey pinstripe he'd refused to change. Around the fire, the girl continued to appear vacant and Oli had turned a pale shade of green, like he'd eaten something he shouldn't have.

'Where's my *mum*?' Eric said more urgently.

'Sebastian,' James began,' you need to tell us where you've been.'

Sebastian blinked in confusion. 'For a walk,' he said simply.

'Convenient,' Abbey grumbled. 'Not much of a cover story.'

'Why would I need a cover story?'

James said, 'Just tell us where you've been, Sebastian.'

'Nobody's kicking the shit out of this prick, I notice,' Sol moaned. 'Why don't you let the freak loose on this one, huh?'

'Let the freak loose?' Sebastian echoed. 'What is it you suppose I've done?'

Sol climbed gingerly to his feet massaging his side. 'I've just been given a kicking for smoking some weed, man, no reason you should get off scot-free.'

Sebastian looked bewildered. 'Free from what exactly?'

'Does that matter?' Sol moaned. 'Didn't for me!'

'You think you frighten me?' Sebastian said calmly, convincingly. 'Any of you, you think you can intimidate me? I've seen things you could never imagine.'

'Is that right, Sebastian?' James challenged. 'Like what?'

Sebastian swallowed hard. 'The kind of things no one should ever have to see.'

'A walk along the beach, Sebastian?' said Abbey. 'You can't do better than that?'

'I don't have to. You asked me where I've been, I told you.'

'For two hours?'

'Two and a half actually. Couldn't sleep.'

The story was weak, there was no denying that, but that didn't make it untrue. Another brutal headache was brewing between James's eyes.

'Somebody want to tell me what I'm accused of? Last I checked, walking along a beach isn't a crime.'

'Oh no?' Anthony had reappeared and moved stealthily back amongst them. 'And how about murder?'

Sebastian's eyes widened, his gaze wandering carefully.

'Now doesn't that look like a guilty face?' said Anthony.

Sebastian failed to defend himself. Instead he stood silently, apprehensively.

'Nothing to say?' Anthony urged.

James didn't know who that question was aimed at.

The decreased number of survivors matched the South African's quiet. Their spirit had taken a hit and nobody seemed to know what to do next. Gradually, quietly, the assembly began to disband, and like the Sebastian interrogation, the crackling fire was abandoned.

James noticed Abbey walk to the water's edge, her shoulders visibly shuddering. He went to her, wrapped her in his arms. She hugged back fiercely. For what seemed like an eternity they stood like this, unmoving, James whispering assurances, Abbey accepting them, not believing them. Further up the beach, Eric had vanished.

47

The fire blazed. Taking solace in the heat, James took healthy gulps from a bottle of Jack Daniels, his head growing muffled and fuzzy. There were no clouds, only a star-studded sky.

Descending into intoxication, his body relaxed for the first time in days. Gibson had been wrong, he was not the hope these people needed, he was not their strength. He was lucky if any of them listened to him at all.

While the rest of the survivors slept, he'd opted to take watch for what remained of the night. Without a distraction he could not switch off, so many blank spaces where solutions should fit perfectly. He believed Sol's drug story, and to a degree he believed Sebastian. His own morality was not unstained either. Nobody here really knew him, nor did they need to.

Movement in the camp stirred his groggy interest; somebody was awake.

'Is this what constitutes keeping watch?' Abbey yawned. She smoothed a patch in the sand and took a seat. 'Getting wasted on Duty-Free and counting stars?'

'A drink seemed appropriate,' he replied wryly, handing over the bottle.

He watched the graceful arc of Abbey's throat as she raised the bottle to her lips and took several long burning swallows. He didn't avert his gaze until she wiped her mouth and handed the bottle back.

'Can't sleep?' he asked.

She shook her head slowly. 'I keep capturing the scene over and over. Elaine just kneeling there, defenceless. Oh, James, the way she fell. What kind of a person does it take to do something like that to another human being?'

'It wasn't your fault, Abbey,' he assured her gently. 'I don't know why Elaine was out there so late, but she must've had her reasons. If somebody was lying in wait, she wouldn't've stood a chance.'

Abbey smiled weakly.

'That kind of detachment,' James went on, 'that level of blankness, he's probably killed so many times it no longer has any meaning for him. It's how some soldiers turn in the middle of a war zone. His country says it's okay for him to kill his enemy, so in war murder is authorized. It's bullshit. A personally tailored justification is a more accurate description. In the end, taking a life harbours no more emotion than drinking a cup of coffee.'

Taking back the bottle, she murmured, 'Where was Elaine's God? All her life she's devoted herself to some higher purpose, some belief that good things will happen if she's a good person. You heard the stories, she's had to work hard to be happy, and then she winds up going out like that.'

Tentatively, James reached over and retrieved the bottle. 'How do you even know it was Elaine?' he questioned. 'You never saw her.'

Focused on the breakers, she replied, 'Then where is she now?'

Perhaps a minute passed in silence, when something occurred that James never thought he would see. Abbey began to cry.

'Don't look at me,' she sniffed.

Glowing under the pallid moon, she seemed so defenceless. He wanted to move closer, throw an arm around her, hug her, kiss away her tears. He stayed where he was, instead handing back the bottle.

She accepted it graciously, took a small sip. 'We're never getting off this island, are we?'

'We have to. I have to return some DVDs before next Friday.'

Abbey snorted. 'I think you're as scared as the rest of us.'

'When you first found me,' he said softly, 'I was paralysed, remember? As I lay there drowning, I kept thinking, *why*? You know, why can't I move? When I came around from the impact, there was this…screaming. I can still hear it now, this awful sound coming from somebody in so much pain. It was a woman's voice. When I found her, I recognised her. She was the stewardess who'd served me earlier. Her nametag said *Heather*. Her leg was trapped beneath a stanchion…' he paused for a pull on the whiskey. '…I tried to calm her down, but she fought me every step of the way. Delirious, she could barely feel her leg and the water was rising around her. If you'd seen her face, Abbey, she was so frightened.

'I promised I'd get her out, promised her she'd be fine, but the stanchion wouldn't budge, not even an inch, and I figured if I couldn't move the stanchion I'd have to move her. So, I grabbed her under the arms. As I pulled she moved with me, came free easily. At first I couldn't understand how it'd been so simple, where her pain had come from. But she was still screaming. Just *screaming*. When I looked down, her leg was completely detached from below the knee. The stanchion had gone right through.'

'My God,' Abbey muttered, closing her hand over his.

'The screaming died off as the shock took over. I could see blood escaping the wound. In the water it looked like ink. I dragged her through the carriage, out into the sea. Halfway to shore, she went limp. I don't know if she was dead. I thought she was, but there was no way to be certain. I couldn't hold on to her anymore, the waves were getting the better of me, so you know what I did? I let her go. I let her go so I could save myself.' He felt his hand being squeezed harder.

'It was a night of impossible decisions for everybody, James, not just you. You did all you could for that woman, and if there was the smallest chance she was still alive, she wouldn't have lasted a day without proper treatment. One life saved is better than two lost.'

Taking another long swig, he said, 'I couldn't move that night because I was punishing myself. I think in some twisted way I wanted to die, to make amends for failing that woman so badly. My brain just shut down. If you hadn't come along when you did…' The sentence ebbed away with the tide.

'The guy I was travelling with, Milo,' she said, 'he had this word-of-the-day thing on his phone. Since we've been on the island, I've been thinking up new ones. Maybe you should take today's.'

Gingerly he laid back and picked out a star. 'That's easy,' he whispered. '*Coward*.'

Heart pumping furiously, she said, 'I'd better have that bottle back.'

'I've tried to forget that night,' he went on, 'no matter how ingrained. But I'm slowly coming to terms with it because I don't have a choice. No matter how distant the light, Abbey, there is still a light.'

She looked sideways at him. 'One of your mum's sayings?'

'One of mine, actually.'

Falling silent, she left her hand on his and peered into his clear blue eyes. Her tears began to well again, the tension hanging densely between them.

Neither dared look away.

They moved closer, their lips mere inches apart. He could feel the soft pulse of her breath against his mouth, the cool evening breeze gliding over them, comforting them in anticipation. As he leaned in slowly, the quiet desperation lingering over them, she glanced away embarrassed, the green of her beautiful eyes clouded with shame.

'I'm sorry, James, I just can't.'

'It's okay,' he whispered, his lips hovering over her ear. 'I understand.'

He could feel her warm breath against his chest. 'Abbey, look at me,' he insisted.

Slowly she lifted her head, fresh tears glistening on her cheeks.

'It's okay,' he said again, wiping the damp marks from her face.

As silence fell weightily between them, they went back to the stars. After a while she leaned over and placed her head comfortably on his shoulder, allowing thirty minutes of serenity to linger. Finally she detached herself from him and climbed quietly to her feet. Without a word, she walked away.

*

Another hour passed uneventfully, the bottle half empty. Thankful for the lack of excitement James narrowed his eyes towards the marginally brighter horizon, the booze encouraging his shut down. He couldn't think of anything but Abbey. The way she'd held his gaze, the feel of her breath against his chest. Never in his life had he wanted to taste another's lips like he did hers.

Reaching for the bottle, he twisted the cap closed and set it down in the sand. 'Room for another?' said an unfamiliar voice.

Startled he sprang back, surprised his body still worked. Standing coyly before him was the girl, shabby brown dress torn up the middle and tied off above the thighs to make shorts.

'Sure,' he muttered, hiding his astonishment.

Taking Abbey's seat timidly the girl stared at him, tired eyes brimming with wisdom.

'My name's Danielle,' she said croakily, her accent broad South African. 'If you were wondering.'

'Danielle,' he repeated. 'Nice name.'

She smiled. 'Hopefully everyone will stop calling me "The Girl" now.'

'I think we can probably come to some arrangement,' he smiled. 'How come you're up so early?'

'Couldn't sleep.'

'Yeah, it's going around...'

Shuffling a little, she said unexpectedly, 'You like Abbey, don't you?'

'How do you mean?'

'I've seen the way you look at her.'

'Hang on,' he said warily. 'Am I being counselled?'

'If we never get home, her husband could remarry or start a new family. Then what?'

'Is there nothing else you'd rather talk about, Danielle? Seriously, first words out of your mouth and you choose to lecture me. You want to give a drunken man a break?'

Probing no further she fell mute again, James no longer finding the silence comfortable.

'Who were you on the plane with?' he asked quickly.

'Nobody.'

'Aren't you a little young to be flying alone?'

'Aren't you a little old to be getting drunk alone?'

'Last I checked...no,' James countered and took another swig.

Danielle frowned. 'If you must know, a friend helped me through the process. I needed to get away.'

'Away from where?'

'Just away.'

Pushing no further, he asked, 'What's in New Zealand?'

'My brother, Neil,' she said quickly. 'He lives in Hamilton. Probably thinks I'm dead.'

'Oh, I wouldn't say that. They won't write us off that quickly.'

'I don't mean the crash,' she said. 'He thought I was dead a long time ago. The two of us grew up in an orphanage after our parents died. They were doing the New York tourist thing on September eleventh, 2001. Never came home.

'Anyway, Neil got out of the orphanage a few years ago, too old to stay. Legally he couldn't take me with him, and so two years ago I ran away.'

'For what reason?'

'It was a Catholic orphanage. I'm not a Catholic. The place was state-run so they couldn't kick me out. I refused to adopt Catholicism, so they treated me like garbage, a real outsider.'

'You didn't report the abuse?'

'Their word against mine. Who was going to believe one kid over an entire Catholic organisation? Besides, I found a better life on the streets. They never looked for me. Probably glad I vanished, but I forgive them. They strayed from God's path, it wasn't their fault.'

Astounded by Danielle's shrewd maturity, he waited for her to continue.

'Eventually I was taken in by a family,' she went on. 'Well, a man named Dominick and a couple of other vagrants he'd taken in. We worked for him on his banana plantation in return for food and shelter. He was kind to us, and for the first time since my parents died, I felt truly safe again. The plantation became my haven. Nobody knew I was there, nobody cared, but that didn't matter, I found my smile again.'

James began digesting. Danielle hadn't talked in four days, he hadn't even known her name, and now here she was, pouring out her soul like she'd known him for years. He needed more. 'What happened in the orphanage that made you run?' he probed gently. 'Did they hit you? Was there abuse?'

'Hit me?' she frowned. 'The years after Neil left I suffered a broken arm, two broken ribs, a fractured collarbone, several bouts of concussion and a chipped cranium. This from the carers and other children alike. I wasn't safe anywhere. At the hospital I was just passed off as a clumsy kid. No matter how much I begged, no matter how long I wept, it just kept on coming. When I began working in the plantation, I healed properly for the first time in years.'

James swallowed hard. The effects of the whiskey wearing thin, he twisted the cap back off the bottle and took a long swig. Finally he said, 'So did you talk to anyone, a friend or something?'

'I did. I gave a detailed report to my closest friend.'

'Who?'

'God, of course.'

Feeling stupid, he said, 'What did God do?'

'It wasn't a question of what God did for me. It was more a question of what I was able to do through keeping my faith. God doesn't perform acts like that, He merely points the way. He led me to the banana plantation, He led me to Dominick. Without Him I would've been truly lost.'

Danielle's behaviour in the clearing now made perfect sense. She'd resisted leaving because she felt safe there. The parallel to her current situation was astounding.

'James?' she muttered. 'Eric told me something yesterday. 'Something you should probably know.'

Sitting up straight, James tried to focus.

'It's about the guy in handcuffs,' she added. 'He told me who was wearing them.'

48

London, 1992

Gradually, the faces of his family evaporated into a funnel of light. He reached out as he raced along, tried to slow down. There was nothing to grip. Piece by piece the bright tunnel transformed into daylight and as suddenly as his journey began, it ended.

Over the precipice of a sheer drop he looked down at his dangling feet, nothing below but rocks and shale. He recognised the place. He'd been there many times before.

Raising his eyes, the rest of the expanse honed into view, awe-inspiring and vast.

'Remember this place?'

'The quarry,' Nicolas York mouthed. 'I loved this place growing up.'

'You did. No matter how much we were warned to stay away, we would always come down here.'

Without replying, York took in the enormity of the abandoned quarry. The place was condemned, a hazard, and so no one stepped foot in there. It was guaranteed solitude; no alcoholic and bickering parents, no demanding teachers.

'Do you remember what happened here, Nicky?'

York nodded slowly.

'This is where you lost your grip on reality, if only for a while.'

Images began seeping steadily through the cracks of his mind: lying alone on his side in bed, crying himself to sleep for months; in class at school, unable to concentrate, freaking out in blind panic in the middle of lessons; thirteen years old, mind fractured.

'Two years you spent in that hospital. But they pulled you back, and you got on with your life as best you knew how. I don't know if you did it intentionally but you successfully blanked out your depression, pushed it down deep. It's been down there ever since, manifesting, thriving on your failures, your losses, your self-destruction.'

'I…I don't feel it,' he whispered. 'I don't feel anything.'

'*That* is your demon, Nicky, buried deep in your subconscious. And the sooner you remember, the sooner you can deal with it.'

'Maybe I don't want to deal with it,' he replied. 'Maybe it's become so dug-in, there is no way to deal with it.'

'What happened that day wasn't your fault. It was me, Nicolas, I was to blame. You blanked everything so effectively you convinced yourself you were somehow responsible.'

'I…I…'

'It wasn't your fault, Nicolas. I was reckless, showing off. '

'But I…'

'It wasn't your fault, I'm telling you the truth…God's honest truth.'

Gradually the voice faded away, filtering into the crumbling image of the quarry. Then…

*

…eyelids like rusty hinges, York prized them open. He coughed, and pain erupted through his side like…he'd been stabbed.

'Welcome back,' said a woman's voice. It sounded like Mason. 'Whoa, whoa, don't try and move. You'll rupture the stitches.'

Slowly the room came into focus. It smelt like the Dungeon. He was lying in a bed of crisp white linen, a bare fluorescent tube hanging blindingly overhead. In the bed to his right was an elderly man coughing, grumbling in his sleep, and to his left was Mason sitting on a plastic visitors' chair, her vaguely masculine features eying him stonily.

'You couldn't get me a room to myself?' he muttered sleepily.

'They wanted to give you one,' said Mason, 'but I told them you'd be much more comfortable in here with Cliff Richards.'

York rolled his head to the sleeping man. 'That's not his name.'

'It's what his chart says.'

York grinned, which hurt like hell. 'How long was I out?' he grunted.

'Couple of days, you lost a lot of blood. Who was it?'

York glanced away.

'That's what I thought. What happened?'

'You don't know?'

'We've checked out the CCTV from the café and some from the high street, but all we can tell is you were in pursuit of somebody. No image is clear enough to make him out.'

'Shocker,' York muttered.

'Yeah,' Mason agreed. 'Who was he?'

'He was *he*, Judy, our Mr Valentine.'

She nodded slowly, unsurprised. 'So fill in some blanks for me. How did you go from jumping into that alley to having a knife in your back?'

He took an aching breath, trying to remember. 'I...I talked to him. Then we fought, and I lost.'

'I figured that much.'

'He was strong, Judy. I mean strong, strong. And he had a knife...I couldn't...wait, how am I still breathing?'

'You don't remember?'

From somewhere in the foggy backcountry of his mind he recalled the mysterious blonde assuring him help was on the way. Mason didn't need to know that. 'I just remember lying there watching him walk away and I passed out. Everything else is kind of...'

Mason squinted as if she didn't quite believe him. 'Well you got lucky, in more ways than one. The blade went straight through the fleshy part in your side, right under your ribcage. It missed all your vital organs and swerved your spine. A few inches to the left and you'd've been in a wheelchair for the rest of your life.'

He lay back against his thin white pillow feeling deflated, relieved. 'And what else?' he asked.

Mason frowned.

'You said I got lucky in more ways than one.'

'We didn't know where you'd gone, Nick. It was half an hour before anybody knew you were missing. Jonathan told me later that you suspected the killer was still in the house and we began to assume the worst. Then we received an anonymous call to the station, some woman telling us where you were, that you needed an ambulance. Without that tip you would've bled out, we wouldn't've reached you in time.'

His eyelids began to feel heavy again. 'What about David Newport?'

'We let him go. No reason to hold him, he gave us a detailed account of what happened when he left the house. His dad gave the same story.'

York nodded groggily.

'Holly's funeral will be next week,' Mason muttered. She shifted uncomfortably on the plastic seat. 'I know you'll want to be there.'

He didn't reply. Something else was coming; he knew Mason too well.

'If you want we can ride together –'

'Spit it out, Judy,' he cut in.

More uneasy shifting. 'Fine. You're off this case, Nick. There's so much at stake here and you're too close to this now. Holly's death is going to mess with your head, no question.'

'I'm fine,' he implored. 'I'm not done with this fucker.'

'Yes you are.'

'No, I'm not.'

'*Yes you are, Nick!* You're done, it's over. And that's not even bringing your addiction into it. I can't even begin to tell you how many protocols you're in breach of by filling your veins with that shit. Tony Braddock's already begun taking over the investigation.'

'Jesus, that cheesy dickhead? So that's it then. This bastard kills my partner, puts me in hospital and I'm supposed to sit here like a fucking melon!'

'I'm sorry, Nick, I know Holly meant a lot to you. And that's exactly the reason you're off this thing.' She stood to leave. 'If you want some advice, take a couple of weeks off, watch some reruns of *Star Trek*, whatever. Recover, and when you come back we'll get you into a programme, see if we can't get you back on track. But this investigation does not exist to you anymore, is that understood?'

Not waiting for a response, she turned silently and left the ward.

Allowing his eyelids to droop, he began to drift again. He tried to put his thoughts in order but his head was fuzzy. He'd been right, already Newport was becoming an icon, a reason for things - a reason for him being off the case. He filed that away, attempted to go back to other things. Moments later, the room dissolved away.

*

When the ward reappeared, Cliff Richards, if that really was his name, was still snoring and fidgeting, his tangle of sheets amassed at the foot of his bed. A nurse was checking his chart.

He looked for a wall clock. There wasn't one. Instead he tentatively sat up wincing at the pain in his side, which had transformed into some kind of dull ache.

'Ah, there he is,' called out a voice from the corner of the ward.

'Shhh,' grumbled the nurse. 'People are sleeping.'

Filling a polystyrene cup from the water fountain, Will Graham held up his hand in apology.

'Get me one of those, Will,' York requested.

Sitting on the same visitors' chair Mason had used, Graham handed over the water. He was smiling. 'Good to see you up, Nick.'

'He's been here for about two hours waiting for you to come around,' the nurse revealed. 'Thank god you're awake, he's been hassling the nurses.'

Graham smiled. 'What can I say, I like a girl in uniform.'

'You're in the right profession then.' Smiling, the nurse replaced Cliff Richards's chart and walked away.

'So, I hear the Pit Bull's been to see you,' Graham said. 'How'd that work out?'

York snorted. 'Like you don't know.'

'Yeah, I'm sorry, man. Really socked it to you is what I hear.'

York shrugged. 'I had it coming.'

Graham leant in. 'Well listen, I have some juicy facts for you. How's your hearing?'

Meeting the technician's gaze, York's eyes widened. 'I'm supposed to be off the investigation.'

'Which is why,' whispered Graham, 'I'm not telling you this stuff. In fact, I was never here.'

York sat up.

'For starters,' Graham began, 'Kilroy took another mould from Janine Bluestock's heart. There were only very slight variations to the mould taken from Harriet Fuller's heart, so he's pretty confident that they belong to the same man, perhaps wearing some kind of mouth guard.'

'What about our guy, has he contacted the station again?'

'Not yet, but get a load of this. I have a fingerprint sample from the last crime scene that Braddock, seconded by Mason, is choosing to ignore.'

'Choosing to ignore,' York echoed. 'Why would they do that?'

'Let me finish. We took the print from the knife that was found…erm, found in…'

'It's okay, Will, you can say it.'

Graham looked embarrassed. 'The knife that was…you know, in Holly. I couldn't work it out, he'd been meticulous so far. Why would he suddenly not wear gloves?'

York knew the answer to that. 'Same reason he didn't take her heart. The whole thing was rushed, bodged. He was careless.'

'We ran the print and it belongs to a Julian Faulkner, owns a house up in Lincolnshire somewhere. His fingerprints are on file because, get this, he tried to burn down his own house. Nothing in the file to suggest why, but I hear he didn't even try to deny it. He had no insurance so no fraudulent charges were brought to him. Guess he just woke up one day and decided he didn't like the colour.'

York pondered briefly. 'So who lives there now?'

'Oh, erm, no one,' said Graham. 'A portion of the house is still fire damaged and no one's ever bothered to repair it. But it's up for sale. So we called the agency it's listed to, and guess what, the contact details for Julian Faulkner have expired. Frank Blithe, the guy at the agency said, and I quote: It's like the man dropped off the face of the planet.'

'So he's just abandoned the house?' York queried. 'Never goes back there?'

'Doesn't look like it,' said Graham. 'Anyway, Mason is considering it a dead end, but I definitely think it's worth checking out. All depends on whether or not you fancy a road trip.'

York glanced over to Richards. 'Like I said, Will, I'm off the case.'

'Well I wouldn't imagine that would stop a man like you now, would it?'

York smirked. 'Where's my hat?'

49

After three and a half days and a handful of blood transfusions, York discharged himself from hospital against the belligerent advice of a German doctor, a couple of well-informed nurses, and Cliff Richards. He told them he felt fine, which was a lie. A smouldering poker was jousting through his side and the painkillers weren't making a dent.

The drive up to Lincolnshire took a little under three hours. The address Frank Blithe had given him directed him to a small town called Market Rasen, a rural diamond with a racecourse and one of those old police houses.

After a healthy-sized gammon steak in a pub called *The Cup of Blood*, he headed out of town. Julian Faulkner's house was a couple of miles further out on the beaten skirts, one of a quartet in a small estate tucked away in the trees, well-trodden dirt track leading up to it. It had been easy enough to find.

The size of the estate was a little over six acres and so none of the four properties were close together. All the surrounding land was used for cultivation and farming, the only things encroaching on private property the grazing sheep and horses.

Pulling over at the bottom of the driveway and climbing from the car, he was hit with the aromas of the countryside. He loved that smell. It reminded him of growing up, his mum and dad taking him and his brother out to the Lake District where they stayed in an old converted barn on Ullswater.

Those memories were his fondest from childhood. His only memories. That was before everything changed. After the incident they never went back there. Like he'd spoken them yesterday, he recalled his dad's potent words: *Everything ends badly, son, otherwise it wouldn't end.* He hung himself the next day.

At the head of the driveway was the agency's For Sale sign and an American style mailbox standing on a post, flap open as if awaiting unwanted mail. The scratched letters of the family name remained stencilled in green onto the box's flank: *F ulk er Resid n e.*

He reached in and pulled out the wad of backlogged post: nothing of interest, most of it junk, damp, or both. The majority was still addressed to Julian Faulkner, some of it to an Arthur Faulkner. His father? Replacing the mail, he locked the car and began up the dirt track.

By the time he reached the house he was sweating freely, the trek mostly uphill and mostly under the harsh afternoon sun. The final section of track was hidden from the sky by colossal overhanging oaks. He was thankful for the reprieve.

Suddenly there it was, the abandoned Faulkner house, a fifteen-minute trek into the woods. For a moment he paused, gawped in awe at the breathtaking sight. The entire right side of the structure was only framework, charred sections of wood and brick lying where they had fallen. The left-hand side of the building was still intact and was overgrown with untamed vegetation, as if the surrounding trees were trying to absorb it piece by dead piece. Next to where he was standing was an old well, wooden pail lying splintered by its side, the only water it saw these days falling from the sky.

He found it difficult to move forward. He couldn't tell if it was his imagination, but something about the house felt…off. Finally he started up to the structure, the black windows staring hollowly back at him. Stepping over blackened debris he climbed up onto the recessed porch, a largely undamaged lounger-bench propped up against the wall, the front door swinging on its hinges.

Gingerly, he stepped inside. A clichéd floorboard creaked under his weight, and his nostrils were invaded by the fusty stink of negligence and abandonment. The house had been gutted. The floors had been stripped leaving naked and buckled wood. Not a single item of furniture remained, and he found himself wondering why the lounger-bench had been spared. Dust mites swirled in the lancing bars of sunlight as he made his way through the house room by room. He found only torn out shells of disappointment. Perhaps Braddock had been right. Maybe the Faulkner home really was a dead end. In the kitchen he paused, standing on a tattered and worn green carpet. It didn't make sense. Why had only this room been permitted to keep its ill-fitting carpet?

He took off his hat and placed it on the sink, wiping the sweat from his forehead with the sleeve of his jacket. At the back wall of the room the carpet didn't meet the skirting-board, its corners curled up. Closing his eyes against sporadic dust, he gripped the green matting and yanked it upwards. It came away easily. He threw it against the opposite wall revealing a small trapdoor in the floorboards, rusted ring-pull embedded.

With a sharp yank the hatch door came up without too much trouble and for a moment he peered into the darkness below, the only light to penetrate creeping in through the hatch. A set of wooden steps led down into the basement and he tentatively took each one until his feet found the concrete floor. He waited a moment for his eyes to adjust and took in the sheer enormity of the underground chamber. Some kind of bomb shelter maybe.

No one had been down there in a long time. Everything was iced in thick dust. Nothing had been moved in months, probably years.

Here: boxes of old LPs, books. There: fusty bedding, pillows. Here: an aging typewriter sitting atop a dusty cabinet. There: plastic storage crates filled with tins of old currency, some battered cine film reels, World War Two memorabilia. Built onto the farthest wall was a stained gun rack devoid of weapons and directly beneath it was a dustsheet covered picture frame.

Gently removing the sheet, he took a step back. The photograph was a sepia image of a handsome man in his early thirties, very stiff and serious. Severely parted hair, crisply starched white shirt and black tie, the man appeared official, almost regimental, though there was nothing in the image to suggest military. There was something very captivating about the man's features, and for a few seconds York felt as if everything around him had dissolved away, leaving only the picture in clear focus. Finally, he tore himself away feeling strangely unnerved.

Replacing the sheet, he picked up the shoebox containing the cine film. He hadn't come all the way to Lincolnshire to go back empty-handed.

Back in the kitchen he threw the trapdoor closed and replaced the carpet. He left the house via the back door, finding himself in a large grassy backyard, that familiar floral aroma all around. About to turn and leave he spotted something at the bottom of the garden that begged a closer look.

As he drew nearer he shivered in the afternoon sun, the monstrous creation entangled in intestinal roots and foliage. At first glance it looked like a kids play unit, on second, it was revealed as the maniacal contraption it really was: a full-sized assault course. Cargo nets, mud ditches, scaling wall, crossbeams, plunge pit, the works. He'd seen this kind of thing a couple of years ago at a military camp in Gloucestershire. They were implemented for young soldiers training to go into Iraq, preparation for integration into *Desert Storm*. But they'd been around since long before that. The question was, what the bloody hell was one doing out here?

50

Four days he'd gone without a hit. That had to be some kind of record on someone's list, somewhere. His dealer was over two hundred miles away. That was probably a good thing.

Back in the small market town, York headed to the main street and parked up. Time was getting on now, the sun much lower in the sky, cooler. Some of the shops on the main street had begun closing up, and Hartford & Clay's Real Estate was following suit. Out in the street was a rotund man in his mid-forties wearing a black shirt and purple tie hauling down the shutter.

'Hello,' York called, startling the man. 'I'm looking for Frank Blithe. He still around?'

The man turned and held out his hand. 'You found him. What can I do for you?'

'DCI Nicolas York,' he revealed taking Blithe's hand. 'I called earlier.'

'Ah, yes.' Turning away, Blithe retrieved a handkerchief and sneezed into it four times. 'Excuse me, Detective, bloody hay fever out here is a killer.'

'I'll bet. Listen, I can see you're locking up, but I was wondering if I could bend your ear for a few minutes. I'm not here officially. Just chasing up a ghost actually.'

Blithe sneezed again. 'Well, sir, if you'd be happy to sit across from me while I indulge in a pint, I'd be happy to talk to you. You haven't sampled England's best ale until you've had a pint around here.'

*

Sneeze.

Sneeze.

Sneeze.

'So,' said Blithe wiping his raw nose, 'Nicolas, did you say?'

York nodded. *The Cup of Blood* was quieter than earlier, the lull period between folk leaving work and coming back later. Sitting at the bar was a surly regular being very vocal about football to the aging landlord. The old guy's face said that he'd heard it all before, a million times over, about a million different clubs. The only other sounds emanated from a fruit machine chiming away in the corner.

Blithe had been right about the ale, it was one of the best pints York'd had.

'You say you're up here chasing ghosts?' asked Blithe. 'Well, if you've been up to the Faulkner house, you already know that ghosts are all that's left up there. The place has been stripped.'

'I saw that,' York confirmed. 'Who stripped it exactly?'

'No one really knows,' said Blithe. 'Pikey's come through here a lot, though. Chances are it was cleared out by them. When they're around they set up camp not far from there…are you okay, Inspector? You're looking a little pasty.'

Sneeze.

'I was stabbed a few days ago,' replied York matter-of-factly. 'So what do you know about the Faulkner family? Did you know any of them?'

Slightly taken aback, Blithe said, 'Erm, yeah, I knew Julian a little bit. He didn't come into town much, and I tended to give him a wide berth when he did.'

'Why's that?'

'Don't know really. There was just something about him. He was quiet but so intense, as though he might explode at any second. His father was more of a mystery, barely left the house. I saw him around from time to time when I was a kid, but I never knew him.'

'Arthur Faulkner?'

'You've done your homework.'

'What about the mother?'

'The mother?' echoed Blithe. 'I never met her. I couldn't even tell you her name. But I know she died of polio. Suffered with it for a long time. I can tell you the nanny's name, though. She used to come into town and run errands for the Faulkners.'

'There was a nanny?'

'Yeah,' said Blithe. 'Margaret Mayfield her name was. Everybody used to call her Maggie May.'

'What happened to her?'

'Nobody knows,' said Blithe solemnly. 'It was a scandal at the time. The woman just disappeared. There was an inquiry but nothing ever came of it. Of course, rumours began floating around that Arthur had killed her and buried her somewhere. When they finally put him away, the rumours strengthened. He denied it, told the police she just wasn't there one day, but no one ever believed that. Unfortunately, there wasn't a great deal of evidence to suggest otherwise.'

York finished his pint and waved to the tolerating landlord to pour two more. 'You still see either of the Faulkners, Julian or Arthur? They still in this area?'

Sneeze. 'Ah, that's where the homework ends, I see.'

'What do you mean?'

'Look, Nicolas, the story of the Faulkner family is legendary around here. The speculation surrounding what went on in that house is breathtaking. You say you're chasing ghosts, then you're in the right place because ghosts are all you'll find.'

The landlord brought the fresh pints over. He lingered slightly. Anything for few extra seconds away from the bar lout, no doubt. When he walked away, York said, 'So start at the beginning.'

Blithe examined his pint. 'You don't give up do you?'

'It's important,' York replied.

'Arthur Faulkner was a World War Two vet,' Blithe revealed. 'I wasn't born at this point, but rumour has it that the Arthur Faulkner who left for the trenches was not the same Arthur Faulkner who returned. I mean, I don't know what happened to him out there, but I heard he was a POW, endured years of brutality…

Sneeze.

'I don't know how much of that is true, but when he returned his mind was broken. I mean, he was *gone*.'

'Gone?' For some reason, York recalled the sepia photograph in the basement of the Faulkner home.

'Yeah,' Blithe muttered. 'There're people around here know more about it than me, but apparently the man could no longer distinguish between civilisation and warfare. The town folk, they tried to warn the local coppers, you know, said he was dangerous, a menace. It went on for years. He lost it a couple of times in town, snapped at locals, threatened to kill people. But no one listened. The police kept an eye on him when he came into the market, but they didn't interfere. And then the worst happened and they had no choice but to lock him up.'

York leaned in, pint forgotten. 'What did he do?'

'He shot the doctor who was at the house treating his wife,' Blithe whispered. 'Shot him in the chest with an old German pistol. Apparently when they took him away he was screaming about *them* coming for him, calling the coppers Nazis and Gestapo scum. His wife was so sick, she died that day. The doctor was on his way to break the news to Arthur, and when he found him in one of the upper rooms, Arthur had the pistol levelled at him.'

'Jesus,' York murmured.

'Yeah. Mid 1960's, Julian would've been eleven or twelve at the time, suddenly parentless. He was taken to an orphanage. Best thing for him you ask me. Stories were, Arthur used to put the kid through hell, training him for combat. You can't've missed the assault course in the back yard.'

'No, I saw it,' he said. 'He used to put Julian through that?'

'And worse. We heard that Arthur locked him in the basement for days at a time with no food or water, and then he'd be dragged out to hunt in the woods for sustenance and the like, anything wild that was edible. And get this, apparently Arthur taught him to not waste any part of the prey. He forced his own son to eat everything, the liver, the heart, the intestines, the lot. Poor kid probably didn't know any different in the end.'

York took a deep breath and shuddered, the image of the teeth marks in Janine Bluestock's heart flashing to mind. 'So no one knows where Julian is now?'

Blithe sneezed again. 'Nah, he's been gone for years. He came back for a while when he was old enough to get out of the orphanage, but after he tried to burn down the house he disappeared. It's like he fell –'

'Off the face of the planet,' York finished.

'Yeah, exactly.'

'And Arthur?'

'Oh, he's still alive,' Blithe declared. 'In his seventies now, I suppose. He's been in Rampton Secure Hospital over in Retford since the incident. They can probably tell you more if you drive up there, but I doubt they'll let you see him. I'll bet the man's in a cell with more padding than a schoolgirl's bra.'

York finished the dregs of his second pint. Blithe sneezed into his.

Julian Faulkner. The Valentine Killer. Trained for combat from an early age. Goosebumps rose on York's arms as he recalled how easily he'd been overcome in the alley and left for dead. The sheer strength and manoeuvrability of his assailant had been astounding. Everything clicked, all the patterns fitting together like pieces in a jigsaw. Only one thing remained for him to do in the East Midlands. Go and see if Arthur Faulkner really was as far gone as Blithe made out.

51

The air had grown cooler now as York climbed out of the car and stepped onto the gravelled lot at Rampton Secure Hospital. The sprawling complex was enclosed inside a twin-rigged chain-link fence a couple of miles from Retford, Nottinghamshire. The foreboding redbrick structure stood ominously alone in Robin Hood's country, secreted away from civilisation much like the minds of some of its residents.

After calling ahead and writing down directions from a guy named Jason McCullick, York screwed up the scrap of paper and slipped it into the pocket of his jacket. His hand brushed against something else. Standing in the subtle breeze of twilight he pulled the foreign object from his pocket and held it at arm's length, scrutinising its existence.

Remember this, Nicolas...Remember me.

On the night of his back-alley scrap with the Valentine Killer, he recalled the blurry image of the blonde woman looking down at him, assuring him help was coming. For some unexplainable reason, he'd believed her unequivocally. As his mind raced backwards, he remembered her sliding something into his pocket. Then she took off and he proceeded to bleed to death.

Keep your eyes open. Help is on the way.

Tentatively, he unfolded the slip of paper and read what was written in neat effeminate handwriting.

Nicolas

If you recall speaking to me on the phone, then you know who I am and what I can offer. I have been watching you. I can only apologise for the cloak and dagger routine but I in turn am being observed. If they see me talking to you, they will know I am not who I say I am.

When the time is right, I will arrange to meet you.

What I said to you on the phone is accurate. Your son is alive.

Below is the address of a house I have had under surveillance for some time. I believe Frasier, amongst others, is being held there by an organisation headed up by someone who goes by the alias "The Face." One wrong move here and he will disappear, and probably so too will your son.

I don't know where else to turn now. I am desperate and you are the one person remaining who might be able to help.

You need only to believe, Nicolas, and you're one step closer to getting him back.

K.

York toppled against the car, a sharp stab of pain lancing through his wound. He bit down on his lip to stop from crying out. A billion questions danced around in his head:

Who was this woman and how did she know these things? Could he trust her, and who were "they"?

How was he the one remaining person who could help her?

Shoving the note down into his pocket he stood up straight and brushed himself off, took several deep breaths. He thought about calling Graham and getting him to run some checks on the address, but the author of the note was right, he needed to play it cool.

Heading unsteadily into the hospital reception, he asked the desk girl for Jason McCullick.

'Someone say my name?' The voice emanated from behind the desk in a small back office. Poking his head around the door, a lean thirty-something with a full head of wiry red hair and matching beard eyed him unashamedly. 'Help you?'

'DCI Nicolas York,' he replied holding up his ID.

'Ah, the mysterious detective up from the Big Smoke,' said McCullick cheerily in a thick Scottish brogue. 'Thank you for calling ahead, sir. How exactly can we help you?'

York plucked off his hat and laid it on the reception counter. 'I'm not even sure you can. I just have a few questions about Arthur Faulkner if you wouldn't mind indulging me.'

'Ah, the illustrious Mr Faulkner,' said McCullick. 'Colourful character, that one.'

'So I hear.'

McCullick looked him up and down. 'You okay, Inspector? You're looking a little ashen.'

'Yeah, I've been hearing that a lot lately.'

Unlocking the door from the inside, McCullick let York into the office and offered him a cup of coffee. He graciously accepted, needing something to warm him through.

'So what exactly is it about Arthur that interests you so much?' asked the young carer.

'Well, that's a touchy subject. Do you care directly for him?'

'We're no wee outfit here,' said McCullick. 'We have over four hundred patients and I myself am merely one of two thousand staff members.'

'You call them patients?'

'Did you miss the sign on your way in saying "hospital?" We run a facility for the sick here, my friend, regardless of what they might have done to put themselves here.'

York nodded. 'And Arthur Faulkner?'

'Aye, Arthur is amongst the sickest, been here since 1966. Totally delusional, hasn't responded to treatment in over twenty-five years. Man still thinks he's being brutalised inside a POW camp, hospitalised a number of the carers believing them to be German soldiers. Last time that happened was over three years ago now, though. These days he just sits at his window and stares out into the day. Man really has suffered.'

He's suffered? York wanted to say. What about the wife of the doctor he murdered? What about the son he tortured? Instead he said, 'Can I see him?'

'Aye,' the Scot replied. 'That is if he's pliant. Spends most of his days pretty zoned out now. He doesn't get any visitors.' Grabbing a large bunch of keys, he added, 'Sign in at reception and pop on this pass. We'll see if the patient is in the mood for company.'

*

As they walked, York wondered why they always painted the walls inside hospitals white. He thought about asking McCullick but decided against it. The moans and voices from some of the cells radiated out into the corridor, echoing eerily back and forth. 'Everyone has their own cell?' York asked.

'My God, yes!' gasped McCullick as though the question was stupid. 'Would you throw a naked flame into a box of dynamite?'

'Got you,' York nodded. 'I guess some people still have imaginary friends.'

'Some people *are* their imaginary friends.'

Other carers roamed the corridors, some with clipboards and white coats, others in navy blue tunics pushing trolleys of meds. They all looked busy.

'Here we are, Inspector,' McCullick declared. 'He's had his medication today so he'll be nice and docile. Just keep your distance and try not to agitate him, okay. I'll wait right in the doorway.'

Sliding the key into the plain white door, McCullick clicked open the lock and pushed it wide.

'Evening Arthur,' said McCullick. 'I have a visitor for you.'

York stepped into the small room, boxlike, one comfortable looking armchair and one bed made up in crisp white sheeting. Just like McCullick said, Arthur Faulkner was sitting by the window examining the dying sun. He looked to be around seventy years old, the few remaining wispy strands of grey hair matted to his head. He wore only a dressing gown and slippers, a thin tendril of saliva hanging from the corner of his mouth.

'Not even going to say hello, Arthur?' said McCullick.

Arthur Faulkner remained still. York wondered if he even knew he had company.

Sitting on the edge of the bed a few feet from the patient, York examined the man's face. The sepia photograph he'd seen at the Faulkner house was some fifty-odd years old, but there was no doubt that this was the same man. The crescent-shaped eyes, the faint hook of the nose, it was easy to tell that Arthur Faulkner had once been handsome.

In the doorway, McCullick waited, eying the scene curiously. 'I don't know, Inspector,' he said. 'Maybe you just caught him on a bad day.'

York leaned forward trying to gain an ounce of recognition. 'Arthur, my name's Nicolas. Is it okay if I talk to you for a minute?'

Nothing, not an iota of acknowledgement; Frank Blithe's words echoed hollowly around in his head: *When he came back he was broken. I mean he was gone.*

'Arthur,' he pursued, 'I don't know if you can hear me, but I'd like to speak to you about your son, Julian. Would that be alright?' The patient blinked, blinked. There seemed to be nothing behind those crescent eyes that remained in the real world, but suddenly Arthur Faulkner spoke, his voice cracked and strained. 'Are you Julian?'

'No, Arthur,' he replied leaning in. 'I'm a police officer. I'm here to talk to you about Julian.'

Faulkner looked confused. 'Who's Julian?'

McCullick raised his hands, palms up: *don't ask me.*

'Julian is your son, Arthur,' he urged. 'Do you remember him?'

The faintest of nods. 'Robert. My son, Robert.'

York glanced over his shoulder. 'Who's Robert?' he asked McCullick. 'He mention that name before?'

'Ignore it, Inspector,' McCullick advised. 'Robert's one of the carers here who regularly looks after Arthur. He's quite fond of him. Over time we think Arthur has come to think of Rob as a son.'

'Arthur,' said York turning back to the patient, 'When did you last see Julian?'

'What did they say to you, Robert?' Faulkner muttered, his eyes flickering left to right. 'What did the Nazi bastards do to you? Did they hurt you, did they hurt me? Oh Robert, oh Robert, *Robert*, how can they justify this. One more day in the box, one more day, one more day, one more day, one more day…'

York waited patiently while Faulkner rambled on senselessly.

'There's a police officer here to see you, Robert,' Arthur Faulkner droned. 'He wants to throw you in the box again. How can they justify this? *How can they justify this?* It's okay, Robert…one more day, one more day, one more day…'

McCullick edged further into the room. 'I think you're out of luck. You're not going to get any sense from him today, he's in the clouds.'

York sighed and stood to leave when Faulkner suddenly reached out and grabbed his arm, the clear definition of a grizzled swastika-shaped scar on his wrist. His eyes came alive and full of wild angst, meeting with York's in a cataclysm of torment. In a moment of lucidity, the patient's frantic eyes cleared. 'You'll never catch him, you Nazi bastard! He's too smart for you, too smart for anyone. He'll find a way, a way out of this hole. You see if he doesn't, you Nazi bastard!'

McCullick came charging into the room. 'Come on now, Arthur, we don't play like that anymore,' he said, prizing his patient's grip from York's arm.

Arthur Faulkner held York's gaze for an intense second longer, his face full of dark determination.

Fighting with Faulkner's grip, McCullick pushed him back into his seat with little resistance and as soon as it began, it stopped. Faulkner went back to staring out of the window as if nothing had occurred, eyes glazed like honey.

'Come on, Inspector,' said McCullick. 'That's enough for one night.'

'Docile my arse,' York muttered looking into Arthur Faulkner's eyes.

'He should've been,' said McCullick defensively. 'I don't know what happened.'

'He murdered his doctor and tortured his son is what happened, Jason! The man is a fucking liability, drugs or not.'

'Which is why he's in here!' McCullick said forcefully.

Physically shoving York out into the corridor, Jason McCullick slammed Arthur Faulkner's door closed and twisted the key. 'Just what the bloody hell are you doing here, Nicolas? Is it an official visit to help with an investigation or do you just want to upset my patients?'

He stared back at McCullick silently.

'I thought so,' McCullick said. 'So how about you tell me what's going on before I call London and report this to whoever it is I report things to.'

*

Back in the reception office York nursed his second mug of coffee. After his visit with Arthur Faulkner, the chill was eating him from the inside out.

Jason McCullick perched himself opposite and took a sip from his own steaming cup.

'What was that, Nicolas? You're going to need to tell me. You turn up here, looking like death I might add, and lay into one of my patients like it's a personal vendetta. Just what the bloody hell is going on?'

'You watch the news, Jason?' York asked without hesitation.

'Aye, sometimes, why?'

York leaned forward and lowered his voice. 'There's a maniac running around London, cutting the hearts out of his victim's chests and eating them. I believe that man to be Julian Faulkner.'

'My god.' McCullick sank into his seat. 'But he seemed like such a quiet guy, pleasant almost. Are you sure?'

'Pretty much. By comparison, Arthur Faulkner is a teddy bear. His son is dangerous and we need to find him. I figured your patient might've been able to help.'

McCullick shook his head from side to side. 'Arthur's been out of it for years. He was never going to be able to help you.'

'What about you? How well did you know Julian?'

'I didn't,' the Scot admitted. 'He used to visit his dad once a month or so, but I haven't seen him in two, maybe three years now. Strange guy, very quiet, but always courteous. Some days he'd sit with Arthur for hours. Not even talking, you know. Just sit there as if he wanted only to be in the man's presence. I wasn't the only one here who found it a little weird. Some other carers were unnerved by him. He was quite a big man in relation to his father, broad shoulders, big arms, and he carried with him this intensity you couldn't ignore. But we never had any trouble from him. He'd turn up, visit Arthur, and leave.'

Intense, thought York. It was the second time today Julian Faulkner had been described that way. 'What did he look like? Can you remember?'

'Not really,' the carer admitted. 'He was fairly plain looking as I recall. I probably have a photograph of him somewhere. As part of the therapy here we take pictures of some of the patients with their family members to encourage familiarity. We show the patients the photographs and hope they can associate.

It wasn't very successful in Arthur's case. He was still living in that POW camp, still is actually. He has no memory of having a son.'

'Could I see the photographs?'

'Aye,' McCullick replied. 'Not the case files, though. You'd need a court order for those.'

'Just the photos.'

McCullick left the room and returned moments later with a large file, *Arthur Faulkner* stencilled neatly onto the front. Delving inside he dug out two snapshots and handed them over. 'That's Julian,' he said pointing out the unsmiling man standing next to Arthur Faulkner. He was taller than his father, broader, wearing plain blue jeans and a white polo shirt. There was nothing joyous about the picture, only deeply etched sorrow of a broken family.

York froze. 'Oh shit,' he murmured.

'What is it?' asked McCullick. 'You look like you've seen a ghost.'

'Are you sure this is right?'

Hoping to god there was some kind of error he examined the photograph again, traced his finger along the tall man's face.

'Aye, that's definitely him, no mistake. Like I said, I met him a few times.'

'In that case,' York muttered gravely, 'I'm no longer chasing ghosts. This man is very real. And I know who he is.'

52

The Indian Ocean, 2011

'Still no sign of Eric,' said Abbey quietly.

'He knew something was wrong last night,' James said. 'We need to find him soon, that front doesn't look pretty.'

Following his edifying discussion with Danielle, Oli had surfaced and took over watch. During the switch the student had been completely non-responsive, his caramel skin ashen. He wouldn't tell James what was wrong, only that he couldn't stop throwing up. Afterwards, James had managed to get a solid three hours of sleep before Abbey woke him with fresh water and fresh concern. Hanging over the horizon was a thick bank of menacing cloud. In the last twenty minutes, it had grown larger. Or nearer.

'If this storm is anything like the one that brought the plane down it's going to rip the beach apart. The tents aren't going to be any kind of shelter.'

Shuffling awkwardly from foot to foot, Abbey looked like she had something to say.

'You alright?' James asked.

She couldn't meet his eyes. 'About last night…'

'Forget about it.'

'I just want you to know that I'm sorry. I was tired, a little vulnerable, and I shouldn't have put you in that position. But you know, if ever you need a late-night drinking partner again, I'd love to oblige.'

'You have some competition,' James revealed. 'Just so you know.' Abbey narrowed her eyes. 'After you left, the girl came and sat with me for an hour. Her name's Danielle. Apparently Eric's been talking to her for a while.'

'Are you serious?'

'She's intelligent,' he added. 'Quite the sassy little charmer.'

For the next couple of minutes he plugged some holes of information, filling Abbey in on Danielle's story. As he talked he realised how low he felt, the lowest since the crash. There was no one thing causing it. It was a general amalgamation of a mild hangover, the storm coming in, the missing survivors, Oli's illness; all paled in comparison, though, to Abbey's rejection. His heart felt flattened, his chest tight. Never in his adult life had he felt like this. It should have been liberating. Instead he felt trampled and discarded. He wanted to say what was really on his mind, what he really thought of Abbey. But when the full Danielle story was out, he clammed up, the words he wished he could say boxed securely somewhere in a remote corner of his littered mind, and without the correct key, that's where they would stay.

*

Heading from tent to tent James woke Oli, Sebastian and Anthony. None were happy about it.

'What's going on, chief?' Sebastian grumbled, flattening his hair and smoothing his crumpled grey suit.

'Things to do, rise and shine!'

Crawling from his tent, Oli said, 'Don't you ever sleep?'

'Half the survivors are out there in the jungle,' James reminded them. 'We don't know where. Eric, Teri, Sol and Elaine are all missing. We need to find them, and as good a place as any to start is where Anthony last saw Elaine.'

Anthony rubbed the sleep from his eyes. 'I can take you back there easy enough.'

'Why now?' Oli whined.

'There's a storm coming in,' James revealed, hoisting a thumb over his shoulder. 'When it hits we need to be undercover. The less exposed the better.'

They spent the next few minutes loading their packs with essentials and brushing their teeth, and then took for the trees in a jarred and despondent line, hours of unrest evident within each turgid step.

Once they were clear of the beach, James leading the expedition, Anthony caught up to him. 'You think you know what you're doing out here, don't you?'

'Not a clue,' James replied boldly. 'I just want to get these people home.'

'There is no getting home,' said Anthony ominously. 'We're all going to die here. I saw the proof for myself.'

James stopped.

'What about you?' Anthony went on. 'Did anybody check *your* hands for blood?'

James met Anthony's glare. 'What are you saying?'

'Nothing, pretty boy. Not a thing.'

'You want to see my hands, you smug asshole! Huh? There, have a good look, tell me what you see.'

Holding eye contact resolutely, Anthony muttered, 'I see guilt.'

'You see hard work and effort, Anthony, nothing more!'

Catching up, Oli and Sebastian stepped into the stare-down.

'What is this?' said Oli gingerly. The kid had vomited twice since leaving the beach.

'Nothing,' said Anthony calmly. 'Nothing at all.'

'Good, cos' I don't like it out here, man!'

Taking the lead, Anthony pressed on without another word, leaving James unnerved. He loitered for a few seconds, tried to process the scarred man's comments. Had he really become a suspect?

Expecting the trek to take them deeper into the jungle, they were no more than six or seven minutes from the camp when they entered the clearing. The barren area was small, no more than fifty feet around. Trees and boulders guarded the perimeter.

'You sure this is the place, Anthony?' James asked. 'Doesn't look like anybody's been here to me.'

'Agreed,' said Sebastian. 'We should probably keep going.'

'Me and Abbey were behind those rocks. And this…' he positioned himself on the opposite side of the clearing. '…this is where our boy was standing.'

'And Elaine?'

'She was here, on her knees. The killer looked right at us and jammed his knife into her throat. She went down heavy.'

'Aren't we missing the big picture here, chief? Call me old fashioned but I thought there was usually a body when somebody was murdered.'

'And blood,' James agreed.

Fresh from the bushes, Oli wiped his mouth. 'We should keep moving. There's nothing here.'

Pressing deeper into the trees, James took the rear. As the trek began turning arduous, his hopes of finding anyone diminished. Reiterating his thoughts, Sebastian said, 'I don't think anybody's out here. They could be anywhere.'

'We'll search till we find them.'

'*You'll* search till you find them,' said Anthony. 'I'm going back.'

'I hear that,' said Sebastian.

'You want to abandon the search?' James griped. 'Go ahead. When either of you goes missing, don't expect us to look for you.'

Sebastian's face turned serious. 'Think about it, chief, Elaine was last seen way back near the beach. We must've walked two miles further. You think somebody carried her out here? Pardon my tactlessness, chief, but Elaine was no size eight. I couldn't have brought her this far and neither could you.'

James nodded. 'You have a better idea?'

'I say we head back this way.' Sebastian pointed west. 'That way we'll cover one big triangle. When we hit the beach, we ride the coast back to camp.'

'Fine,' James conceded. 'Take the lead and head west. We're done here.'

'Hallelujah,' Oli spat. 'Get me out of this sweat pit.'

Pushing through some dense bush, the student disappeared. Only his scream returned.

Scrambling in pursuit James dived through the foliage, arms raised prepared for attack. On the floor at his feet he found Oli, unharmed, next to more vomit.

Strung up before them between two trees was Teri, her tattooed chest on display, mauled. Her head hung forwards as if mounted on a broken spring.

Fighting down the bile James turned away, the excited buzz of flies feasting in the rancid heat.

Anthony and Sebastian joined the scene. Neither turned away, their eyes hazy in fascination.

'Holy shit,' the South African said at last. 'Is that Teri?'

'What's left of her.'

Sebastian stepped closer. 'What happened to her?'

As each of them examined Teri's body more closely, it quickly became obvious what Sebastian was talking about. Right where the girl's heart should be, there was nothing but a ragged hole, gaping and bloody. Oli retched again.

'We're going to need to cut her down.'

The student's eyes widened. 'Don't look at me, man!'

'We can't leave her like this! It's inhumane.'

'Alright, alright' Sebastian interrupted. 'Anthony, you take that side, I'll take this. Chief, you grab her legs. We passed a ditch back there, we can drop her in and cover her body.'

As they worked, Oli watched from a distance, his lips almost white. Nobody spoke. As they lowered Teri's mutilated body into the ground with care, they covered her with whatever they could find. Finished, the four men stood gravely around the ditch.

'Does anybody think we should say a prayer?' Oli suggested.

Anthony's head snapped up. 'What did you say?'

James cringed.

'*Who do you think is up there*?' Anthony screamed. '*Huh? You think anybody is saving us from this?*'

'Not everybody has to believe the same thing as you, Anthony!' challenged Oli.

'Take that back! You take that back right now.'

'Leave it, Anthony,' James interrupted. 'The kid doesn't mean any harm.'

'No, man, fuck that!' Oli protested. 'I want to say a prayer for Teri. Who is Anthony to tell me I can't?'

'And who exactly is it you'll be praying to, huh?' said Anthony. 'Jesus? God? Fucking Buddha? Tell me something, you little *fuck*...'

Lunging for the student Anthony caught him by the afro, jerking his head towards the pit. '…does your God allow that?'

Finalising the point, Oli was pitched to the ground and kicked squarely in the ribs. He rolled onto his side yelping in agony. James dived in, wrestled Anthony to the ground using his weight to stay his swinging arms. Playing gravity, Anthony tried to writhe free, his solid arms like pistons. Sinews taut in his neck, James held fast.

Oli climbed gingerly to his feet, gripping his side, and gradually Anthony realised the futility of the fight and began to calm.

'Can I let you go?' James panted.

Anthony didn't reply. He simply laid still as if in response. Climbing slowly to his feet, James wiped the sweat from his face. He held out his hand to Anthony who openly ignored it.

'Sebastian,' James muttered. 'Take Anthony and follow your triangle back to the beach. Oli and I will look further. Maybe Elaine is around here too.'

'James,' said Anthony menacingly, 'I'm going to pretend for once like you are actually in charge and I'm going to go back to the beach. I'm kind of getting itchy around you, if you know what I mean.'

James didn't.

Let's just *pray*,' added Anthony, 'that you're not next!' and stalked off into the trees.

*

Having found no sign of Elaine, James and Oli arrived back at the camp in time to catch Abbey preparing the others for evacuation. In the last hour the clouds had become impenetrable, sunspots non-existent. The wind too had picked up, palms along the tree line being tugged by their tussled hair. Over the grey horizon clear sheets of tumbling rain fused the sea with the sky. They had thirty minutes at best.

Gathered around the extinguished campfire were the remaining survivors, Anthony and Sebastian too. Pushing in amongst solemn faces, James and Oli received a hug from Abbey and Danielle in turn.

'Thank God,' Abbey whispered into James's ear. 'I was beginning to wonder where you were.'

'Wouldn't miss this party.'

'Is there a plan?' she asked.

'The caves above the lagoon. That'll be the best shelter we'll find. Eric still not come back?'

'Haven't seen him since last night! I feel like it's my fault, James. I never should've blurted out what happened.'

He took her by the hand, cupping it in his own. 'Eric will be fine,' he said softly.

He turned to the others, only himself and five others present. Beneath his colourless complexion, only Oli looked worried.

'Listen up,' he called above the wind. 'The storm's about to hit. We're going to follow the estuary to the lagoon and take shelter in the caves. For those of you coming along, grab what provisions you can and follow me…' pausing, he locked eyes with Anthony. '…Anybody with a different agenda, good luck to you.'

53

Nobody stayed behind. As the first fat splodges had hit the beach the six survivors had fled into the jungle, following James's lead. Laden with packs of bedding and food, they were prepared to get dug in for the night. Halfway to the lagoon, the downpour had hit. There had been no paced crescendo, no gradual increase. One second the drops had been widespread enough to dance between, the next, the sheer velocity of the driving torrents stung their heads and shoulders, the building gusts punishing their exposed skin. By the time they reached the lagoon, they were beaten and exhausted.

Upon entering the caves they had discovered a small network of tunnels leading from the sole entrance. A quick search had determined they were the only inhabitants on a human level, and they quickly chose a moderately dry chamber the size of a small bedroom. Finally they had built a fire and set it ablaze with scraps of salvaged clothing.

In the hours that followed, the storm escalated, the howling wind whistling in through the cracks hauntingly. The temperature dropped dramatically and lightning crashed down around them, followed closely by deep claps of rolling thunder. Each member of the party was huddled into corners, wrapped tightly in several layers, Danielle packed in against Abbey like they were joined in flesh. Everybody else found their own niche, relying on body heat to keep warm. Oli had improved some. Anthony remained ominously silent.

It was a long time before anybody mentioned those still out in the squall.

*

Surrounded by the dank, mildewed walls of the chamber James woke abruptly, sheathed in sweat. His dream had been of bodies and parts of bodies. He was thankful to be awake.

In the remaining firelight he could see Oli milling around, the sheer noiselessness of his actions lost in the trapped banshee of wind. The others seemed to be asleep, or so they feigned.

'Oli?' he muttered sleepily. The student's frantic eyes stared back across the fire. 'What're you doing?'

'I can't just sit here while others are out there in this weather! I'm heading out to find them.'

From the student's tone, it was obvious he was not awaiting approval. Climbing to his feet James whispered, 'You sure you want to go out there? It's not just the elements you need to worry about.'

'I know that,' the student muttered. 'But Eric's out there. He's alone, man. Probably scared out of his mind, the poor bastard. I need to find him, I owe him that much!'

'You *owe* him?'

'I'm going. You can't stop me.'

'Fine, then I'm going with you!'

'You can't go!' cried Oli pointing out the others. 'What about them?'

'You should've thought about that beforehand. I'm not letting you go out there alone.'

'I don't *need* you, James.'

'You think I care whether you need me?'

'I'll go with him,' a third voice offered.

From the chamber's deepest corner, Anthony rose to his feet and approached them. He didn't look recently roused.

'No!' Oli insisted. 'I don't need either of you. You think I'm incapable, just some dumb kid, but you're wrong. This is something I need to do alone.'

'Nobody thinks that,' said James. 'But we all know what's going on out there.'

'Do we?' Anthony said cryptically.

'Look, Oli, people are dying around us. We don't want to add you to that list. Some of us here care about you!'

'You can't change my mind,' the student proclaimed softly. 'I'll be back before sunup.' With no wish to argue further, he began towards the exit.

'Oli,' said James,' 'if you encounter any kind of trouble, anything at all, you get your ass back here, no questions. You're not back by the time the storm stops, I'm coming for you.'

Without a smattering of indecision, Oli left the chamber.

'*Shit*,' James muttered.

'Those who leave alone,' Anthony whispered, 'tend not to return.' The scarred man hoisted his bag over one shoulder. 'I'll make sure he comes back in one piece.'

'I don't think he'll welcome your presence.'

'Well that's the good thing about being me. He won't even know I'm there.'

With no further recommendations to offer, James skulked resignedly back into the shadows and watched Anthony leave the chamber in Oli's wake. With two more souls left to fate and the group of survivors ever more dilapidated, their chances of survival had once again reduced.

Now they were four.

*

Unable to close out the sound of the wind, Danielle was thankful for Abbey's body heat as she lay awake. Her toes were cold, as was the tip of her nose. She could feel the gentle rise and fall of Abbey's chest, just as she could see those of James and Sebastian across the room. Oli and Anthony had left a while ago. She had been awake when they departed, but she hadn't been able to hear them.

The flames of the campfire continued to dance to the silent melody of passing breezes, and she found herself hypnotically lost for a moment in the display. It wasn't until Sebastian coughed himself awake that she snapped out of it.

She watched the big South African pick himself up and move sleepily to the fire, hands forward. Under her breath she cursed. She needed to pee, and for that she needed privacy.

Peeling away from Abbey, she climbed to her feet quietly. Abbey didn't stir, didn't move at all.

'Shouldn't you be asleep?' whispered Sebastian.

Something in the man's eyes told her he was glad she wasn't. 'I need the loo. Wish I didn't, it's freezing out there.'

'So stay and get warmed up for a minute.'

'How come you're up, anyhow?' Danielle questioned. 'Having nightmares?'

'There're no such things as nightmares, only bad dreams.'

'I wish I'd known that growing up. Could've saved me a lot of sleepless nights.'

'You have a beautiful voice, Danielle,' Sebastian smiled edgily. 'It's a shame you didn't start speaking earlier.'

'Thanks,' she murmured uneasily, and took a step towards the entrance. 'I'm going to see about that loo trip.'

'I wouldn't recommend you go out there alone, sweetheart. The storm's raging.'

Danielle feigned another smile. 'I'll be fine. Takes more than a bit a rain to stop a girl when she needs to pee.'

'Then I'll escort you. You shouldn't be wandering around alone tonight.'

'That's okay,' she muttered. 'I'll wake Abbey.'

'No! Erm…what I mean is, there's no point in waking Abbey when I'm already here, right?'

'It's alright, really,' she persevered. 'She said to wake her if I needed anything.'

'Look,' Sebastian whispered, 'I don't even think we need to go outside. There are several other chambers nearby. Besides, I could do with going too.'

'It's okay, Sebastian, really,' she assured him. 'I think I'll just –'

'What's the matter, you don't trust me? I thought we were friends.'

She paused, curious. 'We are…really, we are. I just…'

'Good, so I'll take you. And Abbey can rest.'

Unable to protest further, Sebastian shuffled her from the chamber. She turned reluctantly to see James and Abbey sleeping soundly, and for the briefest moment she could've sworn she saw, in the twisted shapes of the firelight, the faintest trace of a smile resting across Sebastian's lips.

*

For too long he had waited for this moment, this opportunity. He was going to be alone with the girl at last, just like they both wanted.

For days he'd put in the groundwork; sitting on the beach with her, outwardly trying to keep up her spirits, while attempting to steer her affections away from the interfering walking advertisement for brain damage. From the word go Eric hadn't trusted him.

What he had with Danielle was special. The others would never understand. The way she ran haughtily along the beach, the way she flicked her hair; she'd been flirting with him this whole time. His battle with Eric for the girl's attention had been fought, and he'd won.

Eric was too damaged to understand that he and Danielle wanted to be alone.

Up until the plane went down he'd been handcuffed. He knew Eric had seen him at the airport; he just hadn't supposed it would matter. The plane was never meant to crash, just as he was never meant to meet the girl, but during the process he had become free from his bonds, free from the prying eyes which invaded his daily routine, free from restrictions to be handed the beautiful Danielle on a silver platter.

As he led her into the antechamber, his confidence increased. Just like back in Durban where young girls were a dime-a-dozen, and to snare one from the streets was not only possible, it was downright easy. Considering the sheer populous of the region, no one ever missed the odd vagrant. With the promise of money and shelter, they rarely said no to him. If mothers and fathers could so readily abandon their children, somebody had to pick up the pieces.

Turning to her, the whites of her eyes intensified. She looked worried. Just like many before her she was anxious she would not be enough for him, that she would fall short of his expectations. He liked that.

'I think I've got it from here, Sebastian,' she quivered, fiddling with her locket. 'I'll see you back at the fire.'

Playing hard to get.

'You go ahead,' he said softly. 'I'll wait right here, see that you're safe.'

She took a reluctant step forward and turned. 'You don't need to watch me. I'd like a little privacy, please.'

Not eager in response he pushed her further into the antechamber and feigned an exaggerated search. The cave boasted nothing but rivulets of intrusive rainwater and plinking puddles.

'Maybe I should go get Abbey,' she murmured.

The tease.

'I'll take care of you, Danielle,' he assured her. 'Didn't we agree we should leave Abbey be?'

'Well, maybe I'm not so desperate now. I think I'll just head back and sleep it off, go in the morning.'

She turned to leave and the strong arm grappled her from behind.

'Danielle, I'm beginning to think you don't trust me.'

'What, no! Of course I trust you. I just don't need to go anymore.'

Refusing to relinquish his grasp, Sebastian's face changed shape as he considered his options. 'You don't know how long I've waited to get you alone, Danielle. And I know you've wanted it too. I've seen it in your eyes.'

Tearing her arm from his grasp she took a careful step backwards. 'Sebastian, what are you talking about?'

He could feel the erection pressing against his zip. 'You've done nothing but flirt with me since the crash. You're so beautiful, so loving…'

'Sebastian, you're scaring me. Please let me go back.'

'You want to be with me,' he insisted. 'I know you do. Or perhaps…wait, you're not one of them, are you? One of the bottom-feeders. I clothe you, I shelter you, and this is how you repay me, with defiance!'

'Defiance?' she mumbled. 'Sebastian, you're making no sense.'

'You know what I'm talking about, you little bitch. You flirt with me, you flutter your eyelids, and you think you can toy with me, you filthy little *whore*!'

He watched as she retreated cautiously, nervy feet tapping out acoustics.

'Sebastian, I don't know what you mean by all this. Please stay back or I'll scream for the others.'

'You think they'll hear you?' he smiled crookedly. 'Listen to that storm, girl. It's just you and me now. But I don't want you to be frightened, you've got me all wrong. I only want to love you like so many before you. And some of them, they grew to love me too.'

Dismayed to see his words failing, the girl turned and fled, her feet slapping against hollow rock. Sebastian was too fast. He snagged her sweater and flung her to the chamber floor, the puddles doing nothing to cushion her fall.

His erection was raging now, grinding against the brass zipper, aching for release.

Danielle rolled onto her back as he withdrew it, exhibited it.

'There, you see,' he said hopefully. 'Not so bad, huh? I can love you, Danielle, you just need to be a little more open-minded.'

'Please, Sebastian! Please stop. You have it wrong, I don't want this.'

'Sure you do!'

Wrestling the girl's shorts down to her ankles, he dropped to his knees at the girl's scrambling feet, her flailing arms.

Then the unexpected happened, filling his stunned eyes with tears. The thick forearm wrapped around his neck and tugged him to his feet. Danielle scrambled backwards in a flood of tears, pulling desperately at her shorts.

'Like little girls, do we, Sebastian?'

Oh no.

Not again.

He was being dragged away from Danielle. His beloved Danielle.

He knew they wouldn't understand. He knew their dogmatic views wouldn't allow them to see past the restrictions of age.

He was spun around unceremoniously, James's hard face honing into view. 'Sebastian, when you wake up, you're going to have some explaining to do.'

The last thing he remembered was the fist hurtling toward his face.

*

Leading the distraught Danielle back into the main chamber, James reassured her with gentle words. Abbey woke as they entered and produced a blanket, draping it around the trembling girl's shoulders.

'What's going on?' Abbey queried, sitting Danielle down and rubbing her arms.

'Nothing,' said James. 'It's taken care of.'

'What? What's taken care of?'

'I told you, it's nothing.'

Abbey held his gaze. Floating above the noise of the storm was the distinct whiff of deceit. Since she fell asleep, the chamber's inhabitants had halved, and Danielle was a nervous wreck. Logically, "nothing" wasn't going to cut it.

Taking his arm she led him into the connecting tunnel. 'Why are you doing this to me, James, why are you keeping everything from me? Where's Oliver, where's Anthony and Sebastian? Why is Danielle in some kind of shock, and why for the love of God have you been *lying* to me about who *you* are?'

'About who I am? What are you talking about?'

'I'm not an idiot, okay. Oli told me you were secretive about your job, you wouldn't tell me anything about yourself or your family, and I keep catching you looking at me when you think I don't know. Too much doesn't add up with you. I'm scared out of my wits here, so *please*, I'm begging you, let me in.'

She could feel the fresh tears building in her eyes. She watched James turn away and pretend to examine his hands.

'It's probably best if you sit down,' he advised quietly. 'You're right, it's time you knew one or two things.'

She paused for a second then took the advice, picking out a dry spot and sitting cautiously.

'Meeting you at the airport was no coincidence,' he said quietly. 'I've known you for a while.'

Abbey looked on. 'You…what do you… *what are you talking about?*'

He couldn't meet her eyes. 'You asked me what I do for a living? Well…you. You're my job.'

Her stomach grumbled in a lack of comprehension.

'In London I work as personal security for the top end of the market. I'm hired by celebrities, politicians, the monarchy, those kinds of people. A month ago I was approached by a man. He wanted me to watch your movements, remain in the background but be prepared for anything. This guy, he didn't want to alarm you so he asked me not to make contact, just follow you, see that you were okay.'

Abbey ran a hand through her hair, the sensation of violation pulsing through her very core.

'I know all about you,' he said, pacing. 'I know your family was murdered when you were ten, I know you grew up in foster care in Surrey, I know you attained a degree in Architecture from Edinburgh University, and I know that you and Edward were married on a beach in Barbados. Your Maiden name is Fuller, which you still use for work purposes, and I know your birth parents were criminals of the violent porn trade.'

Climbing to her feet Abbey reeled dizzily, rejecting James's steadying hand. 'What about the mole on my inner thigh!' she muttered vehemently. 'You missed that.'

'I understand your anger, Abbey, I really do. I never meant to bump into you at the airport, that was my error, but I –'

'Who hired you? Who was it who told you to spy on my private, my *private* life? Tell me his fucking name!'

James sighed. 'York,' he uttered. 'Nicolas York.'

Again she dizzied, placed a hand against the tunnel wall. Nicolas York was a name she hadn't heard in almost two decades. 'You...you must be mistaken. I haven't seen Nicolas in years, why would he hire somebody to watch me?'

'He believes you're in danger. Nineteen years ago your parents were murdered by the Valentine killer. Nicolas thinks he's back, and killing again. I was hired to make sure you didn't become a victim second time around.'

'No...no, that's impossible. First of all, Nicolas must be sixty now, is he even still active? And secondly, the Valentine killer was caught and tried. He was insane, there's no way they'd ever let him out.'

'York is sixty-one, and yes, he's still working. All I can tell you, Abbey, is that just over a month ago, the killings started again. Bodies have been turning up in South East London without hearts, returned to their residence soon after. York was afraid you would become a target.'

Legs jellying, she sat back down.

'There's more,' he said resignedly. 'Something I haven't told you.'

'More? What else could you possibly know? You just dissected my life in under a minute in the most voyeuristic way imaginable.'

'In the jungle this morning, we found Teri.'

She glanced up.

'She was dead, her heart missing. I think Elaine is dead too, and probably Sol as well by now. York was right, I haven't been the only one watching you. Don't you see, that's how I've known there's no one else on the island. There hasn't been an unknown party stalking the group, it's one of us. Whoever's been killing in London was on the plane.'

Resting back against the tunnel wall, Abbey rubbed her eyes and tried to digest James's words. She wouldn't cry, not this time. Her parents' killer was still out there, nineteen years later, watching her like some caged zoo exhibit. Had he been paroled, declared innocent, or had Nicolas York made an horrific error all those years ago? And what of James? Like the killer, he'd been at the airport solely because *she'd* been at the airport. My god, how much of this was her fault?

She climbed to her feet, unable to quash the sensations rising in her gut. The only reason James was even here was for her, to protect her like some kind of guardian angel.

Pulsating emotions began spreading warmly through her arteries, burning a path into her heart, and right at that moment, she felt closer to James than she ever had to another human being. Slowly she moved to him, slid into his solid embrace like the piece of a jigsaw, hostaged wind ebbing with her emotions, circling them.

'I'm so sorry, Abbey,' he whispered into her ear. 'I never meant for any of this to happen, but I've never had an assignment like this before. I've watched you go to work, I've watched you take your morning coffee in the Starbucks next to your office. I've watched you go about your day, your beautiful world blossoming before me. Never in my life have I felt anything akin to the emotions you stirred when I first saw you…'

She pulled back, their eyes fusing green and blue in the colourless tunnel.

'I don't know if it's love I'm feeling,' he whispered. 'But I don't know how else to describe it.'

Words insufficient she leaned forward and kissed him delicately on the lips, her eyelids drooping as he pulled her in tighter. Sealed into the safety of his embrace, her inhibitions fluttered away on the cacophony of wind.

54

'Wakey wakey, big man.'

At first light, James left the cave into a thick morning mist hanging lazily over the island. The rain had stopped and the wind had idled to nothing. Not even a stirring breeze rustled the trees. The storm was over, and in its wake the island had been abandoned in preternatural calm.

Sebastian was where he'd left him: tied to a tree by the lagoon, his head hanging limply forwards. Scooping up a handful of lagoon water, James tipped it over the South African's head. Woozily he came to, the makings of a black eye gradually forming.

'Morning,' greeted James. Sebastian didn't answer. 'Storm's passed,' he added, looking around. 'How you feeling?'

'The…the girl,' Sebastian murmured gingerly.

'Yeah, the girl. I've got some bad news for you, *chief.* Danielle is strictly off-limits to you now. I know what you are, I know what you *do,* and you don't get to go near her again, understand?'

'You don't know anything about me,' Sebastian countered defiantly.

'I know enough. Like I knew you'd take the bait if I left you alone with the girl.'

'The bait?'

'You think I'd leave Danielle in your care? I've seen the way you look at her, Sebastian. I knew something wasn't right with you, I just couldn't put my finger on it. But when I heard you were the one Eric saw in handcuffs at the airport, I kind of did the math.'

'What *math*?' he muttered miserably. 'What do you know about it?'

'Granted, there are a couple of things I don't understand. Like how did you manage to get free of the handcuffs, and what did you do with Elaine's body after you killed her?'

Sebastian smirked. 'I didn't kill anybody and you know it. I no more killed those people than you did.'

'So molesting minors is okay where you come from?'

'That's a matter of opinion,' Sebastian said wryly.

'It's a matter of the law.'

Sebastian sighed, his head still hanging limply. 'You're just another one of them. You rant on about the law and the rights of others, but you don't see what's going on in my head, the torture I deal with every day. Do you permanently pine for something you morally can't have, huh? Have you ever considered suicide more times than you can count because nobody understands you? I'm guessing not.'

'So make me,' James implored. 'Make me understand.'

Hocking a gob of phlegm to one side, the South African finally looked up. 'In Johannesburg…I was in a maximum-security facility. I was a prisoner to the state. I'm sick, okay. I'm sick because society says I'm sick. I can't help what I am, I was born this way. Adults repulse me. And so they lock me up. I can never be around children. But they have me all wrong, I never meant to hurt those girls, I meant only to love them. Nobody ever bothered to learn that. Instead they threw me into a rat-infested cell and left me to rot. Understand yet?'

'Don't confuse understanding with empathy, Sebastian. The girls you molested didn't have a choice. They didn't know of such things as sex or the kind of relationship you sought. All they knew was innocence, and you stole that from them with your perverted ideas of love.'

Sebastian sneered. 'Preach to somebody who gives a shit.'

Realising he'd become sidetracked, James said, 'None of this explains why you were on the plane.'

'I've been in prison for thirteen years. I expected to die in there. I just considered myself lucky I wasn't castrated.'

'How did you escape custody?'

'I didn't. I was being transferred to New Zealand for my father's funeral. I would've been back in my cell within a week. When the plane started down, the marshal removed my handcuffs so I could assume the crash position. It saved my life. *Un*-fortunately it didn't save his.'

Rising to full height, James scanned the lagoon resignedly. This was getting him nowhere.

'So tell me,' he said, 'where's Elaine's body? It has to be here somewhere.'

The South African frowned. 'I told you, I had nothing to do with Elaine's or anybody's death.'

He slapped Sebastian hard across the cheek, flat palmed. He watched the man's head snap to the side like a jack-in-a-box, watched his eyes swim. 'Tell me the truth!' he demanded. 'Where have you hidden them?'

'I don't know what you want –'

James slapped him again. And again, this time leaving an angry red mark. Sebastian began to cry. '*Please*, I don't know what you want me to say!'

'Who have you killed, Sebastian?'

'I haven't killed any –'

'*Who have you killed?*'

James was screaming his questions now, Sebastian cowering from the torrent of slaps, the crack of each one reverberating across the lagoon.

Crack.

Crack.

Crack.

'*Okay!*' he cried. '*There was one girl. I couldn't help it! Please!*'

James rose to his feet unsteadily. 'What…one girl?'

'Just one!'

'Where? Where was this?'

'In Johannesburg! There was one girl who tried to run away. I chased her and she…she fell down some stairs. I'm sorry…' he began to sob freely now. '…I never meant for it to happen. It was an accident, I *swear*.'

James took a step back, his coercion extracting unwanted information. Sebastian was a coward, a control freak, but it was obvious he wasn't their man. He was a bully only of minors. He wouldn't dare tackle someone his own size.

In the ghostly calm of the morning a resonance swam atop the still lagoon, pricking James's ears – a brittle snap, as if somebody had stepped on a dry twig. He scanned the trees beyond the trio of waterfalls, the image of the light two nights ago driven to his mind's forefront. Oli and Anthony were still out there, Eric and Sol too. Whoever stalked through the mist wasn't far away.

'Did you hear that?' said James quietly.

'I heard something.'

'I should probably check it out.'

'You don't have to be the big shot all the time,' Sebastian advised. 'It's probably nothing.'

Another brittle snap. This time it was no accident. Somebody was baiting them.

'I don't like this, Sebastian.'

'So untie me, I'll go with you.'

James rose to his feet. 'Sit tight, I'll see what's going on.'

'Don't be stupid, James! You don't know who's out there.'

'Shhh.'

'James!' Sebastian growled as he skulked away. '*James!*'

Approaching the far side of the lagoon, James tried to penetrate the thick wall of mist. Somebody was in there, he was certain. Tempted to call Oli's name, he resisted. That's what they did in the movies right before taking an axe to the head.

He pushed through the dense barrier, his arms outstretched. The cave at his back, he was the only thing standing between Abbey and Danielle and whoever was baiting him.

Groping blindly, he searched the mist until he found what had clearly been left for him. Sitting atop a splintered tree stump was the bloody organ Teri was desperately missing.

He approached cautiously, idle footsteps claiming reluctant ground. There was little fluid, only the savaged heart, maimed and shredded from the amateur removal. And then it came, the gory item doing its distracting job. Off to his right somebody broke from the mist, an ethereal shape charging him silently, covertly.

He had no time to react, no time to defend. Propelled backwards he caught the blunt force of something to the side of the head. He was tumbling to the ground as if in slow motion. He thought of Danielle, he thought of Abbey, her perfect lips touching his own, her soft breath against his mouth. In seconds he would be out cold. He knew it was coming, and he was helpless to prevent it. Whose hands was he in now, whose mercy?

God help him.

*

Drifting into consciousness it took a moment for Abbey to remember where she was. A curious fusty odour filtered through the cave, disturbed particles dancing above the dead fire. She and Danielle were alone.

Gently she prized herself away from the sleeping girl and lay her head down on a rolled-up sweater. Gripped by curiosity she left the tired Danielle to sleep and checked the other chambers – all vacant.

Outside she found Sebastian tied to a tree, sleeping head sagging forwards. The dense mist surprised her, the cooling vapour of a trillion raindrops. It hung levelly over the lagoon, conquering her visibility beyond the tree line. No birds were singing.

She was unsure why James had tied Sebastian up out here, and the rising sun was failing to provide answers. Growing anxious she rounded the lagoon and stared into the thick veil of impenetrable mist, the nearest tree branches seemingly powdered with soot, the leaves with charcoal.

Tentatively she toed the threshold of the vapour, probed it with an outstretched arm. She took another step forwards, the mist swallowing her whole. The deathly quiet began to seem unnatural, as if the fog had flattened her senses and shifted her into a two-dimensional universe. Where were the birds' morning songs? Where was the voice of the jungle, hidden animals scurrying in the undergrowth? One more step. Her probing hands found another tree. 'James?' she whispered audibly. 'Where are you?'

From somewhere off to her left, a movement caught her eye. 'James? Is that you?'

Emerging from the fog, a hand gripped her wrist, the scream catching in her throat. She stumbled backwards onto her rump, the agonized face of James staring down at her.

'James! Thank God, you scared the shit out of me.'

Clutching his head, he held out his free hand and helped her up.

'What happened?'

James shuffled her back to the lagoon and took a seat on one of the climbing boulders. His head was bleeding. 'Got KO'd,' he explained.

She knelt above him and examined the wound. It looked superficial. 'Who by?'

'Couldn't tell you. I was checking out some strange sounds and suddenly I was hitting the deck.'

'You didn't see anything?'

'Nothing,' he said resignedly. 'There are a bunch of people wandering around out there, it could've been any of them.'

'Same thing happened to Anthony, remember? He was knocked out before I was abandoned in the chasm.'

James climbed to his feet. 'Why didn't he kill me? I was out cold.'

Abbey stood perplexed. 'Perhaps whoever it was heard me coming?'

James checked his watch. 'I've been out for over half an hour. How long does it take to stick a knife in somebody's chest? I don't get it, Abbey, I was at his mercy. Why go to the trouble of taking me out and then…'

'What is it?'

'Oh no,' he murmured. 'It wasn't me he was after!'

'I don't under –'

'I was just an obstacle.'

'What're you –'

She watched James sprint to the edge of the lagoon. Sebastian was still there tied to the tree. Insidiously, comprehension dawned. Sebastian had not been sleeping when she passed.

James reached for the bound man's shoulder, uttered his name. Then he tumbled backwards, a pathetic groan spilling from his lips.

'What is it?' Abbey muttered.

He met her eyes. Then he turned his attention back to the South African and pressed a hand to his forehead. Abbey recoiled.

Sebastian's throat had been slashed from ear to ear.

*

'What the hell is this, man?'

In the time it had taken for Abbey to throw up, and James to cut Sebastian's corpse free, Oli approached from the direction of the beach looking storm swept. He was alone, and if his gait was anything to go by, he was carrying neither supplies nor good news.

'Is that...Sebastian? ...*Oh my God.*'

Nobody answered, and Oli seemed to physically diminish as James marched to him, face carved out of granite. 'You have three seconds to tell me where you've been...' he demanded.

'What do you –'

'Two seconds!'

'I've been searching for the others,' Oli squirmed. 'Honestly! Where do you think I've been?'

'Don't *lie to me*, Oli!' He gripped the student by the jacket and slammed him against the rocks. 'I'm sick of all the deception. *Somebody* around here is going to tell me what's going on!'

Abbey watched as the tears splashed down Oli's cheeks. 'James...' she began.

'Stay out of it, Abbey! This little bastard is going to tell me exactly where he was half an hour ago.' Then to Oli, 'You hear that, kid? *Speak up!*'

The student shrank back as far as the rocks would allow. 'James, please, I don't know what you're talking about! I've been back to the camp, I've...I've...gone through the clearing, I've been all the way to the north of the island, *that's it.*'

'I left the cave fifty minutes ago! Ten minutes later I was attacked, knocked unconscious, and Sebastian's had his throat cut. *You* were unaccounted for. So, try again!'

Oli's tears were free-flowing now, his afro matted and straggled, his skin still pallid from illness. He tried to force out some words but nothing came. In the end, James dropped him to the floor and backed away.

'It wasn't me,' Oli sobbed. 'I couldn't...I couldn't do something like this...'

As if understanding the student's pain, the birds had finally broken into song. Atop the lagoon Danielle had appeared at the cave's entrance, Anthony standing by her side, his hand resting on her shoulder. True to their quiet natures, neither the birth-marked man nor girl uttered a word.

'Don't bring Danielle down here,' James called out.

Anthony floated gracefully down the boulders leaving Danielle at the cave's entrance. Unlike Oli, he didn't look like he'd been wandering around in a storm all night.

James eyed his marked face curiously. 'When'd you get back?'

Anthony nodded at Sebastian. 'What happened to him?'

James turned to see Abbey flinch. 'Maybe you can tell us,' James suggested. 'Because I have to say, you don't look the least bit sorry.'

'Why would I be sorry?' Anthony questioned steadily. 'The man was a child molester. I don't lose sleep over dead child molesters.'

Another glance to Abbey. 'You knew he was a paedophile?'

Anthony massaged the bridge of his nose. 'There's *always* somebody watching,' he muttered cryptically.

'I don't understand,' Abbey said. 'Why haven't you said anything?'

Anthony shrugged.

Following a moment of apprehensive quiet, Oli croaked out a seemingly unanswerable question. He wanted to know what they were supposed to do next. James didn't have the faintest idea, and his tenuous grip of leadership seemed to be sliding further. Expectant faces looked to him for a response. After all, he was the fall guy, wasn't he, the one who people leaned on when it suited them? 'Why are you all looking at me, huh? Does nobody else here have a fucking brain? You people only turn to me when things blow up in your faces. You've been content to shun my advice since the plane went down, and now, once again, you're looking to me for answers.'

Lines of sadness formed around Abbey's eyes. 'James, we only –'

'You only did what suited you! All of you, and look at us now…'

'That's an interesting thesis, James,' Anthony said clearly. 'At what stage did you appoint yourself saviour?'

'You're missing the point.'

'I don't think I am.'

'So break it down, Anthony. You seem to know what's going on around here.'

'Death follows you around, boy. I don't have any allegiance to you. You're a jinx, a goddamn curse, but most of all, you are superfluous.' Hoisting the bag back onto his shoulder, he added calmly, 'You think I'd stay with you now?' and began towards the trees.

Speechless, James reeled from the savage attack. Gibson Sommerfield's assurances seeped into his head in slow rhythmic drips, every fallacy that had ever left the pilot's mouth. He watched Anthony leave, stalking his black persona into the mist, as if it left a trail of tar in its wake.

He took a seat shakily on the nearest boulder and examined his hands. Anthony was right. He had failed, and his palms were stained with blood.

55

'Don't listen to him, James,' Abbey said. 'He doesn't know what he's talking about.'

Following Anthony's desertion, Oli climbed the rocks and led the confused Danielle back into the cave to collect her belongings. Only Abbey and James remained by the lagoon, emotions raw. Crouching into James's view, she watched his forlorn gaze lying fixatedly upon the palms of his hands. His absent expression left a broken frigidity in the pit of her stomach, though she dared not turn away.

'James?'

No reply.

'James, please,' she urged. 'I can't do this alone. Don't abandon me now.'

'What's the point?' he said quietly, hands still in focus. 'Anthony's right. I don't know what I'm doing. How naive was I to think we could wait this out?'

'Anthony wasn't right, James! There are still three people here who need you to get them through this.'

'Get them through what? Don't you get it, nobody's coming for us. They would've been here by now. I kept telling myself help was on the horizon, that if we could just ride out the storms and find food, it would just be a matter of time. Now people are dead, others are missing. I'm out of my depth here, Abbey. How am I supposed to make this right?'

'Wow,' she uttered. 'Since when did this become about you?'

'What?'

'Look at you. Pitiful and washed up, balancing on the words of a man who's played no part in keeping us going…' she paused to lift his chin. 'Where's my guardian angel, huh? Where's the guy who's kept me safe for *weeks* without me even knowing it? Where's the guy who braved the currents to pull Teri from the sinking wreckage, the guy who's…who's out snorkelling for drugs for a dying survivor? He's the man we need, not this…this *apparition*.'

James went back to his hands. 'You thought of me as your guardian angel?'

Abbey pursed her lips. 'The question is, are you going to continue in your post, or are you sticking with this new pussy persona?'

He smiled.

'Better,' she grinned. 'So get your arse in gear, we have work to do.'

'Anthony's going to get himself killed out there alone,' he said reluctantly.

'I know, and that's why I have to chase him down. He's frightened, James. Frightened and confused, and you were in his sights when he felt like letting it out. If I can find him I can talk to him, bring him back.'

'No, Abbey.' He reached out and touched her face. 'I can't let you become the next *missing person*.'

'We don't have a choice,' she murmured. 'In every second that passes, Anthony puts more and more distance between us. Get the others back to the beach. I'll see you at the camp before the sun sets.'

'Take this.' He handed her a small penknife. 'It's not much, but I'll feel better knowing you have it.'

She palmed the knife and held his gaze as he brushed the hair from her face.

'I can't lose you, Abbey. Not now.'

'You won't,' she uttered. 'I'm coming back.'

He leaned forwards and kissed her forehead, his lips pressing against the taut skin longingly. Then she stood and turned, the barrier of mist looming over her indestructible resolve. Before she vanished, she glanced over her shoulder and caught a fleeting movement in James's lips, his silent words unquestionable.

*

Swirling shapes buffeted her as the mist grew denser. She held her hands out and stepped cautiously, ghostly spectres of Anthony betraying her vision. The sun had not yet cut a path into the fog, stationary clouds tactlessly blocking the day's renewed heat. All around her the jungle was alive with newfound noise, snapping twigs and raindrops succumbing to gravity, her own mind matching the cacophony with a gross collage of images featuring James and Edward, Edward and James.

Her heart was burning with guilt, a sadness lingering there to know that she had deceived her wedding vows, had deceived her husband's trust.

What had she become? How was it that such an intense circumstance could alter one's perception so irreparably? She felt like a gutter-dog, a bitch. A bad wife.

Edward was her life, but she couldn't imagine what the newspapers were saying. If he was reading them, reading *into* them, then she was already dead, and he was already mourning. Had he cancelled her magazine subscriptions, had he halved the milk delivery? Were his friends recommending he move on?

She guessed she must've been half an hour into the pursuit by now, any sign of Anthony non-existent. There was nothing marked in the undergrowth to suggest he'd been there, no footprints, no dense puddles of tar seeping from his persona. She tried calling his name, but only birds seemed interested in responding. She began to wonder if the fog had misled her.

She tried his name again, the silence offering verification that she was lost. She guessed she was near the north of the island somewhere. She imagined Jerry Benton calling for her from somewhere nearby, his trapped skeleton scratching at the wall of his injury-laden cell. Lost in the fantasy, she stepped cautiously into a small valley she'd never seen before, desperate trees clinging to its broad flanks, dried out bed as if belonging to a dormant arroyo. The mist cut a perfect shape to fit the crafted landscape, settling amorphously into the valley.

She pressed deeper, the gorge slowly narrowing with each muffled footstep, until she drew to an unprecedented stop. Something was wrong here, she could feel it. A coppery hue lingered on the air like a persistent fly, the subtly intermittent stench of something unnatural dominating the morning. She took another tentative step forwards and the recoiling sight emerged from the mist. Covering her mouth, she held in her scream. Strung up in the trees were the motionless figures of Elaine and Sol, their shirtfronts dappled with blood.

'I knew you'd come,' said an unfamiliar voice at her back.

Startled, she turned quickly, her throat catching. 'You…' she whispered.

The world fell silent.

'I'm glad you came alone.'

56

London, 1992

Just when he thought no one at Will Graham's house was going to pick up, the phone was answered by Ross, Will's nine year old boy.

After a few short scuffled noises, Will Graham commandeered the phone and asked who was speaking.

'Will,' said York quietly into the mouthpiece. 'It's Nick.'

'Nick!' cried Graham. 'Don't ask me how but Mason's found out what you're doing. She's after your blood, man.'

'She can have it, it's stone cold. Besides, I'm done up here.'

'What did you find? Please tell me you got something, Braddock's arrogance is really pissing me off.'

'Sorry to disappoint. Didn't find a thing. The house is just a shell now, what's left of it anyway. It's been stripped out by travellers by the looks of things.'

Graham's muted sign echoed down the line. 'Bollocks! Sorry, Nick, I really thought we were on to something.'

'Yeah, me too.'

'So what now?' asked Graham.

'I'm just about to hit the road, should be back around eleven. You have any plans for an early night?'

'If I did, I get the feeling they're about to be cancelled.'

'They are,' he said. 'Stay up until I get there, okay?'

After a short pause, Graham asked the question York expected him to, his voice tainted with scepticism. 'What's going on, Nick?'

'Nothing major,' he assured him. 'I found a few reels of old cine film at the house. You still any good at transferring them to VHS?'

'Does a horse piss where she pleases?' chirped Graham excitedly. 'What kind of film is it? Are we talking 8mm, the old Super-Eight stuff?'

'Will, the reason I'm on the phone to you is because I know nothing about it. You want to take a look, or what?'

'I'll wait up,' said Graham and hung up.

Arthur Faulkner's carer, Jason McCullick, eyed York from behind his desk. 'Why'd you not tell him?'

'Same reason the Garden of Paradise shouldn't've had a forbidden fruit tree,' York explained. 'Too much fucking temptation!'

57

The further south York pushed, the worse the weather got. By Milton Keynes there was a sprinkle of moisture in the air dappling the windscreen. By the time he reached Dagenham in east London, the heavens were fully open, the rain battering down in torrents.

Will Graham's house was a semi-detached set back from the road, the contrast of the two adjoining homes astounding. Graham was always going on about his neighbours being reprobates, an unruly bunch that was up until all hours in the morning, the front of their house a state. He could see what Graham was talking about. The front garden was overgrown, a rusty pedal bike rotting against the back fence. A couple of the soffits were hanging from their moorings and paint was flaking away from the overhang. The only thing missing was a burnt-out Ford *Cortina* up on blocks.

The time was eleven-twenty. Box under one arm he darted down Graham's driveway and pounded on the door, thin capillaries of rainwater sneaking under his collar and down his back.

Graham came to the door rubbing the remnants of sleep from his eyes. 'You're erm…late,' he yawned.

'Is the kettle on?' said York pushing his way in.

'Come in, make yourself at home,' Graham sighed.

Placing the box on the kitchen table, York flipped off his hat and ran a hand through his oily hair. Graham followed him through and began making tea.

'Is this it?' Graham asked fumbling in the box. Plucking out one of the reels Graham held it up to the light. 'Oh, this is the old Super-Eight stuff alright. I loved this format as a kid, used to make home movies on it. Made one once of this lad, he had this infection –'

'You're able to convert it?' York cut in.

The forensics man narrowed his eyes. 'You know who you're talking to, right? I'm the Super-Eight master.'

York crossed the kitchen and finished making the tea. 'Where's Ross?'

Graham looked up. 'Where do you suppose he is at half-past eleven on a Friday night, Nick? *I* couldn't stay awake, let alone him.'

'You got him all weekend?'

'Until Sunday afternoon.'

For over a year Graham had been in a legal battle with his ex-wife over the custody of their son. She was an alcoholic. Will was losing regardless.

'So listen,' Graham said, 'this is going to take some time. Have a brew, get some zeds, whatever you need to do. I'll see if I can get this finished before the Pit Bull finds out you're here and hangs me in the second noose along.'

'You worry too much,' York muttered examining his mug. 'Don't fret about it, you're on my side.'

'You know who's in the first noose, don't you?'

'I'll never tell her you gave me that info, Will. You know that.'

'Of course I know that! But she's a shrewd one, that woman. Every single time she puts two and two together she comes out at four. I'd find it only courteous if she could be wrong once in a while.'

For Graham's benefit, York smiled. By his account, keeping Newport on the case made Mason's decision-making score less than impressive. 'So how long will this take?'

Graham blew air out through pursed lips. 'Depends on the quality of the reels. Three hours minimum.'

'Then I'm going to take a quick trip out. I'll be back by two.'

'Where could you possibly need to go at this time of night? It's coming down in buckets out there.'

'Need to go and see a dog about a man.'

Before Graham could protest further York was gone, his tea untouched.

*

Mere streets away, York contemplated leaving the keys in the ignition and driving away. He also contemplated pocketing them and knocking on the red door across the road, its front room lights spilling out though the cheap pink curtains and onto the rain-swept street.

The longer he sat still, the more conceivable his intentions became. Holding his hand out in front of him, palm facing away, he tried to control the shaking. The burning desire in his gut inflamed threefold, pouring out of him in fat globules of sweat. He threw open the car door and stepped out into the drizzle.

He hammered on the red door and waited, the rain sluicing through him. He could hear some fumbling inside and finally the door opened a crack, Tank Henderson's huge squashed face poking through the gap. 'Oh, it's you,' he muttered, taking off the security chain and opening the door wider. A handful of seconds ticked by, York standing fast and staring ahead, the implications of his being there making his heart stammer. He pictured Charles Kilroy's disappointed eyes, but in the face of it, the doctor's Methadone was no substitute for the real thing.

'Yorkster,' Tank grumbled, 'Haven't seen you for a while, I thought you'd kicked it. You coming in or what? Rain's getting on the carpet.'

Swallowing hard, fists curled, York stepped inside.

'Nice hat, dude,' said Tank, and clicked the red door shut.

*

'Where the bloody hell have you been?' said Graham excitedly. 'I've been waiting for you so we can run this bad boy!'

In Graham's hand was a plain VHS tape. He'd written something on the front in white marker but York didn't catch what it said.

'I managed to fit all the reels onto one tape. I almost played it too, but I decided you'd have my balls for a beanbag if I did.'

The digital clock on the wall read three-oh-two. 'Told you, I had to see a man about a dog.'

'Dog about a man,' Graham corrected.

York raised his eyebrows.

'When you left, you said you were going to see a dog about a man.'

'That too.'

Graham's living room was small but incredibly kempt. York took a seat in the armchair almost afraid to touch anything. It looked like no one ever went in there.

Like a kid on Christmas morning, Graham pushed the tape into the video recorder and hit the play button. Then he sat back rubbing his hands together. 'Okay, Mr York, let's see what delectable material you brought us.'

Slipping out of his jacket, he joined Graham on the carpet and watched as the film began rolling. With the remote, Graham fast-forwarded past his homemade title and set the controller on the floor.

Slowly fading in, the TV screen filled with the silent black and white image of a young boy sitting at a wooden breakfast table, bowl of cereal in front of him. He looked to be around four years old, the smooth skin of childhood surrounding a perfectly infantile grin. York recognised the kitchen; he'd been standing in it earlier that day.

'Who do you think that is?' Graham asked.

York leaned in a little, examining the screen closely.

'Nick?'

'I think that's Julian Faulkner.'

'Julian Faulkner?' Graham said aghast. 'The owner of our murder weapon, Julian Faulkner?'

York leaned in further as the child's grin disappeared. Something was happening off-camera to upset him. From somewhere off to the side, a dishcloth was thrown onto the table. After a wandering scan of the kitchen, the child's eyes filled with uncertainty and tears. Then he picked up the dishcloth and wiped up the splashes of milk from around his cereal bowl.

'Why do I feel like you're not being totally honest with me about Lincolnshire, Nick?'

Picking up the remote controller, York hit pause, very aware that Graham was his one remaining ally. 'You're right, Will. I haven't told you everything.'

'Well that's charming. I give you the information, I give you the location and the lead, I convert the film reels, and you're telling me I don't even know the half of it? Jesus, man!'

'I wanted to tell you on the phone, but I couldn't risk putting the temptation into your head. For my entire journey back to London I'd be wondering if you'd gone to Mason with it, and right now, the info I have is enough to bury somebody, someone who is living the perfect lie. But if word got out I had information, this guy could disappear, and I just couldn't allow that to happen.'

Graham glanced at the carpet. 'You still should've told me, Nick, I thought we were a team.'

Looking at Graham's face, he could see what it meant to him to think he was part of York's personal team. 'Will, you have to understand, we're not fucking about here. Are you sure you want in on this? There's no going back once we expose this person. We'll be facing the rap for illegal investigation and it'll be impossible to keep you out of it. The Faulkner info didn't fall into my lap and Mason'll put it together quickly, you can count on that.'

Graham took the remote from him and set the tape rolling again. 'Nick,' he said quietly. 'I'm in, alright.'

Back on the screen the TV faded into another scene. York recognised the backyard of the Faulkner home, far less dilapidated than it was today. Slightly older now, maybe seven or eight, the same boy was standing where the assault course now was, holding up the carcass of a dead rabbit. In his other hand was the definitive outline of a long-bladed knife and around his feet laid the gory entrails of the animal. There was no pride in the boy's face, just blankness, a darkness. Dropping the hollowed-out shell of the rabbit onto the pile of insides, the young boy turned robotically and headed back into the woods, knife in hand.'

'Where's he going?'

'To kill some more prey,' York said softly. 'Probably being fed instructions from behind the camera.'

'Did you see the kid's face?' Graham murmured. 'His eyes looked empty.'

For the third time the scene faded out and then back in almost instantaneously. The camera was focused on the same area of garden, only this time the assault course had been constructed. Scaling the cargo net was the boy covered from head to toe in sludge. His foot entangled in the netting, he fell backwards and plummeted downwards, landing flush on his back. He looked hurt. From the side of the shot, a man entered the scene carrying with him the confident stride of Arthur Faulkner. With vicious force he grabbed the cowering boy by the hair and dragged him to the start of the course, shoving him brutally into the pit of mud. It looked like the boy was being forced to do it until he got it right.

York found himself praying that the boy would make it across this time, but when he failed in the cargo nets for the second time Arthur Faulkner reappeared, almost running to the boy, maniacally eager to reprimand. The frail frame of Julian's eight year old body was lifted from the ground and took the full force of a slap from his father's open palm, before being tossed like a sack of potatoes to the ground. Climbing back to his feet, the stonily resolute boy held in the tears. Keeping a firm grip on the back of the boy's shirt, Arthur Faulkner beckoned to somebody off-camera. As the mysterious third person walked into view York sat up rigidly, his eyes glued to the screen. 'Oh no,' he murmured.

'What?' said Graham, eyes wide. 'Who's that?'

Walking to Arthur Faulkner was a second boy, this one wearing shorts and a crisp white shirt buttoned up to the top. He was dirt-free, as though he'd been spared the assault course. Aside from the blatant difference in cleanliness, he appeared to be identical to the first boy in almost every way.

'There are two of them, Will,' York whispered.

For the first time all night Graham was speechless.

'This changes everything. Remember when you said the teeth marks in the hearts were slightly different? It wasn't the same man wearing a mouth guard, it was two different men.'

'Oh my god,' Graham said softly.

'And what is that?' York hit pause. 'Does the second kid's face look dirty, or is that a shadow?'

Graham leant in. 'I don't think that's mud, Nick, or a shadow. If I didn't know better, I'd say it was a birthmark.'

58

The Indian Ocean, 2011

'All this time,' Abbey murmured. 'It was you.'

Emerging from the mist Anthony's marked face appeared as if in a dream, his left cheek smudged with blood. He glided towards her, his unsmiling demeanour gone, replaced by the confident grin of a man in total control.

'I've missed you, Abigail.' The Deep South American brogue had vanished, traded in for nobleman English, and for the first time, Abbey became aware of her malfunctioning legs.

'Since the first time I saw you, hiding in the corner of that dark room, watching me, I reserved a special place for you in my heart. You don't know how long I've waited for this day. It's our greatest moment, our greatest achievement.'

'I…I don't understand,' Abbey whispered, her voice cracking. 'They sent you to Broadmoor. You're supposed to be rotting in a cell.'

Anthony's left eye twitched as if trying to recall the existence of any such ordeal. 'It destroyed me when I was locked away, because I couldn't be near you,

Abigail. But I knew one day we would be reunited. I have watched you your entire life. I was there on your first day of secondary school, I was there in Edinburgh when you graduated, I was there at your wedding, your honeymoon in Cuba.'

Goosebumps rose on her arms as she listened intently to Anthony as he gave an accurate account of her life. 'You're making no sense, Anthony. If you were in Broadmoor, how could you have been there on all those occasions?'

He looked confused. Then he said, 'Do you doubt me? Is my information incorrect?'

She could not reply.

Moving closer, he said, 'I couldn't believe our fortune when the plane went down. It was like a sign that our reunion was imminent. I'm sure you felt it too. For days I've marvelled at the wonder of it all, the carnage instilled just so you and I could be together again.'

Anthony's words snagged at her seams. 'If what you say is true, you could have killed me any time you liked. The fact that I'm still here contradicts you.'

Anthony's crooked smile dashed her confidence. 'What makes you think I want to kill you? Quite the contra, Abigail, I'd be lost without you. All these others, they have no place here, they don't belong.' Gauging her frown, he said, 'I've become quite fond of you over the years. I don't want to hurt you. That would negate everything we have achieved.'

'Why do you keep saying "we"?' she asked. 'Like I've had anything to do with this. How can you stand there and suggest we're something of a team? Watching me from afar doesn't mean you know me. It doesn't mean you understand me or care for me…'

'I have been more intimate with you than any other individual in your life!' he said abruptly. Anthony flinched. 'You think physical contact means anything?

Edward, James, their love for you is mere smoke compared to mine. And *that* is why our reunion is so important. You belong at my side, Abigail.'

Finally her legs corresponded with her brain and she took a tentative step backwards. If Anthony noticed, it didn't bother him. 'None of this makes sense,' she muttered. 'You had your head bashed in. I carried you back to the camp myself.'

'It's amazing what the human being is capable of,' he said nonchalantly. 'When he puts his mind to it.'

'*What?*'

'Ever tried knocking yourself unconscious with a rock? It's more difficult than it looks.'

'You're insane,' she trembled.

'*No!*' he yelled. 'No, no, no! You don't get to say that to me, do you understand?' He advanced towards her. 'I stood in. I kept my eye on you when your parents died.'

Another step back. 'When you killed them…'

'I *freed* you from them!' said Anthony frantically. 'They were despicable people, Abigail, they didn't deserve you, they didn't deserve life. They grew remorselessly rich by the most abhorrent means. Don't ask me to apologise for what I did to them, they got off lightly. Don't you see, I've been the only solid figure in your life, the only constant. I have been your guardian, your mother and father combined, your brother, your lover, your everything!'

As the day grew warmer, Abbey trembled harder. The mist had begun to lift, the gruesome effigies of Elaine and Sol growing more defined. Their chests on display, it was impossible to miss the ragged hole cut into each. With only a handful of feet remaining between Anthony and herself, she looked back to

Elaine. 'Wait,' she stammered. 'You were with me when Elaine was murdered. We watched it happen together.'

Anthony smiled, calmer now. 'Ah, yes, the irresolute Oliver. Haven't you wondered why the old chap hasn't been looking too great? Needless to say, it's not food poisoning. His quite sickening guttural responses have been down to nothing more than vivid recollections. He even braved the storm last night in search of Eric. Old boy feels kind of guilty, you see.'

'No, I don't see.'

Anthony looked impatient. '*Oliver* killed Elaine. Under my supervision, of course.'

'No,' she murmured disbelievingly. 'He…he wouldn't.'

'He would and he did. I simply told him I'd gut every single one of the survivors should he not do as I ask. It was the perfect ruse, was it not? How could he know that I intend to do that anyway? When only you and I remain, everything will be perfect.'

The sun had begun to dominate the clouds, most of the remaining mist burned away. With no clear path around Anthony, she glanced passively over her shoulder. Where the arroyo ended, the jungle began. There was no easy way out.

'Don't even think about it,' he warned. 'Don't you understand? This is where you belong.'

She said nothing.

One more step.

'I don't want to hurt you,' he assured her. 'But I will. You can't escape this, Abigail. This moment was destined to happen, it was inevitable. You run now, you ruin everything.'

He stepped up to her, brushed a wistful hand through her hair. 'I've waited so long for this moment,' he said softly.

She winced at his touch, tears forming in her eyes.

'That day in your flat…you were unafraid. Now is no different, Abigail, you don't need to fear me. Nobody can hurt you, they never could.'

Her throat was arid, no words would form. She wanted to hate this man, this murderer, but his tenuous grip on sanity dominated her, enthralled her. The black admission sitting deep within her subconscious taunted her, an admission she dared not say aloud for fear of it becoming more real. The words hung there like an advancing cancer, a stain, yet it pushed against her mind's forefront unwilling to be buried: *Anthony made her feel safe.*

Sensing her vulnerability he took her in his arms, her tears flowing freely. She nestled against his shoulder, his protective embrace encapsulating her, his heartbeat thumping rhythmically against her chest.

'What's your real name?' she muttered tearfully.

'Julian,' he replied quietly. 'Julian Faulkner.'

'Julian?' She felt his head move against hers. 'I'm so sorry.'

Before he had time to question the apology, she jammed James's penknife into Anthony's side. She stepped away as he lurched backwards in a trickle of blood, his eyes brimming with disbelief.

'What have you done?' he spat, reaching for the knife's hilt. 'Abigail, *what have you done?*'

'You're insane, Julian. And you're wrong, I do get to say that to you. I didn't ask you to watch out for me, to stalk me, spy on me. You say you're my everything, but you're nothing to me...*nothing!*'

'*You can't do this to me*!' He gripped the hilt and tore the knife from his side in a spray of scarlet. He stumbled backwards steadying himself on a decaying tree, the knife held up bloodily like an object of fascination.

Dismayed, Abbey began to back away.

'You don't know what you've done,' he blurted. 'You've spoiled everything. You're no better than *them*.'

Waiting to hear no more she turned and fled into the jungle, putting the valley and the raging Julian at her back.

Legs a blur beneath her, she ran as fast as the jungle's density would allow. She could hear no sounds of pursuit, no thumping footsteps in her wake. But she was not stupid. Julian...Anthony, whatever his name was, would be coming.

59

London, 1992

The focal point of the dimly lit holding room was the prisoner sitting on the far side of the cell's only table, half of his face bathed ominously in shadow, his expression biased to neither malice nor friendly, just indifference.

Facing the man in custody was Nicolas York and Dr Alistair Woodrow, a specialist from Bristol who had been brought in to document a professional evaluation. He was considered to be amongst the top three psychiatrists in the country. His opinion was vital to the investigation and to any court proceedings that might ensue. Behind the one-way glass, Mason and Graham were standing in morbid silence watching the scene unfold.

'So,' York began quietly, his arms folded, 'what do we call you?'

The subject's face didn't alter, much like the expression of the robotic child with the gutted rabbit. 'It's up to you. We can continue to call you Jonathan Wheeler, or would you prefer Julian Faulkner?'

After Jason McCullick had shown York the photographs of Arthur Faulkner standing morosely with his son, there had been zero doubt that the broad character had been Jonathan Wheeler, their very own audio technician. As he was taken into custody he hadn't fought, hadn't even protested, merely allowed himself to be taken away in restraints.

'I went to see your dad yesterday, Julian,' York revealed. Faulkner's eyelids fluttered. 'Wow…I mean there's fucked up and there's fucked up, but your dad, he is *fucked up*!'

Beneath the table Woodrow nudged his leg.

'I sat there asking him a few questions, you know, just chewing the fat, and he was about as responsive as, well…you! The difference is he was high on meds. Dribbling down his front, jabbering on like an idiot. The man was an embarrassment, you should've seen it. I felt sorry for him.'

Faulkner's face darkened, becoming distracted.

'Bet he wasn't always like that. Nah. He was a veteran, a tough bastard, wasn't he? If he could see himself now, pissing his pants, not able to wipe his own arse, man would be ashamed of himse –'

'You talk too much,' said Faulkner, his tone low and firm.

There was a moment of tense silence, followed by the drumming of Faulkner's fingers tapping on the table.

'Actually,' York corrected, 'you don't talk enough.'

'How's the wound?' Faulkner asked. There was no mocking tone to his voice; it seemed like a genuine question.

'The one from the knife you jammed in my back?'

Faulkner turned his head slowly sideways. 'I like that knife.'

'How?' York asked calmly. 'You mean for hunting animals in the woods up in Lincolnshire? Or cutting out girl's hearts because you like the taste?'

Faulkner's eyes glazed over.

'That's right, Julian. I made a house call yesterday to the home you grew up in. Beautiful area out there, lovely countryside. Wasn't much left of the house, though. You saw to that, didn't you?'

Faulkner stared.

'Why, Julian? Why did you try and burn down the house?'

'If you had the opportunity to erase something from your life that terrified your dreams, would you?'

York pictured the sealed boxes he kept in storage, photographs of his family secreted away inside. Erased? 'Yes, I probably would.'

'Then you don't need to ask me anything more on the topic. Do you?'

'You're not in control of this interview, Julian. Don't push your luck.'

Faulkner smiled. 'Like I said in the alley that night, you need me. I keep you alive. Do you want to become like these people? The Freudian wannabe here, the loyal sentinel on the door? Or how about Superintendent Mason who is no doubt watching from behind the glass? These people are not like you and I. They're as good as dead because they care about nothing but money and possessions. But you and I...you and I, Nicolas, we live for a purpose.'

'Oh? And what is that exactly?'

'The chase,' Faulkner revealed, 'the adrenaline. Have you not learnt anything from me? With nothing left in your life, especially now your partner is dead, it has been me and me alone keeping you alive simply with the power of occupation. Were I not here, you would shrivel up further into your ball and be dead by Christmas. *I* kept you alive, *me*!'

'By sticking me with a knife and leaving me to die?' York challenged. 'Besides, it wasn't exactly you alone, was it?'

Faulkner twitched.

'Where's your brother, Julian?'

'Brother?'

'Or perhaps *his* name is Julian and you go by something else!'

Faulkner appeared genuinely perplexed. 'If this is some type of psychoanalytical test, Nicolas, you will fail. I do not have a brother. I am Julian.'

'I could wheel a monitor in here right now and show a video of you and your brother standing with your father.'

'You're mistaken. Having a brother is the kind of thing a person remembers, would you not agree?'

'Just tell us where he is, Julian, I'm finished talking with you. I just want to go home to bed. The sooner your brother is apprehended, the sooner that can happen. So, one more time, where is he?'

'So it is a test then,' Faulkner decided disappointedly. 'How original.'

'I saw you put through that assault course. I saw your father abusing you, forcing you to do it over and over again until you made it flawlessly to the end. And I saw another boy, exactly the same as you, except he carried a birthmark right here.'

'Change the record please,' Faulkner sighed. 'You and I both know I don't have a brother.'

'You're lying.'

'Am I?'

Doubt began to manifest inside York's gut. The fact that Julian Faulkner was a grade-A psychopath, and therefore one of a very convincing breed, warned him to tread carefully, to avoid being taken in by the bullshit. Or, had there been something wrong with the cine film and some kind of ghosting had occurred creating a second imperfect image of Julian on the reel. No one in Market Rasen had mentioned a twin, let alone a twin with a skin defect.

'Can you feel it, Nicolas?' Faulkner smiled coldly. 'That niggling sensation grating on your insides, telling you you're wrong. It was a fine notion too while it lasted. I would've liked a brother.'

'Fuck,' York muttered and stood to leave. Woodrow stood too, his notepad in hand. 'You're going to tell me where he is, Julian, or this is going to get much worse for you.'

Faulkner scoffed. 'And how much worse do you suppose it can get?'

Out in the corridor, York and Woodrow were joined by Mason.

'Just what the fuck is going on?' Mason snapped at no one. 'Does he not have a brother or is he trying to fool us?'

'I believe the answer is neither,' Woodrow interjected. The man had a squeaky voice that matched his suit.

'Neither?' York questioned. 'That doesn't make sense, Woodrow.'

'It makes perfect sense if you look at it from the angle of the mind,' Woodrow assured them. 'There was an interesting case-study on this subject written up by an incredibly established practitioner named Karl Fiebig fifteen or so years ago.'

'Please get to the point,' York grumbled. 'Does the crazy man have a brother or not?'

'Ignore him, Doctor,' Mason butt in. 'But yes, does the crazy man have a brother or not?'

The timid Woodrow composed himself. 'Have either of you ever heard of a condition called Multiple Personality Disorder?'

'Schizophrenia?'

'No, not schizophrenia, that's a common misconception. A schizophrenic sufferer is born with the affliction. It's a brain disorder that causes hallucinations so vivid the subject could believe he had a demon in the passenger seat of his car, or that a cow had just flown past his window. The sufferer will also be clumsy or struggle to take care of himself. More relevantly, he is unable to plan anything. The man in that room is meticulous, scrupulous.

'Multiple Personality Disorder is very different. Through some trauma, probably in childhood, the subject develops a second or third or twentieth personality to help cope with that trauma. As we've discovered already, Julian Faulkner suffered greatly as a child.'

'Hang on, hang on,' York stepped in. 'What are you saying, Woodrow, that our man in there has multiple personalities? The second boy in that film is right there in the flesh. It's not just a personality we're seeing, it's an actual person.'

'I was just getting to that,' said Woodrow stepping away from York. 'You see, Fiebig's case-study was all about the opposite of MP disorders. It spoke of a theory that stated if one individual could harbour two or more personalities, then the same must be said of the opposite. Julian Faulkner has a brother, he just doesn't know it.'

For a few seconds Woodrow let the officers digest what he was telling them.

'How can he not know?' Mason questioned. 'He grew up with him.'

'The two brothers were traumatised in childhood,' Woodrow clarified. 'Much the same as an MPD sufferer. Only with the Faulkner children, rather than creating *more* personalities to cope with that trauma, they began to share the same personality, until one day they could no longer differentiate. The two brothers are in each other's lives, they know each other, and yet both of them are totally unaware of the other's presence. They think they are one person.'

'My God,' Mason murmured. 'Is this even possible?'

'It's rare to say the least,' Woodrow replied. 'But there are case studies.'

'Wait a minute,' York cut in. 'Julian Faulkner is a psychopath. He could just be telling us what he wants us to hear. He doesn't want us pursuing his brother, he wants us closing the case.'

Woodrow nodded in agreement. 'That's your call, and it's quite possible. But I'm here only to document the interviews and give my professional opinion. And my professional opinion is this: if you drop this now, the brother will walk free. He's out there, and since the two brothers are sharing the same personality, you can bet your bottom dollar he's going to keep on killing. What Julian is capable of, his bother will be too.'

Before York could respond, Graham joined them in the corridor. 'Nick, there's a woman here to see you. She says it's urgent.'

'Kind of in the middle of something here, Will,' said Mason.

York held up his hand. 'Wait, what does she look like?'

'Oh erm, she's erm small, blonde…'

York sprinted from the corridor and disappeared.

*

Apprehensively, York pushed into the briefing room that Abigail Fuller and Roy Sunnily had shared recently. As expected, a woman waited alone, her face shrouded in anxiety. She was not the woman he was expecting. 'Do I know you?'

Like Graham described, the woman was petite and had blonde, almost silver hair. He failed to mention she was elderly, pushing eighty, wearing a tweed jacket and ankle-length skirt.

'I'm so sorry for the intrusion, Inspector,' said the woman demurely. 'I know you're busy. But I wondered if you'd mind sparing me a few minutes.'

'It's actually a bad time right now, Miss…'

'Mayfield,' the woman replied holding out her hand.

'Mayfield?' It took a moment to recall where he'd heard the name. 'As in Margaret Mayfield?'

'Or Maggie May,' she confirmed.

York stood his ground and looked bemusedly into the eyes of the former Faulkner nanny.

'You look surprised,' she smiled.

'Well, Maggie, it's not every day I encounter a ghost. And today I have managed to unearth a handful. You're supposed to be dead.'

'Nothing but the inventive imaginations of small-town people, I'm afraid,' said Maggie. 'No body was ever recovered and so people just assumed the worst. Arthur Faulkner had nothing to do with my disappearance. Well, not directly at least.'

York leaned back in his chair and breathed in heavily. 'What are you doing here? How did you know where to find me?'

'Oh, I'm quite resourceful. Just because I no longer live in Market Rasen, I still hear everything that goes on there. When I heard a police officer from the capital was in town digging up Faulkner tales, I made some enquiries. Didn't take long to find out your name and where you were based.'

'Well I'm glad you found me, Maggie. But I need to ask, where have you been all these years? Everybody thought Arthur Faulkner had murdered and buried you somewhere out in the woods. Why didn't you come forward and let people know you were still alive?'

Maggie's smile faltered slightly. 'You think it was easy, what I did? I abandoned those kids, Inspector…'

Kids…

Plural.

'…and I'm ashamed to say my plan failed. Before Arthur was called up to fight for his country he was such a sweet man, gentle. Mary, his wife, meant the world to him. But when he returned he was no longer that man. The war had twisted his mind. He was evil, and the fact that he's still alive is an insult to me. He deserves to burn in Hell.'

'You say your plan failed,' York stated. 'What did you mean?'

'I couldn't take the way he treated the children. I stayed for as long as I could for the sake of those two boys, but the madness of it all eventually got to me. His favourite was Robert. He considered Julian an embarrassment because of his disfigurement.'

York recalled Arthur Faulkner rambling on about Robert in nonsensical gibberish. McCullick had insisted it was the name of one of the carers at Rampton, but he was wrong. Arthur Faulkner's second son was named Robert, the boy with no disfigurement. Jonathan Wheeler was *Robert* Faulkner, not Julian.

'But that doesn't make sense,' York mused, recalling his conversation with Frank Blithe. 'Nobody in Market Rasen mentioned anyone called Robert. All the old myths and wives tales up there all talk about Julian. How can that be if Julian was the one under lock and key, why is he the brother everybody remembers?'

Maggie smiled a joyless smile. 'Because Arthur called them both Julian to avoid anybody discovering he had two sons. He used to keep poor disfigured Julian locked up in the basement, no light, no food. He wanted no one to know of him because of his defect, and from what you're telling me, he pulled it off.'

'You still haven't explained how your plan failed,' York questioned patiently.

Maggie shifted uncomfortably in the plastic seat. 'Those boys were raised in Hell, Nicolas. Mary, Arthur's wife, was so incredibly ill she was completely out of the picture. But she was so scared of Arthur, of what he'd become, she wanted her boys taken away from him. And in her frail state she asked me to run away, take the boys and disappear. I didn't want to leave Mary with him but I knew she was right. And so that same night I packed up some of the boys' things and snuck them out of the house. We didn't get far. Arthur was waiting for us at the top of the track. I tried to protest, told him the entire thing had been my idea, but he beat the boys anyway, right before he put me in hospital.'

'Jesus,' York muttered.

'When I returned, it was as if nothing had happened. I don't even think he remembered what he did. That was when I came up with my plan to save those boys. After he put me in hospital, questions were raised about what had happened. But I kept quiet. He threatened to kill Mary if I said anything. I just couldn't risk it because I knew he was true to his word. And so I disappeared alone, leaving the boys with their deranged father.

'Questions were already hanging in the air about the sanity of Arthur, and I knew my disappearance would stir all kinds of rumours. He would be investigated and the brutality of the Faulkner house would be blown wide open. I waited for news. Every day I checked the local paper expecting to read that Arthur had been taken into custody. But it never came. Lack of evidence meant the man walked free. That's why I never came forward. Those kids deserved so much more, and I failed them.'

A tense silence hung between them for a few seconds, the room bathed in syrupy quiet. Eventually York broke the spell. 'I'm sorry, Maggie.'

'I know those boys are responsible for the recent murders,' said Maggie. 'They will have to stand trial for atrocities I can't even imagine, and then they'll spend the rest of their lives in a cell. They've been prisoners since birth to a father who never understood them, only how to raise them with brutality and violence…'

'Maggie…' York interrupted gently.

'It's okay, Nicolas, really. I just wanted you to know, that from the moment those boys were born, they never stood a chance.'

*

'So, would either of you like to tell me what I should do with you?'

Standing in front of Mason's desk, York and Graham remained silent. After revealing to Mason their unauthorised operation into the Lincolnshire house, she went ballistic.

'I'm open to suggestions,' she urged.

'Don't suppose it matters that our investigations led to the arrest of Robert Faulkner?' said Graham.

Mason's ice chips locked onto Graham's eyes. 'Is that sarcasm I'm detecting, Will? Because if it is I would suggest you curb it, right now.'

'I wasn't being sarcastic, guv, I was just trying to point out a fact.'

'Which is?'

'Come on, boss,' Graham implored. 'Braddock was not the right man for this assignment and you know it. Taking Nick off the case at a pivotal point in the investigation was a bad decision. I knew it, which is why I fed him the information. Braddock had no interest in following up on the Faulkner house lead and you backed him up, which was your second mistake.'

Mason shot to her feet. 'Will, the ice you're on is wafer-thin. I'd think about getting out of my office before I break pieces of it off and jam them up your arse!'

York expected Graham to scamper out the door, tail between his legs. Instead he strode confidently from the room and clicked the door gently closed.

'Developed some balls recently, hasn't he?' York muttered.

'What the bloody hell is going on around here, Nick? Maybe I have made some decisions lately that you don't agree with, but that does not give you or that pinhead the right to go behind my back and act as you see fit!'

'I know that, guv. And I can only apologise for the deception. But what Graham said was right. Without our unauthorised investigation Robert Faulkner would still be out there, would still be using this very station and watching our every move. Now Julian Faulkner is out there alone and is probably very confused. Without his brother, it won't be long before we find him.'

Mason sat back down and sighed heavily. 'Three weeks unpaid suspension for the pair of you. That's final. By all accounts, Nick, you've both got off lightly.'

He turned to leave.

'Oh and Nick,' she added. 'If I find out that you or Will Graham have been involved in any police work within the next twenty-one days, you'll spend the rest of your careers ticketing vehicles in Peckham, am I understood?'

'Perfectly,' he said.

60

For the hundredth time, York stared down at the scrap of paper in his hand and read the house number aloud. The terrace directly across the street matched the address. He was in the right place, the poor neighbourhood brickwork of a working-class community. The peculiar thing was he'd been parked opposite for almost three hours and there hadn't been a scrap of activity, zip.

Technically staking out a house full of supposed criminals would constitute police work. Still, as much as he had no desire to be demoted to traffic copper, there was nothing on earth could've dragged him away from this place. If his son was inside, he was going in there to get him.

He climbed from the car and crossed the road, a handful of people milling around on the pavements. No one looked in his direction. As he reached the house he snuck a peek into the downstairs window. Nothing, only a beat-up old sofa sitting atop a scabby carpet.

Three doors down, he found the alley leading to the rear of the houses. With no gates to hinder his access he strolled straight through. At the back of the house he found a door built into a tatty kitchen extension. The tiny garden was a mess, overgrown, countless cigarette butts littering the floor around the doormat – a doormat which carried the instruction, *Wipe Your Feet.* He supposed it was referring to the way out.

He checked all the back windows finding nothing still, a slow sinking feeling rising in his gut. 'Oh no,' he said aloud. 'Oh no, oh no…'

No longer caring about the neighbours, he picked up a rock from the garden and smashed one of the glass door panels. As he predicted, no alarm sounded and no one came running.

He reached in and unlatched the door, pushing it cautiously inwards. Matching the garden the kitchen was a state, the worktops a chaos of unclean mugs, overflowing ashtrays, takeaway cartons, and a sink full of plates festering in stagnant water. The room looked lived in, but the rest of the house couldn't offer the same. As he moved from room to room, much like he had at the Faulkner home, he found only disappointment, signs of life having recently moved on. The topmost floor was one large attic space with creaking floorboards and peeling wallpaper, but as he looked closer he found something that made his stomach turn. In a corner of the room was a red and blue painted toy train. He wondered if Frasier had played with it, filling his innocent time, his little mind trying to understand why he was there, what he was going to be made to do.

What he had already been made to do.

What remained of York's fragile walls came tumbling down around him, brick by lonely brick. He slid down the wall in a flurry of wretched sobs, clutching the toy train to his chest. He turned it over and over in his hands, examining every inch of its significance. How late was he – days, *hours*?

Through the blur of tears he scrutinized every surface, every fleck of peeling wallpaper, every dust-laden crevice. If Frasier had ever been here, he was gone now.

*

Leaving the house by the front door he caught sight of the woman perched on the bonnet of his car. Blonde hair bobbed neatly, cute and demure; finally the woman from the alley was making an appearance.

She greeted him as he reached her, her serious face scrutinising his movement. He took a seat on the bonnet next to her, stared straight ahead, the feeling of disappointment dripping steadily into his self-made pool of deprivation.

'What's your name?' he muttered pinching the bridge of his nose. His head was beginning to ache.

'Kellie,' she replied. 'Kellie Carter.'

'Why are you here, Kellie Carter?'

She glanced sideways at him. 'I told you I'd approach you when the time was right.'

'I take it you're no longer being followed?'

'You've been in the house, you tell me.'

'There's nothing in there, Kellie,' he revealed quietly. 'Not a fucking bean.'

At the end of the street, three girls played with a skipping rope, their carefree faces beaming. He watched them for a moment.

'I'm sorry, Nicolas. I didn't mean to give you false hope. But you need to stay strong for the sake of your son.'

'For the sake of my sanity.'

'Frasier is out there,' she assured him. 'I promise you.'

'How could you possibly know that? You don't know me, my past, and you certainly don't know my son.'

'I'm a journalist,' she revealed. 'I've been watching these guys for a long time trying to split open a big story. They're from Latvia, a group of ex-militia who came fresh out of service and into the trafficking business. They were working out of Belgium in '86 but were kicked out after several children disappeared. The Latvians were in the country illegally so the authorities didn't have any legal trouble getting rid of them. After that they set up in Hanover, Germany. They're still operating there now as far as I know, but a group of them broke away and came here.

'One night I got friendly with one of them and he invited me back to his house. He brought me here. Others were here too, and that's when I heard one of them talking on the phone to The Face. I got the feeling none of the men knew who The Face was, but it was obvious he was running the operation. The way they talked to him, there was respect, even fear in their voices. The second and final time I came back here, four boys were being brought in from the backyard. One of them was Frasier. I recognised him from the photographs.'

'Did he look okay? I mean, did he look hurt?'

'He looked confused, frightened. But I think he was uninjured.'

York let the information sink in. 'Wait a minute, what photographs?'

'The ones Holly showed me. She looked up to you, Nicolas, wanted to make you proud.'

'Wait, you're *Kellie*? Holly's Kellie?'

'You sound surprised.' Kellie's eyes began to well. 'I loved her, Nicolas. As immoral as it was with her being married, we spent a lot of time together, and she talked a lot about you and about what happened to your family.'

York's eyes strayed back to the skipping girls.

'Holly had her own problems,' Kellie persisted. 'She didn't want to be with David anymore, but she didn't know how to leave him. I told her I was on the verge of ending our relationship if she didn't make a choice soon, told her I'd met someone else. It wasn't true. I just wanted to hurt her. You have no idea how much I regret those words. The last time I saw her, all I did was ramble on about this scoop, about nailing these bastards down in print. She refused to help me, told me to report it through the proper channels.'

'What happened?'

'I got angry, stormed out. That was the last time I saw her, and I haven't slept since knowing that that's how I treated her at the end.'

York shifted uneasily on the bonnet.

'I want you to know,' she added, 'that you meant a great deal to her. She loved working with you…' She took his hand in hers and squeezed. '…That's got to count for something, hasn't it?' She jumped from the bonnet. 'Nicolas, listen to me, okay. Frasier is out there, I promise you. You cannot give up hope. One day you'll have him back and all this will seem like a bad dream.'

'Uh-huh, and what about the meantime?'

'What do you mean?'

'If you're right, then Frasier is still living this nightmare,' he said softly. 'Do you think it will ever seem like a bad dream to him?'

*

The flat was cold. York hadn't bothered to put the heating on. In the sparse kitchen he sat alone at the bare table staring resolutely at the single item in the centre of the wooden surface.

His arm tingled.

He didn't move.

His hands shook.

He didn't move.

Tick tock.

The tiny brown stone in the table's centre stared back at him. He tried to concentrate and images of the quarry began to solidify in his head. For the first time since he was a child, he started to remember.

'You're finally beginning to see.'

York nodded.

'I knew it would come back. With enough patience, anything can be retrieved.'

York's eyes never wavered from the brown stone. 'It was you, Daniel,' York whispered. 'I told you not to go into that mineshaft. I pleaded with you. But I was just your geeky little brother. You wouldn't listen.'

'Did you forget, Nicky? I never listened to anyone.'

'Everything was so perfect before you died,' he said quietly. 'And then it was just me. Mum became good friends with *Johnnie Walker*, and dad…'

'Dad?'

'You know what happened, Daniel. You were his rising star, his favourite. When you never came back out of that mineshaft he died inside. Six weeks after that, well…'

'He took the easy way out is what he did, Nicky. He left his distraught wife and one remaining son to fend for themselves. He was a coward.'

'He worshipped you.'

'He worshipped us both. You just chose not to see it.'

York reached into his jacket and brought out the syringe kit, laid it gently on the table next to the rock of heroin.

'So you're still going down this route.'

York didn't answer.

'Robert Faulkner was right, wasn't he? You need him. Without him you have no purpose. Without him, you need drugs to get you by.'

'You're wrong,' York said firmly. 'I don't need him.'

'You still haven't figured it out, have you? The demon inside you is crumbling. You know the truth now. You tried to stop me going into that mineshaft and I didn't listen. I was to blame for my demise, no one else, and especially not you. You don't need me anymore, Nicky. I am to become obsolete, nothing but a memory.'

York reached forwards and plucked the brown stone from the table, held it close to his face. Daniel said nothing more.

This was the moment.

This was the milestone.

Slowly, he climbed to his feet and stepped away from the table. He stood calmly at the sink and turned on the tap. His mind was a race of colours, memories, each one better, worse than the last. Robert Faulkner had been right, he *had* needed him, needed purpose. And now that purpose had transformed into something else, something purer.

Slowly he began to crumble the brown stone in the sink, piece by piece. He watched as the water snared the grains and carried them into the plughole in a vortex of purification. It was over.

This was the moment.

This was the milestone.

Frasier.

61

The Indian Ocean, 2011

Stacking full length over a fallen branch, Abbey scrambled to her feet and charged on. She was dizzying, the heat dragging at her heels.

Praying her head-start would be enough she chanced a gasping peek over her shoulder, relieved to see only vegetation in her wake. She had little doubt that Anthony…*Julian* was smarter than she, quicker, more agile. But he was injured, if that counted for anything.

At the north of the island, she was totally alone. Over two miles away, James would be leading Oli and Danielle back to camp. Everybody else was out of commission. She could not afford to fall again.

Then she fell, her arm buckling beneath her as she broke through the green and onto the beach. Crashing through the jungle behind her she could hear the thudding footsteps of her pursuer bounding through the bush. And then he was on her, shirt drenched in blood on one side, bursting through the undergrowth like a possessed predator. His face a mask of rage, she screamed as he pressed the knife slowly into her shoulder, his weight pinning her to the sand. Her flailing arms did little to tip the scales, his bulging eyes bearing over her.

Deliberately he withdrew the knife from the wound, twisting as he pulled.

'I gave you *everything*!' he raged, spittling her face. 'And you throw it back at me! You're no better than the rest of them, just *fucking cattle*!'

Open palmed he cracked her across the face, the splintering slap echoing across the bay. She yelped in pain, the second slap harder still. She could feel his taught body pressing down on her, the sheer solidity of his frame.

Before the third swing she reached up and dug her thumb into his open wound, watched as he arched his back in pulsing agony. With his back raised she crunched her knee into his groin, and before she knew what was happening, Julian was rolling off her and she was back on her feet.

She took off again, the sand hindering her speed. She made it to the rocks at the end of the bay, hurling herself at them, Julian no more than fifteen feet back along the sand.

Unimpeded she made it to the top of the crest, her heart sinking at the sight below. She was back at the chasm, Jerry Benton's smiling skeleton beaming up at her.

'You're all I have, Abigail,' Julian called out, clambering up on the rocks. 'Don't make me do this, I'm begging you.'

He was calmer now, and seemingly not out of breath, though he had grown paler with blood loss, his unshaven cheeks sunken.

'You're going to have to,' Abbey wheezed. 'Because I'm not like you, Julian. You need to understand. If you can't deal with that, you're going to have to kill me.'

'You don't think I will?'

'I'm counting on it.'

He lunged for her, knife outstretched. He missed, sliced through the fabric of her shirt and spun away, circling his large arm around her throat.

Her breath cut off, she grew limp, her feet dangling. With his free arm he brought the knife around and thrust into the same shoulder, inches above the first wound. She cried out as he turned the blade in, twisted it into the bunched nerves. She was mere seconds from passing out. Everything was turning white, the coastline snowing in and out of focus. She couldn't draw breath, couldn't even cough.

She grappled at his arm, tore away fingernails of futile flesh, but there was nothing tenuous about his grip. It didn't react to her flailing, her scratching, as if it felt nothing.

With no options left, she began to relax as her lights dimmed. She didn't want to go out fighting; she wanted to parallel the serenity of their setting. She closed her eyes and allowed the darkness to envelop her, cradle her, a rush of settling nausea embroiling her senses.

She waited for death to grasp the vapour trails of her escaping soul when she felt the sudden rush of cold air passing her, and the sharp pain in her knees. It took only a second to realise what was happening. She'd been dropped to the rocky floor in a crunch of scraping bones.

She scrambled away confused, her lungs padding out with fresh, clean air. There was a grunting over her shoulder, another battle raging on without her. She flung herself over to a picture of the unexpected. Julian was being gripped from behind in a vicious bear hug by Eric. The big man had come from nowhere, hoisted Julian off his feet and was crushing the air from him.

Tears streamed down Eric's face as his enormous arms squeezed the life out of Julian, the audible cracks of the killer's ribs snapping one by one. Eyes bulging, swollen tongue lying idly on his bottom lip, the killer stared at her pitifully as she climbed to her feet.

'I guess you were right, Julian,' she said softly. 'There *is* always somebody watching.'

The spark in Julian's throbbing brown orbs began to fade. Eventually he fell flaccid with one final popping rib, his head hanging limply on his chest.

For a moment neither she nor Eric moved. 'It's okay, Eric, you can put him down.'

Like an automaton, the big man took a few unsteady steps to the chasm's edge and peered at her over his shoulder. She wondered if he was waiting for some kind of approval.

She didn't give it.

He pitched Julian's cadaver in anyway, sickening thumps echoing to the surface with every ricochet of the broken body. Then he turned and looked at her, the tears clinging to his cheeks. Never in her life had she seen an expression so lost.

62

The trek back to the camp was a quiet, disjointed one. Abbey supposed she should try and talk to Eric about his mother's death, but she didn't want to push it on him. She had little doubt that he would ask in his own time, but for now the topic remained buried, right next to her own inexplicable past. Anthony was dead. That was enough for now.

Tearing strips from her blouse, she bunched them and pressed them to the tandem of wounds at her shoulder. They stung like hell, but neither was bleeding too badly. She wondered if Eric was alright. He didn't seem injured, so she didn't ask.

And so they trudged in blessed silence, trailing the island's circumference until they wandered gingerly into the remains of the camp. As they predicted, the storm had torn the beach apart. Not a single tent remained standing, the simple branch framework strewn across the beach amongst a confusion of blankets and meagre belongings. James and Oli climbed to their feet as they spotted the two bedraggled figures sauntering towards them, their passive faces betrayed by their defensive body language.

'You don't need to worry about him,' Abbey said, referring to Eric. 'He saved my life.'

With literally nothing to sit on she fell into James's arms, sagged against him like he was made of stone. She then moved on to Oli and hugged him tightly.

Halting questions and rebounding offers of aid, she hastened them to a sandy perch as she unfolded her account of what had taken place. With Eric present, she left out the bodies she'd seen in the arroyo but included everything else: Anthony Turner's real identity and his death, her lifelong stalker and his unexplained estrangement from Broadmoor, her childhood involvement with Nicolas York almost twenty years previous. She omitted nothing that didn't need omitting, and when she was through, a serene and melancholic silence settled over the group. She didn't fully understand the silence; it just seemed like the right thing to do.

From here onwards she was under little doubt that things would grow more strenuous, their strive for survival unremitting. Julian Faulkner was gone, that box was ticked, and tonight they would sleep soundly in their rebuilt tents under a predatorless sky.

With the sun now at full height, she sleeved the dots of perspiration from her brow.

'Where's Danielle?' she asked sullenly, astonished she'd only just noticed the missing girl.

'We don't know,' James replied almost apologetically. 'We tried to comfort her when we got back to the beach but she took off. There was no stopping her. We followed her into the trees, but she was gone.'

'And you didn't go look for her?'

'She could've been anywhere, man,' said Oli. 'Needle in a haystack, remember? She'll come back when she's ready.'

'Where would she go?'

'Where do we all go when we feel like blowing off steam?' said James.

'The lagoon?'

'Exactly.'

'She's not at the lagoon,' Abbey smiled knowingly. 'She was frightened.'

'So?' Oli questioned.

Walking intently towards the tree line, she said, 'If you were Danielle, where's the *one* place on this island you'd go to feel safe?'

63

'Hi there.'

Sitting down next to Danielle in the shade of the dilapidated hut, Abbey absorbed the banana grove's picturesque beauty. Rays of light speared the remaining clouds gathered overhead, warming spots on the ground around them.

Finally Danielle uttered,' How'd you find me?'

'I'm psychic.'

'James told you about this place, its significance?'

Abbey nodded slowly. 'He did. Nothing to harm you here. That's the idea, isn't it?'

Danielle smiled uncertainly.

'How's it working out for you?'

'What's that?'

'You know, coming here.'

'I know I shouldn't've run from James,' Danielle sidetracked. 'But I didn't know who to trust, even you. From the moment I woke up this morning, everything was just…falling apart. Even from up at the cave I could tell Sebastian was dead. I mean I couldn't see much, but I just knew. And then Anthony took off like he didn't trust anybody, and I figured he had the right idea. If I was alone, I was a whole lot safer.'

'Nobody blames you for running. I would've done the same thing.'

'You didn't do the same thing, though,' Danielle said. 'You went after Anthony. You did your bit, just like James, just like Oli, even Eric. What have I done?'

Abbey didn't know what to say, the question sticking in her throat. 'You survived. Is that not enough?'

Danielle took a heady breath. 'I guess I'll find out.'

Expecting to see tears on Danielle's cheeks, Abbey was surprised to find none.

'I'm ashamed because I doubted you,' the girl went on. 'You and James. You've taken care of me, looked out for me. When I ran, when I doubted you, I let you down.'

For want of a more appropriate response, Abbey said, 'We found Eric.'

For the briefest moment, Danielle's face lit up.

'He saved my life.' Abbey wondered if she'd ever get tired of saying that.

'Saved your life from what?'

'Anthony, believe it or not. But we don't need to worry about that anymore. He's gone, and he won't be coming back anytime soon.'

Danielle didn't comment.

'You know something,' said Abbey, 'it does feel safe here, doesn't it?' The girl shrugged. 'Why is that?' she added perplexingly. 'Why should it feel safe?'

'What were you hoping for?'

'We're in wide open space, no less vulnerable than at the beach.'

'The "why" is something you have to decide,' Danielle explained. 'Follow my reasoning, you'll see what I'm saying.'

Glancing to her left, she eyed the girl. 'I'm not religious.'

'I never said you have to be. I'm more than happy to share my sanctuary with you, Abbey, but you have to have your own reasons for feeling safe here.'

Abbey frowned. 'Like what?'

'Whatever reasons you choose are yours and yours alone. It makes no difference what me or anybody else says or thinks. If it feels right for you, that's all that's important. I choose to speak with God. It doesn't matter to me if you don't believe it. It only matters that I do.'

Abbey smiled. 'This place is your gift. Your gift to us. Muscling in has its uses, but offering hope, that's something else altogether.'

Staring into the wispy, non-threatening clouds, the pair fell silent. As the afternoon hours descended upon the ravaged island, their minds raged like the storm passed, infinite invisible stars hanging over their heads, a different billion marvelling at their twinkling vanity. So many things had been left unsaid, so many unspeakable atrocities that would have to be revisited.

Amidst their oppressive quiet, Abbey felt something being pressed into her hand. She glanced down to see what the girl had given her, the silver chain dangling between her fingers from the sealed locket she'd palmed. She eyed the girl curiously and clipped it open, running her eyes over the contents. Danielle was looking away.

Encased in the small golden shell was nothing but air, an entrapment of falsities and intriguing emptiness. She traced a finger across the locket's defined edges. This was the girl's agenda, her embroiled emotions having thrashed carelessly for interminably long, laying down their weapons and beginning to settle.

Abigail understood. The girl had found her inner calm. The good luck charm had worked for her, now it was for somebody else to try.

Snapping the locket closed, she pocketed it and climbed to her feet.

Danielle looked up at her smiling, eternal wisdom residing behind her tired eyes. 'So…what do we do now?'

Abbey glanced around the clearing. 'Well, we either find a way off this island, or we begin building a new life here...'

For a second Abbey contemplated her own words, their intrusive meaning steamrolling the moment. *Edward. James.*

'…you've found your peace, Danielle, so tell me, what do you want to do?'

Today's word: *Sanctuary?*

End

COMING SOON

The new Thriller from

Jeremy Costello

BREAKING NATHAN

To keep up to date with Jeremy and his upcoming releases, take a peek at his website and hit subscribe.

www.jeremycostelloblog.com

In addition to continuing work on new novels, Jeremy has begun a new blog page called **MindMenace**, which ties together his fictional works with his real life experiences and interests. While **MindMenace** is in its infancy, Jeremy is hopeful that it will develop into a new forum for intelligent debate and conversation.

Thank you

for reading my debut novel Hunting Abigail, I hope you enjoyed it.

If you would like to write a review, either on Amazon or directly to my website, it would be greatly appreciated.

Reviews are the lifeblood of any aspiring author and I consider all praise, constructive criticism and general feedback absolute gold dust.

Jeremy Costello

www.jeremycostelloblog.com
Facebook: @jeremycostellobooks
Instagram: @jeremycostelloblog

About the Author

Jeremy Costello was born in Nottinghamshire in 1979. He is the author of several novels including his debut thriller **Hunting Abigail**, a graphic and haunting story with connotations of stalking and voyeurism. This topic is close to Jeremy's heart due to personal experience and some of the scenes in **Hunting Abigail** are loosely drawn from real-life events.

Jeremy continues to live in the north of England with his family and two guinea pigs, Snowy & Weasel.

Printed in Great Britain
by Amazon